Sheep Gully Road

Laurelle Cousins

Laurelle Cousins

ISBN: 9781763891203
Published by LCP

Cover Design: Laurelle Cousins
Laurelle Cousins Press
Cover Images: Laurelle Cousins Photography
Images: All other images using DeepAI
https://www.laurellecousins.com

To Mike, Corinne, Anna, and Jeremy.
May we always fight to the death in board games and still love each
other, even those who cheat.

Laurelle Cousins

CHAPTER 1

Gus Stevens pulled up at the end of his driveway, forcefully winding down his manual side window and ignoring the way the glass made the rubber seals turn inwards. The hot wind blowing in from the north hit with force, making him recoil. Those winds were never good. But then again, it didn't have to be a fiery day for danger to rear its unforgiving head.

He reached out the ute window, stretching to grab the welded-on fork he used as a handle on his letterbox. With any luck, Patsy might have delivered his mail early.

The letterbox shut with a slap, and he let out a long breath as he stared at his hand. Nothing except another bill. He gave it a fleeting glance before tossing it to the passenger seat, where his blue heeler sat diligently. She sniffed at it, then looked up at him with a big grin, her tongue lolling from her mouth as she panted happily.

'It's okay for you,' he said, reaching out to give her a loving scruff on the back of the neck. 'You don't have to pay them.' He gave her a lop-sided smile, grateful for her eternal loyalty, before sliding the ute into first gear and rolling towards the edge of the road. He was keen to get to town and back before anyone caught sight of him.

Gus swung onto the road, shying from the glaring sun that was popping its head above the horizon. He pulled down his sun visor, not missing the thick smell of black bitumen already heating up.

'Stupid sign,' he scoffed, looking at his dog to avoid the blaring "For Lease" words on the real estate sign pegged tightly in the ground of his next-door neighbour's property. The Pilchers had left just after the accident—he hated how that was so easy to remember—and as far as he was aware, no one had given so much as a side glance in its direction. He might have inherited his run-down property from his uncle, with its sandy soil and copious amounts of coastal heathland in the Otways, but it couldn't have been in a better spot. Not unless he wanted to consider the Nullarbor Plain as an ideal location to exist.

And he had.

But no one in their right mind would ever consider the derelict property. The thought brought a smile as he pushed back a tuft of hair from his face, the wind continuing to whirl inside the cabin, stirring up the sand he'd collected on his thongs. The tree carnage alone from the wild coastal southerly winds was enough to turn anyone away, even if the rent was cheap.

He absently shook his head as the "Welcome to Forest Gully, established 1891, Population 200" sign slipped by him, releasing a disheartened huff. He might not be a bona fide local, but he'd been living here long enough to know most of them. He'd been welcomed with open arms, pouring himself into the community when he'd first arrived.

And now? That's what made it so much harder to stay.

His theory these days was that the less they saw of him, the quicker they'd forget. But would they? He sure as hell wouldn't. Never mind the fact he couldn't afford to leave. The way the town's economy was heading, no one in their right mind would buy his own property even if he tried to sell up.

Nope. He was stuck here for good.

Gus pulled up in front of the General Store, looking from left to right before he forced the squeaky door open and hopped out, making a beeline for the café. Meg knew his order by heart and didn't treat him like some of the other townsfolk. Her smile was bright as he entered.

'Good morning, sunshine. My, aren't we looking attractive today.' She smirked at him with a glint in her eye as she fired up the steam on her coffee machine.

He took a quick glance at what he'd pulled on that morning, pressing his lips together at the sight of his tatty board shorts and T-shirt that had a permanent coffee stain down the front even though he'd tried with several washes to remove it. He'd resisted Nola's recommendation of a good splash of bleach, more than sure it'd only end up looking like a gigantic bird poo. He didn't have too many good tops, and the last thing he wanted was to waste his time on shopping, so it'd have to do.

'Haven't seen you in a while. Same same, or are we feeling like a little change up? I hear a mocha goes down pretty well in the city.' Meg's eyebrows wiggled, hoping to persuade him.

'Nah, just the old old thanks, Meg. Actually, make it a double.' He gave her a weak smile.

'Hmm, we have got a busy day ahead then. What's on the agenda?' Her chirpy attitude was helping his unmotivated mood, but not enough to make him believe he deserved it.

'Nothing special,' he said, giving her a dismissive shrug. 'Although I wouldn't mind getting the old shearing shed cleaned up. Reckon I'll need to think about shearing those cursed sheep soon. I could've done without that particular inheritance from the Pilchers. They're intent on giving me grief and then some.' He shook his head, his wry grin unmissable as she chuckled back.

Meg passed him his coffee, giving him a knowing grin as she caught his eye. 'This one's on the house. You get out there and enjoy, okay?' To her credit, she didn't press him any further.

Gus took the takeaway cup in his hands, wishing he'd asked for an iced coffee once he wrapped his hand around it. 'Yep, sure. You too.' He raised the cup in salute before heading out the door.

As he walked towards the General Store, his melancholy

state of mind improving thanks to his first sip of caffeine, a burly bloke stopped just short of ploughing directly into him from around the corner. Gus pulled up with a jolt, his coffee shooting from the spout and dribbling down his hand with a sting . . . as he laid eyes on Ash Evans.

And as he opened his mouth to apologise, all words vanished.

CHAPTER 2

Kate Harris slowed, leaning over the top of her steering wheel, peering at the small cluster of shops running along one side of the quiet street, squinting in search of the real estate agency.

'It's gotta be here somewhere.' She snuck a look in the rear vision mirror, her enthusiasm taking a swift nosedive at the sight of Riley's melancholy face as he stared out of his window despite the inviting ocean delightfully glistening in the sunlight.

Her mouth twisted as she weighed up the choices of shops before her. 'Maybe if we ask in there.' She pulled out a determined smile, pointing towards The Old Forest Gully General Store. 'They might be able to tell us.'

Putting her blinker on, she swung into a car park in front of the shop, undoing her seatbelt and twisting to face her nephew. 'Wanna come and check it out? There's a café. We can get a hot chocolate.' She nodded, hoping he'd show some eagerness at this big adventure she'd assured him he was going to love. But even now, she could hear his repertoire of responses in her mind. *I don't feel like it. It's too hot,* she silently mouthed to herself as her eyes circled the interior of the car. Was it unfair to expect him to be as excited as she was? Was it so wrong to hope a little of her enthusiasm might rub off?

'It's too hot,' he offered quietly, his vacant gaze holding strong.

Ha! What did I tell you? She shuffled to face the front again, stealing a tight breath as her fingers drummed the steering wheel before letting the windows down. She wanted to bite her tongue so hard she'd be happy to feel the pain, but instead, she hopped out, holding onto the car door and bending to poke her head back inside for one last long shot.

'Aww, c'mon, Riley.' She pushed a smile onto her face, hiding the frustration lingering dangerously close to the surface. He was only eight, and it worried her how withdrawn he'd become. But the moment he laid eyes on where they were going to live, she was sure he'd cheer up. He had to.

Kate looked about her, spying a blue heeler tied to the verandah post of the store by a lead, her tail wagging along the pavement as she watched on. She turned back to Riley. 'Hey, how about you keep this little girl company?' She raised her eyebrows in hope. Riley reluctantly lifted himself in the seat to see what she was talking about. Her face filled with expectancy as he slowly unclipped his seatbelt, no doubt to have her think he was doing this purely as a favour to her when, all along, she knew how much he loved dogs. She whispered a silent thank you to whoever had left the friendly pooch there.

'I'll just be quick, okay?' She shut the door, offered the dog a gentle pat, and then glanced about while she allowed the quadrillion concerns consuming her to fill her mind. How on earth was she meant to look after her sister's child? He'd hardly spoken the whole eighteen-plus hours they'd travelled the last couple of days, and that didn't include his complete silence overnight in the motel room. It wasn't like him; his kid-like bubbliness was normally so infectious.

But one thing she knew for certain. She definitely wasn't meant to be any kind of mother. Not yet. What had possessed Jenna to make her his guardian anyway? Wasn't it enough to have to deal with her only sibling's death? And why had her sister even decided to write a will?

She had no right to die.

Kate closed her eyes against the heat from the threatening tears building behind them. This was her—no, *their* new life. And it was going to be good. It had to be. She just needed to convince Riley of it.

A blistering rush of hot wind whipped at her, making her wish she hadn't worn jeans for the last stint of the trip from Albury, but they'd left early enough to ensure they arrived with time to acclimatise themselves. But as she headed for the General Store, she halted, her eyes narrowing with wariness.

'Well, look who it is—the town hero.'

Kate's brow furrowed as a broad-shouldered man pointed an accusing finger at the guy standing in front of him, his coffee taking a shake as he staggered back.

'I've never said I was, Ash.'

'And you never will.' The man pushed past him, sending the coffee to the ground with a splat.

Kate put a hand to her mouth to hide her shock as the guy blinked at his spilt coffee, shaking the droplets from his arms and slowly bending to pick up the now-empty cup and lid from the pavement. She didn't want him to catch her watching his sad scene unfold, so she moved towards the café, her stride confident despite an image of Riley flickering in her mind. She lifted a smile towards the guy as she moved past, following the delicious aroma of freshly brewed coffee, be it from the pavement or the actual café she couldn't decide. The heat be damned, she needed one.

Now armed with two coffees in a cardboard holder, a two-litre bottle of milk hooked under her arm and a cold can of drink, she stepped outside again, glancing about as fresh disappointment settled on her. The guy she'd seen earlier had worn the face of a disheartened man, and she'd bought him a replacement coffee to cheer him up, but he was nowhere to be seen. But it wasn't like she hadn't downed two coffees in her time, so she shrugged happily and turned towards the General Store. The friendly café owner called Meg had said Nola Richardson would be able to help her.

Kate stopped by Riley, offering him the can of drink, which he accepted with a brief half smile—definitely the dog's doing, Kate decided—before dumping the milk in the footwell of her car. She pushed open the heavy door of the store with her elbow, balancing the coffees with precision as she entered the shop.

It was like any other small-town store, with its shelves full of essentials from packets of biscuits and boxes of cuppa soups to bread and the newspaper of the day. There was a Post Office sign at a separate desk, and further around was a table and chair with flyers displaying properties for lease and sale. She'd come to the right place.

But as she took a step forward, she stilled. In front of her was the same guy she'd seen being given a roasting, now standing with his back to her. With her mouth slightly open and his coffee still in hand, her confidence dwindled. Should she give it to him? She was a stranger, after all. He'd no doubt think she was some kind of well-intended nutter if she was lucky.

A friendly face bobbed around the side of his head with a bright smile, breaking her questioning thoughts. 'Good morning. Can I help you?'

'Um, Nola?' Kate smiled back at the shopkeeper, who nodded and then hesitated as the guy turned to face her, sizing her up and down like she was some secret agent he needed to be highly suspicious of, his sun-bleached locks swinging with him. He comfortably carried that surfy look, the kind she'd drooled over on posters as a teenager.

'Yes,' Nola said brightly and before Kate could convince herself otherwise, she thrust a coffee into his hands in one quick stride, startling him. Her eyes strayed over the deformed skin on his forearms before she redirected her gaze, hoping she'd disguised her curious surprise.

'I . . . thought you could use that.' She gave a little shrug, her eyes cast to the shop shelves. 'Your other one hit the ground rather hard.' Risking a side look his way, she flashed him a hesitant grin but hoped it conveyed what she'd intended. Life was too short. Losing her sister, Jenna, had brought all that home, and she refused to sit back when someone needed a leg up in life or a little friendly encouragement.

'Oh.' He drew his head back, still staring at the coffee cup now in his hand, before he raised dumbfounded eyebrows at the woman behind the counter. Kate recognised Nola's well-there-you-go smile before letting her warm gaze settle back on Kate, a certain glint in her eye.

Well, you've done it this time, Zippy. She blinked at the memories her nickname stirred, ripples of sadness and regret filling her of home and everything she'd lost.

With pressed lips, he moved to step around her, raising the coffee briefly, his perplexed gaze resting on her for an awkward moment before he shook his head ever so slightly and then exited the shop.

Kate took a peek over her shoulder, her eyes following him as he stopped by Riley, smiling, then having a brief conversation with her nephew. Riley gave a big toothy grin back, melting her to the core. Seeing it was like seeing her old Riley, the little guy she had all the adventures with in times gone past. If only she could bottle that happiness and sprinkle it over his head each time he needed cheering up.

Her attention turned back to the guy as he took his dog by the lead and strode towards a beaten-up ute, opening the front door with a distinct metallic squeak and letting the dog jump up before he hopped in.

She stood, fascinated, as he sat for a moment, the puzzled expression he'd carried with him the moment she'd thrust the coffee upon him still lingering on his face before he took a slow sip of his drink. He raised his eyebrows, the crinkle at the side of his eyes softening as he removed the cap, staring inside at the liquid as if it should have bitten him before he licked his lips. His mouth lifted with the gentlest of smiles.

His ute rattled to a start, and it reminded her of home, where farm utes were run with hard love but maintained just enough to keep them climbing the next hill. She gave a soft chuckle.

'And how can I help you, dear?'

The woman's welcoming voice drew her attention back with a jolt. 'Oh, sorry.' Kate stepped forward. 'I'm here to pick up my keys.'

'Oh yes! You must be Kate Harris. It's wonderful to have you move into the community. Fresh blood is just what this place is in dire need of.' She gave Kate a beaming smile.

Community. The word danced in her mind, and she released a slow breath as her shoulders visibly relaxed. Grief had a way of turning things inside out. This change was exactly what both she and Riley needed.

'Thanks. I can't wait,' and she accepted the keys from Nola, tossing them in the air.

CHAPTER 3

'Since. Bloody. When?'

Gus let out a low growl as he slowed in front of the real estate sign, leaning forward to make sure he was seeing correctly. The vintage work truck Graham Richardson was immensely proud of was parked on the other side of the road. He was standing next to the for-lease sign, grinning with satisfaction at his handiwork. Gus leaned back in his seat, his mouth ajar.

'That . . . that's impossible.' The words escaped Gus's mouth in a disbelieving whisper as he looked over at his dog, her tongue dripping with the heat. Graham had to have his wires crossed. He'd just seen his wife. Nola hadn't said anything. He closed his eyes, opening them quickly, fully believing what he was seeing was some kind of mad mistake.

Graham approached, tugging Gus's passenger door open with a loud clunk.

'G'day, son.' Graham's smile had increased to the size of a saucer, but Gus had no words. He looked from the man to the sign and the oversized sticker plastered to the real estate board, then back to him again, dumbfounded.

'Got some good news for you,' Graham continued, seemingly ignoring Gus's apparent state of shock. 'You've got a new neighbour.' The ocean-born creases around his eyes crinkled as he blinked with expectancy, waiting for Gus to respond.

'But?' Gus felt his Adam's apple tighten. This was not the news he'd envisaged arriving home to. He scratched his head. He'd have to think of something quick smart to stop it.

'What's the matter, son?' Graham looked bewildered

before turning back to the sign with pride. ''Bout time we had a newbie in the district. Everyone around here's so starch and stale. She just might breathe a bit of fresh air into this old place, I reckon.' He chuckled good-naturedly, patting the roof of the ute with eagerness, then turning back to Gus, conviction in his eyes. 'Don't you reckon, Speedy?' The dog looked up at him like she was happy to play along. He gave her a scratch around the ears.

Gus had no words for a second time that morning.

And *she*? Gus continued to blink at Graham, unable to relax his jaw before managing to find his words. 'Who exactly is *she?*'

'Kate Harris. And a little ripper if what Nola says is anything to go by. She just rang me on my way back to the shop. Said I'd better put that sticker on the sign because she's here already.'

Graham continued with his infuriatingly chuffed outlook, but right now, that was the least of Gus's problems. The sticker didn't say the Pilchers' place had been leased.

It was SOLD.

'Are people even allowed to do that?' Gus hopped from the ute now parked in front of his beach hut, staring at Speedy, who was standing beside him, wagging her backside, her tail only just keeping up as she watched him like she was understanding every word he was saying.

Gus had previously taken the real estate sign down twice, Graham always managing to set it back in its rightful place on the assumption a couple of local ratbag teenagers were playing pranks on him. Not even hiding it in the undergrowth of the native currant bushes five hundred metres away had deterred Graham from the challenge of returning the sign to its rightful place.

'Bugger me, Speedy, we've got a new neighbour coming.' He rubbed his shortish beard, regretting the fact he hadn't asked Graham when the actual settlement date was. She might be here already, but surely she wasn't going to move in straight away. The place was a wreck, and he still had a lot of work to do before she moved in. Without a fence existing between the two properties, he'd regarded the space as pretty much his own.

But now . . .

Each section of land, while side by side, had an equal expanse of acreage. But both houses were roughly one hundred and fifty metres apart, not visible due to the dense scrubby undergrowth. Each block was basically rectangular, with the backs facing the wild south coast where a sheer cliff face loomed with near-impossible access. That was unless you were Gus Stephens.

Up until now, the absence of a boundary fence had made the management of the Pilchers' property a simple chore. He could stroll amongst the gums and scrub, checking things were in order. The house needed a bit of work, but nothing a handyman couldn't tackle. His interest piqued. Graham had only said a woman's name. Was there a guy with her that Nola hadn't seen?

He shrugged the thought off with feigned nonchalance. If there was a guy, all the better. He could let the two of them sort things out for themselves as long as they left him to his hermit-like—he preferred to think of it as uncomplicated—life.

Gus laced his fingers together on top of his head, uncertain where his thoughts were landing. What he needed to do was think through a quick plan, and the only place he could do that best was eight hundred metres away at the south of both properties.

With his surfboard scraping against the protruding branches, he forged his way through the scrub, his full-piece wet suit hanging from his hips and his free arm pushing aside the branches obstructing his way. The rough ground was hot from the sun's heat as the loose sand, which covered most of the Otway landscape, gathered between his toes over his thongs. He did a short skip, shaking it away. His feet were hardened from his constant trekking to the beach and back, sometimes twice a day, but the occasional stray stone still managed to catch him off guard.

Speedy raced ahead, picking up a scent and scurrying through the bushes for an unprepared mouse or rat, her tail swishing with high excitement for the imminent pursuit.

Gus slowed as he reached the tall edge of the cliff and the near-vertical fifty-metre descent, ignoring the way the hot wind made his skin pinch. The ocean was his, any time of the day he chose. He lived simply. Gone was the future he'd banked on, so future be damned. He didn't need one anyway.

He wove his way down the rough path he'd forged when he'd moved here, embracing the smell of the incoming tide that rolled in below with relentless form, ensuring no mercy was given to the rocks that held back the expansive cliff. The whitewash tumbled and tossed the incoming seaweed, and a sandfly stung the gnarled skin on his arm as he stepped onto the clean sand, kicking his thongs to the side with a smooth flick. He slapped at the bug—not missing the fact it didn't sting like it should have thanks to the scars he wore—keen to get down amongst the action now more than ever. This part of the beach was his own, a place where no one intruded to interrupt his solitude.

His thoughts swung to his Uncle Neil. He tried not to dwell too much on the man who'd become his sole custodian when his mother and father had died in a head-on collision with a large semi when he was a young boy. The memory stirred up mixed feelings. Missing out on the chance to know his mother and father had saddened him. And still did. But if it hadn't been for his uncle, there was no telling what might have shaped him into the person he was today. But moving down here . . . in the beginning, it had been hard. He'd uprooted himself from a full life at Ballarat in the Western District of Victoria, and it wasn't until he'd joined the Country Fire Authority (CFA) of Forest Gully and worked his way up to number two lieutenant that he'd found his footing and purpose within the community.

That's where he'd met Kelly Evans. He couldn't put into words the way his heart had awakened inside his chest the moment her soul-warming eyes had caught his at the working bee. She'd nudged him good-naturedly for jumping the queue, the excuse of a barbeque hamburger seeming as good as any just to stand beside her. They'd hit it off straight away and had been inseparable. His chest grew tight as his heart gave a sad pang, loneliness jolting him yet again.

The cold chill of the ocean spray clawed at him despite the heat in the air. He laid his board at the water's edge, steadying it before he wrestled the rest of his wetsuit over his upper body, grateful it not only allowed him to stay in the ocean longer but because it hid the scars—his constant reminder.

He sucked in a tight breath. The sooner he got into the water, the sooner he could breathe.

With the surf picking up pace thanks to the afternoon ocean winds, waves built in sets that had Gus picking and choosing the best of them. Gliding into shore, he about-faced and paddled out once more, this time resting on top of his board, his feet dangling either side in the water. He faced the cove—his sanctuary—the place that had saved him from complete despair on more than one occasion. But a fresh thought worked its way to the forefront of his mind. What would he do about this new neighbour?

He licked the salt from his lips as Speedy stopped abruptly, staring out at him before turning and chasing down the froth from the next wave that tumbled onto the shore.

And what about his own life? No longer did volunteering

hold such importance. In fact, the less he did of it, the better. He didn't need that in his life.

Ever again.

And it wasn't like he needed much, even though Nola had told him off only that morning for the skin hanging from his bones. His best mate, Hughey, passed on cuts of meat to him most weeks, and Patsy dropped off a box of veggies from her impressive garden every second week or so. He quite enjoyed playing Russian roulette with his meals, and he was interested in finding out what he could come up with, given what was in his fridge from week to week.

These were the people who still included him as an acceptable local, including Meg, of course. But Ash Evans and the brigade boys, all except Graham, he could do without. He was over their judgy attitudes and high horse motives that they liked to push with their so-called good works. He'd joined the team because he wanted to make a difference.

Now, there was no difference left to be made.

He shook his head, his locks sticking to his shoulders as another wave swelled beneath his board, lifting his feet. Keep it simple, stupid; that was his approach. But he'd silently adjusted the saying, making his own version.

Keep the Solitude Secure. That was his forever motto to live by from now until the day he saw Kelly again.

CHAPTER 4

Kate could hardly hide the excitement bubbling inside her as she slowed, pulling over to the side of the road and staring at the gigantic sign next to her new driveway.

'Here it is, Riles, our new home. Well, the front entrance anyway.' She shifted in her seat to see Riley staring straight through the "sold" sticker. She gave way to her shoulders, allowing them to droop as she looked out the windscreen once more, her own enthusiasm feeling like it had a chink struck from it. A driver coming in the opposite direction acknowledged her with his hand on the steering wheel, and she smiled, enthusiastically waving back, there and then determining to make this sea change work for them both. It was exactly what they needed.

Kate scanned the landscape, relieved that her trees and shrubs looked flush and alive, unlike the blackened bushland she'd travelled through earlier as she'd approached Forest Gully. Narrowing her gaze, she looked to her right for a fence to indicate where her property boundary was. Her gateway and the neighbouring one were separated by a lone post, so it had to be somewhere nearby. A rabbit darted from the cover of one bush to the next.

But where exactly was their house? Pinning all her hopes on the perfect home for them, the one she'd dreamt of, she'd assumed it might be near the front gate. She had twenty acres to do with as she pleased, and she couldn't wait to start growing things. Regardless of Riley's "who cares" attitude, she was going to make a go of this. And he'd love it. Eventually. All she had to do was give him time, as much as he needed, to make this his new home, to fall in love with it like she was more than ready to. One walk along the beach and he'd be hooked … she was sure of it. She contemplated even driving back to the main street later so they could do just that along the beachfront opposite the shops, ice cream in hand after a refreshing swim. She couldn't think of a more perfect introduction to their new life.

Kate edged into her driveway, her anticipation tangible. Her small car bumped and tossed from side to side as she inched forward. Was this some kind of inland safari track where you needed an off-road vehicle and a driving permit to get in? She chuckled to herself, keeping an eye out for their home, complete with rustic views and serenity just like the website had promised.

Stopping mid-way down the drive, Kate jumped out to tug another rogue branch lying across her access to the side of the driveway. When she returned to the car, Riley's expression was less than impressed as she put the car in gear again. But that's what kids did, right? Made your life a bit hard, to begin with, then loved you with all their might? He'd definitely scored eleven out of ten on his current scorecard.

She'd been the favourite auntie—the only one, actually— and he'd been a kid who'd always wanted to explore. And she loved him for it, taking him on auntie-only adventures all over their farm in Queensland, thanks to her love of the wide-open spaces and stock. But now, with the disaster still fresh in their past eight months on, he'd lost that love and his unfaltering love for his auntie, so it seemed.

'Why'd you even bring me here?' He crossed his arms over his chest, his cheeks ballooning with air as he frowned out the window, his body rocking with yet another tree root curling its way across the driveway.

'Because we need a fresh start.' Kate paused to gather her thoughts, wishing she could convince herself it had, in fact, been the right thing to do given the way he'd been acting the whole way here. 'And because we'll be able to go to the beach whenever we like. Won't that be incredible?' It was a far cry from the dry, inland environment they'd known.

The answer she got was silence.

A glint of tin reflected in the sun as the house roof came into view, and she sat taller in her seat, excitement building. 'There it is, Riles,' and she couldn't help but point. The online images had spruiked a four-bedroom house sporting acreage and the smell of fresh sea air. She'd been well assured by the agent, seemingly a biased local from what she was currently looking at, that it had everything she was looking for.

Instead, what she was greeted with was the last thing she'd anticipated.

'Baaaaa. Baa, baaaa, baaaa.' Several sets of eyes analysed her arrival as though visitors weren't expected or welcome and would be delighted if she could about-face and vacate *their* premises.

'What?' Kate's mouth grew wider the longer she eyed the scene. Cautiously hopping out of the car, she hesitated, unsure what to make of, let alone what to do about what lay—quite literally—in front of her. What was meant to be her verandah was currently overrun with a multitude of woolly bodies, clearly prepared to hold their ground as they watched her with scrutinising stares.

'Baaa.'

Kate's head drew back, that bleat the full stop to her thoughts. And then she saw it, her home. Her heart plummeted two feet below where she stood.

This is what I've bought after all my effort and planning. Her chest could have caved in if she hadn't managed another sorry breath. It looked more like a demolition job with a tree trying to grow through the verandah roof, a busted gutter and a door that hung wide open like it was a free-for-all backpackers lodging.

'Huh. So *that's* what they meant when they said it was rustic.'

She stood back, only rousing from her disbelief when Riley spoke, his words giving rise to the trickle of optimism still clutching tight inside her.

'Auntie Kate, I don't reckon sheep are meant to live inside with us.'

Kate looked at him, then the doorway where a sheep's backside casually disappeared inside. A giggle flowed from her mouth before she burst out laughing, looking back towards her nephew. And he laughed too, the sight of it filling Kate with so much love for him she could almost burst.

'Maybe it's a pet sheep like Nosey,' Kate said, remembering the way the lamb wouldn't drink his bottle from anyone other than Riley.

Riley nodded, heading towards the animals, unphased by their presence. He was a true farm kid in every way, and it warmed her to watch him move so as not to spook the sheep, who, in her opinion, were far too chilled around humans. Their home had to be somewhere close by. But that could be worked out tomorrow. Right now, she was bushed. All she wanted to do was unpack their basics, then sit down with a cool drink and simply enjoy her tranquil surroundings. This was their sea change for a brighter future.

Besides, if the sheep were, in fact, hers, she simply had some tenants she could work with. Some extra revenue would be perfect, and these sheep could be just that. She'd make the best of it, showing Riley that it was all about your approach, not what you viewed as a lack thereof.

'Shoo, shoo! Go on, get outta here,' Kate said good-naturedly, making her way through the sheep poo rolling about her feet. The sheep resting near the doorway begrudgingly stood, shifting further down the verandah while others stared at her contemptuous audacity. She pushed through the half-open door with Riley close behind, keen to get inside for a look-see when she abruptly stalled. Their verandah guests were only the start of it.

Spider webs draped the ceiling from end to end, and wallpaper peeled freely from the walls. The skirts and architraves were manicured perfectly to knee height by precision teeth marks. And what was meant to be their dining table had an extremely content, fat ewe relaxing on top of it like she was the queen of her kingdom, chewing her cud. Her bright eyes blinked at Kate.

'Well, at least the place looks like it's been loved,' and she gave Riley a humoured nudge with her elbow, hoping to keep his recent good mood intact.

Humph. Nope. Not one ounce was left if his disapproving face was anything to go by.

'Okaaay,' Kate said, her raised eyebrows taking in the five-star sheep accommodation once more.

'Are we meant to sleep in here tonight?' Riley's wavering voice disarmed her good intentions, and she closed her eyes tight to blot out the sight of her dust-infused kitchen, now understanding why there hadn't been a photo of it online. She made her way down the hallway, finding beds in each room. At least that part of the ad was correct, if you could call a bed with three legs a functional piece of furniture. Kate huffed a disbelieving chuckle. Maybe her royal highness had servants residing in this part of the house.

All aspirations for the ensuite were dashed the moment she turned on the taps at the vanity. Brackish brown water chugged from pipes that reverberated from deep within the walls, the smell old and disused. With her face turned aside, she held her breath and left the tap on, glancing a peek with one eye after a minute.

Finally, clean water flowed from the tap and the smell, while not completely gone, was improved.

'Right then, lets choose a room for you, young man,' and with her best motivating voice and an encouraging hand on Riley's shoulder, she steered them down the hallway. They chose the cleanest room with the nicest view. Beginning to think nothing would sway him, it was a no-brainer to give up the best space. One day he'd appreciate the stunning views of the trees or enjoy watching a kangaroo while lying in bed.

Returning to the large living area, her gaze narrowed on the ewe still eying her from her throne as Kate headed towards the front door, keen to grab their luggage. As she took two suitcases in her hands, she turned to face her new dwelling, mustering a renewed outlook. It has good bones, she tried to convince herself. And that equalled potential, be it with a mountain of hard work. But she'd never been afraid of that. It was Riley who she was more worried about right now.

Kate swished at the flies circling her with unrelenting interest as she stood at the boot of her car for her second load, staring over the top of her mound of doonas, pillows and her backpack. For a place that looked wild enough, it could have passed for being undiscovered since Adam was a dot; why was there someone walking through her property . . . in half a wetsuit?

Tugging her eyes away, guilt swamped her for gawking at the strong, tanned torso with long locks trailing over his shoulders, his defined biceps flexing with his movement. But no sooner had she shifted her gaze aside than her eyes were bouncing back with interest to the surfboard now disappearing into the nearby scrub. She stooped down for a better look, risking toppling her load. Who was that? And he had a surfboard? She swiftly dismissed her interest, telling herself it was probably just some random teenager. But if he was here, did that mean the beach was accessible from their place? Having it within reach sounded amazing, but as for people waltzing through her property . . . not so great. Finding the fence line outlining her property raced to the top of her to-do list for tomorrow.

Riley interrupted her musings, ducking his head inside the car to grab his Lego. That had to be a good sign, she tried to convince herself.

'Hey, bud, see that rock next to the garden shed?' She pointed to a wooden building all but falling over next to a broken wheelbarrow. 'I've put a spare key under it, okay?'

Riley gave a disinterested nod before heading back inside, leaving Kate wanting more but feeling empty. She swung her gaze back to the track, but the surfer had vanished, a frown burrowing into her brow. She headed back inside, pushing past the sheep attempting to re-settle themselves in the afternoon shade of her verandah right in front of her door.

With a determined glare at the ewe still atop her table, she headed for her room, dumping her armful onto her lop-sided bed before marching back to the living room, her objective clear. There were going to be two of them living in this house, not three, and an eviction was about to take place.

'Right, Monica. We need to have words.' The ewe turned towards her like it was the most natural thing to do as she continued chewing. From the corner of her eye, Kate saw Riley look up with mild curiosity as he tipped his Lego onto the small table covered in coffee ring stains in front of the fireplace.

'You see what you're sitting on?' Kate made a circle with her finger and gave the ewe a nod. 'Well, it's our dining table.' She drew out the words, hoping the sheep would get the message from her tone.

The ewe continued to chew, blinking.

Kate leaned forward to ensure the sheep didn't miss a word. 'And you know what goes *on* a dining table? Dinner. And if you don't move your cute woolly bum off there right now, you just might be our next meal, so move.' And with that, Kate shoved the ewe with greater effort than she'd first thought might be necessary until the sheep casually jumped to the floor with a thud before ambling towards the open door, but not before giving Kate one last brown-eyed glare.

'Go on. *Out!*' Kate gave the order with her finger, pointing to the door, and she followed the sheep, pushing her hindquarters outside and shutting it with a heavy nudge, but not before another barrage of uninvited visitors arrived by the dozen. Flies, the size of mice according to Kate, flew in, claiming the air space as their own and swarming around her face like they were expecting to sample some delectable treat from the corners of her mouth.

'Argh.' Kate swiped at them wildly, her patience now at an all-time low.

She marched to the kitchen and searched the drawers for a swat; the only thing remotely useful was a crusty old tea towel that smelled of dust and used dishes lying on the sink. She twisted it into submission and began flicking at every surface they landed on, counting it a double win when she swatted two of them in the act of hanky panky, which apparently seemed to be all the go. The heat inside was stifling, but if she left the windows open, without flyscreens, they'd be harassed all night, let alone what other creepy crawlies might decide to pop in and check out the new digs. The only blessing was the working ceiling fan that rocked back and forth with a bothersome rhythmic beat.

The evening air was cooling as Kate propped up her bed with an old stump she'd found underneath a tree outside, made the beds and cleaned down the kitchen to a workable state. They had slim pickings for their tea with the butter a melted slosh from their trip even though she'd put an ice block in the esky that morning, so she made up two sandwiches and glued them together, one with peanut butter for Riley and the other with vegemite for her. The two of them sat in the stillness, listening to the cicadas' thrum and the birds ready themselves to roost for the night. It was music to her ears.

CHAPTER 5

Kate dragged herself out of bed thanks to a somewhat predicted lousy sleep. Between the frogs croaking in some nearby waterhole—she was certain should have dried up with the heat they were sweltering under—and a continuous shuffling and scratching she could only assume were her bed and breakfast guests on the verandah, she was overtired and more than a little cranky.

She shuffled out to the kitchen and put the kettle on, desperate for a coffee. As she waited for it to boil, she opened every window she could to let in the cool early morning breeze before it heated to another thirty-eight-degree day and the flies arrived in droves once more.

She had her lips wrapped around the rim of her mug, ready to take her first sip when Riley called from outside. Kate almost dropped her cup as she shoved it towards the table and ran to the door, fearful of what she might find, but to her relieved disbelief, Riley was grinning as he cuddled what looked like the beautiful blue heeler they'd seen yesterday, who in turn was welcoming him with a luscious lick.

'Can we keep him? Pleeease, Auntie Kate. He's lost.'

'Well, it's actually a *she* and I don't think she's a stray, Riley. She's too well fed.' So were the sheep that had planted their fine tushes on her doorstep. She scanned the scrubby bushland. 'Which direction did she come from?'

'This direction.' The attractive voice resonated from deep in the bush, and Kate took a half step back, more than a little wary as a broadly built guy approached them from what appeared to be a worn pathway through the scrub. Was it considered normal to have men waltzing through her property like it was a freeway? She resented the calmness with which he strode towards her, appearing more handsome than should have been allowed as recognition dawned.

'It's . . . you.' Her voice hesitated, then a smile found her lips as she put her hands on her hips and straightened. 'So, how'd you enjoy the mocha?' A hopeful smile rose on her lips as her eyes fell on what looked like a shark tooth on a black cord around his muscular neck.

'Not bad. Not bad at all. Can't say I've had one before. Meg's been trying to twist my arm, though. I might just have to surprise her and order one next time I'm in town.' His lips rose but not enough to indicate he'd actually liked what she'd done for him. His smile was the kind you showed when life had worn you down. She recognised the look all too well.

Kate nodded slowly, trying to decide why the random guy she'd bought a coffee for only the day before was now standing on her property, looking like he knew his way around.

'I'm Kate, and this is Riley.' She took her nephew by the shoulders warmly, sensing him stiffen beneath her hands but her eyes remained glued to mocha guy. 'You've got a beautiful dog. I think we met her yesterday.'

This time, he smiled as if he found it hard to receive a compliment. 'Name's Gus, and yeah, she is.' He glanced down as his dog wagged her tail enthusiastically, keeping an eye on him but more than happy to accept as many pats as Riley wanted to give. 'That's why I named her Speedy. Should've been a beagle the way she puts her head down and just goes.' He gave a half chuckle as he focused on his dog like that was easier than keeping his gaze on her. Kate watched him curiously.

'Speedy's a cool name.' Riley pressed his face into her neck fur, his grin saturating Kate's heart. Seeing her nephew acting like he used to back on the farm laid the foundation of relief in her soul, which she was so desperate to find. But she pulled herself up quickly. Some of those memories were too hard to face just yet. She needed this new home to take the time to breathe before she could start the full path to healing.

'So, you've bought the place.' Gus made a big gesture of scanning her property, tipping her off-kilter a little by his tone. 'I live next door.'

'I have. Is . . . that okay?' she said tongue-in-cheek. 'You don't appear too excited to have a new neighbour.' She sensed she was pushing, but she didn't like the feeling she got, as if he wanted her to pack up and leave.

'That all depends.'

'On what?' She stood a little taller.

'Are you going to stay? I mean, check the place out,' he said, swinging his hand around in front of him. 'It's way past its use-by date. It'd be hard to bring it back to its former self and cost a pretty penny, too.' He took her in with a disarming calmness.

'So, was it you walking through my place last night? Did you trip? I mean, since it's so bad, your words, not mine.' She smiled, the faint twitch of his eyes telling her she'd snookered him.

'She's a rugged place, that's all. You'd have to be desperate to want to live here.'

'You do.'

He nodded, defeated. 'Listen, I was only coming over here to get my sheep off the place, so if you don't mind, I'll—' His tone turned defensive. Had she overstepped some unspoken line?

'*Your* sheep? No, they're actually quite comfortable where they are.' She turned from him to her verandah as Monica bleated loudly at them both. He could take his good looks and march right back home. For good. 'They came with the property, so—'

'Look, Kate, it's not all it seems. The sheep are part of what the last owners left behind, for me. So if you don't mind, I'll take them home now.' He moved towards them, keeping his eyes off Kate as she eyed him, trudging past her.

Kate stayed silent, more than sure his chances were Buckley's and none, unable to hide her pleasure when she was proven right. The guy couldn't shift sheep in a pink fit, and these girls were going to be harder than most. Being around sheep most of her life had taught her a thing or two.

'I see that's working for you,' she said as she folded her arms across her chest, finding it hard to resist smirking as he flapped his arms in the air like a scarecrow with Speedy barking at him, not the sheep.

She paid attention to the way he lifted his chin and let out a frustrated puff of air before speaking.

'It's too hot to shift them anyway. I'll do it another time.'

'Let me know, and I can help if you'd like.' Only, a small hunch told her this guy didn't ask for help too often.

'Nah, I'll work it out.' He called his dog as he disappeared down the mysterious path he'd emerged from.

Kate brushed her hands clean of the dust in the air and of this *Gus* who'd managed to intrigue and confuse her all at once. '*His* sheep. Well, we'll see about that,' she said before calling Riley in for breakfast. After that, she was going to find a good spot to dig a veggie patch.

Bloody sheep.

Gus leaned against the verandah post of his hut, a coffee brewing in his mug as the new day's heat began seriously rising.

They were more than a nuisance; they were the bane of his life. A soft memory danced to the forefront of his mind.

'Look, Gus.' Kelly pointed to the lambs racing about in a paddock they drove past. 'Aren't they so sweet?' She turned to him, her eyes full of determination and exhilaration. 'Let's have some sheep of our own one day.'

If it weren't for Kelly, he'd be glad to let his new neighbour have them. But because of her, he couldn't let them go.

An image of this new woman's gratified grin alongside her irritating assurance she was keeping his ewes filled his mind, suddenly making him more determined to get them back to his place. That was if he could work out how he'd get them home without her help. A deep groan rumbled from within his chest as his head tilted upwards.

And besides all that, what had gone so wrong with what was meant to be a flawless plan? Telling her how precarious the property was had kept more than four couples from leasing the place in the past, scared off by his embellished stories of wild pigs and possums that would nest in the walls and roof. And it was true . . . at least about the possums. Maybe that'd be all it would take, and he quietly chuckled to himself. She might appear strong on the outside, but could she survive the strange noises of the night? He'd have to wait patiently, but give it a good week or two with no sleep, and she'd be running from the place faster than he could shift his sheep. Well, perhaps that wasn't the best example to use, but regardless, she'd be gone, and he'd have his peace and quiet back. Guaranteed.

The clouds were white and fluffy above, but on the horizon threatening plumes were building. If he wanted to clear more of the scrub on their boundary so the sheep would have a new paddock to actually *stay* in, he'd have to start now. If rain rolled in, he might not be able to get the trailer on the ute for a couple of days, thanks to the sandy soil, and he wouldn't have the luxury of time, thanks to her unplanned arrival.

With that thought, he contemplated his situation. This woman called Kate could stand firm for as long as she liked, but that would change once she understood how hard it was to live out here. Without a tractor or the know-how, she was never going to survive, and he had bets on that she was the kind of woman who had no clue when it came to living on the land.

Gus pushed himself off the post, flicking the dregs of his cup towards the small garden he'd poured his heart into so there was some semblance of "home" to his dwelling. 'Rightio, Speedy, let's get some work done,' he said, leaning down to stroke the top of her head. He put the cup on the table under his small verandah, retrieved his boots from beside the door and pulled them on with a couple of hops.

His poky shed housed most of his livelihood, including a motorbike that didn't work, a wheelbarrow, and a few handy tools. It was all he needed. More stuff just meant things got more complicated, and the less of that, the better off he was.

The ute gave a bang as it came to life, and he thumped the dashboard with his fist to curb the consequential new squeak that had turned up a week ago. 'C'mon, old girl. You've got it in you,' he urged, and with a jitter, he backed the vehicle towards the trailer. He tossed a spade and a weathered wooden-handled mattock in the back with a thud before heading off down the rough track that should've been the boundary fence line between his place and next door.

He'd just started digging when Speedy gave a sharp bark, taking off through the scrub. When she returned, she had a friend with her.

Gus stood, smiling as he balanced his weight on his shovel with one foot.

'G'day, Riley. How are you? Sleep okay last night?' The kid looked a little quiet, but maybe he was just shy.

'Yep. I'm good.' Riley reached Gus and bent to pat Speedy, his face a little solemn.

Gus tilted his head to the side. Hmm, had either of them slept okay? The kid's drooping eyes suggested otherwise.

'Does Mum know you're over here?' He was certain she wouldn't be too happy if she did, given the reception he'd received last night. But that was exactly what he'd wanted, right? If it all looked too hard, she could still move on. The thought gave him confidence.

'Nah, she's busy. I just wanted to find out what had made that loud bang.' He glanced around him. 'Did you hear it?'

'Yeah, buddy, I sure did. Old Bertha here doesn't like early mornings. She doesn't like mid-mornings, afternoons or evenings either.' He gave a soft chuckle. The kid didn't crack a smile.

'She's not my mum.' Riley's voice faded away as he feigned interest in the trees to his side.

The comment threw Gus and he cocked his head to the side. 'She's not?'

'Nope. She's my auntie. We're starting again, so Auntie Kate says.' The way he said it piqued Gus's attention, not missing the quiver in the boy's voice.

'Oh, right.' Gus nodded. Curious but not wanting to pry, he began to dig another dead bush out, Riley's words churning over in his mind. Why would he be living with his auntie and not his mother? Was she sick? No one would choose to take their nephew from their sister for no good reason.

The big stump wasn't about to give up without a fight, and Gus worked up a sweat as the sun drained his energy. With one final tug, the roots lost their grip, and Gus stepped back with a steadying jolt.

'How long have you been out here?' The question threw Gus, and he extended the time he had to respond by heaving the cumbersome bush into the trailer and stopping to wipe the salty sweat from his brow.

'Long enough.' This had been his new start, too. His jaw clenched. Look where that journey had got him.

His Uncle Neil came to mind. Sure, the old guy might've been a bit of a fuddy-duddy and a whole lot of cranky, but he'd loved him more than he could say out loud to anyone. Regardless of how his life had turned out, he owed the old man big time.

Gus's narrowed lips sucked in a long breath as if it might cool his racing heart, and he reached for his cold bottle of water in the shade of the wheel arch on the trailer. He took a long slug before wiping his mouth with the back of his hand, eyeing the boy with interest.

'Hey, can I show you something? I've done enough digging for now. It's getting too hot.'

Riley stood, his face a mix of uncertainty and curiosity.

'Can you hear that sound?' and Gus pointed over his shoulder, his hand still holding the water bottle. 'Would you like to see the ocean?'

Riley's eyes lit up as he stood, Speedy licking his hand for more attention.

'Yeah.'

For the first time, Gus spied a glimmer of the boy's face filling with interest.

'Well, come on then.' Gus motioned for Riley to follow. He pushed past the many metres of wayward branches, holding them back for Riley as they moved through the crowded foliage. When they stepped into the clearing, Gus's chest filled with anticipation as Riley squinted against the blustery wind so typical on the oceanfront.

'She's a rugged coastline, but she's beautiful.' Gus allowed himself to be transfixed by the moody waves breaking against the rocks far below. It wasn't the first time he'd been captivated by the cliffside with its fragile rubble cascading down to a heaped pile at the bottom.

'Wow. It's incredible.' Riley didn't hide his eagerness. 'Can we go down there?' He moved to go.

'Nah, buddy. It's not safe,' Gus replied, reaching out to scruff the boy's hair good-naturedly. His gut told him it wasn't the best idea to show Riley how he got down to the water. But it didn't help that Speedy was now already halfway down the cliff using their usual path before she glanced back at him, tilting her head to the side in confusion when he called her to come back.

'We'd better get you home, or your Auntie Kate will get worried.' He motioned to leave but paused as Riley shook his head, studying the rocky ground at his feet.

'Hey, are you okay?' Gus moved towards the boy, but before he could reach him, Riley began to follow silently.

And all the way back to the house, he couldn't help but wonder why such a young kid was carrying the weight of the world on his small shoulders.

CHAPTER 6

Kate stood up, the sweat beading down her face beneath her wide-brimmed slouch hat. Her cheeks filled with air as she moved her shoulders in her sweaty t-shirt, squinting against the sun.

'Riley? Where are you, buddy?' She put her hands on her hips, circling a full 360 degrees. It would do him a whole lot of good to get out and investigate the place, making an adventure for himself around their acreage with hidey holes and hidden treasures waiting to be discovered. After what he'd gone through, he needed as much kid chill time as he could get.

She had no clue what time it was, but thirst was driving her towards the house. The faraway ocean roared on the warm air, and Kate stared at the sky in the west with a wary eye. Definite clouds were building, looking suspiciously like they intended some kind of business, the kind she'd worked hard to shove to the deepest depths of her mind.

Monica greeted her atop her dining table with a long baa as Kate stepped inside. With hands on her hips, she moved towards the fridge, shaking her head, be it with a small smile tweaking her lips. 'You'll keep, young lady.'

The glass beaded as she skulled the cold water and poured herself a second glass, poised at her lips when the door burst open.

'Auntie Kate, Gus showed me the ocean.' He pointed at the side wall of the house as though she should be able to see through it. 'It's incredible.'

Kate lowered the glass, her emotions swelling hard and fast. Seeing that smile on his face said it all. She'd done the right thing, coming here. 'That's nice.'

Any further words or thoughts of them tangled themselves in her mouth as Gus stepped inside after Riley, his face widening in a grin as he looked all damned delicious in a windswept kind of way. Kate made eyes at Monica; the kind you gave your best friend when a gorgeous guy showed you the remotest bit of attention. The ewe baaed a welcome to their guest, and Kate looked to the ceiling, cursing the sheep under her breath for giving away all her secrets, just like Jenna would have done.

'I see *Baabra* has made herself at home.' He chuckled, obviously happy with his woeful pun.

'Oh. So, you two are friends?' She waved her finger between them both before eying Monica again. 'Traitor.' She turned her attention back to Gus. 'And her name's Monica, by the way. We had a rather long chat last night—although we're yet to come to any firm agreement. Beats me why she thinks our dining table is better than yours.' She quite enjoyed showing him the smirk lifting her cheeks.

'Well, that's easy. Baabra has particular tastes. Your table is more spacious than mine.' The way he lifted his eyebrow as his face remained deadpan smacked of smugness, but she wasn't going to be defeated, not by a long shot.

'I'm sure we could acclimatise her to your table.'

'Nah, she knows you're soft. I don't have an open house policy like you do.' A tiny smirk nicked the edges of his soft whiskered lips.

But before she could retaliate, Riley peeled out the door again.

'Hey buddy, where are you off to?' Kate strode past Gus with not so much as a side glance, concern keenly replacing her enjoyment of their banter. Riley had been so excited to tell her about the ocean, and she'd zoned out on him, Gus taking her attention as fast as one of the quad-zillion flies still buzzing about inside the house. Her unease turned to annoyance, not at Riley, but at Gus. She couldn't afford to let him take her focus so simply, no matter how her heart skipped when she watched the way his gaze danced on her, which she had a hunch it was. She was here for one thing: for both her and Riley to heal.

The inside of the house might have been hot, made bearable only by the clackety ceiling fan. But outside, the sun continued to belt out a blazing heat, scorching her body as she moved back under the shaded relief of the verandah, nudging another reluctant sheep out of her way with her foot.

Riley knelt beneath the shade of a huge tree not far off where Speedy was lying, slapping her tail and making plumes of dust that puffed into the air. The darkening sky was creeping ever closer as Gus stepped up beside her, and she tugged her concern back to the dark depths, attempting to mask it with a smile.

'Looks like I'm not going to get the space for my veggie patch cleared out after all,' she said, risking another glance towards the threatening sky.

He nodded as he, too, looked to the sky. 'Storms 'round here can be pretty wild. Only last week, we had a—'

'Well, there are plenty of other things to do. Come on, Riley. Gus and Speedy need to head home.' She marched towards the door, fighting the imminent fear building inside her.

'But can't they stay for tea tonight?' Riley begged as he ran back to the house, Speedy hot on his tail. His face urged her to agree, and she considered the options. If he stayed, she'd just get more annoyed at him, not to mention the fact she still only had peanut butter and Vegemite for a meal. She'd overlooked the state of their food situation when inspiration to begin growing food for them had taken over.

If he left, he wouldn't have to see her body stiffen with sheer panic as she clambered underneath Monica's table. And

Riley—she shied away from the debilitating thought. The last time they'd been in a storm, only two of them had come home alive.

'I think—'

Gus saved her.

'I'll head off then, leave you two to it.' Before she could stop him, Gus called Speedy, and the two of them walked away with an ease she couldn't fathom through the growing rumble in the sky.

Gus took a hard left-hand turn off the track and came out at Shark Tooth Corner, his own personal place where the peak of the rock pointed to the Southern Ocean. A ship was sailing on the far horizon, perhaps heading for Hobart as the choppy seas rose and fell to their own rhythm.

He pushed his hair from his face as a distant flash of lightning illuminated the clouds around it. He'd seen enough storms to pick when they'd be turbulent, and at a guess, this one was all bluff with no bite. But still, it worried him. He hadn't missed the way Kate had stopped and listened intently as she studied the sky, rubbing her arms as if they were cold against the heat of the sun still shining in front of the approaching storm clouds.

Nah, they'll both be okay. He shook away his fleeting apprehension as a strong gust rocked him on his feet, indicating the air was changing.

But still, that nuisance tree that had planted itself right next to her house worried him. It had grown like a mushroom before he'd realised it was too late to simply tug out. Now its roots would be set deep below the verandah concrete, its leaves no doubt filling her gutters. He should've taken care of it long before anyone had arrived. He knew the risks. Now he'd put his CFA training to shame. If it came down on her, he wouldn't forgive himself and he'd done enough of that for one lifetime already.

'C'mon, Speeds, we'd better get home and buckle down.' He hoped Kate and Riley were doing the same.

CHAPTER 7

Kate cringed beneath the damp bedsheet she gripped around her mouth, unable to sleep due to the unbearable humidity and the lightning that continually lit up the room in unfriendly shapes thanks to her gaudy orange threadbare curtains.

A whimper sounded at her door, and she sprang from her bed, grabbing Riley and tugging him to her in a protective hug, hiding him from the lightning with her body. The poor kid. She'd never been surer about moving, and then her new neighbour mentioned that storms passed through the area most seasons of the year. How had she not thought to check a statistic like that out before committing to such a big move?

She pressed her cheek to Riley's head, kissing him. 'Love you to the moon and back, bud,' she whispered into his hair, the quote she'd read to him most of his life thus far.

Guess How Much I love You. It had been their book, an anthem vowing their love and loyalty towards one another. And now, she needed to be strong for him. But instead, all she was doing was making a huge mess of everything. She drew him closer, believing everything would be okay in time. If she didn't believe that, she'd have nothing to pull her through.

Why, Jenna? Why me? Mum and Dad would've been so much better at this child-rearing caper. A tear rolled down her cheek. *I'll never be the mum you were born to be.*

There had to be a reason why she'd been entrusted with this crazy child-rearing role, and she found some way to navigate it. She'd managed to be an auntie successfully up until Jenna had died. So why was she finding this role so hard? And if she didn't, she'd have to turn around and head back home. She'd promised to let her parents raise Riley if she couldn't. And she'd agreed with their deadline of six months, the start of June. She couldn't fail.

Daylight washed into the room, her broken sleep all too real as her eyes fluttered open and her body cramped with pins and needles. They'd camped in the doorway of her room since midnight, protected by the hallway walls while the storm had raged outside. She had no desire to contemplate what had happened out there or how Riley might respond to seeing it.

Kate eased Riley from her, gently laying his head on the teddy Jenna had given him for his last birthday. She laid him on the floor. Sneaking to her suitcase, she snatched the nearest shorts and T-shirt, then took a deep breath before heading to assess the damage. Monica was standing in the middle of the dining room and turned, offering a good morning bleat before following Kate. The front door was wide open, and Kate rolled her head in dismay.

'How did that happen, Monica? I thought I'd locked you out.' She put it down to the rough winds that had blown most of the night.

When Kate stepped outside, she was greeted by several baas of high and low nuances as she wrenched on her boots. 'Morning, ladies. Did you have a better sleep than me? I bet you did,' she grumbled to herself.

She stared wide-eyed at the open sandy space that had been promoted as her backyard. The rich earthy smell of rain oozed from the sodden ground. Besides a lot of leaves and debris, nothing appeared to have been destroyed. Even her car had narrowly avoided a fallen branch, much to her relief. She needed to head into town for supplies if she was going to feed them better than the gourmet menu she'd relied on so far.

The cool stillness of the morning was a relieving change, and she decided to treat herself to a coffee at Meg's instead of the dusty-tasting instant powder she'd brought with her. She also planned to visit the small hardware store, hoping to buy some seeds and seedlings if they sold them. Then, this adventure would feel like it had really begun.

'Good morning. Nice to see you again.' Meg's cheery smile radiated friendship, giving Kate the permission she'd been looking for to breathe. 'How have you been getting on out in the sticks?'

Kate walked to the counter, Riley dragging his feet in tow.

'Hi, Meg. Not too bad.' If she didn't think about last night for too long. She grinned down at Riley, who'd slow-stepped up beside her. 'This is Riley,' she said, ruffling his hair only to have him shy from her touch. A fresh cloud of rejection parked itself over her.

Meg offered an encouraging nod his way. 'Great to meet you. Would you like a hot chocolate? I always add marshmallows,' she said, wiggling her eyebrows to entice him. 'Lots of them.' It worked, much to Kate's relief, even if it was only with a slight head nod.

'I'll have a latté, please,' Kate said as the door opened again.

Meg glanced up and then let out an impatient huff. Kate took a curious peek over her shoulder, unable to resist a small giggle at the guy who clearly had all eyes and more for the café owner.

'Morning, Megsy.' He moved forward with caution as his attention shifted to Kate, offering a friendly grin. 'Kate,' he said, holding out his hand. She took it, perplexed that this stranger knew her name and turned to Meg for answers. She knew all about small towns, but she'd been here less than twenty-four hours. Had the bush telegraph worked that fast? She was almost impressed.

'This is Hughey, our local butcher.' Meg offered him an impatient glare. 'And the local who won't take no for an answer.' She placed Riley's hot chocolate and Kate's latté on the counter and set her hands on her hips. 'He doesn't know when to stop.' She poured another slosh of milk into the jug with a splash, sticking it under the coffee machine while glaring at him.

Kate couldn't make out what was going on between the two of them. Were they having a little lovers' tiff? Or was he wanting a relationship with her? Her eyes narrowed as she studied them both.

'But we'd make such a great team.' Hughey's hopeful eyes begged Meg to reconsider.

'Not on your nelly, Hughey. And what makes you think I have the spare time or the money to shift my shop? I'm kinda busy here, barely making ends meet as it is.' She eyeballed him harder.

'Um, oh good, I need to visit you next,' Kate broke in, hoping to defuse the tension between the two. She turned to Hughey. 'Got to get a few things for the freezer.' She gave an overzealous smile at them both. Was her interjection too obvious? But that next coffee was going to burn the top of someone's mouth, namely Hughey, if Meg didn't remove the milk from the steam soon.

'Can I have one of those raspberry and white chocolate muffins too? Riley, what would you like?' Kate went to scruff his hair good-naturedly again, but as her hand hovered above his head, she thought better of it, giving him a rousing nudge instead. He pointed to a chocolate brownie, turning to her with weary eyes, begging her to say yes.

'Great choice, Riles.' The cool auntie inside her jumped for joy. Anyone who didn't want chocolate for breakfast had no clue how to live. She nodded at Meg, grabbed a copy of the Forest

Gully Times sitting on the counter and moved to a table near the window so they could sit and watch the slow-moving town steadily come to life. Someone waved to her through the window as they walked by. Her eyes lit up as she waved back. It seemed she was as interesting as the local news today.

Kate hesitated as she entered the General Store, the concern in Nola's voice unmissable.

'No, Graham, we can't ignore this. We have to face facts. If things don't change around here, we'll all be shut in twelve months' time, if not less.'

'It can't be all that bad.' Graham shook his head. 'Tourists are dropping in more and more, and Kate has bought the Pilchers' place. It's not doomsday, sweetheart.' His voice was light with a touch of gentle, intentional humour.

'But you're wrong, love. We're barely taking a salary between us.' She moved to the back of the store, talking as she went. 'Heaven knows how we're meant to retire at the rate we're going.'

Kate let the door shut, allowing the small bell hanging above it to signal she'd arrived. They swung around towards her, suddenly all smiles.

'Good morning. How's it going out there in the sticks?' Nola said.

Why did everyone refer to her place like that? It wasn't that bad.

'Did you get any damage from the storm last night?' Graham piped up. 'I can swing by with my chainsaw and tidy up for you if you'd like.' His smile was as generous as his girth and her heart skipped. It was hard to talk about it but having someone willing to help mattered more than she could say. Her throat tensed.

'No, we were lucky, I guess. But a few trees are lying about that could do with a trim if you wouldn't mind. Then I'd be able to move them, maybe even have them for firewood come winter.' But would she get to stay that long? She glanced at Riley trailing behind her, studying his feet.

'Not a problem. I'll drop by this afternoon. Now what can we do for you?'

'Just grabbing a few essentials,' she smiled, taking a basket from the base of the counter to roam the aisles. But rather than look for what she needed, her mind drifted to the conversation she'd walked in on. What had they meant when they'd said things weren't okay? A twinge of doubt wiggled into her mind. This town might be small but it had more going for it than some of the towns she knew, especially some of the smaller ones back home. All it took was everyone rallying together to make it come alive.

Kate strolled up, meeting Nola's friendly face as she placed her basket on the counter. 'Can I ask? Do any of the shops here need another pair of hands? I was hoping to get a bit of work.'

'Well now, there's the positive spirit,' Graham said, side-eying Nola pointedly.

'Of course there is, love. Last I heard, Nige at the hardware store was keen for someone to do some hours part-time. Would that work for you? It could be while your little fella,' Graham gave Riley an encouraging wink,' is at school.'

Kate liked the thought until she saw Riley's downcast face. His head shaking fervently had her heart plummeting as she heard his mumble.

'I don't wanna go to a school here.'

Kate found it impossible to hide her concern. But what was she meant to do with a comment like that? Head back home? That wasn't an option. Or dare she think of it, home-school him? Heaven forbid. She was having enough trouble trying to win him over as auntie without adding that into the mix.

'Riles, this is our home now.' Kate spoke gently but cringed through what felt like a distinct mix of mortification, embarrassment, and discomfort over what she'd imposed on both of them by making this big move. She hated that she might be coming across as unfair, and a tad selfish if Jenna were able to give her opinion right now. But what else was she meant to do? To her, Jenna was irreplaceable. But being a mother, well, that's what she had to be now, even if it did look a little—or a lot—different. All she knew was how hard she would work to make things better for Riley than they currently were.

But what about her? Could she still have her own dreams? Or should they be pushed aside—now she was in this parent role? And yet, as she focused adoringly on her nephew, reality hit. She'd effectively done just that, dragging him away from everything he knew . . . and loved, assuming the changes she'd made were going to be good for him, because they were good for her. Her heart ached with heaviness, both for the life she'd always dreamt of and for the loss of her sister. Things had turned out so differently from how she'd imagined they'd be.

Kate dredged up an unconvincing smile, turning back to Nola and Graham.

'Oh, well, I might call in there then,' she said with the cheeriest voice she could muster. If she had a job, that could be just the thing to keep her distracted from her inadequacies right now. She slid one of Riley's favourite chocolate bars into her basket and paid for their few groceries. She might not be the world's greatest substitute mother to the world's most despondent kid, but she wasn't above using a bit of hardcore bribery.

Their next stop was the local primary school. As Kate and

Riley were shown through the rooms, Kate smiled, noticing the way the kids were engaged, chatting as they did activities. On the oval, surrounded by tall tree ferns as a backdrop, a class was playing baseball.

'Look, Riles, it's your favourite game.' She silently thanked the teacher for choosing to play it.

As she reached to put a hand on his head like she'd always done, he pulled away from her touch, his action hitting its intended mark with a sting to Kate's heart. But for him to be choosing to observe by watching the game rather than staring at the ground was a major step forward, right? The school bell sounded and the kids cheered, sprinting towards the locker room for their snacks for recess. Having noticed them, the teacher strolled over, closely followed by a handful of kids lugging the equipment from the finished lesson with effort.

'Hi. Nice to meet you. I'm Judy Hemming, the Grade Two/Three teacher.' She shook Kate's hand. 'And who might this be?'

'I'm Kate and this is Riley. He's excited to begin school with you next week. The principal mentioned you'd be his teacher.'

Kate looked down at Riley, ready to prompt him to say hello but to her pleasant surprise, he'd already engaged with the children, listening to a boy and girl and nodding as though he spoke their language. A small smile found its way to his lips. He took a step towards the children, their easy chatter happening comfortably.

Kate exhaled slowly, her hand on her chest. He wasn't thrilled about moving here but he might've just made a couple of friends. With any luck, starting school would be the medicine he needed and she could work out what was next for them in Forest Gully.

52

CHAPTER 8

The weekend had been taxing on Kate's muscles thanks to the many shovels of sandy earth she had heaved aside before adding fertilised soil to the garden beds. She'd created them by using the dead tree trunk branches strewn about her property, and she was proud of her efforts. Nothing quite like a bit of upcycling, she'd thought to herself as she stood back to admire her handiwork. Riley had been exploring their property, his spirits visibly lifting each time he came home with Speedy by his side. It was pure relief to see, even if it caused her mind to drift to her next-door neighbour more often than she had agreed it should.

The little hardware store on the main street was small but stocked the basics—enough to get anyone started. If someone wanted more, they'd need to visit Geelong.

To her disappointment, Nige—Patsy's husband and the owner—had informed her that they had decided to stick to a tight budget and not hire any new help, but he assured her they would call if their situation changed. However, that wasn't going to stop her; she had another idea brewing.

Kate drove towards Geelong after dropping Riley off for his first Monday at school. She was excited to visit the nursery she had researched over the weekend on her phone, her ideas bubbling and her list for what she wanted to buy as long as any Santa list she'd ever written. This nursery looked nothing like the one back home she'd worked at in Tenterfield, but it promised all the veggies and roses she could wish for.

The winding Great Ocean Road stretched for kilometres as the water stayed in view, the waves rolling to the shore in gentle flushes. The breeze was pleasant as she drove with her window down, soaking in the smell of the sea and admiring the way the huge rock edges stood up to the continual wear and tear from the boisterous elements during rougher times.

As she strolled inside the entrance of the nursery, she slowed, marvelling at the beautifully laid-out assortment of potted plants—a cottage garden in one area and a local native space in another. Paths of red scoria trailed all over the grounds with tiers of plants displayed, and there was an array of vegetable seedling varieties so vast she sensed her list growing quicker than her bank balance.

Roses had always been one of her favourites, thanks to her mother's and grandmother's love for them; they had been beautifully displayed in an established rose garden where they'd lived before selling the farm. Although they might not be able to face working a property that held such tragic reminders anymore, Kate was keen to recapture some of its elegance.

She stood in front of the rose section, so overwhelmed by the choices on offer that she found herself pulling out her phone to make a call.

'Hey, Mum.'

'Hi, darling. How did Riley go?' Kate could hear the concern almost verging on tears in her mother's voice.

'Okay. Quiet, like usual. But I've made it to Geelong without a call from the school, so that has to be a good sign.' She gave a light chuckle. 'Just hope it stays that way.' She slowed to admire the roses in front of her blooming in the summer sun. She cupped one in her fingers, breathing in its delightful fragrance.

'What was the name of Nanna's favourite rose?'

'It was a Double Delight. Smells just like lemonade.'

Kate browsed the plants until she found one. 'Got it. Thanks, Mum.' She was ready to finish the conversation when she halted. 'Hey Mum, I miss you.' Her voice faltered; fresh emotion thick. She wasn't sure she'd ever get used to not having her family close by for moral support or the hug she so desperately needed right now.

'Oh, honey, I love you too. And remember, not a moment goes by when I don't think of you both.' A slight sniffle sounded down the line. Like Kate, her mother hadn't understood why Jenna had left Riley to her and not them.

Kate had known all along that it was a risk to ring on such an emotional day, and her mother's words threatened to tip her over the edge. Before the tears building in her eyes had a chance to fall, she whispered the word 'bye' and hung up, sniffing abruptly as she did. Her parents hadn't loved the idea of her taking Riley away, but it was the unblemished new beginning she'd needed. Only Riley refusing to pardon her for taking him away from everything he'd known hadn't been an outcome she'd expected.

With a twitch of her nose and a brisk chin up, she moved about the nursery like a woman on a mission, her ideas brimming. By the end, her car boot was full of numerous seedlings, packets of seeds, fertilisers, and an assortment of rose bushes surpassing her already generous Santa wish list. What a surprise, she mused to herself. She had plans, big ones, including a picket fence at the entrance of their property. Then, no one would be able to miss seeing her new venture, which she'd decided to name The Seaside Bouquet farmgate.

When Kate arrived back in Forest Gully, she pulled over on the opposite side of the road in the main street, jogging over to the bakery. The thought of a pie for lunch was calling her, plus she hadn't met the shop owner yet.

Pushing the door open, her momentum came to an abrupt halt as she laid eyes on a pair of strong legs in boardies she found all too delightfully familiar. He turned at the jingle from the door, and she rapidly exhaled at this town's excessive use of loud doorbells, which announced her arrival at every turn, mainly when Gus happened to be in the shop she'd called into.

'Well, hello neighbour,' she said, happy to allow a trickle of friendly stirring to shine through in her voice. 'Managed to round up those sheep of yours yet?' She cocked her eyebrow as he stared at her. The shop door shut behind her with a clunk.

'Monica likes it at your place a whole lot more than mine. She sleeps way better, and I wouldn't want to break her heart or her habit.' As his grin grew, so did the unchecked flutters inside her. Since when had she allowed a guy to stir feelings in her other than mild interest and curiosity? She glanced around the shop with caution, hoping no one else in the shop recognised the heat winding its way up her neck, soon to engulf her whole face.

'Well, the sooner you come and collect them, the better, or you'll be coming over every morning to sweep my verandah. I've had just about enough of their extended sleepovers and leftovers.'

Kate moved to the display cabinet, ignoring her increasing excitement as she got closer to her good-looking, cool-as-a-cucumber next-door neighbour. If she didn't let her eyes stray his way, he wouldn't be able to see the effect he was having on her. She focused on the lush custard tart calling to her, fully knowing if she was asked what her order was, she'd be pointing its way, completely tongue-tied.

In her peripheral vision, she saw him keep his eyes steadily on her, her gaze narrowing as he smirked in her direction before turning his focus to the display cabinet.

'Thanks, Lexi. I'll take the last custard tart, too. Wouldn't want it to feel lonely.'

At his words, Kate swung around, her mind buzzing with frustration and annoyance, and, well, something, she just didn't know what.

'You didn't seriously do that.' She placed a hand on her hip. 'You saw me looking at that custard tart, didn't you?' she added, narrowing her eyes at him suspiciously, her annoyance building faster than the heat from Meg's coffees.

'Sorry?' He angled his shoulders towards her, his face almost unreadable, but she could see the smugness hidden below those gorgeous whiskers. He knew exactly what he was doing, and it annoyed her to recognise that it felt like they were definitely mixing some flirting with their current grievances at one another, regardless of how nice it felt.

'I don't know what you're talking about. But if you're quick enough tomorrow, you might get one—unless I beat you to it again.' With that, he gave her a cheeky, far too cute for his own good lopsided smile, snatched up his takeaway bags from the top of the counter, gave her a nod, and left the shop.

Kate rolled her shoulders, dismissing his way too cheery charm that distinctly unsettled her in more good ways than bad. Gus Stevens had artfully rattled her. He might portray the all-round quiet guy on the outside, but inside, there was definitely a man that found it desirable to tease her—even if it was good-naturedly—at every given opportunity. And she wasn't quite ready for the delicious yet confusing feelings that came with that attractive fact.

'Listen, Hughey, there's no way I'm going anywhere near the fire station, training night or not.' Gus stalked back inside his beach hut, Hughey hot on his tail. 'So, stop asking me.'

'Hey, I get that you don't want to, but we need you, Gus. We're a man down now that Jim and his wife have left for their whirlwind trip. If a fire roars over the hills through here, I don't have to tell you what it's gonna look like without that extra set of hands on the team.'

A shiver ran over Gus's body despite the stifling heat. To turn up for training after all this time, he'd only be inviting the inevitable. To be judged beyond reproach. Ash wasn't the only one who didn't need reminding. They were both still alive, and Kelly wasn't.

'I'm not setting foot in or near the depot ever again. You try and tell me the fire captain would be happy to have me there.' Gus snatched a stubbie from the fridge, squeezing it tight as he fought with the idea of not offering his best mate one after what he'd suggested. But that wasn't who he was so he slid the bottle down the kitchen bench towards Hughey. It pulled up just short of Hughey's hand as he reached into the fridge, seizing another for himself.

'Ash knows we need you.' Hughey popped the bottle top and Gus watched him glug the liquid down hard. He remained quiet as he took a slug of his own, pressing his lips tight, the alcohol failing to offer him the relief he was looking for. His scrutinising gaze remained on his long-time friend.

'Have you forgotten how Ash and his buddies regard me? Last week, Fred saw me coming and stood, dusting his hands exaggeratedly before he shot me a disgusted look, then left the table out in front of Meg's. He hadn't even half finished his coffee. I'm that piece of chewing gum you get stuck to your boot and can't get rid of.' He turned his head aside. 'They're never going to let me have a life.'

'You're my best mate and I get it, I do, but we need—'

'No, Hughey, you *don't* get it,' he said as he turned back to him. 'She was going to be my *wife*. I couldn't save her. Ash will never condone my actions and rightfully so. How do you expect it'll look if I try and kid myself of that fact, then waltz right on in like everything is okay? It doesn't matter how long it's been. Time's never going to fix what I've done.' His voice hitched as the emotion of the past surged inside him, and he turned his head from Hughey for fear that his mate might feel sorry for him. That was something he didn't deserve.

'Aren't you forgetting who you did save? Carl wouldn't be here either if it weren't for you.' Hughey stepped closer. 'I know you've heard Carl wants to join the team.'

Gus took a rushed swig, wishing the icy cold liquid pooling against his teeth could help him forget what Hughey had just said, appalled this conversation was even happening.

'I failed, alright! It wasn't enough to only save one.' His hollow gaze dropped to the floor. If he'd done a better job of shutting the conversation down sooner, maybe this round of guilt could've been avoided. He hid his face in his hand, sucking in a shuddering breath as regret ached behind his closed eyes.

'I couldn't do enough.' A soft sob left his lungs. 'If I'd only got her out first, I could've saved them both.' He pressed fingers to his eyelids, the sting behind them nothing short of what he deserved. Nothing would fix what he'd done.

Ever.

'But you don't know that. Shit, Gus, the forensics said her legs were pinned. Even if you had more time,' Hughey's voice softened, 'she was never getting out. Not before—'

'Don't say that!' Gus spun on his best mate, pointing a shaking finger. 'If I turn out for a job with the team again, there's no way they'll be sure I've got their backs. And you can't say I'm wrong because you know I'm not.' He turned away, determined to hide the tears now trailing down his cheeks. He swiped at them in frustration with his fingers. 'I'm useless to the team. Can't even pick the one who needs saving first.' Saying those words out loud hurt like hell, but he had to continue. Hughey needed to understand. 'The team are better off without me.' He shook his head, moving towards the lounge and sinking into the couch with a slump, wishing he'd thought to pour himself a glass of cold water to settle the beer now churning inside him. But he didn't have the energy to stand up again.

'I get it, but . . . I was there too,' Hughey said with gentle care. 'I saw the way the car went up in flames. There was no way either of us could've got her out before the explo—'

He stopped, the glare Gus fired in his direction halting his words, and Hughey grimaced, casting his eyes down as he retreated to the seat opposite. He drew in a bolstering breath. 'I won't forget either, but I won't let that stop me from helping someone else.'

Hearing Hughey's words made Gus blink hard behind the cover of his hand. He didn't want anyone else to get hurt ever again. That's why he had to stay away. He wasn't convinced he'd be able to cope if he failed someone a second time. He rocked his head in slow arcs, mindful to keep his eyes from straying over his forearms. On the surface, they were healed. But his heart remained exposed, raw and full of the same pain. The only way he could guarantee something like that wouldn't happen again was to never participate in an emergency, no matter what.

CHAPTER 9

Kate's enthusiasm was running high, matching the feverish heat of another hot Sunday. She had successfully installed a watering system yesterday. Now, with fresh manure—thanks to Gus's sheep providing quite the supply on her verandah—her garden bed was ready.

At the mere thought of Gus, she gave a miffed huff, and removed her gloves to cool her hands. The man was infuriating and yet completely charming, even though he made a point of avoiding people, except her—clearly. She couldn't manage to frequent a shop without him appearing from nowhere, successfully proceeding to send her equilibrium haywire. She'd always thought of herself as an early riser, but he'd even managed to beat her to Meg's café this morning. He'd levered the door open, leaving her with the imprint of his suntanned cheeks, dancing eyes, and carefree hair in her mind before she'd grabbed the door in the nick of time, scurrying inside the shop before it slammed shut on her foot. Not before he'd saluted her with his cup in the air and a pleased smile as he left. How did he continually hold the upper hand in this tug of, what was it, witty one-liners and smug looks they seemed to be keeping alive between them?

But there was no way she would let herself get mixed up with that man, or anyone else for that matter. She had enough on her plate without that complication. Annoyed at herself for even thinking this, she shoved her spade into the sandy dirt with gusto, making holes for the roses she'd meticulously laid out in a hit-and-miss fashion. With violas growing at the base of them for ground cover, it would look like the perfect cottage garden she could take pride in each time she tended it.

She dug the last rose bush in, kneeling back with a smile. 'This one's for you, Jenna,' she said, brushing aside the slow-falling tear with the back of her glove. The Double Delight took pride of place as the centrepiece.

After a good watering with some liquid fertiliser, she stood back, admiring her handiwork.

'Not bad,' she nodded to herself as Riley came up, followed by his ever-present shadow, Speedy.

'Hey, girl.' Kate bent down to stroke the dog's head, immediately rewarded with a little jump that caught her cheek with a lick. 'Bet you wouldn't steal my custard tart, hey?' She grinned, pretty sure she was wrong.

'Auntie Kate, can I go down to the beach?' Riley asked, keeping a loyal hand on Speedy's fur coat, his voice but a whisper as his hand gently ran along the dog's back. Kate stood, glancing towards the sky out of habit before listening for the sound of the ocean.

'What if I came with you? I'd like to see it too,' she said with a smile, beginning to gather her shovel and gloves, relieved this might be her opportunity to make up for not paying attention to him the other night when he'd mentioned it. She had to believe that while things looked different now, she was his sole carer, she could still be fun to be around. But before she could stand, Riley spoke up.

'No! Um, Speedy will come with me.' He looked down at the expectant dog, her eyes trained on his as she panted patiently.

'Well, what if after I get these veggie seedlings in, we go for a swim near the shops? We can grab some lunch from the café too, if you'd like. Remember how we used to do that?' She'd often taken Riley into town back in Tenterfield where they'd catch a movie or go ten-pin bowling. It was their "thing" and it had always been important to them both.

'But I've found a spot—'

'Listen, mate. I'll be done here in no time. You go inside and get your boardies on, okay? I'll be in soon,' she said, pumping her fist in the air with enthusiasm, waiting for Riley to return it excitedly like he always did when a special outing was planned. But her hand fell softly away as he gave a slow nod towards the ground before turning back to the house with Speedy trotting beside him.

Her chest clenched. What was she meant to do? With her hand on her hip, she blinked as she watched him disappear around the side of the verandah. She was all for Riley setting out on adventures. But she wanted to let him know she planned on being in his life too, if only he'd let her. How was it fair that circumstances so far out of her control had the power to change the course of their lives so dramatically?

With one last squint in their direction, she snatched up the hose and hurried to wet down the next garden bed, putting in the spinach, tomato, and zucchini seedlings and covering their bases with sugar cane mulch. The seeds she'd bought could wait until tonight when the sun had gone down. Keeping her promise to her nephew before he changed his mind or refused to go at all was so much more important.

As Kate rushed inside, she faltered, her hand gripping the door handle as her eyes locked onto a sheep she thought she had dealt with. Monica chewed her cud contentedly on their freshly cleaned dining table, having knocked the vase Kate had displayed in the centre to the floor, water pooling beneath it. The ewe had settled in for a comfortable few hours under the fan.

Of course she had, Kate sneered, her arms lifting and slapping her sides in frustration.

'Oh no, you don't, Miss Monica.' She marched over to the

table, pushing the ewe's backside with everything she had. But now that Monica was facing the familiar action of being shoved over the edge of the table, she scuttled to her feet and leapt off, walking towards the open doorway with her ever-present poise.

'Cursed hand-reared crossbreds,' Kate growled, dusting off her hands, hot on the heels of the ewe, closing the door on Monica's retreating rear end.

'Morning, Meg,' Kate said as she entered the café and drew in a dreamy breath of coffee and fresh muffins, which she now spotted sitting atop the counter under a glass dome.

'Kate. Hello.'

Meg thanked the customer she'd just served. 'Have a wonderful day. Don't forget to visit The Point. The view is amazing. Just don't get too close to the edge. The cliffs around here are known to be treacherous.' She offered the customer a reminder wave of her finger. 'Oh, and drop in again sometime. I'd love to know what you think.'

Kate greeted the stranger with a friendly smile as they passed one another, while Riley lagged behind like something the cat brought in. At the counter, she was pleased to see he was already taking an interest in the cake display. She placed her hands on the bench top, leaning in towards Meg. 'That was wonderful. Do you say that to all your customers?' She glanced over her shoulder once more before giving Meg a "go-you" smile.

'What do you mean?' Meg shrugged before grabbing the cloth to begin cleaning the coffee wand. 'Got the urge for a mocha?'

'Of course. Do you even know me?' Kate said with a teasing grin, and the two women giggled. They'd hit it off from day one a week ago. Kate had visited for her latté every day since.

'But seriously, Meg, telling that guy about The Point? It's great for visitors to know the attractions Forest Gully has. I haven't got a clue where it is, and I'm a local,' she said, tongue in cheek with a good-natured flick of her eyebrows, now eying off the chocolate brownie slice she'd pinned as hers. Meg followed her gaze.

Riley looked Meg's way, curiosity in his eyes.

'What would you like Meg to get for you, buddy?' Kate looked down at him with all the expectation of a perfect date for them both, one just between the two of them. If this didn't work, she wasn't sure what would.

The shift in Riley's focus was subtle, morphing from thoughtfulness to what appeared to be genuine pleasure. Kate let her suspicion about his sudden change of spirits slip away, appreciating the small thrill her heart skipped. Had he acknowledged her, let alone been pleased with the thought he was choosing something to take to the beach with them? Could she dare to dream?

'Guess what I've done this morning?' Kate's shoulders danced as she looked at Meg while waiting for Riley to choose.

'Slept in?' Meg said with a giggle. 'You're late today,' and she began to warm the milk.

'Absolutely not. I'm a country girl, remember,' she said, trying for a mock offended look. 'You should see what I've done to my garden.'

'Ah yes, the sea change.'

Kate spun around at the deep voice, the café door clunking shut, the pesky bell jingling as if it were Christmas even though the holiday had already been gone six weeks ago. Her neighbour strolled towards her, sending a nervous shiver over her body.

Kate turned back to Meg. 'I'm not the only one who slept

in,' she said loud enough for him to hear, and they giggled, Kate acutely aware of his presence and her rapidly heating cheeks. According to Meg, he'd been in every morning before her, and she was secretly pleased to finally have one up on him.

'I'll have you know I planted all my roses and seedlings. I'm going to have myself a productive veggie patch with plenty to share,' she said with a determined grin and a nod for good measure.

'Don't know why you'd bother. Nothing will grow out there in that sandy soil. They'll shrivel up and die within minutes.' He turned his attention to the hot food counter with a subtle shrug. 'Everything does.'

Kate couldn't hide her disbelief, frowning at Meg as she handed her the mocha. She turned to face him, hoping the flush on her cheeks might be mistaken for the heat of the morning, or the mocha, or both. If she didn't know better, she'd think he was still trying to get rid of her.

'From what I can tell, things are pretty alive around here. What's got up your nose?' Meg let out a snort of laughter as Kate's brow lifted in front of him, perplexed by his apparent eagerness to undermine her plans while Riley slipped to the other side of Gus.

A swift shaft of pain stabbed her in the chest as her eyes locked onto Riley's hand. He reached for Gus's as he would've hers in times gone past, not so long ago. *But why?* She'd known him all his life.

She directed her glare at Gus. 'Why do you have to be such a negative Nancy?'

That's when Kate glimpsed it. First the indication of shock on Meg's face as she turned to Gus, then shied away. And as Kate held firm, his eyes dulled, his brows knitting together hard and tight as though he was remembering something with a jolt.

Something . . . painful.

She'd unknowingly managed to overstep the mark. She blinked rapidly, remorse rushing through her as she fiddled with her wallet to get out her card, giving herself time to think. If she'd known he'd become so distressed at her words, she would never have said them. But he'd been so rude.

'Can I get you anything else, Kate?' Meg continued the conversation as if nothing untoward had happened, saving her from further discomfort. The brownie Meg placed inside a paper bag suddenly lost its appeal. 'Just a chocolate muffin for Riley, thanks.'

Riley stepped away from Gus, turning to Kate, his face serious and confused. 'But I wanted a doughnut.'

'You'll be fine with the muffin for now.' She waved her card and paid, desperate to remove herself from Gus. She could accept that he'd been hurt by her words, whatever the reason. But for Riley to side with him over her? From now on it would definitely be better if they kept their distance from their new neighbour.

'Thanks, Meg.' She gathered her items and left, a small part of her relieved that she didn't feel sorry for not saying goodbye to Gus. He'd be the town grump in no time if he continued to carry on like that. Then again, he could have already been that.

The sand was hot beneath her feet, making her toes curl as she called out to Riley who lagged behind. Throwing down her towel, she immediately felt the relief from the stinging sand as she jumped on top of it before tugging on Riley's towel, doing the same for him. She sat down, sipping on her cuppa, her shoulders visibly relaxing as she looked up as Riley came up beside her. She patted his towel, smiling. 'C'mon, buddy. Let's enjoy the waves.' He held his paper bag limp at his side, his soft drink in the other, his lips downturned.

'Hey, what's up? Don't you want to sit next to the best

auntie of all time?' She spoke it with as much enthusiasm as she could summon despite the residual bad taste in her mouth from her encounter with Gus, but by the look on Riley's face, it wasn't close to hitting the intended mark.

He glanced to his right before he spoke. 'Can I sit over there, in the shade. It's too hot here.' His attention swivelled everywhere but on her.

'Oh, um, yeah . . . sure. Would you like me to help you move?' She went to hop up, but the way he rocked his head told her to stay put. She slowly lowered herself to the towel again, the following sip of her mocha failing to ease her concern or the sense of rejection. If her heart could have erupted from her chest, it would have.

Without another word, Riley picked up the corner of his towel, slowly dragging it to the shady tree a few metres away. It left Kate feeling alone, exposed and disquieted that if this didn't work out for her, she'd be bound for home long before she'd had a chance to prove she was up to the huge task of mothering him.

CHAPTER 10

Gus stood quietly, his fingers softly thrumming on the door handle of his ute, his gaze drawn to the scene unfolding across the road. Kate sat alone in the sun while Riley dragged his sandy towel some distance away, setting himself up in the shade. If Gus was right, Riley had chosen a spot as close to the sand dunes as possible. The boy's shoulders were slumped and his head was down, his paper bag untouched beside him.

And his heart threatened to break. Over the past few days, he'd been enjoying hanging out with Riley both before and after school, and when Riley had come over to ask if he could take Speedy for a walk.

Riley had a disposition that made Gus want to put his arm around his shoulders, comforting him until the boy had the courage to let his smile shine again. He didn't say much but Gus liked his company. Other than his dog and those pesky rogue sheep that he was supposed to be taking care of, there wasn't a lot of manly presence around him except for Hughey until Riley had come along. Not that he wanted company. He didn't. It only brought him trouble. Maybe it was because Riley was a kid that he made an exception.

Gus watched on, wrestling with whether he should go over and see if he could help. But the thought held him captive. He was still reeling from Kate's remark which he recognised was unintentional. But he had every good reason to be negative.

Then Riley had taken his hand, holding it tight right in front of Kate. But what could he do about that? He wasn't about to shun the kid's affections, even though he could see the pain in her expression. And now, if he approached them, who would he sit with? His eyes slid from Kate to Riley and back again, the space between them as vast as the view of the sea in front of them. If pressed, his allegiance was with Riley. That woman was beginning to ruffle his feathers in ways he wasn't appreciating. She was forthright, fair, and kinder than some in this community. But what he'd gone through, how he'd suffered . . . well, that was none of her business. If she did know, she'd only feel sorry for him and do exactly what Hughey had done to him the previous night. He wasn't hearing any of it. How could he? Kelly would still be here if he'd followed the fire brigade's lifesaving protocol.

Gus turned away, hopping into his car and pulling onto the road. What he needed was a good surfing session to rid his rampant and confronting thoughts of this annoyingly beautiful woman. All she was doing was disturbing his sleep and messing with his firmly-held ideals.

Gus got home and changed into his wetsuit, lifting it as high as his hips. Speedy bounced on the spot, an excited bark leaping from her before she ran ahead, scooting through the foliage as Gus picked his way down the dodgy path towards his tranquil beach, his feet slipping every now and then on the loose stones. The surf was slow so he left his board on the sand, opting for a walk instead, the sun's warmth the reassuring balm he needed.

Speedy ran up to his feet, dropping the ball she'd left on the rocks many walks ago, and Gus picked it up, tossing it up and down in his hand. Speedy let out a shrill bark, planting her front feet on the sand in front of him, bowing as she begged him to throw it. He grinned, leaning forward towards her. 'You want it? Well, here you go,' and he threw the ball more than thirty metres ahead, his cricket arm still in fine form. Sand kicked up from Speedy's back feet as she tore away, chasing the ball down before the wave coming into shore sucked it about with the incoming tide.

He walked the beach patiently, silently, picking up the ball as Speedy pounced about over and over, desperate for him to throw it again. He must have thrown it more than eighteen times when, as he stood once more, a familiar figure walked towards him.

He forgot to breathe.

'Hey, Gus.' Riley skipped towards him, unable to hide his excitement. Speedy dropped her ball and tore towards him, skidding to a sandy stop, and he knelt down for a cuddle and a sandy slurp on the face.

'Hey there, bud. Does Auntie Kate know you're down here?' He frowned, a strong hunch telling him she wouldn't approve if she knew how steep these cliffs were. Only yesterday he'd seen rocks fall away from the sides without warning. When she didn't appear, he scanned the heavy shrubbery for movement. But there was none.

'Um, she said I could go exploring.' Riley ruffled Speedy's fur on her neck before he stood, and Gus sensed the kid wasn't telling him all the facts, but he let it slide. At least with him here, Riley would be safe.

'It's so cool down here.' Riley looked at Gus with eyes that held glee, and Gus had to admit it was good to see his neighbour's nephew so happy. But he couldn't shake the niggle that the kid was definitely hiding something. He couldn't dismiss the hunch, eying the top of the cliff one more time before reluctantly shrugging his apprehension aside.

Riley ran along the water's edge, kicking at the waves as Speedy excitedly snapped at them. Riley puffed, slowing to catch his breath as Gus jogged, catching up, the arms of his wetsuit swinging beside him.

'You're right. I always think this beach could go on forever,' Gus said as he reached out, scruffing Riley's hair cheerfully.

'Around that bend.' Gus pointed as he leaned towards Riley. 'It has a private beach all of its own when the tide comes in. There are caves and climbing rocks. It's pretty cool.' He nodded at Riley, enjoying the interest on his face.

'No way. Can we go there?'

'Nah, mate, the tide is already in. It's too dangerous. Maybe another time.' He picked up the sticky, sandy tennis ball gingerly in his fingers and tossed it as far as he could for Speedy. Riley ran after it and Gus took a deep breath, delighting in the fact he was finally sharing this special place with someone. It was beautiful, and it was dangerous. But as long as he taught Riley how to respect its many varying moods, there'd be no harm.

They were walking back towards the path on the beach when Riley broke the extended silence Gus was rather enjoying.

'Gus, can I ask you something?'

'Sure.'

'How did you hurt your arms?'

Gus instinctively ran his right hand over the worst of his injuries on his left arm, the skin puckered and pronounced. Memories came flooding back in a rush and a knot tightened inside his chest. So many memories, some brand new at the time, and hundreds unfulfilled. Would the pain ever lessen? He wished he knew.

'I got burnt.' Gus's eyes hung over his hand, but a side glance at Riley broke the reverie before it gripped him any further. He quickly removed it, raising a smile as he sized up Riley's reaction. Would he be repulsed? Would he ask any more questions Gus couldn't be sure he could answer?

But to his relief, the kid just shrugged, his friendly smile reaching Gus's heart with a warm tug.

'I like hanging out with you, Gus.'

'I like being with you too.' He blinked at his new little

neighbour. 'How are you settling in? Liking it?' Not for one minute did Gus think Riley was happy, let alone satisfied with his new home.

Riley studied the sand at his feet, kicking a piece of seaweed in his way. 'It's okay, I guess.' He shrugged. 'I wish we never had to move, though.'

'Why did you?'

''Cause Auntie Kate wanted us to. Said we needed a fresh start.'

Speedy took off at a frantic pace, chasing a pesky seagull that had the audacity to land on her beach, but all Gus could do was stare off into the distance. A fresh start away from what?

'They can be good.' He kept his voice upbeat, but did he honestly believe that? His own fresh start had begun with expectation and ended in tragedy. And here he was still stuck with only a handful of memories, sadness, and a title he didn't deserve. But he couldn't move on. The Pilchers had struggled to sell and that was with a house. No one in their right mind would buy his shonky shack with non-existent fencing, even if he offered the sheep for free.

'Why does Auntie Kate look after you now?' He didn't want to push Riley but he'd lain awake, curious about their story.

The boy went quiet and Gus immediately regretted asking. 'I'm sorry, bud. I shouldn't have asked.'

Idiot. What had he been thinking?

'Auntie Kate and I loved camping, and we begged Mum to come with us. We knew if we pestered her enough, she'd eventually give in. Grandma and Pop lived on a big farm in Tenterfield and we found a neat spot near a waterhole and set up our tent.'

Riley looked down, considering more dried seaweed as they stopped. Gus put a reassuring hand on his shoulder. The kid was struggling with what to say and Gus didn't want him to feel he had to continue, nor did he want him to stop if it meant it could help by talking about it.

Riley sniffed. 'That's when Mum died.' His soft sob was so quiet that Gus squeezed his shoulder a little tighter, watching him intently. Riley was hurting from the memory and Gus knew all about that, his chest clenching tight, realising just how much the two of them had in common.

'Riley, I'm so sorry.' Gus leaned in closer, fighting away the dampness threatening his own eyes. He waited for Riley to tell him what happened, but he didn't, so he didn't press the subject. The kid had been through enough.

He clamped down on his own memories, refusing to allow them power, instead squinting to shake them free. Would there ever be a day he could live released from the bondage of guilt that gripped him?

'Grandma and Pop sold the farm just before we came here. Auntie Kate calls it our sea change 'cause it hurt too much to stay.'

Sea change. Immediate regret hit him with a distinct queasiness. He'd tried to stir her earlier at the café but she hadn't reacted. He'd been avoiding people for so long, he'd lost his social cues as to when a word might hit below the surface for someone. Regret filled him.

All Gus could do was nod, the lump inside his neck stabbing hard. Speedy licked Riley's hand and Gus forced a smile as the kid broke free of his reverie, beaming at his dog. She was the right kind of medicine for Riley. So why wasn't she enough for Gus to push past his own pain? Because he could never picture himself loving anyone the way he'd loved Kelly, ever again.

'Auntie Kate got lots of money for our town back home. Everyone called her Zippy 'cause she did things real fast.' He looked down at the sand, giving it a light kick as he shrugged. 'It was mum's nickname for her.'

Gus did a take-two on the subject change but kept listening. He wanted to learn more about this woman who, at the mention of her name, made his heart skip a little faster.

'She made things happen. She'd round everyone up to help. That's who she is.' Riley shrugged his shoulders dismissively before picking up a piece of driftwood for Speedy and tossing it. The dog tore away, sand flicking in the air again.

'They always loved it when she helped with the school fête. She would dress up as Shaun the Sheep and convince everyone they needed a mystery jar to take home.' He gave a light smile. 'No one escaped. She wouldn't let anyone leave before they had a go at Lily Pads either.' His eyes lit up as he looked at Gus. 'You had to throw coins onto these floating leaves in toddler wading pools. If you landed on the smallest leaf, you won a *whole* block of chocolate!'

'No way!' Gus leaned back as he grinned.

Riley had effortlessly convinced him it was the best thing that could ever happen to someone before he pressed his lips tight, turning away once more. 'But when Mum died, she stopped doing it.'

Gus stared at Riley. He and the kid were not that dissimilar. They were both lonely and felt like they had no one they could rely on. He knew, without a doubt now, that Riley was still struggling with immense grief. He was just smart at concealing it. And on top of all that, they'd both experienced what a broken community could look like. Gus ran a hand through his hair, deep in thought.

The incoming tide was making the shoreline slim and on glancing at his watch, time was getting on. He would lay odds that Kate was beginning to worry.

'Well, little buddy, let's head back. My stomach's rumbling.'

Riley took another deep breath, nodding, as they continued walking. He broke the extended silence. 'Thanks Gus.'

'For what?' and Gus frowned at him.

'For getting me.' Riley shrugged as he smiled up at Gus before taking off, jogging towards the exit with Speedy barking at his heels. And it almost broke his heart.

CHAPTER 11

'Where have you been? I've been looking for you everywhere. I was worried sick.' Kate squatted down in front of Riley, giving his shoulders a quick squeeze, her eyes dark and full of concern before he wriggled free. She glared at Gus as she stood. 'Has he been with you this whole time?' There was a quiver in her voice as she stood back with her hands on her hips. Riley's wide eyes swept from hers to Gus's.

'Yeah, sorry. My bad. I should've told you. We were just, you know, having guy time, and I forgot how late it was getting.' His mouth crinkled at the corner, and she couldn't tell if he meant what he'd said or if he was trying to save Riley's skin. Never mind the fact it kinda looked cute.

'Please give me your phone.' She put her hand out, offering a less-than-pleased smile, her expression struggling to hide the worry filling her. Riley might be safe now, but what if—

She gleaned a small amount of satisfaction in his hesitation before he eventually tugged it from his board shorts and handed it over. With it in her hands and one final glare, she was relieved to find he didn't have a password. She tapped away.

The responsibility given to her for Riley's well-being was weighing heavier and heavier these days. To fail . . . her mother would be having serious words with her if it even looked like she'd lost him.

'Any time you feel the need to wander off with my nephew for hours, please text me.' She handed back his phone.

She loved the way Riley lit up around Gus. But how could Gus be okay with this scenario? For all she knew, Riley could have been trapped somewhere, and she'd have no clue where to start looking. She thought of Jenna, glaring down at her with her angry pointy finger poking her way for her irresponsibility. It was a trait she'd so often teased her about, ending with them both laughing. But this wasn't about babysitting her nephew anymore, not since she'd become a custodian. She had to be his mother and provider. That meant protecting him no matter how he felt about it. Her insides churned.

Kate brushed aside Monica's pleas for attention as she turned and walked towards her veggie patch, hoping Gus might disappear amongst the shrubs for good. The sun was nestling down on the dusk horizon, and she needed to bring her packets of remaining seeds inside before the rabbits could develop a taste for them. She'd already covered everything as best she could with shade cloth to keep them out.

There was no sound behind her, and she turned, forcing her frustration both at herself and Mr Too Cool to—be it reluctantly— simmer down. 'Riley, come on.'

Riley and Gus shared a wary gaze before they followed cautiously. She let a rush of air fly from her lungs.

Kate didn't stop until she stood in front of her new garden beds, rather satisfied as she raised an I-told-you-so eyebrow Gus's way. 'See, things can grow here.' She allowed her shoulders to straighten as interest flickered across his face. Surprise was precisely what she was aiming for.

'Wow, this is impressive,' Gus said. 'They're still alive.' His smug grin made her wish she could push him all the way back to his shack with one gigantic shove.

'Auntie Kate, can Gus stay for tea?'

What? Now that was taking things a bit too far, wasn't it? After every anxiety, every worried thought she'd just gone through.

She eyed Gus with a narrowed stare, hoping she'd masked her inward pleasure at the idea despite how she was telling herself she should feel.

'Well, I don't have to stay for—'

'Can heee? Pleeease, Auntie Kate?'

Kate's eyes moved from the sweet face of her nephew—wanting to say yes to everything he ever asked for—to the neighbour she couldn't decide if she wanted to be around or not. She fought with herself for a reason to say no. Anything. But the longer she paid attention to them both, the more her grievances subdued. It was futile, and she sighed.

'Okay, fine,' she said, her shoulders failing her by falling into a defeated slouch. 'But you, young man, need to get inside for a shower first, pronto.'

'Yay.' Riley jumped in the air before taking off, Speedy in hot pursuit. Kate watched him heading towards the house, and warmth surged inside her chest. Seeing Riley with a friend, be it of the canine variety, meant he was happy, something he needed most in his life right now. As for his friendship with Gus, only time would test the endurance of that relationship.

'Thanks, Kate. I am sorry. I'm so used to doing things on my own. It didn't occur to me until it was too late.'

And there it was, that sheepish grin she'd seen when Riley had invited him to tea. To his credit, it looked like he carried a hint of reluctance about the invite, piquing her curiosity.

'I'll keep a closer eye on the time when he's with me from now on.'

She fidgeted under his keen eye as her foot made shapes in the sandy soil, letting puffs rise into the air. She couldn't quite explain it, but she did trust him.

'And I'll text, I promise.'

The smell of lamb chops sizzling on the barbeque had Gus looking up from his post at the Lego table with regularity, his belly offering up a deep growl. He was a whatever-cuts-of-meat Hughey gave-him-to-eat kind of guy. What didn't sell at the butcher shop that week was his bonus.

Kate strolled inside, full of purpose as she covered the cooked meat with alfoil, setting it aside to rest. She placed the salad she'd put together earlier on the dining table.

Speedy's eyes moved back and forth, watching all three of them, her head remaining on her paws as she lay next to the coffee table.

'Who's hungry?' Kate said.

'Me!' Riley jumped from his knees to his feet in one hit, making Gus wish he still had it in him to do the same.

Gus couldn't hide his smile as Kate stopped mid-scoop of the salad she was dishing onto the plates, staring at her nephew with an enchanted gaze as he raced to the table. His insides skipped as she turned to him, her smile effervescent and genuine, holding him captive. If she watched him much longer, he'd turn beetroot red beneath the beard he'd trimmed that morning. He stretched his legs so he could get up, the pins and needles in them buzzing from the punishing cross-legged position he'd held for too long. But regardless of his resolve, a flush of heat still warmed his cheeks.

'Smells good.' He pulled at his collar as he wobbled to his feet, recognising from the length of her gaze that there was more going on behind her eyes. Her smile had stilled. Had she thought twice about him being there? He could leave if she wanted him to. He'd been close to turning down the invitation in a moment of panicked realisation that he was starting to like their company . . .

a little too much.

Time passed quickly, and it was after nine-thirty when Kate asked Riley to head to bed.

'But can't I stay up a bit longer? I'm not tired.' His sweet face was working hard to convince Kate, and Gus was intrigued. Would she melt under that innocent charm?

'No, sorry, buddy. It's past your bedtime as it is. You've got school tomorrow.'

Gus smiled to himself.

Riley blinked slowly before saying good night to Gus. He didn't offer Kate the same gesture, and a shimmer of guilt ran through him. But he couldn't control how her nephew responded in any given situation, so he hid his unease by looking down at his hands, resting palm down on the table before he regarded Riley.

'Night buddy. Let's catch up again soon, hey? Might need you to help dig out some more of those shrubs. What do you say?'

'I'd like that,' Riley said with a smile, then, without a second look at Kate, shuffled down the hallway.

Kate made them a cup of tea and they retreated to the couch, kicking aside the stray Lego under the table.

'You're good with him. And he likes you.' There it was, that disheartened voice and Gus worried she might tear up. She kept her eyes on the haze rising from her mug.

They sat in the peacefulness of the humming cicadas as Gus toyed with whether he should bring it up. If he heard it from her, perhaps he could help.

'Riley told me what happened to his mum. I'm so sorry.' And he was. Unbelievably. She had to be hurting too.

Kate held his eyes with a start. 'He did?' She turned her pained expression away from him. 'He won't talk about it.' Her voice softened. 'He won't talk to me at all. I don't understand why.' Her head shook in sad confusion.

'Give him time. He's just a kid who hasn't worked out where he fits yet.'

'I thought I was doing the right thing bringing him somewhere new. We both needed a chance to start over. Or so I thought.'

He studied her as she stared into the fireplace still smothered with burnt ash and coals from the last winter it had been used by the Pilchers.

Gus gave her time to go on, but this woman—who wasn't afraid to give as good as she got—remained silent.

Kate's eyes widened as she continued to stare, now gazing at the fireplace mantle. She shied away, blinking back the moisture in her eyes, and she shook her head. 'But all I am is a bad reminder that Jenna is gone, and I'll never be his mother.'

A lonely tear toppled over the precipice of her lower eyelid, trickling down her cheek. Gus rolled his lips as he fought not to reach out and wipe it away.

'And I'm not trying to replace her either,' she interjected as though she was reading his thoughts. 'But no matter what I do, he hates me.'

'No, he doesn't.'

'But you're wrong.' She shifted, turning her body towards him now. 'You don't see the silence I get when I suggest we do something he used to love doing with me.' She pressed a hand to her chest as she leaned forward. 'He loved hanging out with me.' All expression fell from her face. 'Now, it's like he wishes I never existed.'

'No. The kid's gone through so much. How long has it been?'

'Nine months.'

'That's why, then. He's still grieving, and not just over his mum. He's lost his friends, his grandparents, and the only home he's known. You can't expect him to adjust to all that by shifting two states away,' he said gently, but the moment she held his eyes, he wanted to retract it or at least have chosen his words better.

'So that makes me a terrible auntie for doing that to him?'

Speedy lifted her head from her paws, glancing from Gus to Kate, her tongue curling as she yawned.

Gus wanted to gently remind Kate that Riley had lost his auntie too and that he knew for a fact that Riley missed that person and wanted her back.

'Kate, I didn't say that. I just think—'

Kate stood, moving to the kitchen counter before she turned to face him, leaning against it. 'Please take your just thinks and head on home, and don't trip in the dark on any of those never-ending tree roots lining every damn path around here because I'm clearly not much help if you need it.' She straightened, rendering him speechless and unable to ignore his pounding heart as Kelly appeared in his mind. That, alongside the internal ache for the way he'd made Kate feel, well, it really would be best to leave. At some stage during the past couple of weeks, he'd managed to switch off the aches in their varying forms, but now they had reignited with a vengeance.

So he gave a resigned nod, rising to his feet. Speedy jumped up, following her master into the dark.

A shimmer of annoyance filled Kate as she fought against the urge to clench her fists at her side. She glared at the dinner dishes soaking in the hot water as if this was all their fault. Here was a man she hardly knew, getting along with her nephew as if they were forever best buddies. It didn't matter what she did or how hard she tried, Riley showed little interest in her anymore. He simply refused to love her, and there wasn't a thing she could do about it.

Well, she'd just have to try harder. What other choice did she have? She couldn't return the favour and give him the cold shoulder back. That would only make him feel even less loved. She thought back to the ways their mother had reared Jenna and herself. She'd been firm with them, getting cross with their father when he'd played the clown when they were supposed to be going to bed, but high as a kite from the shenanigans he liked to turn on just for them.

Riley simply resented her when she was the parent, and when she reverted to being the good-time auntie. Gone were the days when he giggled and ran around the house as she chased him. She didn't have time for that anymore. She had responsibilities that sucked her time dry and her enthusiasm thin. She was so out of her depth.

The following day started out a little cooler as she woke, slightly puffy-eyed from the tears she'd shed before she'd fallen asleep. She stretched her arms above her as movement from the open bedroom door drew her attention. And they weren't Riley's feet clip-clopping down the hallway.

Kate leapt out of bed; her eyes suddenly wide as a certain woolly butt strolled towards the lounge. 'Monica! How did you get inside?'

The ewe paused at her name or Kate's screechy voice—she didn't care which—swivelling her head back with a certain ease Kate was resenting all the more. But all she could do was stare in shock and confusion. She tipped her head to the side, swivelling as Riley approached, causing Kate to skip out of the way as he strolled right on past, heading for the lounge.

'I . . . um?' She stared with her mouth hanging open until she could gather her words. 'Riley, do you know how Monica got inside? Was she in your bedroom with you?' Was that even an answer she wanted to hear? Kate rubbed her brow. Was there ever going to be an end to the ongoing mischievousness of this ewe?

Not waiting for Riley to answer, mostly because that was easier, Kate ushered Monica out the front door with a nudge from her knee and a shove with her hands. She stopped at the entrance, greeted by numerous faces turning to watch her as they stretched their legs and stood on her verandah, ready to begin their new day.

With a clenched jaw, she secured the door shut with a firm push, testing it before heading to the kettle, a huff on her breath.

There was a trail of droppings leading down the hallway to the dining table where Kate could only assume Monica had set up camp overnight. 'Damned sheep,' and she shook her head, her lungs deflating. When was Gus going to get his act into gear and relieve her of his rent-free tenants who had no regard for her efforts to keep her verandah clean after they sauntered off for a casual morning smoko and a drink?

Speaking of which, she grabbed her phone, glowering. And damn it. She'd given him her number, and he hadn't bothered to do the polite thing and text her so she'd have his. Her hand flopped to her side. Had she not been running short of time to get Riley to school, she might've marched over there and made him take his annoying sheep back right now.

Riley slipped out of the car at the front of the school gate without a word, and Kate caught sight of the two children running up, offering him a Monday morning greeting like no other. Her heart ached. Not all that long ago, it was she who was giving the kind of greeting that had him exploding with energy and excitement in response. They'd high-five each other after he'd jumped to reach her hand, and then he'd run ahead, looking over his shoulder to urge her to play tiggy.

Kate took a sobering breath before heading straight for Meg's.

Hughey was coming out of the café wearing a decidedly smug grin when Kate stepped up, holding the door open for him thanks to his hands being full of coffees.

'Mornin', Kate.'

'Hey, Hughey. You seem happy with yourself.' She considered him. Was he going an ever-so-subtle shade of pink? 'I'll drop in soon. Just getting one of those for myself first.' She nodded at his takeaway cups.

He saluted her with the one in his hand, then crossed the road back to his shop.

'Goood morning,' Kate said, overemphasising her welcome while eyeing her friend with certainty. 'What's going on with you two?' She waited at the counter, holding Meg's shy expression as she watched her squirm a little.

Meg brushed her words off with a wave. 'What are you talking about?' She moved to the coffee machine with zeal, starting the drink Kate hadn't ordered yet.

'Oh no you don't. No fibbing to me, young lady. No one could miss the way Hughey was blushing as he left the shop.' She waggled her eyebrows, receiving a dirty glare back.

'No, you've got it all wrong. I'm not willing to fraternise with the one person who is relentlessly pestering me to join ranks. He reckons I have all the time in the world, so much so that I can afford to close shop long enough to do a reno next to him and re-open months down the track with no income in between. Honestly Kate, the man has sand in his brain.' She slammed off the frothing wand, wiping it clean as though it was dirtier than a grease trap.

'So why do you think he wants you to move next door? He.

Likes. You.' Kate took a sip of her mocha, cringing as the milk burnt her tongue. Meg had to start reining in her frustration over Hughey when she was making coffee, or someone was going to lose their taste buds for good.

'Oh.' Meg waved her hand in the air again. 'He has some grand scheme in his head that we could join shops down the middle and make it a café come larder come butcher thingy,' and she brushed the concept away. 'Personally, I can't picture how it would work. And as if anyone around here would want an eatery like that. This town is so close to falling asleep I wonder if it's worth staying open sometimes.' Meg leaned forward, resting her crossed arms on the counter. 'This place is only for the locals, and by that, I mean the old ones. Sometimes, at our Country Women's Association meetings, we joke that it's like living in a retirement village. No young people, except for you—' she smiled— 'want to live here because it's got nothing going for it. Some people left after the last big fire we had.'

Kate recalled the blackened trees she'd seen on the outskirts of the town throughout the bushland. 'That fire must've been a long time ago. The trees have got good regrowth.'

'They do. But look around. It's summer. The place should be swarming with visitors.'

The door swung open, and immediately, Meg's eyes widened before her chatty expression shut down, and Kate stood taller, perplexed by her friend's reaction.

'Morning, Ash.' She livened her face with a professional smile. 'What can I get for you this fine day?'

The middle-aged man slowed as he reached the counter beside Kate.

'Oh, Kate, this is Ash Evans. He's a local.'

Kate offered a welcoming smile. 'Nice to meet you.'

'Yeah, you too.' Ash cut any further friendly chit-chat off

with his folded arms and stern face that focused on Meg's sleek black coffee machine.

'Rightio,' Kate mouthed as her eyes widened at Meg, who appeared unsurprised by his behaviour. She couldn't be sure, but he looked like the guy who'd bailed up Gus the day she arrived. 'I'll catch you later, Meg. Bye, Ash.'

Ash acknowledged her with a half-nod. If this was how the community of Forest Gully was determined to be, then they really needed a firecracker up their clackers.

CHAPTER 12

'You've gotta be kidding me,' Kate said before exhaling a breath as she pushed the door open to the butcher's shop. Hughey was standing in front of the chilled display cabinets, directing Gus—who just happened to be wearing a white apron for some strange reason—as to where to place specific meat trays.

The shop smelled of sawdust and fresh meat as Hughey greeted her, his generous smile something she'd begun to associate with him. But it glided into a frown as Gus looked on, considering her with a lazy blink. It was plain to see from the tweak of his lips that he was aware she was annoyed at finding him here.

'Didn't know you worked here,' Kate said in a forced light voice as she approached the counter like a ram to his feed bucket. At least he had the good manners to appear a little shamefaced.

'Yup.' Gus took a sip of the coffee Hughey had brought in, its bitterness hitting his features immediately.

'So, when are you going to take your sheep home? Monica has made a nasty habit of stalking me in my sleep.' She maintained her sweet smile. Before the end of this day, those sheep would be back where they belonged.

Hughey snorted a chuckle but smothered his grin in a flash as Kate turned on him.

'Good morning, Kate,' Hughey said. 'Lovely to see you this fine morning. What can we get for you?'

Hmmm, sweet as pie, she muttered under her breath, her surprised eyebrow rising at the word 'we'.

'Definitely not lamb,' she said, eyeing Gus with a cynical glare once more. 'I've already threatened three of them with the deep freeze compartment if they continue to trip me up as I head to the car.' She didn't care if Hughey was standing there or not, ignoring his chuckle. She wanted to know if Gus planned on mentioning it last night. One itty-bitty word, perhaps? Being irked with him was starting to feel rather satisfying.

'I'm sorry, but I'm working on it, okay?' He put his palm up, asking for her patience but it was wearing thin.

'Have you owned sheep before?' She put her takeaway cup on the bench and crossed her arms, eying him sceptically.

His lips pressed together like he couldn't decide how to convince her, giving her time to take in his features. He still rocked that sexy surfy physique, broad shoulders and bronzed cheeks that she'd seen rise in the warmest of welcomes when he wanted to give one. So today wasn't one of those days? She waited for him to answer, her finger tapping slowly on her crossed arm.

Time's up.

'Can you tell me what breed they are?' She *so* had him.

Her peripheral vision hinted that Hughey was attempting to mouth something his way but she let it go. And in the time she'd waited for his answer, a new directive played into her mind.

'Hughey, what's the best kind of lamb to buy, if I did want to buy some?'

'Crossbred.' Hughey shifted from foot to foot. 'They're bred for their meat.' She didn't miss the way he emphasised the word crossbred and was still trying to catch Gus's eye.

'Okay. And do you source your stock locally? You'd be able to prepare them on-site, right?'

'Yeah, sure. I've done it for a few of the locals from time to time.'

'So, Gus, why don't you sell Hughey some of your sheep? You'd make some money and solve my problem.' Eventually.

Kate considered Gus's puzzled expression as he stared in

confusion at Hughey. After some time, he focused on her. 'You mean you want me to feed the local community with my sheep?' There was a certain horror glued to his face.

Kate nodded. 'Kill two sheep with one stone if you get my drift,' and she couldn't resist a chuckle at her pun. But as she said it, all she could conjure in her mind was Monica staring at her with those damned trusting eyes. And that was precisely why she'd never been allowed to have a pet lamb back at home. 'Everyone gets attached,' her father had said. 'No one likes to eat a sheep that has a name.' Now Kate was beginning to understand what he'd meant.

'No.'

'No? That's it?' Her head pulled back of its own accord.

'Yes, that's it,' and Gus moved towards the back of the shop, not giving her a chance to engage any further in their discussion.

'Hey, hang on. We need to work out what to do with them, and I'm trying to help. You work in a butcher's shop for heaven's sake.'

Kate raised an eyebrow at Hughey. What was so wrong with the proposal? The sooner, the better, in her opinion. Then Monica wouldn't be inducted into her own hall of fame where a portrait of her would live above the fireplace, haunting her forever.

In all truthfulness, the lamb was what she was craving, but beyond Hughey's shoulder, all she could see was Gus as he busied himself, shifting tubs of meat with what appeared to be little purpose.

'Just some chicken thighs, thanks Hughey,' Kate said as she looked back at the array of cuts on offer in the display cabinet. If they managed to talk later and she had, in fact, bought lamb, well, she'd find it hard to escape his scrutiny if Gus chose to serve her with a plate full of his attitude.

And as Hughey wrapped her chicken up in butcher's paper, Gus continued to poke about at the back of the store, looking more and more like the proverbial lost lamb. Now she did feel a little guilty.

Kate said goodbye to Hughey, resisting the urge to call out to Gus. She wasn't happy with him, but she didn't intend to be rude. Even when Hughey called him to help when two more customers entered the shop, he didn't turn around.

Outside the butcher's, with the package in her hands, a tickle of excitement grew. She turned towards the General Store, waving to Meg through the café glass doors as she strode past. She pushed the door open, smiling.

'Hey, Nola, Graham. How are you?'

In unison, the couple said hello back, making them all laugh. But she wanted to cut to the chase.

'I have a question for you both. Where can I get some chickens?'

'Oh, that's easy. Go see Patsy. She loves them,' Nola said.

'Has way too many if you ask me,' Graham said, shaking his head. 'She lives next door to us, and her damned haughty roosters wake me up at four a.m. with their crowing and carry on every damned morning. Can't get back to sleep again for love nor money.' He shook his head despondently.

'Oh, they're not that bad,' Nola chided, swatting him good-naturedly on the arm before she smiled at Kate. 'You know Sheep Gully Road? Just head on up there and go past the giant ash tree on the left-hand side.' Nola gave a broken-hearted glance towards Graham before continuing. 'You can't miss it. She's the next house on the right. You should be able to catch her now that she's finished the Road Side Delivery mail run for today. But look out. She'll want to make you a cuppa.'

'Thanks, Nola. I might drop by now.'

'Just beware, she'll chew your ear off,' Graham said, this time earning himself a swift nudge in the side from Nola's elbow. But it didn't stop him. 'All the CWA women have a knack for doing that super well,' and he sidestepped out of the way, avoiding the next swipe from Nola's hand.

'Speaking of,' Nola said, 'you should come along to our next gathering. The women would love to meet you, and we could do with a new face to look at. We've all been here a long time, and you'd understand how it gets when suggestions for activities start to run dry.'

Kate couldn't miss the optimism in Nola's expression. And what could it hurt? She'd been wanting to get to know the community, and this was the perfect way to start.

'Sure. I'd love to. When is it?'

'Wonderful! Tonight. Our place at seven. Bring a plate to share.'

And with that, Kate left for Patsy's with a skip in her step.

Kate moaned as an obtrusive sound disturbed her, turning over in bed and falling back to sleep before the sound trumpeted a second time. She pried one eye open, staring wearily through her bedroom door as she tried to work out the source of the noise. The distinctive clippety-clop footsteps she expected to hear were absent. But there was no mistaking it when it roared to life the third time.

Kate sat up with a start, her hair cascading over her face and a what-have-I-done expression matching it. In all her wisdom—which clearly wasn't much at this unruly hour—she'd not only brought home six "point of lay" chickens, but Patsy had convinced her that a Sussex rooster would give her wonderful chickens.

But as the bird crowed towards a crescendo in his unrelenting joy for the dawn, Kate ripped her pillow from under her head and planted it on top of her face, hoping the wretched animal wasn't waking Riley also.

We'll get so used to him we won't even notice in a couple of days, she muffled into the pillow, still able to hear with acute clarity the cock-a-doodle-dos hollering through the early morning air, the echoing vibrating her headspace when the feathered brute took a moment to catch his breath. She peeked out of one eye at the window, a deep growl murmuring through her lips.

She rolled onto her front, drifting in and out of sleep until the dark morning light filtered in through her window, unsure how much extra shut-eye she'd managed to catch after the late night with the CWA ladies when Riley knocked on her door. She pulled her head out from beneath the pillow, roughly brushing her tussled hair aside and lifting her neck. With squinting eyes, she tried to focus on him, albeit blurrily. He'd been less than happy sitting amongst a group of yabbering women all trying to talk at once, but she'd promised to make it up to him today with a swim after school.

'Auntie Kate. That chook is really noisy.'

Kate let her head flop back to the mattress, closing her eyes and pointing her index finger in the air towards him. 'That he is, but you can make some pocket money from his offspring. Won't that be fun?' she said in a groggy voice. Hearing his feet padding away, she lifted her head once more, one eye open before releasing a weary groan.

Flopping onto her back, she urged both eyes open at the rich orange glow from the sky demanding her attention. And it should've been a beautiful sight, the kind you'd race out and take advantage of with a camera. But to Kate, it sent a shiver down her spine, waking her up more effectively than she'd want anyone to know. A red sky at night was okay. It was a red sky in the morning that made her shiver with apprehension.

CHAPTER 13

It was now or never. Gus slugged down the dregs of his coffee and clutched his hair back in a rough man bun as he stood at his kitchen bench. Speedy meandered in through the open door, moseying over to him for a pat as her backside swaggered.

Outside, the sky held striking tones amongst intimidating clouds. A start like this usually meant it came with a storm of some kind. The radio station weather forecast had said the chance of one was on the cards, and although he loved to watch a good lightning show, he had too much to do to be held up by one today.

The sheep under Kate's verandah baaed incorrigibly at him as he quietly approached, rising to their feet. He nudged some of them with his foot to make his way to her door. He knocked, leaning to his right to look in through the loungeroom window for any movement.

All was silent, that was, other than the maddening rooster that had rudely shown up at her place yesterday. He'd tried to block the noise with his pillow, eventually tossing it aside and getting his coffee an hour earlier than his usual rise-and-shine time. He was already feeling the effects of a too-early wake-up call, and he hoped this wasn't a sign of things to come.

He was scratching the side of his face with a yawn when Kate opened the door, all dishevelled and, damn it, disturbingly sexy in her pyjama shorts and matching T-shirt. His brows rose as he locked eyes with her, and she offered a deflated sigh. His Adam's apple tightened as he squashed down his desire to reach out and brush aside the tassel of hair delicately hooked over her nose.

'Good morning,' Kate said in a sluggish tone. 'If the rooster woke you, you weren't the only one, so don't go feeling entitled.' Her words took him by pleasant surprise, and the side of his mouth lifted as he chuckled. She sure was cute when she was tired, with her hair sticking up in all directions.

'Yeah, he did. But that's not why I'm here.' The surprise on her face and the way he'd managed to stir her attention so quickly appealed to him, sending a pleasant rush of warmth through him. 'I've been clearing the boundary between us, and it's ready to fence. I was hoping you'd like to help me do it today?' He'd put odds on she'd be more than happy thanks to the way she was wearily staring at the sheep at her feet.

'Now?' Her eyes were still trying to hang out of her head, and she rubbed them with the backs of her fingers, pushing that pesky strand of hair into submission. 'And how are we doing this? I'm guessing we're going halves?'

'You don't have to worry about that. I've got it taken care of.'

Her body leaned sideways, her shoulder resting on the door jamb as interest settled across her face. 'This wouldn't be your way of apologising for bagging out on my veggies, would it?' She tipped her head forward, a teasing smile pinching at the corners of her lips.

Gus glimpsed the wariness in her widening eyes and snuck a look behind him. 'I reckon there might be a storm on the way and—'

'Yep, let's do it. Come on in for a quick coffee, then we can knock it over before lunch,' and before he could remember what else he was planning to say, she gave him a brisk nod towards the kettle before marching herself back down the hallway in what felt like a rush.

Gus stepped inside, closing the door on Monica's insistence

on gaining entry.

'G'day, Riley. How's your day so far?'

The kid was sitting at the dining table eating Coco Pops, and while he waited for Riley's answer, Gus glanced around the lounge room. He hadn't noticed it before, but it was clear her feminine touch now lifted the once dreary space. Simple touches like a throw over the old sofa and some bright cushions all made for a homely feel, even if the furniture was old. The newly begun crochet project sitting on the coffee table caught his eye before he shifted his attention back to Riley.

The kid shrugged his shoulders as he turned his cereal with his spoon, watching the chocolate-coloured milk dribble back into the bowl. 'Okay, I guess.'

'Well, I say the sooner you get to school, the sooner you won't have to listen to the ruckus that's going on outside,' and he thumbed in the direction of the blasted rooster still making his presence known. Riley chuckled with Gus as the rooster's crows grew more determined if that were even possible.

'But Auntie Kate did say I can sell the chickens which would be fun.'

Gus smiled at the liveliness in Riley's voice, his peripheral vision alerting him to Kate pausing at the hallway entrance, holding up the architrave with her shoulder as she listened. Gus gave a slight nod her way, a thoughtful look on her face before she glanced about for her shoes. He tugged out his phone and texted her. If she had his number, it wouldn't only have to be for her to contact him about Riley.

'C'mon, buddy. Let's get going.' Gus turned to head out the door.

'I'll make us some to-go coffees, since you didn't quite make it to the kitchen.' This time, when she looked up, her teasing grin was unmistakable, and a warm buzz rushed through his core.

'Yeah, sorry 'bout that.' His grin was sheepish.

'I'll head out to the fence line soon,' she smiled.

'Do you know where it is?'

'I wouldn't have a clue.' Again, that adorable grin that threatened to challenge his self-imposed motto. But keeping the solitude secure was the only way he could protect someone, especially another woman he had growing feelings for, from getting hurt. But how was he meant to achieve that if his stomach remained a fizz of excitement at the prospect of spending the whole day with her? But he didn't want to miss out on her help either. The storm was still a way off, and a fence was the answer to keeping their neighbourly relationship somewhat amicable.

'Just listen for the post driver, and you'll find me no worries.'

She nodded. 'C'mon, Riley or we'll be late.' Kate headed towards her car as Gus ruffled Riley's hair.

'Have a good one, buddy.'

'I will,' Riley grinned, hopping in the car so Kate could drop him off at school. Gus grinned at Riley, but it was Kate's relaxed smile that won out, snatching his attention. And if he had anything to do with it, he'd ensure that it made a regular appearance, especially around Riley.

Half an hour later, Gus looked up to see Kate approaching him, and he laid the post driver on the ground, tugging off his gloves.

'I see you cheated.' Gus reached for the cup she was offering and took a long sip of his latté, unashamedly gazing at her with a glint in his eye. He looked down at her lips as they parted in a soft smile, making his grip on his cup tighten. He swallowed hard, forcing down the desire to kiss her there and then by swiftly looking at his feet.

'Meg would be upset with me if I broke my record and

missed a day.' They chuckled together.

With their coffees kicking them into full gear, they worked hard to line the star posts up. Kate held each post with the oversized leather gloves Gus had lent her as he drove them hard into the ground. By late morning they had the length of the fence line done.

But she'd been keenly distracted most of the time, unable to look away from the developing clouds with uneasiness in her movements and expression. Gus figured it was time for a distraction. 'Feel like a break?' By her look, he'd hit the nail on the head.

Kate had brought with her some home-cooked scones with jam and cream for morning smoko, which she'd kept in a cooler bag in the shade of a shrub. They sat beneath a leafy tree as they ate, the silence between them easy. Gus accepted the scone she offered, breaking a piece off and tossing it to Speedy as she lay beneath a bush nearby, her eyes trained on both of them for the next piece they might throw her.

'So, Tenterfield, hey? Did you like it there?' Why would she move to a quiet town like Forest Gully? He didn't get it.

Kate reached for her bucket hat, refitting it snugly to her head as, yet again, she eyed the ever-blackening clouds as if they fascinated her in some curious way. If she was uneasy with storms, she was hiding it well.

'Yeah, it's got a nice little cricket club. Dad used to play. We'd always stop what we were doing to cheer him on every Saturday afternoon, rain, hail or shine.'

She took another bite of her scone, the cream lining her top lip, and she rushed a hand to her mouth, licking it away. It had his insides in a tangle, unable to make himself look away.

'So, why all the sheep? Need them for friends?' The question came across as light, but it left him in no doubt she'd never understand why he might keep sheep. He was well aware he didn't look like any sheepman he'd known back home.

She ran a finger over her lip to catch the jam, and this time, he did look away, not because he wanted to, but because what she'd said had been correct in a small way. But what idiot would admit to a fact like that? Her words saved him from his urge to lean in and kiss the skerrick of jam still nestled on her upper lip.

Instead, he decided to come clean with the truth.

'They were given to me. When the Pilchers moved, they told me they were my inheritance for looking after the place until someone leased it.' He looked up, holding her gaze. 'Or bought it,' he corrected, recognising that speaking the word out loud induced annoyance within him once more, even if it was a little less than when she'd initially moved in. 'They were heading to a suburban house block.'

'But—and tell me if I'm wrong—you have no clue about sheep, do you?' Her interest zoned in on him, making him feel a tad foolish even though it was delivered gently.

'You obviously know a thing or two about them,' he said, admitting defeat. He subtly shook his head as he studied the remainder of his scone resting between his fingers, the cream wilting in the ambient heat.

'I knew it,' she giggled, slapping her hand on her thigh. 'You were never going to round them up the other day, were you?'

A wall of defensiveness tightened his back, even though it was clear she intended to understand him. He wished he understood himself more some days.

'I'd have given it a crack. But you were watching, and well, I didn't need to shame myself any more than was necessary.'

'I'll admit it was funny to watch,' she said, her giggle settling.

The sparkle in her eyes sent a nervous quiver to his voice.

'So how come you know so much, Miss Smarty-pants?' He grinned, hoping his attempt at lightly winding her up would disguise his sheepish embarrassment. 'Monica has taken a real liking to you.' Could she hear how loud his heart was thumping?

'She's Miss Queen Bee to you.' Kate offered up another heart-warming grin, freely and unconditionally.

Gus chuckled back, unable to stop himself from studying her finer details. She had the cutest eyebrow wiggle that dared him to kiss it. He really needed to stop thinking about kissing her or he might actually follow through.

'That's a perfect name for her. She does like ruling the roost.'

'Don't remind me.' Kate shook her head, tossing her eyes to the tree above them, the gum leaves shuddering with the growing wind gusts. She redirected her gaze to the parched sandy soil in front of her feet. 'I grew up on a sheep station. Merinos and crossies. That was our main income.' Her interest turned to him. 'When are your girls due?'

'Due for what?' He lifted his eyes with a start. Where was this conversation heading?

'To . . . have their lambs?' Her confused expression had him baffled, alarmed and fearful all at once.

Speedy thumped her tail on the ground in dusty bursts, watching them closely.

'Um.' He rubbed his jaw. 'Are they close?'

Kate nodded. 'You'd get good dollars for those lambs when they're on the ground. There's enough of the ewes in lamb for you to put up a decent-sized pen at the market or sell them directly to Hughey. Have you thought about him promoting your local meat? And who knows, sales could pick up. The locals might love it.'

Ash and his loyal followers wouldn't touch the meat if they knew it was from him, and Kelly would turn in her grave if she thought—

No, no more thoughts, Gus. Shut this down now.

'So, why'd you leave to come here? I could think of better places to choose from, like Hawaii.' He grinned, happier now the conversation was less focused on him.

Kate's face stilled at his joke, although well-intentioned, now lost in the moment. He let his gaze drift to the ground beside him. He should've been more sensitive.

'It was my sister's choice to work on the farm. Me, I've always loved the country, but I needed to do it somewhere else after . . .' She drew in a steadying breath. 'After the accident happened. So did Mum and Dad. It was the right thing for all of us to do.'

But was it right for Riley? Gus had his reservations but kept them to himself. The kid was lonely. She'd gone ahead and made a decision for both of them, giving him no say in it. He was concerned Riley wouldn't be able to move on if he didn't have a choice—no different to him.

'So, moving here is enough . . . for both of you?' It had been for him, until Kelly had died. Now nothing would ever be enough if it didn't carry with it some kind of dream for him to live for.

'Yeah, it is. We have the beach and all this space around us.' She brushed her hand towards the land in front of them. 'I'd like to get some livestock down the track.' She studied him, the intensity of her gaze threatening to urge him to spill his deepest secrets. He gulped quietly. This was a superpower he wanted to learn.

'This fence will help with that.' She didn't hide her engaging smile. 'Might even be able to get a pet for Riley.'

A far-off rumble vibrated in the distance, and her face shifted from tranquil and in the moment to defensive as her voice cut short. She stood up quickly, gathering the food and shoving it back in the esky. 'How about we get this finished, hey?' She glanced at the sky yet again.

Gus followed her gaze. The clouds were upon them, dark and angry, although the impact of the impending storm was still some time off.

'Let's roll out the ring lock. We might be able to get the top strand attached to the posts before that arrives.' Gus gave her what he believed was a reassuring smile.

Kate's nervous glance back had him quickening his steps. She was on tenterhooks so the sooner they got this done, the better.

With Kate on her side of the fence and Gus on his, they managed to attach the wire like Gus had planned, and as Kate held it taut for him to do the last knot, her arms began to shake, her eyes glued to the sky rather than the wire he was fixing off.

'Hey, it's okay. We're nearly done.' He reached out, placing a gloved hand over hers as they continued to shake. Where was the woman who didn't balk at revving him up with her witty comments all while challenging his convictions? Where was the woman who wouldn't let him show her up?

'Riley.' She sucked in the word with instant concern even though it carried tenderness and love.

Gus leaned in a little closer. 'He's okay, he's in school.' He squeezed her hand.

'But he'll be scared.'

Glancing up, Gus noticed the way the moody clouds were rolling over one another with vigour, the scent of rain thick in the air. 'The storm is heading out to sea, not towards the school. He might hear something, but it won't be close to him like it is to us.'

'To us?' Beads of sweat trickled from her forehead as she nodded, her brow creasing tight, and he couldn't unsee the way she blinked in the direction of her house, hidden amongst the scrub and bushes. Did she want to make a run for it? The storm was close and even though her house was a stone's throw away, running in and out of the tight bushes would slow her down. There wasn't enough time.

He wanted to reach out, to comfort her with a reassuring squeeze around the shoulders to ease the fear her body pulsed with, but somehow, it seemed too soon, mostly for him.

A memory flashed into his mind of Kelly. He was taking her for a celebratory picnic at the Stony Creek Swimming Hole, a spot he'd taken her to for their first date.

A soft smile crept up his lips.

Kelly reached out, taking his hand in hers as he drove, holding her left hand to the sunlight shining in through the windscreen. Light shimmied off the clustered diamonds, catching his gaze. He turned to her, beaming back at her dancing eyes and sweet smile only for him.

'I think we should head back. The lightning's close,' Kate said, her voice tight, and she lifted her leg over the wire, her feet scrabbling to his side of the fence. She shrunk as a flash lit the sky, a crack of thunder arriving only seconds later. Her eyes widened, begging him to listen.

He looked away, shaken by the memory and the feelings it stirred, as though he was betraying Kelly by spending time with Kate. But it was so they could live their own lives, on their own side of the fence. His fingers clenched inside his gloves.

The rain didn't begin with soft droplets. Instead, it came with a sudden downpour that Gus heard coming with a roar, and the thunder rocked above them relentlessly. Kate threw her hands over her head as she cringed forward on the spot.

'C'mon, follow me.' Without a second thought, Gus took her hand and the esky in the other, and they ran towards his hut.

They reached his small porch as lightning electrified the air, an immediate crack deafening them, and Kate dove into his chest, hiding her head beneath her clamped arms as her body shook with involuntary waves. Gus wrapped protective arms around her, holding her tight as he turned his back to the elements, the rain drenching his T-shirt and shorts beneath the shallow verandah as he rested his chin on her head. He breathed in the fresh scent of her shampoo, silky and soft against his skin, and found himself resting his cheek on her hair, drawn by its comfort as he closed his eyes.

She was shivering despite the steamy air, and he roused himself enough to reach for the door handle, ushering her inside. She'd feel safer with walls around her, he hoped. Speedy gave a quick shake as she trotted in after them.

Inside, Kate stepped from his hold, her cheeks flushed and her hands still clamped around her body as she gave a coy glance his way before taking in his abode.

His house wasn't much. All he needed were the bare necessities. He considered what she might do with her soft touches to the place.

Kate took a deep breath and held it as another clap sounded above them and he could see she was doing her best to fight reacting. What he saw between sharp cracks of thunder was a woman lost in her surroundings as she fought to slow her breathing in an effort to relax.

'Here, have a seat.' Gus ushered her towards the couch. He went to the fridge and grabbed two cold bottles of water, passing her one. 'Let me.' Gus took back the bottle from her shaking hands, prying off the cap, saving her the embarrassment.

'Um, I'm sorry about this. It's not like me.' The slow rock of her head said more about her disappointment in herself. 'It's the storm. Kind of brings back bad memories.' Her expression was tense. She placed her bottle on the floor beside her.

'I get that.' He nodded, hoping it might reassure her as he

sat on the couch opposite, not daring to sit closer in case he couldn't stop himself from pulling her to him once more. Speedy nuzzled Kate's hand for a pat as though the dog knew exactly what she needed. Kate gave a melancholy chuckle at the dog's affection, the sound somewhat of a relief after the expression he'd watched on her face.

Fresh brilliance filled the windows of the beach hut, followed by more distant rumbles. This storm, like so many around here, was but a flash in the pan. There hadn't been a dinky-die storm for more than five years, from what Graham knew.

Kate waited a moment, running her hand down Speedy's back before she continued, Gus sensing her breathing steadying.

'Every time one comes over, all I can focus on is the loud crack before—' She stopped speaking, and her hand stilled on top of Speedy's head. 'Gus, it wasn't the thunder that made the sound I'm talking about.' She went quiet, and Gus leaned forward, resting his elbows on his knees as he contemplated her, urging her to continue with his undivided attention. Even with all the fear and pain she was displaying, damn it, she was beautiful.

'It was a branch. A huge one. It came down on the tent, onto Jenna.'

Kate sucked in a sob as Gus reacted physically to her words, his forearms tensing and his knees pressing together as he sat taller. He looked down at his arms, remembering.

'I can't imagine what you went through.' Only he could. The circumstances might have been different, but the brutal threat towards someone you loved so deeply . . . was a pain you could hardly describe going through. At least now he could better understand the reason behind her pent-up fear alongside the wariness in her eyes. No matter who you were, you couldn't always save the ones you loved. He knew it. Only he wasn't about to believe it for himself.

The floor threatened to suck him downwards as Speedy left Kate's side to join him, urging her head in between his legs as her big seal eyes locked onto his. How did she always sense when he needed her most?

The rain on the roof softened, giving the indication they'd be able to resume work. He opened his mouth to speak when she beat him to it.

'But the firies were incredible.'

What? Did she mean her local Country Fire Authority? He marvelled at the strength she was drawing on to talk like that. But he couldn't, so this conversation needed to end.

For good.

Her gaze lowered to his arms, his skin flinching with the weight of her questions and scrutiny she no doubt had rumbling about in that pretty mind of hers. Her eyes gently slid to his and he sat up, wishing he'd hidden the scars he'd never let anyone touch since they'd healed.

His heart lurched. But if he'd thought she was waiting for him to fill in the silence between them, he needn't have worried.

'Having a small, tight-knit community is the best. They got there so fast. Riley and I pulled so hard, trying to lift the branch from her.' Her words slowed. 'But even if we'd been able to, it wouldn't have made any difference. She didn't have a chance.'

She'd stumped him with two mighty swoops. If this had been a larger community, then perhaps Ash wouldn't have had the power to ruin his life as he had.

And she'd died on impact? Gus's whole body ached with pain and anger and fear as cramps in his muscles began to grip him, but he forced himself to remain stock still. Kate's sister might have died a horrendous death but at least it was quick. Why did Kelly have to suffer like she had?

A vision came back to him, Kelly's fearful but brave eyes

locked on his as the flames increased around her, all while Hughey fought to hold him back from running to her as the rest of the team raced to douse the fury of flames viciously engulfing the car.

Her eyes were telling him she loved him with everything in her. She'd also nodded, letting him know it was okay to let her go.

Gus covered his grief behind his hand.

Their resources had been overstretched at the time, with a roaring bushfire already tearing up the mountainous hectares of bushland in the summer heat. But when the Forest Gully team heard over the CB radio that it was Kelly and Carl, they left their post immediately.

Gus pushed a hand to his neck, desperate to hide the raw emotions yelling at him to let them escape, even if it was in front of Kate.

He would have died alongside Kelly if he'd been able to free himself from Hughey's arms. And for so long, he'd wished he had because nothing was worth living for without her in his life.

Until perhaps now.

The sharpness wedged inside his throat thickened, and he gave a quick sideways glance at Kate's fingers as she fiddled with them in her lap. What she and Riley had suffered, would anyone ever grasp the full extent of it? He had to believe someone would, but sadly, it might likely be because they'd suffered something similar.

Like himself.

And even more than all that, how was she able to stay so positive? Were those CFA members from her life back home able to attend another incident when they knew one day it could mean yet another local—a friend—was potentially seriously injured? Or worse, find ways to deal with it? How could they continue doing that?

He sure as hell couldn't.

Gus put his bottle on the floor before rubbing his face with both hands, hiding from Kate and, even more than that, hiding from himself.

Kate broke the silence of his anguish.

'The community was incredible, rallying around us and providing food and support.' She took in a resounding breath. 'That's what a community should be,' and as he looked up to see her gaze settle on him, he remained speechless. 'Mum and Dad still live in the main township. But they'd have Riley back in a heartbeat. I promised I'd return home if I couldn't make it work here.'

Whoa. All this emotional stuff was too much. He had to find a way out of this conversation.

'Right, the storm's moved on. Let's get this fence finished. Then we might be able to convince Monica's crew to come home.' Gus stood, striding to the door, not waiting for her to follow.

CHAPTER 14

Speedy disappeared from view, returning with Riley as Gus was twisting the wire knots for the fence he and Kate had run out of time to complete. The cliff edge hung not ten metres from where they were standing.

'Hey, buddy. How was school today?' He gave Riley an encouraging grin as he tied off the last wire on the star picket, then checked the fence for tension with a tug, happy with the result. He was grateful his uncle had taught him how to fence while they were running the stock feed and supply store in Ballarat. Not every farmer wanted to bother with fencing work when they had enough to do chasing stock and dealing with good and bad weather during cropping seasons. It was the one thing Gus had taken on the side as a money-making venture.

Riley gave an unenthusiastic shrug at the question, and Gus stood to full height, his muscles relieved from having the chance to stretch out.

'That good, hey?' He couldn't help but grin at the kid who reminded him of himself more and more each day. 'Wanna take a walk with me? I've been working on something for you.'

Much to his relief, Riley showed interest, his eyes focused on him. 'C'mon, then.'

Riley walked in front as they headed towards the rugged track Gus used for access to the beach. As they approached the path, Riley turned back to him, grinning.

'You've begun making steps down there!' Right there and then, Gus realised what his efforts truly meant.

'Yup. This way I know it'll be safe for you.' In reality, he should've done this a long time ago, having had his fair share of slips and sprained ankles he'd had to hobble home with. It was for him as much as it was for Riley. And it warmed him to think it would give Kate peace of mind.

Riley began to make his way towards the beach and Speedy darted to the right, her nose down in pursuit of a tantalising scent.

'Whoa there, buddy. Take it easy,' Gus called, picking up his pace to catch up to Riley. 'It's a long way off finished. You have told your auntie about going down here, haven't you?' He ran a hand through his tussled locks.

The waves were rough, the remnants of the storm now well out to sea, but the winds, still riling from it, worked to knock Riley off his feet as he stepped onto the sand. Gus ran up, catching him from behind before he toppled over.

'I love it down here,' Riley said as he beamed at Gus. 'Thanks for making it easy to get to.'

'Well, buddy, don't you come down here without someone, okay? You've seen for yourself how those gusts can try and knock you over.'

They walked in silence as Speedy tore along the shoreline, seagulls flapping above her reach as she playfully snapped at them.

'Gus, can we go around that corner?' Riley pointed to the end of the section of sand where tall rocks hid the view beyond. 'The tide's out.'

Gus soaked in the sight of the ocean as if he depended on it, the translucent sky blanketing them. He nodded. 'Okay, but we'd better not be too long. I don't need any more trouble from your auntie.' But the thought did tickle his fancy. Seeing her riled up, even if it was at his own expense, did give him the kind of smile he hadn't basked in for a long time. Only he wouldn't let Hughey know. When that guy got hold of something, he didn't let go.

'She always worries,' Riley said as he bent down to investigate what was under a large wad of seaweed.

'I've noticed. Hey, how about we climb those rocks? Want to check out one of those cool caves I told you about?'

'Yeah!'

Gus loved the way Riley appeared expectant, even joyous, dare he say it, as he took off and ran towards the rocks.

'Hey, wait for me.' Gus jogged after him, keeping a close eye on Riley as he clambered his way around the bend, judging the angles with surprising steadiness. He'd been just the same as a youngster, desperate to experience independence and unearth the undiscovered.

'Gus. There it is.' Riley gave him a quick glance before disappearing through the opening. A pool of crystal blue water, calm and inviting, rested at the bottom of the cave, full from the last time the tide had rushed in. Riley perched himself on the edge, his feet swaying in the cooling water. Speedy sidled up beside him, nosing the water with interest, her tail wagging. Riley ran his hand down her back.

Gus smiled. Riley wasn't just patting his dog. He was protecting her so she wouldn't fall in.

'I call this Shark Tooth Corner.' Gus lowered himself into the water opposite Riley, its radiant warmth similar to a heated pool. Gus closed his eyes. It was here he relaxed best.

'Are you coming in?'

'But there's sharks.' Riley's voice was high-pitched, concerned.

Gus peeked through one eye, chuckling good-naturedly.

'Oh, no, buddy, there aren't any here. But I did find a shark's tooth at the bottom of the pool once.' Riley's wide eyes hung on his every word. 'It must have washed in with the tide. That's where I got the name for this place.'

He looked about him, the rock walls well above his height as his hands floated on the surface of the water. Like the beach, this was a place he could catch his breath when the voices inside his head were too loud, reminding him he wasn't the kind of man others regarded well. He hated the terms *before and after* the accident. All he'd wanted was to live a life that gave him purpose and helped others.

A life so different to the one he was living now.

Riley let his body flop into the water, doggy paddling around the edge, glee oozing from his toothy smile. Speedy barked as he splashed water her way.

'I found this cave when I first moved here,' Gus said as he admired the crustaceans glued to the rocks. 'I wish I'd had somewhere like this to go to when I was your age.'

'It's so cool. I wanna come here again.' Riley giggled as Speedy lunged for a piece of seaweed he'd tossed to the side.

'Well, only with me, okay? It's dangerous when the tide comes back in. You can get trapped until it goes back out. And that's hours.' Riley nodded, relieving Gus. The last thing he needed was for Riley to go missing.

'Let's head back, buddy.' He ruffled Riley's hair as they hopped out of the rock pool.

As they reached his hut, Gus's phone pinged with a text message. He grabbed it, suppressing his smile as he saw the ID.

Is Riley with you? I can't find him. Should I be concerned?

He's here having a cool drink. I'll send him home in ten.

Want to come for dinner? I'm doing homemade pasta.

Wow, now that was unexpected but a nice surprise all the same, and his stomach grumbled instantaneously. He grinned.

Sounds good to me. See you soon.

Gus put down his phone, brushing off the temptation to add an *x* at the end of it, only because it was the friendly thing to do of course. 'Okay, buddy, let's head to your place. We're in for a pasta treat.'

'Are you coming to dinner? Yay!' Riley bounced to his feet, sending Speedy racing to the door. She shot out, spinning around to check they were following her, like she knew the plan. They weaved their way to the well-worn spot at the fence where it was easy to hop over, saving the long walk down to the gateway he'd left space for at the cliff. Speedy slinked under the fence.

Monica baaed as they approached, turning her nose from the closed door she'd been fixated on to watch them. As Riley pushed the door open, she took the lead, waltzing in before he could stop her.

'No, Monica. Out!'

Gus smothered his chuckle behind pressed lips as Kate glared at the ewe, pointing towards the door with the wooden spoon dripping sauce. He stepped in, angling the ewe's head in the direction of the exit and shuffled her back outside, much to her objections.

'Honestly, that sheep is beyond words,' Kate said. 'Does she waltz in and take over your place? Given half a chance, she'd be sitting at, or should I say *on* the dining table, eating with us.' Kate chuckled as she started serving up the piping hot carbonara, grating fresh parmesan cheese on top before finishing it off with a sprinkle of homegrown parsley.

'No, she never visits me. Must've heard I was after her hide thanks to our chat the other day.' He smiled, his eyebrows angling high as she glanced up at him, holding his gaze with a delighted grin of her own. He wasn't sure he'd be able to come to the idea of selling the lambs once they were born. Thankfully, there was plenty of grass in his paddocks past his hut, which would keep them happy until he decided what to do. With Kate here, he was starting to appreciate some things from a different perspective.

And he'd make some money to boot, a thought he couldn't disregard.

Gus took a seat at the dining table, and Riley went to the kitchen to help with the bowls of pasta, managing to earn Kate's surprised glance. He disengaged himself from their conversation, instead looking about him, hoping Riley was telling her about the beach.

The crochet project sitting on the coffee table was steadily growing, and a reticent smile rose on his lips as he ran a finger over them.

'I see Nola has got you off and running with the wool. It's coming along well by the looks.'

'Urgh. Don't ask me how many times I've undone and begun again.' She shook her head in dismay. 'I had to drop into the shop just to get her to start me off again yesterday. Those CWA women are a force to be reckoned with, a lot like the ones at home, although I've managed to avoid the crafty side of things until now. This lot seem to think I'll be a natural. They're setting themselves up for major disappointment.'

'Nola has a knack for doing that,' he started, smiling before he continued. 'She'd had Kelly knitting scarves and baby blankets—'

Gus stilled. Had he just said all that about his fiancée without so much as a second thought, in front of Kate no less? Where had that come from, and what had he been thinking? He didn't do that around anyone, including Hughey and Meg.

Kate cocked her head to the side, her genuine interest clear.

His brow tightened in a whirlwind of memories and sadness and long-gone plans for a future as his mind travelled back to the funeral. He saw Kate's brief frown, but luckily for him, she changed tack. She knew the severity of such sadness and pain, perhaps choosing to save him from further angst. He was grateful.

'Well, I do make a mean sticky caramel cake.' She stood. On request, her mother sent some copies of Kate's most loved recipes in the post, and Kate was excited to pull one out and give it a go.

'Don't mind myself a bit of cake.' He nudged Riley. 'How about you?' But all Riley could do was nod enthusiastically as he chewed on his pasta, eagerness glowing in his eyes.

'So, what were you two boys up to earlier? Have fun?' Her gaze settled on Gus, but with his mouth full, Riley answered.

'We finished the fence. Now Monica can go home.'

'Thank goodness for that.' Kate looked to the ceiling as Gus chuckled, hating to admit to the thrill rushing inside him at the way she'd teased. If this kept happening, he could see himself as an undone man sooner rather than later, and that wasn't such a good idea. He worked to rein in his emotions by chewing another mouthful but couldn't help himself.

'I reckon she's going to miss you. Your house is her new shed,' he said. They locked eyes, the zinging spark between them threatening to zap every ounce of his resolve. Did she feel it, too?

The conversation slowed, and Gus waited for Riley to fill in the silence, fully expecting his excitement about the cave to be at the forefront of what he wanted to talk about next, but instead, the boy shovelled another forkful of dinner into his mouth.

'We went to the beach, didn't we, buddy?' he began, nudging Riley to continue. But it was Kate who spoke instead.

'Oh.' She smoothed the wooden table with her hand slowly, and Gus could tell what he'd said had hit some kind of wound. But why?

Riley endlessly twisted the remaining pasta with his fork.

Gus blinked.

Kate stood, taking their plates to the kitchen. 'So how did you come to live here, Gus?' Her voice was strained as she forced herself to sound cheery.

'This was my uncle's place. I used to work with him back at his stockfeed store. He died just before we were about to leave for Forest Gully. He left this place to me. I was like his kid, I guess.' His voice softened. 'When Mum and Dad died, I was still little. He took me in. He was all I had.'

Casting her eyes upward, Kate had stopped scooping the ice cream into the bowls, her full attention on him.

'That must've been hard for you.' She took in Riley's despondent gaze as he studied his Lego booklet resting beside him at the table as if it was the key to his whole future. He waited silently for dessert.

Gus nodded a thanks for her sympathy. If anything was going to shake a kid up, it had to be your parents dying before you were old enough to know them. He looked to Riley, holding himself back from placing a hand on his shoulder in front of Kate. This heavy conversation needed a positive spin.

'Uncle Neil wasn't exactly thrilled to have a kid to suddenly care for when he'd been a bachelor his whole life, but he did it and he was good to me.' The light chuckle he gave caught unexpectedly at the sound of Kate sucking in a tight breath. He'd simply been reflecting on how his past had evolved. But now, with her tight brow shaping her saddened eyes, it dawned on him that he should've thought it through before speaking.

'Hey, I'm sorry for what I said the other day, you know, about the fire brigade guys from home.' Kate stared at her feet. 'I didn't think.'

Ouch. And she'd recognised he'd changed the topic to avoid talking about it any further. He had to get better at this conversation stuff.

'It's fine. I've accepted it and grown up,' he said with a soft smile but his attempt at a little light humour seemed to miss its mark.

But then her beautiful face lifted in a gentle smile, having the mixed effect of making his heart race and his chest pinch. He didn't need anyone feeling sorry for him.

'So, where's this dessert? I'm ready to critique it.'

And as he ate, memories surfaced of a future he no longer had and a past he couldn't find a way to let go of.

CHAPTER 15

'The Seaside Bouquet?' Gus blurted out the words on Kate's look-at-me-right-now sign as he skidded to an abrupt halt at the end of his driveway, leaving a shower of gravel skittering to the side of the road in his wake. Wasn't it enough her exasperating rooster had announced his hearty rise-and-shine call at an all-time new ungodly hour this morning?

Kate stood at her gate, stacking cartons of eggs onto the shelves of her rough-and-ready new farmgate stall she'd had handmade from wooden pallets. Impressive. He hated to admit it.

She stood back with her hands on her hips, admiring her handiwork with an approving nod, ignoring Gus's terse tone.

'What's your problem now?' Kate said airily, refusing to meet his gaze, instead placing a couple of buckets on the shelf, stuffed full of bunches of her roses and some bags of kale that were growing out of control in her veggie patch, her smile unmistakable. Graham was standing next to her with his hammer in hand, finishing off the picket fencing.

Problem? Yes. He had a big one. And it was standing right in front of him. Did the woman not comprehend the fact he insisted on his peace and quiet?

'You do realise no one comes along here? You'll never sell anything.'

'And how's that a problem for you?' Her sweet smile didn't fool him as she tossed it over her shoulder in his direction. And he wasn't about to be lulled in by her more-than-reasonable comeback, which, incidentally, riled him all the more.

'If I didn't know better, Gus, I'd think you might be jealous you didn't think of this first. You're welcome to buy from my stall. It'd save you going into town, which I know you like to avoid at *all costs*.' She spun towards him, her gaze tenderly penetrating.

Had Meg told her? Hughey? She'd become way too friendly with his friends, and if he weren't careful, there wouldn't be any left.

'Would you like me to write you a note to ask for your permission? Oh, and let me guess, you'll get back to me when you're good and ready, like you have about the sheep. I've just finished sweeping up after Monica and the crew this morning.' Her head tipped towards him, her smug lips pinning him to his seat.

What happened to the woman last night who apologised? He liked that version way better than the one that had him on the back foot, regardless of the way she was rattling his heart with her seductive wit.

'I don't want people parading past here on a regular basis and blocking my driveway.' There, that'd do it.

'No.' The word was excruciatingly polite as she gave him a congenial smile and showed him her back once more as she fiddled with her rose display. 'This looks great, Graham. Thanks for your help. Grab a carton of eggs. I'm sure Nola could use them to make something for CWA tonight. And tell her I'll be there. I've nearly finished my crochet square.'

'Thanks Kate, that's mighty nice of you.' Graham took a carton and held it in his hands. He offered her a wave before acknowledging Gus with a she's-totally-got-you smile, then headed back to his truck.

Got me? She had him in more ways than he was managing to cope with right now. Flustered, he sharply rubbed the back of his neck. What was it with this woman? The locals were flocking to her like a hot chip they couldn't resist. And she was way too close to breaking the boundaries of the low profile he'd happily festered in. No siree. There'd be no more sharing any more of her impromptu dinners, regardless of his mateship with Riley. Letting his guard down too often around her was becoming costly. He'd become too careless.

Gus took off at speed to retrieve his mocha from Meg's. Then he'd check on Hughey and find out if he had any leftovers. Then grill him about what he'd been saying to Kate before he went to the hardware store. He suddenly had some renos of his own to do, including a functioning front gate. People might come to her place but they could stay the hell away from him.

'Woohoo, look who's here. The man who's romancing the stone with his cute next-door neighbour.' Hughey's laugh was jovial and hearty as Gus stomped into the shop.

'Knock it off, alright.' Gus shook his head in dismay, letting the door clunk, wholeheartedly regretting stepping outside his front door this morning.

'So it's true then.' Hughey chuckled some more.

Gus pressed a hand against his mouth as he considered his options. This whole town was like a colander, letting every tiny morsel of information trickle through their mouths until not only had it made its way to the ears of the least discerning counterparts, but they'd managed to elevate it into some imaginary truth where no one could be swayed otherwise.

'Please.' He took a long breath. 'Just give me what you've got left over and I'll get outta here.' But Hughey wasn't ready to be that sympathetic.

'Well, she is a bit of a looker. So, what's stopping you? Meg says—'

'Meg. Says. What?' Gus found himself glaring at his best mate.

'I dunno,' Hughey said, immediately feigning innocence. 'Only that Kate is the catch of the century. Reckons she's going to hype this place up. And Meg is on board. Even the CWA women are getting excited.'

What the . . . 'About what exactly?' Gus's narrowed eyes intensified.

'Oh c'mon, mate, making blankets and those crafty things women like making, like . . . you know, booties 'n' stuff.' Hughey lifted his palm into the air. 'You know what I mean,' and he pulled out a tub from beneath the refrigerated counter full of meat leftovers waiting for Gus.

'No, I don't know,' and he didn't want to either. All he knew was that his next-door neighbour had only given him constant, pounding headaches since she'd arrived.

After that nightmare of a summer where a fire had ignited when some idiot decided it was a bright idea to weld on a thirty-five-degree day with ferocious northerly winds, and on top of that, Kelly losing her life, none of them should be ready to forget and move on. Kelly's memory deserved so much more than that.

Gus had had enough. 'Meg has been chatting to you then?' He was impressed he'd turned this conversation back onto Hughey's interest in Meg.

'Cor, it's nothing like that. I just need my coffee in the morning, and she's the one who gets it for me.' Hughey fiddled with Gus's meat, putting it into a plastic bag, all the while turning a steady shade of iridescent red.

'Ha! I knew it.' Gus pointed a satisfied wiggling finger at his friend. 'You want to ask her out, but you're too chicken.'

'And you're too spooked by your past to give Kate a go. I'm telling ya, she likes you, man. Meg knows these things.'

Meg *knew* that? How? Had Kate said something to her? And if she did, how did he feel about it? He'd been running from his feelings for so long that he wasn't even sure he could trust them.

Kate walked into the hardware store and halted, disbelief filling her mind at the sight of Gus's strong tanned legs clad in board shorts facing her. She clenched her teeth, wanting to march straight back out the door, but that would only be admitting he was getting in her head—which he was, in all the wrong ways.

So, she didn't. The man might be irritable and irrational, but that wasn't going to stop her from living her life the way she wanted to in this town.

She marched to the aisle where the terracotta pots lived, grabbing several from the shelf before heading to the counter. Placing them down without—she tried to convince herself—so much as a second thought regarding her neighbour, she fought to block out the weight of his eyes now on her.

'Nice pots.'

What? Was he being nice to her now, after his ridiculous tantrum earlier? The man was insufferable. 'Thanks. They'll do nicely at my farmgate,' emphasising the word for good measure, 'with marigolds in them,' as she turned to glare his way.

'You'll wanna hope they don't break when they fall over in the wind.' He held his smile off, but she could see it, desperate to escape his firm hold.

'What's it matter to you, with your new gate to shut you in?' She made a show of looking at the gate she'd spotted at the doorway, his name written on a tag. 'You won't need to go out ever again. Thanks to me.' Touché.

Patsy's husband, Nige, let his eyes skim from her to Gus, then back to her again, a smirk teasing his cheeks. 'So, who am I serving first?'

'Gus. He's got to shut everyone out with that gate and he'll need the rest of the day to do it.'

Gus didn't say a word, just waved his card over the EFTPOS machine, then dragged his gate with him through the side door. With any luck, she wouldn't have to run into him again anytime soon.

When she opened the door to Meg's café, she was greeted with more enthusiasm than usual. Her friend's smile was downright smug.

'Okay, sit down and spill.' Meg brought over two fresh coffees she'd obviously made in anticipation, placing them at the window table.

'Noo. Just forget it, okay.' She waved Meg's nosiness away, handing her a bunch of her roses, hoping the woman could be guilted into changing the topic. She should have known better.

'Oh wow, these are incredible, Kate. Your garden is going great guns.' Meg soaked in the fragrance.

'I know things have been tough for your business. I just wanted to give you something to cheer you up.'

'Aww, Kate, that's so lovely.' She put the roses aside and took her mug in her hands, refocusing. 'Now, come on, it's quiet in here at the moment. Tell me all the goss.'

'What goss? There's none to tell.' She could play this game too.

'Oh no, you don't.' Meg shook her head. 'There's something going on between you two, so spill.'

Kate put her hand to her heart, her eyes widening with what she hoped was honest innocence. 'There's nothing going on. We fixed the boundary fence—'

'Whoa. Hang on a minute. When did this happen? Even Hughey doesn't know about that.'

'So, you two, who are supposed to be sworn enemies thanks to your business ideas clashing, are comparing *notes* about what we're doing?' Kate made a show of letting her mouth fall open.

'Well, you two have got the town talking, which in itself is a pleasant change. Gus hasn't been seen, other than to get his coffee from me, for months. It's only because I was Kelly's best friend that he knows I don't blame him for what happened, unlike some of the locals around here.' The frustration on Meg's face was plain to see.

'Who's Kelly, and why would Gus allow himself to become such a recluse because of her?'

'Oh, I've never told you.' her tone softened. 'Kelly was his fiancée. He lost her.'

Fiancée? Had her inward shock shown on her face? She had no right to react to something like that. So why had she?

'That's terrible,' Kate said. 'Can I ask, did it happen down Sheep Gully Road?' An image flashed in Kate's mind, of the tree on the side of the road with a cross nailed to the trunk and fresh flowers surrounding the base. She'd seen it on her way to Patsy's to buy her chooks.

'Yeah. It's been two years, but things haven't been the same since. It doesn't help that Ash Evans was and still is the CFA captain. Kelly was his daughter.'

'Oh no.' It made so much more sense now.

'But I'm telling you, Kate, Gus really likes you. I haven't seen him like this in so long.'

'What? He does?' Kate gave a small smile, the warmth inside her almost making her giddy.

The door chime rang, and Meg moved to stand up and serve the next customer. 'Don't give up on him, Kate. He's one of the good guys.'

CHAPTER 16

Kate raced home after school pick-up. There wasn't much time before the CWA meeting tonight. She pulled up at the front of their driveway, twisting in her seat towards Riley. 'Hey buddy, would you grab the honesty box sitting on the shelf, please?' Riley offered up a weary gaze, then slowly opened his door, retrieving the box and hopping back in the car.

'Wanna check how we did today?' From what she could tell, only a couple of cartons and one bunch of roses had gone, but it was exciting to find out anyhow. Kate passed him the key.

'There's a twenty-dollar note in here.'

'Really?' She was sure she hadn't sold enough to have earned that much.

Kate rushed to make their tea—toasties with ham and cheese—before giving the garden a quick sprinkle. They flew out the door so fast that even Monica didn't have time to stand up and push her way inside when the door opened.

'Do we have to go?' Riley's voice droned like a winding-down bagpipe, and Kate fought against the annoyance flaring inside her.

'Yeah, buddy.'

He nodded slowly, carrying his box of Lego and sliding into the car.

'I promise there'll be lots of yummy treats for you, and I won't watch while you help yourself. How's that sound?' She had to try something, anything to get him to want to go. If sugar freedom was what it took, then she was on board.

'Good.' The word didn't carry the chirpiness she'd

anticipated. This kid was a hard sell, but she refused to bail on the ladies.

On her way to Nola's, a sense of loss filled her. She'd freely admitted to being well and truly over the sheep waltzing around like they owned her place. But Gus had texted, telling her he'd collect the sheep tonight. Now, she couldn't offer him a hand—which she was in no doubt he'd need—but more than that, she couldn't farewell them. She hated how contrary that sounded.

Kate presented Patsy with a terracotta pot full of daisies as she opened the door for them.

'Oh heavens, Kate. Whatever is this for?'

Kate's chest filled with satisfaction as Patsy beamed.

'You gave me such a wonderful deal with the chickens. I wanted to thank you.' Even if her eyes said out loud she was regretting taking home the rooster.

'Well, I love it. I'll put them right here at the front door for everyone to enjoy.'

With their first round of cuppas in hand and their knitting and crocheting underway, Patsy stood, drawing their attention.

'So, ladies. We want to support our fire team this year by raising money for equipment of some kind. What good ideas can we do for the day? Whatever we decide on, it needs to be interesting if we want plenty of people to support it.'

'I love this idea,' Kate said. 'We can make it a town fair to gather everyone, locals and beyond.'

'I'll start,' Jenny said, the mother of one of Riley's friends who'd begun coming to their gatherings after meeting Kate. She put her knitting down on her lap. 'What about a Little Miss Ocean Princess pageant? We could have all age groups up to twelve years old, and they could stand on the back of Graham's vintage truck and walk around it like a catwalk. The girls need something in this town to show them they're beautiful and special.'

Kate wasn't sold on this idea but then again, she'd never been a girly girl. Maybe it couldn't hurt.

'And the boys, or anyone actually, could have an onshore fishing competition. The winner is anyone who catches a fish.'

Everyone laughed. That only happened on the rare occasion when Graham was exceedingly lucky.

'Oh yes, that sounds great,' Patsy said. 'We haven't had a fair for so long.' Her voice faded, and the ladies quietly nodded to one another before taking sips of their tea or a nibble of their slice. Nola picked up pace with her crocheting.

'What about lucky jars?' Kathleen said, one of the quieter women in the group and heavily pregnant with number five. 'We could have three sections: boy's jars, girls' jars, and a selection for the adults to choose from. If we wrap the jars up and price them, people can choose. Erin can help me because it might be a little tiring if I do it on my own.' Kathleen beamed, patting her belly and smiling at Erin, who gave an approving nod back.

'A cake stall is always nice,' Nola said, gaining several enthusiastic nods. 'Oh, and what about a chook run? We could line up competitors and when we let the chooks go, everyone has to catch a chicken. Anyone who manages to get one can take it home.'

'That sounds like so much fun,' Kate said. 'It would be a hoot to watch the adults chasing after a chook.' She tried to picture Gus scrambling for one, the thought nestling into her mind.

'What if we sell some chickens?' Everyone went quiet, looking over at Riley, who was now standing by Kate's side and gazing up at her.

Kate's heart stilled. She'd promised him that would be his pocket money. But here he was, forgoing that to help the fire brigade? A proud tightness gripped her throat.

'What a wonderful idea, Riley. How would you like to be

in charge of that?' Patsy said. Riley looked pleased and nodded.

'Oh, and what about a gumboot toss?' Lexi from the bakery chimed in. 'The men will get involved if there's something like that. The prize could be a voucher from Nige's hardware store.'

'I'll make it happen,' Patsy said.

'And a two-legged race and a sack or wheelbarrow race would be fun,' Brenda said, an honest-to-goodness CWA lady from way back. She was eighty-something, but nothing was going to stop her from joining in the fun.

'How about some kind of dog challenge?' Kate suggested, thinking of Speedy, secretly wishing that might be enough to lure Gus along. He needed to hang out with others more, or he'd become a grumpy old bachelor just like his uncle.

Meg nodded enthusiastically at the women. 'What if everyone could bring their dogs for a high jump and a race for the fastest dog to get to its owner?'

'So, it's settled then. We have lots of ideas, all of which I think will be perfect,' Patsy said. 'Mid-May should be lovely weather for it. Let's make this happen.' The ladies clapped; their fervour high.

After two more rounds of cuppas and a whole lot more chatter, they called it a night. Riley had fallen asleep on the couch after eating more than a week's worth of sugar. Kate couldn't help herself; she'd had to watch, and she hated having to wake him now. Nige saved her, picking him up in his arms and taking him to the car.

The house appeared stark and lonely as she quietly rolled in, the odd rabbit darting in front of her across the driveway. The verandah was vacated except for the remaining sheep poo left there from their efficient day's work.

Kate exhaled, a sudden stab of loneliness hitting her. When she cleaned the mess up in the morning, there'd be no more. But it was for the best, she tried to convince herself. They were Gus's stock, and he needed to take responsibility for them.

CHAPTER 17

'Riley? C'mon. You'll be late for school.'

Kate sat in her car, tapping the steering wheel. She glared at the doorway as if it would make him appear faster. She was about to hop out when Riley appeared with his backpack and a scowl that could compete with the weather they'd been having intermittently of late. When he hopped in, she didn't dare say another word. The kid was bottoming out after last night's feast, or the late night, or both, and Kate was hit with a strong twinge of guilt for taking him out to the meeting. That hadn't been her best parenting moment.

Slowing at the gateway, she hopped out to replace the honesty box in position. Taking in the sun in the cloudless sky, she sensed it bite at her skin, making her rub her arms against the sting. She'd been so focused that she almost missed Gus at his front entrance as she headed back to the car.

'Good morning, neighbour.' She smiled, but he declined to meet her gaze.

'Yep. It is.' He wrangled the twelve-foot gate towards the peg it needed to sit on at the post.

Kate nodded slowly. 'What's got your jocks in a tangle?' Was it that he was concentrating, or was he still salty with her?

'Humph.'

'Do you need a hand with that? I can—'

'Nope.'

Hmm, yup. Still grumpy. But he'd get over it. She offered him a wave but once again, he kept his eyes on the job.

Kate strode into Meg's café after school drop-off and had

to wait her turn. Some unfamiliar faces were ordering all manner of things, including breakfast muffins and hot drinks.

'Oh, these are lovely.' The woman leaned forward to smell the roses.

'Aren't they? And the one who grew them is just behind you.' Meg angled her head past the lady, and in turn, the woman engaged Kate's gaze.

'Are they Double Delights?'

'Yes, they are.' Kate smiled, an added dart of emotion catching in her throat.

'I thought they were. My mother used to grow them. The fragrance is so delicate. Just like lemonade.'

'You can buy some for yourself,' Meg piped up. 'Kate has a farmgate market out the front of her place just down the road.'

'Wonderful. Steer me in the right direction, and I'll grab myself a bunch before we head home.'

'This might help,' and Kate handed the woman a flyer she'd managed to print up for her farmgate a couple of nights ago.

Kate beamed at Meg as the folk left, stepping up to the counter. 'Well, that was a nice surprise. And thank you.'

'I hope you've got more of those.' Meg eyed the papers in Kate's hands and cleared a space for them. 'Here, put some on the counter.'

'Have you got time for a cuppa?' Kate had some burning questions she wanted Meg to help with.

'I sure do. The rush hour has subsided. We had four couples dropping through on their way to the Twelve Apostles. Pity they didn't want to stay a night or two. I did quite nicely out of their impromptu drop-in, though.'

A haughty crow strutted along one of the outside tables, harassing the few remaining customers sitting outside. Meg glared at it.

'I've already shooed that incessant bird away this morning.' She shook her head in frustration. 'I wouldn't be upset if someone overfed him and he sank to the bottom of the ocean.'

They both giggled as Meg finished making their lattés, and they took their seats at the window table before Kate turned serious.

'Meg. How did Gus hurt his arms?' She hadn't been able to free the question from the forefront of her mind since she'd seen them that first day, handing him his mocha. Even when she'd risked revisiting her grief and told him about Jenna during the storm, she'd believed he might have felt safe enough to open up. But he hadn't. He was a closed book, and it was obvious to her that he treated everyone around him the same way.

'There was a fire.' Meg's voice petered away like the vapour rising from her latté.

Kate waited, unsure if Meg would continue.

'At the accident.' Meg's voice softened. 'You remember how I told you he lost his fiancée?'

Oh no. Did she actually want to know those finer details and find out more about a woman he'd loved? The word fiancée continued to leave her feeling—what was it? —uncomfortable, sorry . . . and with a heartfelt yearning to hope she could say that about herself one day. But she wanted to understand him, especially when he'd seen her looking at his damaged body and hid it from her.

'Was Gus a member of the local CFA? He'd shut down on me when I was telling him about our crew at home and how incredible they were.'

'I'm not surprised he did.' Meg continued to stare at her drink. 'He hasn't talked to anyone about it. Refuses to have anything to do with CFA now.'

'So, what happened?' Kate gripped her mug tightly,

desperate to understand why.

'A wombat was heading towards the undergrowth at the side of the road, running from the impending smoke of the bushfire chasing it down. The air was thick, and Kelly couldn't see the animal until she was almost on top of it. She swerved, slamming into that big tree near Patsy's. She had her younger brother, Carl, in the car with her. Gus had been put in charge by Ash to make sure they got out safely. He tried to get Kelly out, but she was stuck.'

Meg stole a quivering breath. 'She insisted he get Carl out first. He had a broken arm.'

Meg's eyes welled up, and she sniffed, her obvious pain enough for Kate's own eyes to fill. She reached forward, putting her hand over Meg's and squeezing it as she empathised with her pain.

'I'm so sorry.' She didn't want to guess what had happened. It was enough to know the misshapen skin he wore day and night had to be a hideous reminder. That was pain on a whole new level she truly didn't understand. She drew in a shaky breath.

'He saved Carl, pulling him through the passenger window as the flames overtook the car,' Meg continued. 'And when news spread that Kelly hadn't made it, well, Gus worked to make sure that no one could ever remind him of his failings again by avoiding everyone. It's been more than enough for him to live with how he let her down, and Ash, every day since.'

Kate sat back. Now she understood his choice to live out in the sticks, alone. He didn't feel worthy of anyone's trust. No wonder he pushed her away like he did. He couldn't even trust himself.

CHAPTER 18

Gus's mood stooped from ground level to fifty feet below it as he tried to get the second gate he'd purchased to sort out his problems with his nuisance next-door neighbour to work. And it didn't help that every nosey parker using the road was slowing in front of his place to find a spot to park. Kate might've wanted it, but he sure as hell didn't. Shouldn't she have asked him first? Wasn't that the neighbourly thing to do?

He stood as the seventh car for the morning arrived, finding it hard not to roll his head in frustration as they waved an oh-so-warm welcome before heading over to Kate's farmgate. He smiled through clenched teeth. Why were so many people finding her farmgate anyway? It wasn't like they lived on a main road.

Gus scratched his head as the woman told her husband to put some money and a tip in the tin. He watched her breathe in the fragrance of her bunch of roses before her husband carried an extra terracotta pot full of pink daisies back to the car.

Nodding as they waved a friendly goodbye, all smiles—way too many for him this early in the day . . . or ever—he got back to work. But her neat setup niggled his curiosity. What was so damn good about her farmgate that everyone wanted a slice of it? Gus glanced to his left and then his right before edging his way to the road. Doubling back on his glance to be sure no one was coming from either direction, he tiptoed to the shelves at her entrance.

Eggs? Her chooks had started laying already? And he hated to admit the flowers looked healthy and fresh. He had to give it to her. She wasn't the kind to sit still. But even so, his hackles rose.

She had no right to invade his privacy. Things were fine just as they were.

Distracted by his stomach and the eggs he was almost tasting for his lunch, he missed the sound of a car approaching until it slowed in front of him. Gus jumped a step back as Kate turned into her driveway, spinning his back to her to hide his face, his eyes racing over the dirt at his feet. What was he supposed to do now? A rush of heat prickled at his skin. He'd been caught red-handed *and* looking interested in her farmgate produce . . . Did the universe offer no sympathy?

Kate wound down her window, her insufferable smile like a sprinkling of salt on his parched tongue as he gave her a side glance before looking away again.

'What are you going to buy? I promise I'll give you a neighbourly discount.' Her voice was way too cheery. He rounded his shoulders.

'I'm good, thanks. And I'd appreciate it if you could take your farmgate somewhere else. It's been like peak bloody hour all morning. Can't get a thing done in peace.' If he was going to buy her eggs, which his hunger pains were screaming out for him to do since he'd missed breakfast and one of Meg's coffees—something he needed urgently—it would require going about it under the cover of darkness. He'd starve before he let her see him buy anything, especially after he'd grouched earlier, which he now regretted. Mr Keep the Solitude Secure—as much as he didn't want to admit it and couldn't stand the taste of kale—saw the positives in having goods to purchase without the risk of running into the brigade guys, who right now ran a close second to Kate.

'You haven't got your gate finished? I could help you if you'd like.' The twinkle in her eyes doused a fresh dose of infuriation through him.

'No thanks. Wouldn't want to hold you up. Catch you

later,' and Gus marched back to his problematic gate, frustrated he'd just turned down a pair of hands he should have accepted if he was going to get the bothersome thing up at all.

'Are you sure? I'd be happy to.'

'Yes, I'm sure,' and with that, Gus picked up his tools, abandoning his gate and marching back to his hut.

The midday sun streamed down on him as he bypassed the hut, opting for the well-worn path to the beach, Speedy trotting beside him. He'd do some more work on the steps this afternoon, but right now, he was in desperate need of a cooling off, both for his body and his ragged mood.

A scrubby branch jabbed at him, and Gus gave his arm a brisk wipe. The scratch wept slowly, but he turned a blind eye to it, not wanting to touch his forearms. If he did, he'd remember.

The ocean salt stung the cut, and he embraced the feeling, the waves tumbling around him as he body-surfed back to the shore in his boardies. He stood in the shallows, scrubbing his face with his hands. Speedy danced at the water's edge, panting as she waited for him.

'Why has she got under my skin, Speedy?' Gus gave his dog a quick pat on her side as he snatched up his raggy T-shirt, and they headed towards the steep track back home. It wasn't like she meant anything to him, he tried to convince himself. And yet she still managed to drive him to distraction in every waking moment and dream. Just that morning, he'd sat bolt upright in bed, a vision of her all too cute little smile taunting him as she returned his sheep for the umpteenth time. Couldn't his dreams even allow him one win over her for once?

Gus was halfway to the top of the path when he stilled, his attention drawn to a distant noise, and Speedy slowed, turning back to look at him.

What was that? But the afternoon wind rustled the leaves

around him, so he dismissed it, convinced it was nothing more than a bird whistling. He shook the salty droplets dripping from the ends of his hair as they stuck to his neck, and he began walking again.

But on the wind, he heard the sound, faint but unmistakable. It was the fire siren.

Gus's heart thudded in his chest, the siren the one thing he'd stop everything to answer in times gone past.

Should he go?

Would he be welcome?

Hughey had said he would be. Refusing to let his mind question itself, he took off up the slope at a run, cringing at the rocky sand poking into his feet as he urged himself to the top. He stopped. Listened.

Speedy gave a shrill bark, and before he heard it, he saw it, thick black plumes rising into the sky like overbearing clouds.

Gus rushed a hand through his hair as he fought to compose his breath.

The smoke, intense and wild and positioned directly over the main street, had Gus's hands punching his thighs in a mixture of doubt, confusion, and worry. The ominous colour told him the fire had not long ignited and was burning with rage. He pictured it licking at anything it could use as fuel to keep it alive.

They were one hand down, his mind told him. He had to go. He had to try. He couldn't push aside the urge to help whoever was in trouble, even though it filled him with misgiving fear.

Gus ran to his hut, locking Speedy inside so she wouldn't follow. He leapt into his ute, unexpectedly skidding at the end of his driveway. 'Stupid damn gate,' he cursed, and his nuisance neighbour. He never would have put one there in the first place if she'd not bought the Pilchers' property.

He heaved the lopsided gate aside. About to get back in his

ute, he stilled. More sirens in the distance, the crews from Apollo Bay and Glenaire no doubt being hailed too. With at least three turnouts, it had to be serious.

The engine roared as he over-accelerated, and he had to slam on the brakes as cars and utes streamed past in front of him, thumping his steering wheel with the palm of his hand in frustration. Some of them were volunteers he knew well—many of whom no longer talked to him. Others were turning up to have a good old sticky beak. There had been several occasions when Gus had needed to ask onlookers to get out of the way at a scene they'd been working.

The smoke was giving way to tall, licking flames as Gus approached the main street, and he slowed, his heart beating wildly. It was a shop going up. But not just any shop.

It was Hughey's.

Gus's eyes were glued to the building.

He pulled over on the nature strip in front of the beach and jumped out, holding the door as he frantically scanned for who was in charge or what was even being done. But his heart wanted to explode. If Hughey was inside . . .

Without a second thought, Gus ran towards the fire truck with no gear or helmet in hand. He'd arrived without a plan, so much like when he'd tried to save Kelly. But he came to an abrupt stop when he was intercepted.

By Ash Evans.

Ash stepped in front of him, his face set and determined. 'Don't you bloody well go near there. Having the likes of you amongst the action is a danger to the scene. Go home to your shack in the scrub. We don't want you here.' He pointed directly over Gus's shoulder at his ute.

But the shop, Hughey. What if his best mate was still inside?

But the moment the thought struck him, the fear he'd allowed to fester for what felt like an eternity took an even higher leap, much like the roaring flames, their wild anger heating his body even from such a distance.

Ash was right. He'd been no good to anyone last time.

How would it be any different now?

CHAPTER 19

Graham stood in Gus's lounge room, staring out the window with a cold stubbie glued to his hand. 'None of it could be saved.' He cast his eyes down before he took a seat.

Gus shook his head in denial. 'How'd it start?'

'They're suggesting it could have been an electrical surge, making the power point spark. They were installed back in the early 1900s, so it wouldn't surprise me. Didn't take much for it to light up inside the walls. Hughey was cutting up meat with the bandsaw and had no clue till it was too late. He was lucky he got out when he did.'

Gus took a seat before his legs gave way. He'd only been in the shop yesterday, helping out Hughey by giving him a few hours. It was the one safe place for him in town because it was mostly the wives of the firies that came in. But had he missed something? Could he have done anything to prevent it? Why hadn't he thought something like that could happen any earlier? But then again, neither had Hughey.

But regardless, it wasn't fair. Hughey was making a real go of things. The town didn't need this setback.

'Okay, ladies,' Patsy said, gathering their attention with a clap at the impromptu meeting held especially for Hughey at her house. 'Let's put our plans for the fire brigade fair on hold. What are we going to do for our wonderful butcher? We all need him to keep his business running. Nige will twitch if he can't have his Thursday night steak.'

'How about,' Kate said in between mouthfuls of Nola's scrumptious peppermint slice, which she was going to make sure she got the recipe for before they were finished, 'having an outdoor cinema night? We can take the story to the local news. We might even promote the fair on the side. If folk from bigger towns pick up that things are on the move in Forest Gully, they may come for a day drive or even stay over.'

'What a great idea,' Patsy said. 'And the sooner, the better. How about we set the date for three weeks? That should give us enough time to put plans in place. Nola, would Graham be happy to use his vintage truck as the platform for the screen? I think it'd look a treat.'

'Yes, definitely. Any excuse for him to show it off,' Nola replied, and they all giggled. Graham was renowned for driving it to their letterbox—not one hundred metres from the house—if he didn't have any other excuse to use it for the day.

'I have an idea for a film,' Kate said. 'What about the *Barbie* movie?'

This raised some serious eyebrows, some excited and some not so. She felt the hard sell coming on. 'I've heard it's a hoot, and even the men have enjoyed it. Why wouldn't they when Margot Robbie is the golden girl in a short pink skirt?'

'I love it,' Meg said. 'Who doesn't want to see a girl go after exactly what she wants.' She eyed Kate suspiciously. She got Kate's shut-up-right-now glare in return, making her smother a giggle.

There was still mixed reservation over the film choice, but Kate wanted to seal the deal with an extra sweetener.

'I've also got something for you all.' She gathered a stack of plates from the kitchen, placing them on the dining table before retrieving the plate she'd warmed up in the microwave. 'Have a try of this, ladies. And don't hold back on me. I want to know exactly what you think.'

She served up her sticky caramel cake with a drenching of caramel sauce on each plate and passed them around. The only noise to be heard was the clinking of spoons on crockery. Kate gave a satisfied smile as she snuck a spoonful herself, dying to hear their feedback.

'Mmm, this is amazing, Kate. You need to make this for the café. I'll pay you.' Meg shovelled another spoonful into her mouth, closing her eyes in ecstasy as she chewed slowly.

That wasn't something Kate had been expecting. She'd been hoping for a simple "it's really yummy."

'Bring it in tomorrow, and I'll—'

'Whoa, hang on a minute, Miss Meg. It's definitely more appropriate for the bakery,' Lexi said, licking her spoon with dedication as she kept a close eye on her rival. 'Something new is exactly what the bakery needs. I've been at a loss for a bit of inspiration lately.'

Kate smothered the giggle urging from her throat. 'And what am I supposed to do with all that, ladies? Do I sell it to both of you?' She'd been getting a few shifts at Meg's to give her friend a break. It would make things more than a little busy if she had orders for them both, but it couldn't hurt the purse strings.

'How about I make one and drop half off to both of you? Then both stores would get the opportunity to see how it sells.'

Fervent chatter began again as Kate returned to the kitchen and flicked on the kettle for a third round of hot drinks. Meg followed, pressing her shoulder close to Kate's as they stood at the kitchen sink. 'I'm feeling guilty.' Her voice was a low whisper.

'About what?' Kate said, unsure why they were whispering and she gave a questioning frown.

'About the fire and about being mean to Hughey all this time. I've turned him down flat about his business concept so many times, and now look at what has happened. My shop is fine, and his is, well, soot.'

'You can't feel guilty over that. It could've happened to anyone.'

'But my shop is older. How hasn't this happened to anyone before?'

'Maybe this is a sign.' She gave Meg a teasing poke in the arm. 'Maybe there's a future larder-come-butcher-come-café for Forest Gully in the making after all,' and she wiggled her eyebrows at her friend.

'No, it'd never work,' Meg whispered, a little more sharply.

Kate watched her friend, hearing the sincerity in Meg's voice as she shook her head sadly. Now that was an interesting step up in events. She'd never seen Meg offer any sign of regret or concern for Hughey. Or had it been a cover-up, Meg liking him after all?

'He'd drive me mad, Kate. The man doesn't let up. And he calls me Megsy. I *hate* that name.'

Then again, maybe not.

'That's because he *likes* you.'

'No, he doesn't, so don't even say that,' Meg whispered then stood taller, taking a step backwards and casting an edgy glance over her shoulder at the women basically dribbling over Kate's dessert. She turned back, giving Kate her signature hairy eyeball, the one she usually reserved for Hughey, before tossing teabags into the mugs with more gusto than was necessary.

'He's been the bane of my life, ever since primary school. Do you know he put a mouse in my lunch box once? I screamed and threw it sky-high the moment I opened the lid, and the teacher told *me* off for wasting my lunch.'

Kate couldn't hold back her chortle, and Meg stopped, pointing in Kate's direction. 'And you want to know the worst part? For the next week, he planted a life-like toy mouse, like the ones you buy for a cat to play with, on my desk, in my locker, and in my pencil case. He even sat one on my head while we were sitting on the floor and the teacher was reading a storybook. When I threw it back at him, it landed on Julie Walker. She squealed, and I was sent to the principal's office for bad behaviour. And all Hughey did was laugh.'

Meg crossed her arms with indignation as Kate poured the hot water into the cups, struggling to stifle the giggle desperate to break free.

'Well, he got your attention.' She gave Meg a teasing wink, her constrained smirk now soft.

'What he did was make an enemy for life. I won't, Kate. Not on your neat little Nelly, thank you very much.'

But regardless of her friend's animosity, Kate was determined to see this setback for Hughey as an about-face, no matter how it turned out in the long run. There was no point wallowing in all the wasn't-it-terrible commiserations the ladies had begun the night with. What they needed to do was focus on their let's-do-this-now attitudes.

CHAPTER 20

'No, no, nooo!' Not only had Gus's sheep managed to find their way back under her verandah again, but her veggie patch was ravaged.

Kate spun around, both hands on top of her head as she stared at Monica, who offered up an inquisitive gaze and a loud 'baa'. Her mouth flattened as she glared at the ewe. '*Not. Happy. Jan*,' she growled at Monica, using her finger to circle her own face, ensuring the ewe knew exactly how she felt. 'You need to stay *out* of my garden, or we won't remain friends. What am I going to have to eat or sell?' And as she said it, she turned to her roses, their flower petals and leaves also decimated, the leftovers scattered over the garden bed. Her shoulders slumped. 'You have got to be kidding me.' And just when her farmgate was taking off. But there were some buds still closed that hadn't been munched. With any luck, in the next few days, she'd have at least a few roses to put up for sale again.

She marched back to her verandah and stormed inside, disregarding the door still ajar. Monica waltzed in behind her, making tracks for the dining table. Kate swivelled around at the sound of her hooves. 'Oh no, you don't, young lady.' She wrapped her arms around the ewe's torso as Monica lifted her front feet to the chair beside the table, ready to hop up.

'Out, out!' Kate spun the ewe towards the door, resisting slamming it shut like she really wanted to before thundering towards her phone, hitting call with a determined punch of her finger. What was his excuse going to be *this* time?

'Are you missing anything?' She didn't even give him a

chance to say hello.

'What do you mean?'

'Like some . . . oh, I don't know. *Sheep*?'

Was it necessary to have to spell it out? Had he not paid attention to the fact that they weren't in his paddock?

Several loud bleatings erupted outside her window and Kate spun around. 'Oh no you don't,' and she marched towards her kitchen as she peered out its window, the sheep marching back towards her garden.

'Oh no, I don't what?' The confusion in Gus's voice was clear, but she chose to ignore it.

'Monica, get out of there! And all your friends, too.' She raced with her phone still at her ear, flinging the front door open and chasing his sheep from her remaining rose buds, which they were about to wrap their succulent lips around.

'You had better get your butt over here right now, Gus Stevens. Your girls have discovered my garden and developed a taste for it. How did they get off your property anyway?' She puffed as she shooed the sheep back towards the verandah. They'd cause less damage there but how long they'd stay put was anyone's guess.

'Okay, I'm coming now.'

Her phone went dead and she stood behind the sheep, not prepared to move in case they tried another swiftie on her. Five minutes later, Speedy trotted through the scrub with Gus hot on her tail, a sheepish grimace on his face.

'Look,' he puffed, 'I'm sorry. Beats me how they got out.' Gus scratched his head as the sheep relaxed under her verandah, astutely watching proceedings.

Working together with Speedy trotting beside them, Gus and Kate steered the sheep towards the lower paddock gate. Kate couldn't help but do a double take when she laid eyes on the expanse of the cliff's edge.

'Wow. That's impressive . . . and steep.' She took a tentative step closer, grasping the fence for stability so she could watch the waves frolicking below.

'Yeah, she's beautiful alright.'

That all too familiar funny stirring filled her tummy as she listened to him speak of the ocean, like it was a part of him, as though there was no better place to be than in amongst it.

'We're so close to the edge.' She gazed in awe.

Kate ebbed her way through the gate cautiously. As long as Riley didn't discover this spot, she'd sleep easier.

'I don't get it,' Gus said as he stared at Kate, rubbing the back of his neck. 'The chain was hooked up. They shouldn't have been able to get out.'

Kate clapped her hands loudly, urging the sheep deeper into Gus's property, throwing her arms in the air as she stomped the ground for them to keep moving. But the sheep were in no hurry. Speedy managed to head one off when it about-turned, heading towards her side of the fence once more.

'She doesn't make a bad working dog, considering she's hardly been around sheep,' Kate said.

'Yeah, you're right.' His gaze settled on her with the kind of ease that said he liked what he saw. How did she respond to that? By going red, of course, and she turned away to link the chain back through the gate herself so she knew it had been done.

It was almost March and stiflingly hot, her drying sweat irritating her body. Gus stood to her left, his long locks draping over his well-formed muscles beneath his almost threadbare T-shirt as he offered her a smile that threatened to melt her on the spot. Why did she have to keep on noticing that?

'Would you mind helping me walk them up to the shearing shed? I hate to admit it but I'm gonna need all the assistance I can get.'

'Asking for help now?' she teased. This was a side of him she could get used to. 'You have a shearing shed? Do you know what it's used for?' She playfully nudged him in the side with her elbow as she brushed past, unwilling to stay and see what might happen if she lingered. There was a definite zing pulsing in the air, and for a stark change, she wished she could say it was a storm setting off her out-of-control heart instead of her conflicting feelings for her neighbour. Did he feel it too? His darkened pupils suggested yes, but was that even what she wanted? Coordinating Hughey's fundraiser and the CFA fair and being a mother to Riley was all that should matter. Even then, did she have them in the right order? A twang of guilt flooded her.

The fundraiser. Thank goodness she'd remembered it now.

'I've been meaning to ask you for your help.' There was no better time than now. She waited, not missing the frown that flashed over his brow at her words.

'We're organising a fundraiser for Hughey to get him back on his feet. The town needs him.'

She hung back, reaching out to tap one of the slower-moving ewes on the backside, encouraging her to hurry up.

'We're having an outdoor cinema night. You like the movies, right? All the proceeds are going to Hughey.' She flashed a hopeful glance Gus's way but he returned it with a vacant expression.

'I don't like movies. Sorry,' he said, effectively shutting the discussion down with the turn of his back.

'But he's your best mate.' Her hands hovered on her hips, and she stared at him, long and hard. What was going on in that frustrating head of his? He was impossible. If she needed to, she'd drop it for now. But this discussion was far from over.

They worked the sheep into the yards, Speedy barking as

Kate closed the gate on them. 'Well, they won't get out of here,' she nodded with satisfaction.

'Thanks for this. They must've found out I'd booked a shearer for tomorrow. Any wonder they took off to your place.' His heartening chuckle did funny things to her insides.

She staved off her small smile, his neatly kept beard completing his handsome appearance. She'd always been a sucker for one. Made a guy look rugged and farmy somehow, like the fellas back home, not that anyone had taken her eye.

Aware her gaze was on him longer than the recommended dose she'd allowed herself—three seconds, four at max—she bit her lip, racking her brain for some new topic. Anything. If she continued looking at his dreamy eyes and stepped closer, she'd—

That's enough, Kate. She hopped over the yard railing to put some distance between them.

Kate bent down, peering under the shed. 'Check this out. There's a heap of sheep manure under here. You could bag it up, sell it at the open cinema night, you know, like a side stall. We're going to be doing a barbeque and selling popcorn too.' After all, this was a country fundraiser for a butcher.

'Where?'

'The fundraiser for Hughey, at the showgrounds. This would be perfect. It's a little old and crusty, but it would be great for someone's garden.'

'You sure know a lot about sheep shit.' The glint in his eye was unmissable, and her body urged her to move closer to him like some troublesome charm, but she kept her feet planted exactly where they were.

'So, will you do it? Riley could even help you.'

What was it with this woman? Couldn't she leave well enough alone? There was no way he was going anywhere near a mob of townsfolk for a money-raising event—even if it was for his best mate. All it would do was leave him open to more scrutiny and jibes if Ash's crew were there. And they would be. He'd forgotten his self-imposed vow once with Hughey's fire. He wasn't about to do it again.

'I've got some chaff bags lying around inside the shed. I'd be happy to help Riley bag it up.' *That's all.*

'Great. So that means you'll help? I'm sure having his best mate there will lift Hughey's spirits.'

'Ah, I didn't say I'd—'

'Speaking of which,' Kate checked her phone, 'I'd better head off and pick Riley up. I can send him over when we get home from school if you'd like?'

Gus gave a slow nod, unsure what exactly he'd agreed to. Speedy nuzzled his hand and he gave her an affectionate rub down her back.

'Kate, I—' He stepped towards her, fully intent on telling her he couldn't turn up at the movie night because it was too hard, and no one wanted him there anyway.

But this woman was ruffling all his securities. No one had done that since . . . Kelly. She'd been the one to show him how to love deeply, meaningfully. Uncle Neil had done his best, but, being a bachelor, he hadn't wanted to talk to Gus about the loss of his parents when Gus asked. Men, especially farming ones, held it all inside. And now it was threatening to tear Gus apart.

He'd loved Kelly with all his heart, but she was gone, and against his better judgement, it was feeling like Kate was beginning to fill a part of his empty heart.

Kate stilled, the interest in her eyes deepening as she watched him intently, no doubt pondering why he'd moved closer.

He wasn't sure himself, but he continued towards her as though his legs had a mind of their own. With one last step, he studied her eyes, her nose, and her softly-parted lips.

Her neck was so elegant as she swallowed slowly. He could feel it, like electricity whirring between them. It had his heart racing and his mind hurtling, with all the reasons why he shouldn't want to do this. But he couldn't stop himself.

With only inches between them, he moved, watching her intently for any resistance as he neared his lips to hers, feeling their softness as they met his. He closed his eyes as he began to be rescued from his guilt, instead taken to a place of warmth and nurturing and dare he think it, peace.

Her hands rested on his forearms and he fought not to pull away. He'd believed it would repulse and repel, not attract someone.

But when he opened his eyes, hers were still closed, a dreamy expression on her face. Could she actually be interested in him? Against everything screaming inside, he'd let her fingers move tenderly over his bumpy skin, and she hadn't flinched.

He gently drew away from her, watching her eyes flutter open.

He smiled.

She grinned back.

'Ah.' He took a step back, her hold slipping away as he awkwardly ruffled his hair with one hand and struggled to muster the courage to continue. 'Could I ask what you're doing tomorrow?' He frowned, shying from her, the heat beneath his whiskers rapidly moving towards his exposed cheeks.

'Ask away.' She showed no hint she wanted to leave. That had to be a good sign.

'Any chance you could give me a hand with shearing tomorrow? Last year, I hired a contractor in to do the lot. I don't need to tell you I have no clue how to recognise one end of the fleece from the other.' This time, his smile was coy. He knew his limits.

'Sure. I can show you how to throw a fleece. I loved doing that when we were shearing back home.'

Her welcomed acceptance relieved him no end about how he was going to cope tomorrow with zero experience and a shearer who expected him to help. But better than that was the chance of working alongside the woman he wanted to be around more and more.

'Great.' His lips lifted, and his old smile returned; the kind Kelly had said always encouraged others to return it. How long had it been since he'd allowed himself to do that? Way too long. And he liked the thought of it sticking around.

CHAPTER 21

'He kissed you! It's all over your face, girl.'

Kate's eyes widened. How had Meg worked that out from what, her expression?

'Aww, c'mon,' Meg teased. 'You've got a poker face if ever I've seen one.' She shot around the counter, hooking her arm through Kate's as she directed them to the window table.

'Okay, spill.' Meg leaned forward eagerly on her seat, her arms crossed.

Kate sat mute. She'd walked in to get her coffee, and now she was facing a cross-examination about her love life, the one she didn't have. Did she?

'I knew it the moment you opened your mouth to order. Since when have you done that in the last two months you've been coming in here?' Meg raised her you-can't-fool-me eyebrows in Kate's direction.

Okay, so she had her. The woman was sharp.

'Listen, all we did was—'

'Yes, yeees?' Meg leaned even further forward, causing the table to tip towards her.

The memory of Gus's lips on hers was, well, perfect. She couldn't describe it any better. And he'd let her feel his arms. She'd sensed the slightest of flinches to begin with, but it had settled. Touching him that way was like having a view of the inner him. It was a mark of his resilience and his dedication to someone he'd once cared for. It showed how deep his heart could genuinely love.

'Shift sheep. If you'd let me finish, you could've saved

yourself a whole lot of pent-up excitement.'

Meg sat back in her chair, arms straight, wearing a blank stare as her hands lay face down on the table. But Kate knew better than to think she'd give up that easily.

'Oh, don't give me that.' She rolled her head all knowingly. 'Something happened, and you're going to tell me.' Even if a customer did arrive, Kate wasn't sure a bomb beneath her friend would move her.

'We did. And I convinced him to bag up the manure below the shearing shed for Hughey's night.' Kate grinned, satisfied with her comeback. If she allowed herself one more thought to the way Gus's lips had melted her insides, heated her skin and made her want for more of the same, her friend would be onto her like an intrepid seagull.

Meg's eyes narrowed, unconvinced. 'Well, that's a good thing. Did he say he'd come too?' Her gaze was less than convinced.

'No, but I assume he will. Riley's over there helping him now.'

Meg's fingers thrummed the table as she sized up Kate one more time before begrudgingly getting up and moving to the coffee machine. It was just on closing time and she wanted to make them both a latté.

'Your sticky caramel cake was a hit by the way.' Meg eyed Kate as the aroma of coffee brewing filled the air. 'Has Lexi said how it went at the bakery?' Kate didn't miss the scrutinising curiosity lacing her words.

'No, but I haven't gone in there. Why?'

'Oh, no reason,' Meg said, now the one feigning disinterest in what her competitor was up to. 'I just know having a warm sticky caramel cake with hot sauce oozing all over a plate, *with* a dollop of double cream, would be a *lot* more enticing than a cold one handed to the customer in a paper bag.' She gave Kate a wicked smile.

'You two would compete over who had the ugliest jumper if someone showed interest. Have I created a monster I'm unsure how to tame?'

Both women laughed as Kate sipped on her coffee and Meg switched off the machine and the lights for the night.

'Hey, wanna come over for a barbeque tonight?' Kate said. 'I'm trying a new recipe for dessert. Plus, I have a weakness for Hughey's homemade chicken, fetta, and chive sausages he's been making with a machine he's borrowed from a mate. Were you aware he's been making them from home and sharing a small space in Lexi's bakery?' Kate studied her friend carefully for any reaction. That had to get a mildly shocked glance from her. Or at least she could hope.

'Will Hughey be there?' Meg's eyes focused on her takeaway cup as she pulled the door shut behind them, and Kate huffed indignantly.

'Oh, come on. He's a good guy. If you want, I'll invite Gus too.'

'Good. Then I'll be able to prove something *is* going on between you two.'

Kate grinned. The thought of Gus coming over had her tightly reined-in butterflies fluttering about wildly again. But having them all together was a good plan. There was no way Gus wouldn't do something for his best mate and she was going to make sure she got him to the movies.

Gus wished he hadn't said yes to the invite, not because he didn't want to see Hughey and Meg, but because too much was being thrown his way, all when he hadn't asked for it, and he wanted to make it stop. But running out of feed did help increase the motivation.

Riley was like a little mate now, and they'd already had a man-to-man chat about the girls in his classroom who were leaving him little notes in his school bag. Then there were the boys who were being butt heads by not letting him join in with their footy match at lunchtime, and his teacher who loved maths a whole lot more than Riley did.

Was Kate privy to any of this? He assumed so.

He nodded a greeting to Hughey, stepping forward to give him a welcoming handshake. Hughey's affable nature took everything in his stride, not appearing to be anxious over the fire only a week ago.

But Gus was.

With fresh memories of Ash branding his chest with his firm hand, he'd felt helpless all over again. When was he going to stop toying with inclinations that got him nowhere? He couldn't turn back time and he could never make it right.

The night was warm with a light breeze as they sat around the empty fire pit the Pilchers had built. Gus drowned his sausage in bread with sauce and took a bite, gazing up at the stars. Nothing could beat the open space and a sky that went on for miles.

'Hughey, these sausages are my absolute favourite. If there was a silver lining to losing your shop, the fire may have given you a newfound niche. You need to experiment with more flavours.' Kate licked her fingers, and Speedy sat at her feet, waiting for a stray morsel or more.

'What about smoked meats? Personally, I'd love to buy some salami. We never get those yummy things unless we go all the way to Geelong,' Meg said, and Gus watched on as Kate choked on her mouthful, eyeballing her friend in amazement. He'd seen it too. Was that a slither of encouragement for Hughey? Wonders would never cease. He caught Kate's eye and they shared a smile that sent ripples through him. He looked down to tame his desire to admire her delicious smile longer.

'Yeah,' Hughey said. 'And I want to make some spicey sausages, and I thought about making a range of kabana too, like chicken and garlic and pork and chilli.' His enthusiasm was irresistible.

'Yes, please,' Kate said as she took another bite, moaning at the deliciousness.

Gus remained quiet, his belly full and his interest waning. He was considering hopping up to say goodbye when Riley came over with a new Lego masterpiece.

'Do you like my fire truck, Gus?' Riley beamed as he admired his build. Gus fought to keep his mind from the thought of never being a brigade member again. It hurt. His award for bravery and dedication before the crash meant diddly-squat when Ash had shafted him to the lowly ranks of unwelcomed and disgraced.

'She's a little beauty, Riley,' Hughey said with an impressed grin.

Gus's glance swept upwards, watching his best mate, a sincere sadness washing over him. Hughey's face shifted to thoughtfulness as he gave Gus a nod that spoke of regret, remorse and gentle encouragement. It was a good thing he'd finished his food because the lump in his throat was making it nearly impossible to swallow. His eyes rested on the truck again.

'She's a beauty alright,' Gus urged his constricted voice to say, giving a nod. Riley's face lit up, his approval clearly meaning more than Gus had realised.

'I'm going to drive the fire truck when I'm big enough.' Riley focused on his creation again, lowering it to the floor to adjust a few pieces.

What? Where had Riley come up with an idea like that? And more so, what was Gus going to do about it?

'That's great,' Kate piped in before he could respond. 'You'd make an excellent fire captain.'

Gus's stomach pitched as Riley looked up at her, his face radiant. He couldn't deny it was a relief to see Riley happy with what his aunt had said, but there was no way he could encourage his little mate to do that.

'Hey, Gus, I forgot to tell you,' Hughey began. 'Carl Evans is joining the crew now that he's old enough. I reckon he'll be really good at the job. He—'

'What's he wanna do that for?' Gus's tone was harsher than he'd intended, the lump still jagged inside his throat.

'I thought you'd like to know, that's all.' Hughey went visibly pale, looking down.

How could Ash's son want something like that when he'd barely escaped a fire himself? Did he want a second death wish on himself? Gus bit the inside of his lip, avoiding all eye contact as he stood.

'I'd better head off. Got an early start in the morning.' He sent a bashful glance Kate's way. Would she still come and help with the shearing? He'd be best to assume not.

'I'll be there as soon as I've dropped Riley at school. You'll have to survive the first run without me.'

'Really?' The word came out before he could stop it, shocked that she would still help.

'You'll be okay 'til I get there.' Her smile, her words holding such promise, he had to believe her.

His mouth lifted in a hesitant crooked smile, his half-nod to them all signalling their departure. Speedy stood and trotted off in front, ready to head home too. And even though the roots of the shrubs were catching his thongs in the dark, he didn't bother turning his phone torch on.

CHAPTER 22

'Pick the wool up by the back legs, squeeze it together between each hand and lift it on top of the fleece still in front of you. Then pinch it with your fingers and lift, like this.'

It sounded so easy.

Gus scratched his neck. He couldn't tell the front legs from the back ones, let alone manage to pick a fleece up without it slipping through his hands and falling in a mess on the floor, which he'd successfully achieved many times over before Kate had arrived.

'It's harder than it looks,' she said, her cheeks softening with a warm chuckle as her eyes danced all over his face, making him squirm.

'You're telling me,' he said with a rueful smile. 'Whoever said rousing was a cinch had to be drunk.' He'd already bent over for two hours and could feel his muscles objecting. What would he be like by the end of the day?

'Don't worry,' Kate said as she carried the fleece to the small wool table, tossing it like a pro. 'It took me lots of practice before I was doing it with relative ease.' She moved to one side of the table. 'Even then, I still have my misfires. Help me skirt the fleece on your side like I showed you, then you can throw the next one.'

'So, what are we going to do with the wool when we've finished?' He'd managed to stack the fleeces in the corner of two walls but was fast running out of room.

'I'm putting it all into that old wool frame over there and we'll change it as it fills. You don't have enough to sell at auction so we'll need to take it to a wool merchant somewhere. There should be one in Geelong.'

Everything was sounding so foreign to him. How had the simple act of saying yes to inheriting eighty sheep and then their lambs become such a time-consuming job? She must've seen his glazed eyes as he looked about him.

'Don't worry. We'll find one. Then you'll have a bit of spare change to use for fixing up this shed.' He watched Kate as she studied some of the missing floorboards, letting in dust and any creature that wanted a cosy home.

'I'll take the wool off your hands.' The shearer looked up with a smirk on his face as he continued to shear. 'Won't charge you a thing.'

Gus liked that option until Kate's gaze widened, and she shook her head when the shearer looked down again. She leaned over the wool table towards him, the fragrance of her perfume sending his heart skittering.

'No, you won't do that,' she whispered. 'He's trying to rip you off. He'll sell the wool himself and take home the money instead of you. And that's on top of what you're paying him already.'

She pulled the fleece towards her, placing it into the wool frame and leaving Gus feeling empty for her closeness.

The whole job only took half a day, thanks to a fast shearer and help from Kate. He didn't doubt he'd have been there all day if she hadn't been available.

'Thanks.' The shearer held the cash Gus paid him in his fist. 'Are you sure you don't want me to take that wool? It'd make life a lot easier.' His lips curved in a joking smile.

Gus looked over to where Kate swept the shearing board extra clean with gusto.

He offered the shearer a grateful smile. 'Nah, but thanks.'

They shook hands, and the shearer left, leaving Gus with those telling hazel eyes that could read him better than he could read himself.

'Well, I'd better be off. Gotta drop what's left of my flowers off to Nola before I pick up Riley. It's her birthday today.'

Was it?

'What about your farmgate? The bunches were disappearing mighty fast last week.'

'Ah, Mr Stevens,' she said smugly. 'I knew you were taking notice. And here I was thinking you were attempting to avoid it with your big new gate.' With the emphasis on those last three words, her mouth twitched in a smile, pinning him to the floor.

'Let's just say I had to work on that project longer than I'd planned.'

'Hmmm,' Kate said as the little smirk she gave made him weak at the knees. She had an assurance that disarmed him, and yet, when it came to Riley . . . something in their bond was missing.

Kate waved goodbye before hopping over their fence and disappearing into the bushland, leaving Gus feeling all of a sudden . . . lonely. The bushy scrub between their houses had given him a sense of privacy he'd thrived on when he needed it the most. It had allowed him the distance from others he wanted to get his life back in order. And now that he'd done that?

A fierce sting stabbed inside his chest. Was he any better off for keeping himself estranged from the only community he'd once considered his family? And what had happened to him since his next-door neighbour had intruded on his personal space and, dare he admit it, a decent-sized wedge of his heart? A deep longing for a companion settled inside him.

No, *Keep the Solitude Secure.* He'd do well to remember because it's all that mattered. And if Carl Evans wanted to be a firefighter, then Gus wouldn't have to watch it happen.

What was the point of a motto if you couldn't keep one?

Mid-afternoon, the open-air cinema loomed large with warm sunshine and a refreshing breeze. A handful of leaves had begun to fall from the deciduous trees Gus had planted near the house. But his brow was covered in sweat as he stalked about his house like a grizzly bear ready to tear it down. What had possessed him to agree to this?

One simple answer. Riley.

Gus tramped to the front door, perplexed by the sight of thirty bags of Sheep Poop—as Riley had named it for the stall— that they'd collected, lined up in neat rows underneath his verandah.

'All for a great cause,' Kate had said before he'd been lured in by her energetic charm and sparkling eyes that had made him kiss her.

His heart sped up at the thought. Her lips had been soft and magically impatient as he'd become lost in the moment. And where had it left him? With no choice but to deliver bags of sheep manure to town.

'Cursed woman,' he said to Speedy, who tilted her head to the side as she watched him back and forth. But if this was the way they could get behind Hughey, then how could he say no?

But the thought begged consideration, if he rang her . . . Kate could come and get them. Easy fix. His finger hovered over her name, but he let the phone fall back to his side, frustrated. This was no way to treat his best mate, and there was no way she'd have time to pick it up. A picture of her formed in his mind. She'd already be there, a bundle of organised drive and unvoiced impatience as she directed people to where they had to be. He couldn't even ask Riley to go with him as his right-hand man. The kid was setting up their stall right now, waiting for the grand "Sheep Poop" delivery. He'd even made a huge sign to hang on the front of their open tent.

Oh man.

The buzz of anticipation in the main street had floated in the air each day this week when he'd ventured in for his mocha, not to mention the townsfolk queueing for Kate's farmgate. Getting to his letterbox was becoming a game of hide and hide a little harder.

Gus's phone rang in his hand and he tried to ignore it. There was no doubt who it was, checking up on him to make sure he turned up. He had to give it to her. She knew him better than he'd realised.

Guilt nestled inside him as he lifted the phone to his ear, not bothering to check who was calling, ready with his unenthusiastic, "Yes, I'm on my way" line, but he was pleasantly surprised by the voice. It was Mark Twigg, his mate from back home.

'Hey, Mark. Nice to hear from you. How's things?' His mood lifted considerably.

'Not bad. I'm on an overdue break and thought I'd drop by to say hello. I'm almost in Forest Gully now. Got time for a catch-up?'

Have I? You bloody betcha. He wanted to kiss Mark for his superb timing. With him there, Gus might be able to forget about Ash. And it wouldn't hurt to have a Senior Constable standing beside him, even if he was off duty.

'I'm on my way to an-open air cinema night for my mate, Hughey. Wanna meet me there?'

'For sure. I've seen some posters for it, and with the stream of cars in front of me right now, I reckon if I follow them, I'll end up at the right place.'

'Great. See you soon.'

'Right,' Gus said, pushing through his front door, heading for his beat-up ute, Speedy racing him to it. She jumped onto the ute tray, spinning around, her tail beating back and forth, her tongue lolling.

'Quit with the grin, girl.' Even so, a smile curved his lips, and he scruffed her neck fondly.

Gus landed wearily in the front seat, having loaded all the bags, their weight sure to put his squeaky suspension to the test. Speedy sat beside him in the passenger seat, breathing heavily out of the open side window as the sun streamed down through the windscreen.

For a rare change, Kate's farmgate was quiet, so much so that Gus edged towards the roadside, peering past the scrub shared between them both to make doubly sure no traffic was coming. These days he expected to be blocked inside his property by a car parked in his drive.

The full weight of Gus's cheek sat neatly in his palm, his elbow on his open window ledge as he gripped the steering wheel with his left hand, feeling the weight of the heavy burden upon him. The movie night was being held at the showgrounds because of its ability to park a large number of vehicles. But it meant he'd have to pass one more hurdle, the very thing he'd managed to avoid for so long.

Gus pulled over to the side of Sheep Gully Road, allowing a string of cars to pass. Up ahead, on his left, the mountain ash loomed large and tall. And at its base, a small white cross sat, hammered to the trunk with fresh flowers circling its base. His jaw tightened.

Leaning forward, he narrowed his eyes. Were they Kate's

roses around the base of the tree?

He sent his ute skidding back onto the asphalt between cars, the smell of rubber from his tyres filling his nostrils. Was he losing his marbles by doing this?

He had to be.

CHAPTER 23

Where is he? Kate had one hand on her hip and the other shading her eyes as she scanned the showground oval, cars of all descriptions parked in the designated area. Graham's truck, with its large white screen on the tray, was positioned in front of the small stadium, and people were filling its rows while others were setting up camping chairs in front. Riley was standing at his and Gus's stall tent beside it, his face sullen as he, too, gazed back and forth.

'It'll be right, mate. He'll be here soon.' He had to be. She'd promised. If he backed out on his word, she was acutely aware Riley would blame her, not Gus.

Instinctively, she moved to put her arm around Riley's shoulders, but he slunk from beneath them, conveniently disappearing into the crowd. Not even the popcorn table held his interest.

Streams of people were arriving from surrounding townships, all supporting the effort to raise money for Hughey. His reputation as a butcher was well established, but somehow now—most likely thanks to his new Instagram account Kate had set up for him—his popularity had grown even more. His sizzling sausages cranked out an aroma to die for. Early evening was upon them, and the queue hadn't let up.

Kate sucked in a worrying breath. Several people had dropped past Riley's tent on a second visit, hoping to buy his five-dollar bags of poop for their garden. *Turn up, Gus. Pleeease.*

It was fine for him to let her down, but how dare he do it to Riley? She found herself pacing back and forth, the opportunity to call him one last time well past. The film would be starting soon. After that, she doubted people would bother coming back.

Brenda walked over to Kate, her knitting needles click-clacking in her hands, and the footy scarf she was making was almost finished. How she did that was beyond her.

'This is a hit, Kate. I'm tickled pink by how many people have come to support the cause. It's gone beyond my expectations.' They both admired the continuing stream of people willing to pay a fifteen-dollar entry to participate.

But just as Kate's worry began to resurface, the sight of those muscular shoulders and long strong legs in fitted denim jeans that could have been made especially just for him strode towards her, two big bags balancing either side of his neck. His direct gaze had her sucking in her breath.

He slowed in front of her with a directness she wasn't used to seeing from him.

'Gus, you made it!' Riley ran towards him, his face overjoyed. 'We've got lots of people wanting poop.' He jigged on the spot, and Kate's heart melted at the joy he displayed.

'Okay, buddy. I'll go and get the rest. You start selling them.' Gus lowered the bags of sheep poo, and Riley lunged at him, hugging him around the waist in a fierce grip.

Gus held a hand to his hair, his straight teeth offering a deep, genuine smile before stepping away for another load.

Riley sold his first bag to a waiting customer, his smile generous and utterly delighted.

But Kate's was long gone. Unable to take her eyes off Gus's retreating form, his streamlined hips moving with his casual gait, her heart ached. It was as if the man was some damned lure, drawing Riley to himself.

She shifted from one foot to the other, contemplating her options. But there were none. She had to face facts regardless of how much they hurt. Riley would always love his own mother more, and she'd never be able to be the jovial auntie she used to be.

Ever again.

CHAPTER 24

Regardless of the sting from the direct sun, Gus couldn't ignore the tantalising smell of gourmet sausages as he hauled the last two bags of manure onto his shoulders and approached Riley's tent, relieved he'd finished the job. He'd done his part. Now, he could get out of there. He'd high-fived Hughey on his last walk back to the ute, more than sure his best mate was grateful he'd made the effort, even if he did look a little surprised.

He looked about, keeping an eye out for Mark amongst the people milling around Graham's truck. Excited chatter and the clunking of food trays and drinks before the film started filled the atmosphere. It was a bigger turnout than he'd expected, and he marvelled at so many unfamiliar faces. How had Kate pulled this together at such short notice? She didn't know these people. She was still a newbie herself.

Dumping the last of the bags to the ground and winking goodbye to Riley, he walked over to Brenda, the beginnings of a soft pink masterpiece emerging as she knitted blindly.

'Hey, Brenda. Is Kate around?' He shied from her interested gaze as warmth flooded his already hot and bothered body, making him wish he hadn't stopped to ask. Brenda had lived in Forest Gully all her life and could sniff out the possibility of a fresh relationship like a truffle dog.

'Now, why would that be important to you, young Gus?' The sparkle in her eyes burned into Gus's inner motives, and he wanted to turn there and then and escape her scrutiny. But he had to believe he was a better man than that.

'Just need to tell her that's the last of the shit—' he hesitated, noting Brenda's disapproving tut-tut alongside her raised eyebrows; 'um, sheep poop,' he corrected. 'And that I'm heading home.' He glanced up at the roar of a loud engine, shying away quickly. It had only been a red flash in his eyes, but it was enough to send a wave of sickness through his gut.

'Are you sure that's all you wanted to tell her?'

Brenda's probing had his shoulders tightening and he stretched his neck to each side, releasing the tension gripping them. His eyes narrowed on her. Had Kate said something to her about him? Or was she just an old sticky nose? Had she picked his look of disappointment?

To his relief, she let him off the hook. 'She's gone to Meg's stand to grab a latté for the two of us. You can find her there.' Brenda's eyes danced over him, making him squirm.

'Nah, just say goodbye for me. Thanks, Brenda,' for nothing, Gus growled under his breath as he stalked through the busy crowd, still keeping an eye out for Mark. If he knew his mate, he'd be in the huge queue at Hughey's stall, lured by the aroma, or already finding himself a spot to sit down with two loaded sausages in hand. The guy was never one to miss out on a gourmet meal.

It was only when he felt a slight tug from behind that he slowed. Gus turned. Riley was jigging with exuberant excitement.

'We just sold all our bags of poop, Gus. Isn't that great?'

The kid's face was brighter than the glare from the sun setting over the horizon, and Gus gave an approving nod, offering a high-five his way.

'That is, bud.' He squatted down, opening his arms as Riley launched into them, grasping him like he might never get the chance again.

'You've got some nerve turning up here.'

Gus stiffened, blinked slowly at the ground in front of him, and then stood slowly, his guarded eyes turning to Ash Evans as

Riley looked at each of them, gripping Gus's hand in his.

Carl stood alongside his dad, and Gus dug deep to offer him a friendly nod. 'So, you're one of the team, Carl.' Unable to muster the resemblance of a smile, the hesitation in his voice said it all as he looked down at Carl's arm, a soft scar all that remained from where a plate had been inserted into his badly broken wrist.

'That's no business of yours, Gus,' Ash interjected. 'Why don't you head back to that hobo you call home? And don't show your face around here again.'

'Gus helped me sell sheep poop for Hughey. He's allowed to be here.' Riley stood tall, his tone sunny, direct, and protective. Gus raised his hand, resting it on Riley's shoulder protectively as nausea swept over him.

'It's okay, Riley.' But was it? Yeah, it hurt, but he couldn't change any of it. If only they could fully grasp what he'd genuinely give to bring Kelly back.

'But he's wrong, Gus.' Riley looked up, pleading with him.

'Good to see you, Carl.' Gus eyed Ash one last time before taking Riley's hand in a firm grip and striding back to Brenda and Riley's stall. Just past where she was sitting, Gus spotted Mark waving with a sausage in hand and a large bag of popcorn slung under his arm.

'Riley, you need to stay here, or Kate will get worried.' He clutched Riley's hand as he squatted down to face him, hoping it would inject the importance of what he'd said, his own need for his little buddy to listen now higher than ever. He forced out a smile.

'She doesn't care what I do,' Riley said dejectedly, kicking the dirt with his shoe. 'She's too busy.'

'That's not true. She loves you, and you did a super job here for Hughey. I'm really proud of you.'

'You are?' The loneliness in Riley's expression threatened

to break Gus, and he leaned in, drawing him in with a deep hug, whispering in his ear. 'If she hadn't done any of this, Hughey wouldn't be getting a second chance to start all over again. You don't want to miss out on his famous hamburgers, do you?'

Riley gripped Gus, shaking his head unconvincingly as he burrowed into his shoulder.

Mark strolled up to them, greeting Gus with a firm handshake as he stood. He looked a little surprised to see Gus was hugging a kid.

'Mark, this is Riley.' A rush of warmth filled his chest.

'Nice to meet you, buddy. These sausages are amazing. When will the hamburgers be ready?' Mark gave Riley an eager nod, but all Riley offered back was a shrug, and his eyes remained downcast—a look passed between the two men.

'Aren't you staying for *Barbie*?' Riley looked up with pleading eyes at Gus.

Why had his day become so much more complicated than it had been one hour ago? Was the world out to get him? He urged Riley's attention by squeezing his shoulder as he leaned forward.

'No, bud, but just wait 'til we get all the proceeds in and tally up how much the town has made for Hughey,' Gus said to both Riley and Mark as he stood again, keen to make his getaway. 'We might have to celebrate that with a surf. What do you say?'

'Promise? Can you teach me?' Riley's voice bubbled with fresh hope, his legs doing a little hop on the spot as he looked at Gus.

'Yup, I sure will. And I'm past halfway with the staircase down the cliff. I can't wait for you to tell me what you think.'

Feeling a tad guilty for having to leave Riley, the urge to continually glance about him had him toey. He'd done what he'd promised.

Waving goodbye to Riley, he nodded at Brenda, her gaze

still sparkling like she was privy to something juicy as he turned to walk to his ute, Mark by his side.

They were almost back at their cars when Kate came running up, her breath puffed.

'Gus, I wanted to thank you.' She slowed, reaching a hand for his arm. He gently pulled it out of reach. 'It meant the world to Riley that you brought the manure and I know Hughey is stoked you helped.'

Was he? All he'd done was let his best mate down at the shop fire.

'No worries, wouldn't have missed it,' he lied. Her head tilted as she regarded him. And as he held her probing gaze in return, the temptation to take the one step forward required for her to be in his arms, his face close to hers, his lips . . . kissing her . . . it was all too real. So, he stepped back, increasing the distance between them and his need to smell her perfume, which was already playing havoc with his thoughts. He flicked a glance at Mark, sensing his curiosity.

'Ah, Kate, this is Mark. Mark, Kate.' His head bounced between them as their focus went to each other and off his heated neck.

'Well, we've gotta head off, so I'll catch you later, Kate.' He gave her the lightest of smiles, as if it meant nothing more than being polite. Mark was staying the night, and he was looking forward to having a friend to hang with. He gave the nod to Mark and headed for his ute, hopping in with what little dignity he had left.

Kate slid in behind the table she'd set up for the movie, frowning as she slumped into the camping chair.

'Now, what's that face for?' Brenda's all-seeing eyes held hers.

'I just saw Gus and, oh, I don't know—' Kate's contemplation drifted so far away that she forgot about her hamburger she'd placed on the table. It was like Gus was a man of exasperating mystery. One minute he was showing deepening feelings for her, and the next, he was pushing her away like she was some disease he'd die from. She'd pretended that the way he'd moved his arm before she could touch it hadn't stung.

Besides, he'd made it clear he was uncomfortable being there. But he'd agreed to come even though he was late. She would've skinned him alive if he'd let Riley down.

'Auntie Kate?' Riley moved beside her, and she could pick up the concern in his soft blue eyes.

'Hey, buddy, what's up?' She bent forward, reaching her hand softly around his waist and to her relief, he didn't shy away, his little body so near, giving her the crumb of reassurance she was desperate for. He absently jiggled the bag of popcorn he'd bought.

'Does Gus like me?' He stared at the dirt around his feet.

'Of course he does.' Where was this coming from, and where was it going? The bigger worry on her mind was Riley preferring Gus over her as a parent. She rubbed his back with tenderness. He still didn't move.

'Mr Evans doesn't like me. He doesn't like Gus either.'

'What are you talking about?' Kate glanced across at Brenda whose attention suddenly focused on her knitting. She gave the woman a suspicious frown.

'Mr Evans told Gus he shouldn't be here.'

'Tut-tut-tut,' Brenda said as she glared at her knitting like it was about to smoke. Kate spun at her murmuring. The woman was clickety-clacking on triple speed. She'd have three beanies finished by the end of the night if she kept up that pace.

'What do you mean?' She turned back to Riley, puzzled.

'He told Gus he was a hobo.' Riley's gaze was quizzical, probing Kate's eyes for answers. 'What's that mean?'

'He isn't a hobo, sweetheart, and you don't need to worry. How about you go and check in on Meg. I know she's saving you the biggest triple choc chip muffin at the coffee stall.' She urged a smile into her voice, hoping it might redirect his thinking. She stood and Riley gave an encouraging nod, his head downcast as he turned away.

Patsy hopped up on Graham's truck, standing in front of the screen and holding a mobile microphone to her mouth. Kate glanced at her before taking a seat next to Brenda, still distracted by Riley's dejection written all over his body language. It was enough to have her eyes stinging.

'Okay, Brenda. You'd better fill me in.' She inhaled deeply as Patsy's voice spoke to the audience. So far, she'd sensed acceptance from the community, especially for the event tonight. She wanted to understand what was going on with this quirky small town that held their cards close and their opinions loosely.

Brenda's needles never slowed, not even as the crowd murmured with anticipation and expectancy. Kate heard a 'Woo-hoo!' holler out in the audience, followed by wolf whistles and cheers amongst the hundreds of fairy lights that lit up the seated pavilion. It was Hughey pumping everyone up for their first glimpse of Margot but she let out an impatient breath, desperately trying not to roll her eyes.

In the distance, the local fire truck eased to a stop and children clambered down from the back cabin. Her genius idea of a gold coin donation in exchange for a ride around the showgrounds had kept a steady stream of passengers lining up until the film started. Had Gus seen it?

'Not until you relax those wire-tight shoulders,' Brenda

scolded, waiting for her to do as she was told. Kate made a show of relaxing them.

'There was an accident.' Brenda's voice softened, and her knitting needles eased their frantic pace. Kate turned to listen before following Brenda's line of sight. She was staring at the fire truck. Kate's interest piqued.

'I know. Meg told me.'

Brenda sucked in a laboured breath, the click-clack of her knitting needles resuming.

'That young man lost everything in the fire that day, including his reputable standing within this community, thanks to some.' Her mouth pinched tight. 'I wasn't sure I'd ever see him turn it around, but—'

Brenda now had Kate's undivided attention.

'He's braver than most. He couldn't have done anything more to help without getting killed himself, which he nearly did. Ash Evans has no right to treat him like an outcast. But he and his staunch fire mates wanted to blame someone. It was a horrid incident that was never going to end well.'

The whole community had ached alongside her father, mother, Riley, and herself as they'd said goodbye to her sister. They'd rallied around the Harris family, understanding their decision to leave the farm. To Kate, the community was her extended family, who had each other's backs in everything, both good and bad.

'Did you know Gus was quite the volunteer once?' Brenda's eyes danced at Kate's intrigue, and Kate sat up, alarmed by her own reveries and the change of subject.

'Oh?'

Brenda continued knitting. 'He coached the kids at the local cricket club. Young Carl was in the team. Gus was devoted, spending hours helping them perfect their batting and bowling techniques.'

Kate frowned.

The old woman nodded, mostly to herself, because Kate remained silent, staring without seeing the pink beanie taking shape on Brenda's lap.

Brenda continued. 'Carl's joined the brigade now. Not sure how that will go down.' She shook her head. 'Ash won't like it. Couldn't imagine him wanting his son to relive the atrocities of the accident or risk his life another time over.'

Kate watched the ants hustling about her feet, a little thrown by the point Brenda was trying to make. The poor old dear did have a track record for waffling on, missing the fact people weren't following her gist. Kate's mouth slipped open, ready to ask a clarifying question when Riley bounded up.

'I just went on the fire truck. It was awesome.'

'That's great, buddy.' Kate's heart triple-skipped, his excitement overwhelmingly infectious, having a soothing effect on her. Instinct kicked in to touch his hair, soft and short from the haircut Meg had given him a few days ago, but she reined it in. For now, him looking at her with those adoring eyes she hadn't seen for so many months mattered more than anything.

'Gus might want to go on it with me. He might still be here.' Riley spun around, desperately searching the crowds that were now all but a murmur. Another wolf whistle echoed in the air, bouncing around the louder cheers erupting as Margot appeared on centre screen, looming over all the little girls in her curvy striped one-piece, oh-so-long legs and a luscious smile that had the men swallowing back their tongues.

A distinct breath of impatience burbled from Brenda's mouth but Kate ignored it. She was more concerned about letting down her nephew yet again as he looked back at her, his eyes eager. This was the part she didn't understand how Jenna had done. Letting him down hurt her more than it would hurt Riley, she was sure of it.

'I'm sorry, bud. He's gone home.' Her throat closed around her words. 'Would you like me to come with you?' Her face crinkled against his impending disappointment and her own rejection.

Riley stopped jumping. 'No, it's okay.'

His words were the knife that stabbed her directly in the heart. Why did he refuse everything she offered? How long would it take before he let her in again?

'How about we take the money you've made today over to Kathleen?' With her due date getting closer, Kate was a little worried about her friend being able to manage. 'I'll check how it's going, then we can have takeaway for tea. Lexi might still have some pizza to sell.' She brightened her voice, her smile lifting, unconvinced it was tempting Riley in the slightest.

But there it was again, that agonisingly slow-moving nod he'd perfected so well, particularly since living in Forest Gully. Kate closed her tired eyes to block out his rejection and her own despair. Was it possible it was going to be like this for the rest of her life until he grew up and left home?

CHAPTER 25

An eerie shiver slivered down Gus's back despite the profound heat hovering in the still night air, perfect for the event. He hadn't wanted to turn up, but somehow, Kate's magnetic charm had worked its power over him, now leaving him with the angst of driving past the tree that haunted him almost every night, all over again. But he was certain he'd done right by Riley, and that was what mattered. The kid was a dinky-die mate, be it in miniature, and Gus's affection for the boy was growing rapidly.

Having gone out with Kelly, Gus had been acutely aware that Ash had tended to be overly protective of his only daughter. She'd been the school captain in both primary and secondary school, and not because she manoeuvred her way there. She was that genuine, lovable girl everyone wanted to be friends with and for reasons he'd never entirely understood, she'd chosen him.

Gus's chest clamped hard around his heart. Now, what did he have? Nothing but everlasting guilt over failing her when she'd needed him most. After that, reality had set in. Ash might be unwavering in his opinion about him, but he deserved it.

Every bloody bit.

Ash had bailed him up at the scene of the accident as though Gus intended to let the love of his life die right in front of him. He still woke in a cold sweat some nights with the image of Ash screaming in his face. The man had made it no secret that his ugly lesions were well deserved. He tried to hold to the notion that it was a father's grief that had been speaking, but since then, the man had made it his personal mission to hold Gus accountable. He'd received several icy glares from the fire crew today—nothing new—as he'd walked through the crowd. In better times, he'd been a team member and more than well-respected. Those people had been his friends.

Gus drove without seeing, his thoughts all-consuming as Mark drove behind him. Riley had begun to fill a space in Gus's heart that included trust, loyalty, and friendship, the kind that came along when they walked in silence down the beach. Each of them letting the sound of the waves override the sadness and pain meant more than words could say. And even if he couldn't fully put it into words, Riley was helping him.

As the memorial at the base of the tree loomed closer once more, Gus pushed his foot down on the accelerator, focusing straight ahead rather than risk seeing it again. He fingered the knot in his shoulder muscle, desperate to ease the tension clinging to him like a long-lost friend.

'Well, ladies, it was a huge success.' Kate beamed at them all. 'And not just because Margot stole the boy's hearts.'

'Ryan Gosling wasn't any slouch,' Brenda said with a cheeky grin as she picked up her knitting. The other women giggled, their tea cups saluting the air at the fun the whole night had been.

'We raised four thousand, eight hundred and seventy-six dollars and forty-five cents for our wonderful butcher,' Kate said. 'Everyone rallied, and I'm so proud of you all.'

'Hear, hear,' Patsy said, raising her china cup in the air for a second time.

Kate smiled as she watched the reaction of the ladies, the clatter of teacups being placed back on saucers filling Patsy's living room. The women nattered amongst themselves, expressing salutations to their fundraising efforts and nodding approval as they passed around the plate of Jenny's fruit cake. It was a meagre start to Hughey's comeback but, nonetheless, a huge help while he waited for his insurance to come through, which he'd been told could take several more months thanks to the police wanting to rule out foul play.

'Now we can resume our plans for the fire brigade fair,' Patsy continued. 'It'll be here before we know it. Are there any ideas about what we could do with the money we raise?'

'How about a new fire truck? One isn't enough with the bushland surrounding us,' Erin said.

'Great idea. I can get onto the Forest Gully Fire Brigade's Facebook page and start promoting it. Never hurts to let people know what's coming up in a few months,' Meg said as everyone except Brenda resumed their clickety-clack with their knitting needles.

'I couldn't agree more,' Nola said. 'Graham is always grizzling about needing another truck. But Fire Rescue Victoria won't help us unless we raise a significant amount of money ourselves.'

'How much would that likely be?' Lexi asked as Nola typed on her phone.

'I've just texted Graham,' Nola said, looking back up. 'He'll find out for us. I should have the figure by our next meeting.'

'Good. I don't want to relive another fire,' Brenda said, her voice trembling slightly as she recommended knitting.

Kate's gaze rested on her, getting the feeling there was more to the woman's determination than that of a fire. Since when had Brenda put her needles down for any issue before now?

'So, ladies, I have another something for you all to try.' Kate waggled her eyebrows to get their undivided attention, hoping her idea might lighten the mood. 'And yes, it has something to do with the fair.'

'Honestly, Kate, you're putting us all to shame with these yummy treats, not to mention widening my waistline. Heaven forbid, I might have to take up running,' Nola said, and they all giggled. The first time she'd given it a go, Graham had needed to close the shop to pick her up with a sprained ankle. She'd never run again.

Kate headed to Patsy's kitchen, talking over her shoulder as she went. 'I've got a new choc chip recipe for you all to try.' She headed back to the lounge room, a large plate in her hands. 'Mind you, I don't want any of you to get out of sorts when you have to agree these are pretty good.' Her mouth twitched with a smile.

Brenda sat a little taller in her seat, eyeing Nola with a that's-not-even-possible glance. Kate hadn't needed to live in the town for long to understand there was fierce rivalry between the two women when it came to their biscuit recipes. It was high time she put an end to the belief that condensed milk was the only answer for a good choc chip cookie.

The women each took a biscuit, taking a doubting bite.

'Kate, you have to give me this recipe.' Meg closed her eyes in sheer pleasure as she took another bite, groaning as she savoured the chewy deliciousness to make it last longer.

'Is it better than the sticky caramel?' The biscuit recipe had been Jenna's favourite, making her rather protective over it. If she were going to divulge the secrets to its success, she'd need to be sweet-talked incredibly well.

'No,' Meg said, annoyed by her question, making it clear Kate had spoiled her ecstasy moment. 'This biscuit is in a whole new category of its own, and I'd love to put them next to my cake selection. I could even have pieces for customers to try as they come to the counter. They'd buy them, for sure.' If Meg's pleading eyes were any indication, her friend was prepared to beg, then deep grovel, if required.

'Maybe I'll just hold it to ransom a little longer. I might enjoy teasing this one out.'

'But you won't even give me the sticky caramel recipe.' Meg feigned offence, much to Kate's delight.

'Of course I won't. I need to hold something over you in case you decide to take your café elsewhere.' Kate chuckled, and Meg snorted a giggle, splattering a mouthful of tea down her front.

The evening was rolling in, and Kate thought of Riley's school day the next day. She glanced over at him, her head tipping to the side as he pushed the fire truck he'd constructed about him. How he managed to make whatever came into his creative mind was a marvel to her, reminding her of her father. He had the uncanny ability to rig up a solution to any mechanical problem they'd had on the farm. Had it not been for his father—her grandfather—wanting him to work beside him, he would've done engineering. Kate couldn't help but question if he was sad about not achieving his dreams. But her father had never suggested so.

But would Riley? Kate stared blankly, visualising Riley as a grown man, the one who would likely disown her the moment he could fly the coop. Her heart stilled, the ache sure and heavy. What did the world have in store for him? She wished Jenna was here to see his ingenuity unfolding and take over the motherhood role she felt so useless at. All she'd succeeded in doing was letting the kid down, dragging him across the countryside, far away from everything he knew and loved. It had sounded so right in her mind at the time, with new faces, new friends and, all importantly, an opportunity to put his tragedy behind him. But had that been the best way for him to deal with his loss? She doubted he'd ever forgive her.

But for her, these women were fast becoming her friends and her lifeblood. And even more so than back in Tenterfield, she realised that to thrive, she needed these comrades with a common thread to stand up for one another and to fight for causes dear to the hearts of the community.

And to convince her non-committal neighbour that he needed them as well. Then perhaps he'd recognise he needed her, too.

Kate beamed at Hughey as she stood inside Lexi's bakery, the yeasty smell of freshly baked loaves making her tummy grumble. She'd just handed him an important piece of paper.

'Nah,' he said, flabbergasted. 'They couldn't have raised that much.' Hughey's eyes goggled over what he was seeing.

'They did. It's all there.' Kate pointed as if she needed to convince him that the printout she'd done on the computer to show him the final amount was, in fact, fair dinkum.

'Well, that's better than a slap in the face with a dead fish,' he said, still not completely convinced it could be right.

Mark pushed the door open and strolled up beside Kate. 'You're up nice and early,' she said.

'Yeah, thought I'd get some breakfast for Gus and me before I hit the road.'

'So, you're a cop, I hear?' Kate couldn't hide her curiosity, only finding out minutes earlier from Meg when she'd dropped the coveted plateful of choc chip biscuits in for her to sample and sell, not believing Meg wouldn't eat them all before they were offered to customers.

'I am. I'm meant to be on holiday. Thought I'd say g'day to Gus while in the area. We grew up together.'

Finally, a piece of Gus's past, Kate thought, studying Mark with a curious smile. 'Was he always quiet and elusive?' The question gave rise to an intrigued smile from Mark.

'No, quite the opposite. But he always loved the beach, so I'm not surprised he moved down here.' Mark instructed them to move to the door with his thumb, and all three stood in front of the charred building, the old brick walls standing precariously. 'Mind if I take a look at the remains of your building, Hughey? I've checked the report. I hope you don't mind. Once a cop, always a cop.' He gave a light chuckle. 'They've confirmed it was an electrical fault thanks to the past-their-use-by-date plugs.'

'It's a wonder it didn't burn down any sooner, I guess.' Hughey's mouth tightened, and Kate reached a hand to his forearm, giving it an I'm-so-sorry squeeze. He offered her a sad smile, staring at the blackened remains, the donation certificate in his hand flapping in the gentle sea breeze.

'It might look bad, Hughey, but you'll come back bigger and better than ever,' Kate said, hoping her positive vibes would transfer to him. 'And with all those exciting propositions you've got, you could put this town on the map.'

His shoulders rose to his neck, a weak smile creeping onto his face. 'You're right, Kate. I reckon I'll give it a crack anyway.' He tossed a defeated gaze towards the café.

Kate looked too, spying Meg shooing away the crow before busying herself at the outside tables of her premises, wiping the overnight sea mist from them in readiness for the new day. She swivelled back to him, her mischievous grin unmissable. 'I'm positive you will, Hughey. And I reckon I know the right people to get around you to make it happen.'

Hughey's engaging smile hung on his lips like warm honey. 'Just gotta convince her.' He blinked thoughtfully at Meg before focusing on Kate, his expression less than assured.

'Don't worry about that. We'll get her over the line. She just needs a bit of gentle convincing.'

'A bucketload if you ask me.' Hughey looked back at Meg once more, his lovesick gaze just about breaking Kate's heart as his expression grew sombre.

Kate had to do something quickly. Hughey's earlier excitement over the money they'd raised was fading fast.

'Right, text me your bank details, and I'll get the fundraising money put into your account. Then you'll be able to buy the next bit of equipment you need. It's not much, but it all helps.'

'Too right, Kate. I've got my eye on a second-hand mincer in Geelong. Reckon I'll shoot down there today and take a squiz.'

'That's the attitude I like to see.' Kate waited for Hughey to text her, then made the transfer there and then. That way, he could buy anything he wanted immediately.

'Thanks again, Kate. This is better than I could have imagined. This town sure did need someone like you to come along.' He reached out, slinging his arm around her in a warm side hug.

He and Mark walked back to the bakery, chatting amicably, and Kate's gaze slid over to the schoolyard where recess was underway. Kids were kicking footballs and playing cricket. But over in the far corner, Kate picked out the outline of a small figure sitting beneath the shade of a large pine tree. The child's face was downcast as they concentrated on something in their hands.

Kate's feet stepped forward, curious as to why a child would choose to sit alone when there were so many others to play with, and as she moved closer, she momentarily forgot to breathe. Not only did she hurt for this child, but she knew who it was. And he appeared more alone than she'd felt the day they'd arrived in Forest Gully.

She waved, his name catching in her voice as she called out. He looked up, but not because of her. It was the school bell calling the children back to class.

Her heart missed a beat.

Kate stood listless as her nephew dragged his small feet across the oval towards the classrooms. A slow tear trickled down her cheek, and she bit her lip.

It wasn't fair seeing Riley so sad. But were tragic memories better off being lived with from a distance or close by? The answer continued to evade her.

CHAPTER 26

Gus had enjoyed reminiscing over better times with Mark, but it was time to say goodbye.

Mark had returned from the bakery with two quiches and steaming hot coffees from Meg. They'd enjoyed breakfast at the table beneath Gus's verandah.

Gus waved him off as the gums swayed in the gentle breeze. It had felt good to see an old friend, a fact that pleasantly surprised him. But even more so, he was looking forward to dropping in to see Hughey.

Gus left straight after, heading directly to Geelong and the wool merchant he'd found on Google. With any luck, this year's wool, along with the long-forgotten bags of wool he'd come across when cleaning up the shed, might amount to a decent bit of pocket change.

A little over two and a half hours later, he eased up in front of the bakery. Kate's car was parked out the front of Meg's café. He tried to kid himself the shimmer of excitement racing through him was only about giving Hughey his gift. But her name danced in his mind like gentle butterflies flitting above his head, making him giddy.

He stepped from his ute, patting the envelope tucked safely inside his shorts pocket. According to Kate, he'd shorn his sheep in the nick of time. His ewe's girths were expanding at a rapid rate thanks to the ram Graham had dropped off five months earlier, like in previous years for the Pilchers.

The thought of lambs stalled Gus. Hughey's enthusiasm had been high as he'd pitched to him the benefits of marketing his own fresh local meat. Hughey was sure the paddock-to-plate concept could be a Forest Gully winner.

Kate had been on board with the idea too, and he had to admit, she did know a thing or two about sheep. As if on cue, his heart drummed at the thought of her like so often these days. She'd effectively wriggled her way under his skin when he'd refused her permission to do so. He smiled, then checked himself with a drawn-in frown as he stepped towards the bakery. He didn't need any more of Hughey's ribbing, especially with Lexi listening on.

Hughey was tied up with a customer when he pushed the heavy shop door open, the smell of cinnamon doughnuts immediately playing havoc with his wannabe self-control. So, he did what any reasonable person should do, headed straight to Lexi's hot display cabinet, his eyes firmly set on at least three of the little beauties. He'd managed one bite when Hughey swivelled towards him.

'What about this idea?' Hughey said to Gus as though he was continuing on a conversation. 'We can supply Lexi with the mincemeat she needs for her meat pies from your sheep. Why hadn't I thought of that before? What do you reckon, Lexi?'

Hughey gave her a you-can't-possibly-resist-such-a-great-idea gaze.

Gus's eyes widened in angst.

'I love it.' Lexi smirked at Gus's look of horror, the sugary crumbs hovering on his lips dropping as he rushed to hang his chin over the paper bag. 'How many lambs do you think you'll have, Gus?'

Gus choked on the doughy goodness now glued to the roof of his mouth and teeth, raising the back of his hand to his lips. 'You're looking at me like I should know,' he spluttered, blinking at both of them. He still wasn't convinced he could let any of the mob go, especially that way.

Hughey and Lexi shared a good-natured laugh, although he was certain they didn't realise his misgivings about their new idea.

'No matter,' Lexi said. 'We'll work it out, and we can always buy from my other sources where we need to, depending on how else Hughey plans to use the meat.'

He'd always been someone who enjoyed a good roast, but somehow, hearing Hughey and Lexi talk about his sheep as their next meal made his insides coil with tension. He couldn't deny the sheep had driven him more than a little mad with their unsolicited drop-ins to his neighbour's lodgings. But the more he'd worked with the small mob, the more he began to recognise many of them and their particular quirks. He couldn't imagine parting with Monica's unborn lamb. But he wasn't so sure Kate would feel the same way, given their rent-free history.

'You'd better get your neighbour to check on them. Reckon she's the one who'll know what to do.'

Gus didn't miss the twinkle in Hughey's eyes before he returned his attention to Lexi. To her credit, all she offered was an agreeing nod.

'Oh, I nearly forgot,' Gus said, dusting his fingers free of the sticky sugar on his shorts before reaching into his pocket. 'This is for you.' He pulled out the envelope and handed it to Hughey.

'What's this?' Hughey's voice rose a notch as he stared down before looking at Gus again.

'Open it and see.' Gus couldn't hide the smile swamping his cheeks.

'Where'd this come from?' Hughey pulled out a wad of one-hundred-dollar bills, his mouth agape.

'Kate suggested I sell my wool in Geelong. Not too shabby for a motley mob of sheep, I don't reckon.'

'Not too shabby at all.' Hughey lifted his eyes from his hand. 'Are you sure?'

'Yup, I am.'

Hughey shook his head in slow degrees, counting the money. 'Thanks mate. Honestly, I'm speechless.'

'That's a first. Does it mean I have to pay you to shut up from now on?'

The three of them laughed. He might not have all the friends he once had, but a few good ones meant the world.

Gus froze as he stepped from the bakery out onto the pavement, his eyes darting to his left. The loud roar of the Forest Gully fire truck's engine slowly rumbled along the road in low gear. It drowned out the sound of the exuberant waves washing ashore as the tide rolled in. The doughnut sat heavy in his stomach.

Gus took a swift step back, unconsciously pressing himself hard against the shop window as it drove past. He knew the drill after an event or call out: checking all the gear was intact and without damage, washing the truck, and then taking it for a spin to refuel before returning to the station. He watched the guys inside the cabin, chuckling at some dad joke Graham had no doubt just told.

Ash was in the driver's seat, his eyes focused hard and fast on the road ahead, ignoring the cabin carry-on. He'd always been the serious one, but these days more than ever.

Gus took the breath he'd been holding as the right indicator lit up, and the truck swung into the station.

Memories rushed at him, much like the buzz of adrenaline in his arms and legs every time the siren sounded or a call on the fire pager hailed them. He watched, unable to tear his eyes from the members as they walked back and forth, their mood still high from the previous day's events.

Gus's chest pounded at the heightened emotion that came over him every time a fire broke out or someone needed assistance, wearing the sheer fear like a second skin. Last night may have only been a fundraiser, but the Fire Authority was the lifeboat of the town, ready to take on an emergency in a split second, and they'd been there for Hughey. They didn't need to be told twice to drop what they were doing and race to the station when hailed. Most of the participants carried their firefighting gear with them 24/7, especially during the hotter months. Security and reassurance were what the people of Forest Gully and surrounding townships needed, with a dependable team to protect them.

But not for Gus. He hadn't been able to do a thing for his parents, and he'd been stopped from trying to help Kelly. Dependable no longer lived in his vocabulary anymore.

The sight of little white bodies leaping and frolicking out the front of her house was enough for Kate to let her next-door neighbour off the hook about his mob's most recent visit, at least for now.

'Riley, can you see them?' Kate slowly rolled her car to a stop, pointing in the direction of the confident lambs racing around their verandah while the ewes stood nearby, bleating their objections to the unruly antics and calling them back. Thank goodness she'd fixed up her front gate. The ewes liked her house so much—she rolled her eyes at the mere thought—they didn't stray too far, but lambs, especially when they got older and asserted their independence, were a whole new ball game.

Instinctively, she rested a hand over her heart, relief filling her as she turned in her seat to watch Riley giggle at their playfulness. These ones were almost a week old, full of confidence and loads of attitude.

He jumped from the car the moment she braked. A grin filled her face as he walked quietly up to them, only metres away. The lambs stopped their play, staring at him before one called out to its mother, tearing back to her for a reassuring drink.

Kate was impressed. Her nephew might not have had much time to experience the farm and learn its ins and outs, but he had a natural way with them, knowing when to stop so they wouldn't take fright. There was definitely some serious Harris stockmanship blood coming out in him. Jenna would be proud.

But as Kate slid from the car, pausing to enjoy the way the stock moved in a mob, vigilant and watchful, a looming question chiselled into her mind. How had they got into her place again? Was there a hole in the fence they'd missed? There couldn't be. She'd walked it herself to check. Had Gus left the gate open? But that didn't make sense either, considering the whole point of the fence was to keep them on his side.

She grabbed their groceries from her car boot and lugged them towards the front door, giving Monica a gentle nudge as the ewe attempted to push her way in. A conglomerate of flies helped themselves inside as she bustled through, pushing the door shut. The day had been temperate thanks to autumn hitting its straps, but the fly-breeding season was exploding. At least the mozzies had backed off, thanks to the constant coastal winds they'd been experiencing more regularly over the last few weeks.

Kate had been so preoccupied with unpacking groceries, getting the chicken ready for tea, and catching up on the mountain load of washing she'd turned a blind eye to for the previous five days, that two hours flittered by until her stomach reminded her they might need to eat. She stilled, enthralled by the dusk sky closing in with colours of pretty pink and orange hues, imparting a welcomed calm inside her. More and more, Forest Gully was becoming home.

Walking to the front door, Kate swung it open, biting back her niggling concern with her teeth against her lip. Where was Riley? As far as she could remember, she hadn't seen him come inside after they'd arrived home. She'd encouraged him to scout out where the sheep might be getting in, but he'd been gone far longer than the half an hour she'd suggested.

The trees were rustling in the strengthening breeze and Monica nosed her way towards Kate's leg, nudging it. Kate was convinced her wide belly was harbouring twins, shaking her head in defeat as she allowed the ewe to pass before she moved over to the gravel driveway. She'd become soft and it was all Monica's fault.

Gathering her hair in a ponytail as she scanned to her left, then right, the daylight was rapidly dimming. She'd been sure she would find Riley watching the lambs, but they were curled up asleep next to their mothers.

Her mouth motioned to call his name when Riley emerged from a track in the scrub she'd never paid attention to before.

'Where have you been?' She forced herself to offer a pleased-to-see-you expression despite the anxiousness flowing through her. The thought of losing him sent a wave of goosebumps over her arms.

The wind kicked up another notch and the gum leaves rustled with hurried urgency. She stepped towards him, not missing the wariness within his eyes.

'I went to say hello to Speedy.' He looked down at his grubby toes housed in his thongs.

'Uh ha.' Kate dragged out her words, never taking her eyes off him. Was he hiding something from her? It definitely felt like it. 'Well, you'd better get inside and have a shower. Tea is nearly ready.'

Riley found a sudden level of enthusiasm, and he ran

towards the door. Kate's narrowing gaze followed him, and she couldn't decide if it was because she hadn't growled or that he'd just got away with something, but he was safely home, and that's what mattered.

Staring back into the increasing darkness, a rummage of questions took precedence over the chicken on the stove that could well be burning at this point. If he'd gone to visit Speedy, why hadn't the dog followed him back here if the gate was open? Kate flapped her arms in the air before heading inside to sort out exactly what her nephew had been up to. No doubt she'd lose another round of points, her negative tally increasing, all in the name of trying to protect him. She silently marvelled at her own mother for managing to raise two daughters to adulthood. At the rate she was going, she'd be sacked and heading home before her deadline.

CHAPTER 27

'What the heck?'

Gus scratched his head with one hand, his coffee balanced in the other as he stood under his verandah, scanning his empty paddock that should have been filled with his sheep. Unconvinced his eyes were telling him the truth, he walked to the shearing shed, glancing about him as he went.

Still nothing. But how could they have gone missing?

Speedy raced ahead, her nose to the ground, only stopping to turn and check he was taking up the rear as they began to hunt through the scrub. Imprinted in the sandy soil were plenty of hoof marks, but that didn't answer his confusion. There was no way they could have—

Gus walked the boundary fence between him and Kate, the footprints pointing in one distinct direction, the same one that had his heart deflating with speed. His head tipped to the sky, resting on his shoulders. He drew in a long, slow breath, standing straight once more as he took a long sip of his coffee. If the day was headed in the direction he was guessing, he'd need every drop.

Foraging beneath the dense scrub with Speedy darting in and out as they went, it wasn't until he turned for the gate at the cliff's edge that he halted. It was wide open, several hoofed footprints leading through it . . . to Kate's house.

'Ah, damn it.' Gus pushed the hair out of his face, now not as concerned about his missing sheep as at the reception he was going to receive if, in fact, they had made themselves at home at their old haunt. How exactly had the gate been opened? Hadn't Kate secured it?

The closer he got to her house, the faster he walked, and the tighter the grimace clenched his face. These pesky sheep were causing more trouble than they were worth. Maybe Hughey's grandiose scheme was worth consideration after all. A quick sale with him or even through the market would solve a lot of his problems.

Muscles tensing, he approached the house, the oh so familiar sight of the numerous faces as they turned towards him at the sound of his footsteps not surprising. Why had he agreed to take on these creatures with agendas of their own and a fetish for a homestead verandah that wasn't his?

'Baaa.'

'Shhh!' He inched his way closer, bent forward and tiptoed as he pulled his hand towards him over and over, urging his sheep to stand up and come with him. All he needed was for Monica to behave for once, and they'd all follow. But where was she?

'Woof.'

No, no, no. 'Speedy, quiet.'

The happy dog bounced around him, circling him with glee, anticipating the game he was suggesting they play.

One ewe stood to her feet with effort, her round belly impossible to miss. She bellowed again at Gus.

Gus ducked for cover behind a wide-trunked gum, snatching a breath before stealing a peek around its side, feeling distinctly more like a sheep burglar than a sheep wrangler.

Kate's car sat in the driveway, and the kitchen light was on. But there was no visible movement inside, only the tantalising smell of chicken something on the air. She was a good cook, and his appetite grizzled in response.

'Baaa.'

'Shhh, will you,' he whispered with a frustrated tone. 'I'm feeling bad enough as it is. You shouldn't be here,' and he waved his hand in the air again as he glared at his sheep. 'You need to get home, now.' He pointed towards his house. If he asked nicely enough, maybe they'd obey him and hop up on command. If he could move them without any disruption to Kate and Riley, he'd likely win back points of some kind. Any kind would do, actually, only he wasn't sure how far in the negative he was right now thanks to the sheep crossing boundaries that were supposed to be impossible.

'Maybe they like me more than you.'

Gus jumped at the words as he stood, whacking his head on a low-lying branch. 'Ouch.'

There was a distinct hint of humour in her voice, even a smugness if he thought about it long enough. He winced, giving Monica, who had walked outside the now open door of her own accord—a first, he was sure—a this-is-all-your-fault glare as he rubbed his hand on his head.

He about-faced with stealth, willing himself to look in the direction of her voice. Was she mad? He expected her raised eyebrow and blank expression to greet him, but to his surprise, he received a smirk, making him feel like a mischievous kid caught trying to skip class.

'You do realise there are easier ways to get an invite to dinner.'

There it was, that alluring eyebrow raised in a tall arc as she stood with arms crossed, her teasing smile twitching her sweet pink lips. Again, his gaze settled on them, remembering their tenderness and their enthusiasm matching his.

His breath hitched, and he forced himself to look at the ground in front of her. This woman rattled him, enticed him, and stopped him in his tracks at every turn. And right now, he wasn't sure if he was grateful to his rogue mob of sheep for making him turn up at her doorstep unannounced and scoring a dinner invite or if he wanted to wring their necks for dobbing him in.

'Kate, I don't have a clue how they managed to get over here. I'll take them home right now.' But as he turned back, they'd started settling in for the night, camped under her verandah like usual.

'That's not the best plan right now.'

What? Why? Gus angled disbelieving eyes at her, his head flinching back ever so slightly. 'But I thought—'

'See that ewe over there next to the tree?' She pointed to one pawing the ground and walking restlessly back and forth in the same spot, away from the mob. 'She's going to lamb within the next hour. She'll be vulnerable if you move the mob, leaving her exposed to a fox or a stray dog. I doubt she'll follow the mob, but if she does, you'll disrupt her labour. It could put the lamb's life in danger.'

Gus opened and then closed his mouth, struggling to find the right words as he instantly worried for the ewe. He considered Kate. What was he meant to do then?

'Leave them be for the night. I'll keep an eye on the ewe about to lamb, and if she's settled by morning and no one else starts lambing, we can move them to your place then.'

This time, her expression told him that she wanted to help. And it mattered more than he could find words for. Gus glanced about him, strumming his lips with his fingers. He turned back to her. 'Are you sure? I swear, I don't know how the gate got opened.'

'So, are you coming in? There's plenty. Riley would like you to.'

Quick change of topic, he mused. But he liked the way her smile reached inside his chest and warm-squeezed it. It was genuine, although somewhat tired, but it held sincerity as she waited for his answer. He desperately wanted to say yes, but he wasn't in a position to accept her hospitality, not when he was the one causing trouble for her again. But he breathed in another waft of whatever chicken surprise was in her oven, and his hunger voiced its opinion through the stillness of the evening.

'Is that your answer?' A teasing grin radiated over her face.

He grinned back coyly, with a touch of hesitancy. Whenever he was around her, it was as if his life grew more complicated by the second and yet became freer at the same time.

'There's more than enough if you like chicken with homemade gnocchi.'

Homemade? Was she for real? Since when had one of his favourite meals been made for him at home, and her home no less? He only had that dish when he was back in Ballarat and went to Roberto's, the little Italian restaurant he loved.

His belly whined again, making her right cheek softly lift in a grin. 'I think that's your answer.' Her eyes twinkled with teasing as she walked past him towards the front door, his feet following her and his brain trying to catch up on what had just happened. 'Oh no, you don't, Miss Monica.' Kate shoved her knee towards the opening of the door, blocking the ewe.

'C'mon,' Kate urged, 'or else Monica will be another guest *on* the table.'

'Gus!' Riley leapt to his feet from the coffee table, smothered in Lego projects and ran, bouncing up and down in front of him like he was a gift on Christmas morning. Kate's eyes slowly dropped from Gus to Riley before they slid to the Lego pieces strewn on the floor, her smile barely visible. Today was the first anniversary, and with so many memories resurging, she fought back the painful sting of tears.

She'd been the first one to have a cuddle within one hour of Riley being born. She'd taken him on all the adventures he'd ever known, like Lilo rides down the creek that flowed through their farm after a decent rain. And yet, right now, in front of her, as he was bubbling with excitement at seeing Gus, the only thing on her mind was the failure she'd somehow effortlessly fallen into.

Where had the fun, cool auntie gone?

And who was her nephew?

Why had she even thought she could be a mother to him? When Jenna had asked her all those years ago the day he'd been born, she'd said: 'For sure.' But never in her wildest dreams had she believed it would happen. A kid was never meant to lose a mother so early in life.

'Look at the plane I've made, Gus.'

'Wow, buddy, that's incredible. Where are we going to fly to? I reckon it'd be pretty cool to go to Wet and Wild. We could go down that giant waterslide.'

'Yeah,' Riley beamed. 'I've always wanted to do that.' The moment between their interaction subsided as his smile faded, his eyes sliding up to look at Kate before dropping again.

Riley dragged Gus over to the Lego pieces, urging him to sit down and help him finish off the plane's wings with him.

Gus agreed to it, then glanced over at Kate, offering her a reticent smile as he dutifully followed. She repaid the gesture and then turned to focus on the gnocchi she needed to put into the pot of boiling water, her eyes heating with moisture. Riley had mentioned wanting to go there a year ago when Jenna was still alive. She'd promised to take him. And now? If she did, she'd also have to visit her parents. And if she did that, they'd see just how unhappy Riley was with her. That risk was too high. She needed more time to convince her nephew he could love her again like old times. But she had to stay in Forest Gully to do it.

Riley was a bubble of words and ideas with Gus as he motored into his tea with an enthusiasm Kate found hard to find.

'How was your day at school?' Kate urged a smile she didn't feel on the inside as she focused on Riley.

'Good.'

That was it? She gave a sad nod, tossing her gnocchi with her fork. She put a piece in her mouth, the taste lacking its usual deliciousness.

'I like maths more now, like you, Gus.' He looked up brightly, but in the next moment, his face turned sombre and his focus moved to his plate. 'But the other kids tease me.' He gave a despondent shrug. 'They say I'm nerdy. Did you get teased too?' He looked at Gus, his pain obvious.

Kate forgot to swallow. He'd been at school in Forest Gully long enough for her to see him have two haircuts, but he'd never mentioned anything about this. He'd never told her much about anything, full stop. How much more did Gus know that she didn't? It suddenly rankled her that Riley spent most of his days after school over at Gus's, and she immediately hated herself for not making more of an effort. But that was impossible when everything else needed to be done to keep their house functioning. And in that one brief moment, her heart longed for the days when all she'd been responsible for was herself. She knew it was selfish, but back then, Riley had loved her. Now? She'd be lucky to get a half-hearted like.

She allowed herself to slide back into their reality, focusing on Riley as he continued to chat with Gus. Wasn't she supposed to be the one who should've been told he wasn't fitting in? That kind of stuff was meant to be shared with the one person in his life who would always be there for him. If her nephew couldn't thrive in school, it'd be on her. She needed him to start telling *her*. Not someone else. Not Gus.

And there it lay, the core of her problem. Did Riley no longer have faith in her? When she'd simply been his auntie, he'd told her everything, and Jenna complained about the same thing. Was it something that went with the territory of being a parent that made kids reluctant to confess their hearts to them? Did that mean he'd never confide in her ever again?

And Gus . . . Kate lifted her gaze to him, recognising he was avoiding her by his narrowed eyes concentrating on scavenging the remaining sauce on his plate with his fork as he chased it with the last of his gnocchi. How could he have kept all this from her?

And for no good reason at all, she suddenly had the urge to speak up, not thinking ahead as to how it might come across or how Riley might respond. She knew it was irrational, even assuming, but she had to. She'd had enough of Riley ignoring her no matter what she did. And as for Gus, she was definitely going to have words with him also.

'Riley, you left the gate open after visiting Speedy yesterday. We've put that fence up for good reason. The sheep are Gus's and they need to stay on his property, not ours.' Her plan to keep her voice calm was rapidly failing.

'But I didn't—'

Kate put her hand up, not prepared to listen to any more of his excuses.

'Now we have to wait until the ewes have a break in between lambing before we can return them. We won't be able to sell any more flowers or veggies at the farmgate because they've munched through our produce, and at this rate, you might not get to go on that school camp I saw that note for.' His face was aghast.

Money wasn't tight. She just had to be careful. The farmgate was beginning to help but now there'd be nothing to sell for another four to six weeks until her plants had a chance to grow some produce again. And with the cooler weather creeping in, growth would slow down even more. At least the chooks were still laying well.

A bright idea struck her, and she sat a little taller. Gus clearly recognised her shift from personal A-grade grump to fierce leader by the way his eyes widened. Why hadn't she thought of it before? The school had recently posted a request for any interested personnel to begin a school vegetable garden. It was a paid position, which would be ideal. But more than that, it would keep her closer to Riley. Maybe he would show an interest in her if she was more available this way.

Warm excitement simmered through her right up until the moment Gus chose to speak.

'We can't work out how the gate got opened, buddy, but I'll make sure it's latched properly when I take the sheep home.' Gus ruffled Riley's hair, offering him an it'll-be-okay wink before he cautiously glanced at Kate. In return, she eyed him with as much vengeance as she thought she could throw at him without Riley noticing it. Talk about ruining her I've-solved-all-my-problems moment. And how could he make it sound okay that stock could roam as they pleased? Riley had grown up opening and closing gates in paddocks back home.

Kate stood and gathered the dirty plates, dumping them in the sink with a distinct clatter. She yanked the ice cream from the over-frosted freezer drawer and not so subtly put it on the bench.

'It's ice cream and topping for dessert. Who wants some?' She hated the tone she was using, but she couldn't stop. What with Riley lying and Gus sticking up for him, she was done with both of them. In fact, she was over this whole night. What she wanted was to go to bed. But before she could bail on them, Gus spoke up.

'Uh, none for me, thanks. Better head off.' He walked to the door, avoiding the killer glare she offered him, scooting out through the opening as she called out.

'We need to talk.'

All he offered back was a reserved nod, shutting the door behind him.

CHAPTER 28

Late on Saturday afternoon, Gus decided to face what he'd known all along. He'd been avoiding Kate Harris since yesterday. He'd only caught the tail-end of the death glare she'd thrown his way last night as he was leaving, but that small glimpse was enough to be sure he was securely in the doghouse. Consequently, he hadn't shown his face that morning to help shift the sheep.

And now remorse wanted to chew him up and spit him out because they were back in his paddock. Lambs were curled up next to tufts of grass, sleeping in the warm glow of the morning sun as the mob meandered nearby.

Pressing his lips firmly together, he watched them grazing contentedly. How did he manage to complicate things so well, especially around this woman? It wasn't as though he *liked* her. Kissing her had been a mistake, no matter how good it had felt. She was just a neighbour he had to be friendly to, mainly thanks to his wayward sheep. But if he sold them, he could end that tie. Maybe he could embrace the idea after all.

Monica looked up, her gaze trained on him as if on cue, and she let out a long 'baa', remaining still as she waited for a reaction from him.

'Geez.' Gus gave a disbelieving shake of his head as he stared back at the ewe. How was it that all the women surrounding him made it impossible to live life how he wanted? Monica blinked one last time before putting her head down to graze again.

He slouched against his verandah post, watching the antics of half a dozen lambs as they stood and stretched, then jumped in the air as they found their feet and confidence. The new lamb born last night was curled up against its mother's side as she rested, her eyes continually watching for any sign of threat to her baby. His cheek wedged in a small smile.

Gus's mind drifted to Kelly and how she would have loved this sight as they'd sat at the table with their coffees, watching on. Sorrow threatened to overwhelm him.

And what did Kate say last night? Something about wanting to talk to him? He had a hunch he was in trouble again for something he had no clue about. He'd known from the day they'd met that allowing himself to feel friendship, kindness, a crush—because that's all it was between him and Kate, and ever could be—should've been nipped in the bud right there and then. Getting to know her and Riley . . . was precisely why he'd tried to avoid people. He pressed his fingers to his forehead, rubbing his dull headache.

'Hey, Gus.'

Riley's timely, bright voice had him pushing himself off the post and shaking away the mood he was happily going to wallow in only moments ago. There was something about this kid, and his cheeks rose, more than happy his little mate was swinging by for a visit.

'Wanna go down to the beach?' Riley's expression lifted, and Gus marvelled at the simple thought that had his mood lifting immediately.

'Sure. I've got something to show you.'

Riley's face lit up. 'Have you finished it?' He leaned in, his eyes widening, desperate to hear Gus's answer.

'I sure have.' Speedy raced by Gus's leg, stopping at Riley's side with overwhelming excitement, licking his hands as he tried to pat her on the head. Riley giggled, turning his face from her as she expertly reached to slurp his face.

The sand was warm underfoot, and their walk along the

beach, peaceful. The waves gently lapped at the sandy edge rather than rolling in with their usual vigour.

Gus broke their silence. 'There's nothing better than taking a board out there and catching some waves.' He said it more to himself as he stared out to sea, its peace filling him with welcome relief.

'Can I learn to surf? Will you teach me?' The hope in Riley's eyes was unmissable.

'Sure I can. But you'll need a wetsuit. It's pretty cold right now, especially when you hop out and the wind is blowing.'

'I can get one.' Riley nodded like his head was about to fall off.

'Okay, you do that. I have a spare board you can use.' Gus chuckled; pleased Riley was excited about something. He'd like nothing more than to help him learn. But more than any of that, it was a tonic for him, giving him the confidence that he might actually make a difference in someone's life.

An hour later, Gus and Riley climbed back to the top of the cliff edge, having had a man-to-man discussion about footy, the best surfing waves to catch, and, of course, their usual topic: girls. Gus took in a weary breath. If only he could talk to Riley about his auntie and maybe find out what made her tick. He'd already worked out she was the girl who arrived at the drop of a hat where there was a need.

But him? To do that kind of thing again would mean copping scrutiny from the Ash Evans band. They'd never asked *him* what had happened *that* day.

'Gus.'

Riley's voice broke his introspection, and he fought to retrace what they'd been talking when they reached the gate.

'Yeah, bud.'

'I didn't open it.' Riley fiddled with the chain, studying it, clearly puzzled.

Gus was stumped. If Riley hadn't, and he believed the kid because the concern on his face was all too real, then who had?

'I didn't want to say anything last night because, well . . .' Riley kicked at a small rock before he continued. ''Cause if I did, Auntie Kate would've found out I'd been down at the beach alone.' He wore the face of a guilty kid who wrestled to confess his sins.

Gus counted himself lucky that Riley was secure enough with him to do that despite feeling sick at the thought. If he'd been put in the same situation, he more than likely wouldn't be confessing any such thing to his uncle, who would have grounded him for a month.

'Would she disapprove?' Gus couldn't believe Riley hadn't told her about their beach walks.

'No. But she'd want to come with me.' He looked up at Gus, his gaze desperate. 'I don't want her to come because it's *my* thing.'

'So, the beach is kinda like your secret place, hey?' The kid needed to have something to call his own. Now that he understood.

Riley nodded vigorously.

'Did you go to Shark Tooth Corner?' Gus eyed him with a guarded look.

Riley gave a guilty nod, unable to look Gus in the eye.

Gus scratched his neck before he stepped closer, reaching a hand to Riley's shoulder.

'Your secret's safe with me,' he said, giving Riley the nod that said it was secret men's business. 'But I don't want you to come down here alone again. Okay?' He didn't think his heart could take it.

Even though Gus was less than happy about what Riley had done, at least he knew. And he'd make another point of talking to

Riley soon about being careful on the rocks. The waves pummelled Shark Tooth Corner savagely when the wind blew up, causing boulders to fall without notice, the thought making him cringe. He forced a reassuring smile to mask his apprehension.

He scanned the sky closing in with dusk tones that always had a way of comforting him no matter the mood they carried. The clouds were heavy but without any suggestion of rain.

Riley smiled up at him, sincere and genuine. 'Thanks, Gus.'

'No worries. Now let's get back before that auntie of yours has our hides because you're home late again.' He offered Riley a good-natured wink before they headed towards her house, and the dressing down he was sure to receive from the woman he couldn't shake from his mind or his heart, it seemed.

CHAPTER 29

'Don't worry. I'll be your guinea pig any day.'

A week later, Kate waved goodbye to Hughey, stepping from the shop with a basket full of his gourmet sausages and a selection of Lexi's leftovers. Kate had arrived in the nick of time to give them a good home. Riley loved Lexi's custard tarts too, and Kate was beginning to get desperate enough, prepared to use regular bribes to win his heart with food, as her mother had told her would work with any male. He was having a growth spurt, devouring everything within reach, and she'd taken to hiding things she wanted to keep for a later date or special occasion. The lamingtons were destined for the CWA meeting tonight. The long-awaited plans for the fire brigade were underway.

'Do I have to go? I am nearly nine, you know.' Riley moaned the drawn-out words like he was in pain, reluctant to look her way as his hands flopped by his side like a limp fish.

'Ah, yeah, I'm more than sure about that, buddy.' As if she would leave him home alone. He disappeared way too often when he was under her nose as it was. How did parents give enough freedom to their kids and yet have an invisible string tethered to them so they could tug them back when the time was right? The frustration of it all nipped at her conscience.

Riley looked her way and gave a top-notch eye roll she'd award an A plus to if she were his teacher before stalking towards his room, his dejected body slumping behind his closed door.

'He just wants a bit of independence,' Meg had told her at the café earlier that day when she'd arrived for her caffeine fix and a chinwag while he was at school.

Kate tightened her fingers in her hands, wishing she had a straightforward answer before responding to his effective non-verbal comeback. 'You might be nearly nine years old, but I'm still responsible for you.' She half-heartedly jabbed a finger at the hallway, lowering it in defeat. 'So, get ready for tea because we'll be leaving soon.'

She turned away, chastising herself for failing to keep the aggravation from her tone. He was a good kid. She just had to find a new way to reach him.

Kate spun around and headed back to the kitchen, inwardly kicking herself for forgetting Lexi's goodies sitting on the dining table. She'd planned to offer Riley one, but when their conversation took a turn up crooked avenue, she'd clean forgotten. Attempting to ease the headache that had a knack of turning up every time she needed to parent Riley, she moved to the kitchen and reached for a glass, filling it with tap water. She took a gulp, then stared out the window at her pillaged veggie patch. The fun police had taken sunny Auntie Kate away, and it worried her that she might never make an appearance again.

'Hey, Riles, I've got a treat for you,' she called from over her shoulder, listening for his door to open. But all remained quiet. She bit her bottom lip, instead removing the meat from the fridge for tea.

With sausages in bread tucked neatly in their bellies, Kate snatched up her basketful of lamingtons, heading for the door.

'C'mon Riley, or we'll be late.' When she'd asked him to clean his teeth, she didn't think it would take him a whole ten minutes and once again, the familiar niggle of guilt wriggled inside her. He didn't want to go. She wasn't looking forward to when he was a teenager, taller than her and prepared to stand his ground like she'd done to her parents.

Kate opened the front door and stilled, the absence of Monica causing an unsettling sense of loneliness she wasn't expecting.

She's back where she belongs, and that's a good thing. She nodded to herself. As annoying as the ewe was, she'd now given Gus an excuse not to drop in. But it was for the best, she convinced herself. She needed him out of the picture if she was going to have any chance of reconnecting with Riley.

When she'd moved the mob back to his home paddock early this morning, she'd been sure to latch the gate securely, dusting her hands with satisfaction. There was no way they could return unless someone—namely Riley—left the gate open.

Riley moved painfully slowly, stopping as he reached the front door, looking like he was about to be asked to forgo lollies forever. Kate's heart clutched tight as she stood at the open door of her car as it warmed up, offering a cautious smile. Why was he stopping?

'Could you take me to the surf shops in Torquay? I wanna get a wet suit.' His sad eyes pleaded with her.

'Why do you want one? No one swims this time of year. It's too cold.' Kate couldn't hide her surprise. Where had this come from?

'That's why I want one.' The frustration in his voice was building, and Kate bobbed her head back, staring at her nephew. What had got into him? He'd never asked to go to the beach when it was warmer. Why the sudden interest? Then it dawned on her.

'Gus said he'd . . .' Riley's voice trailed off, and he studied the verandah.

Kate left the car and went to him, bending down to reach for his hands, trying to catch his eye, but he shied from her, stepping away.

'Doesn't matter.' Riley shook his head as he moved past her to the car, his backpack dragging in the dust.

The drive over to Patsy's might have only taken ten minutes but it was a painfully quiet one. When Patsy opened the front door as Kate was reaching for the handle, her bright smile was exactly what she needed.

'C'mon in, Kate. Hi Riley.' She beamed down at him, his face still downcast.

Kate was relieved when Riley eventually lifted his head, offering Patsy a whisper of a smile as he stepped inside and found the beanbag she had ready for him. He plonked himself in it, staring at the puff of dust it stirred up in the air and Kate gave a helpless frown. Patsy patted her on the arm.

'Leave him be, love. I'll get Roger Dodger on the job. The poor old fella won't believe his luck being allowed inside. Ten to one, he'll lick Riley to death.'

Kate's cheeks were drawn downwards, but she nodded, sincerely hoping Roger could work his magic on Riley. Patsy went to the outside kitchen door. Before she'd fully opened it, the chocolate-coloured dog had pushed his nose through the opening and raced over to Riley, showering him in sloppy slurps and kisses as only a labrador could give.

Her breathing stilled as her nephew not only smiled but giggled freely, turning his face away as he tried to pat Roger. No one had warned her parenthood would be so tough, expecting she'd know what to do thanks to having lived with her nephew all his life. How had Jenna managed to survive while making it look so easy?

The chatter amongst the women held a constant hum, and Kate chuckled as Patsy's husband, Nige, poked his nose through the door to check on proceedings. He was a quiet man, the kind who avoided fired-up nattering women—at all costs. But the temptation of sweet treats was too much to pass up, and he slinked alongside the dining table, reaching for a lamington. No sooner had he taken a bite than the eagle eye of his wife, with her hands on her hips and her brow raised in his direction, had him making himself scarce once more.

'Okay, ladies, we should get down to business.' A hush came over the group and all the women turned their attention to Patsy. Brenda continued knitting.

'I'm relieved we're raising money for a new truck, I must say,' Nola said. 'I'm more than a little worried about the upcoming fire danger.' She took a sip of her tea before continuing. 'Graham keeps saying there's too much undergrowth.'

'Not to mention all the paddocks not being grazed around here,' Brenda chimed in. 'Gus needs to breed more sheep.' Her knitting needles click-clacked as she frowned, casting her gaze over the group. Several heads bobbed in agreement.

'It was only by luck that we weren't set alight again last summer,' Nola continued. 'Graham and the team ran around like jackrabbits putting out the embers from the Apollo Bay fires. Devastating business.' She shook her head. 'They were exhausted.'

'So, my question is, are we going to get enough money from a fair for a truck? They cost thousands, and it's not like the council, or the government for that matter, are going to buy us one. If we want a second truck, we're going to have to raise enough money to show them we're serious.' Nola paused to gauge the feeling in the room, looking at each of the women seated in a semi-circle. 'But Graham's gone over the books. He says we've only got a few thousand dollars and we need every cent of that for new hoses.'

Sensing an injection of enthusiasm was needed, she

continued. 'Remember all those terrific ideas we had, like cake stalls and the Forest Gully Princess pageant? I particularly want to see people chasing chooks along the beach. So, what ideas do we want to run with?' Nola looked expectantly around the group.

'I really want to watch the gumboot toss,' Kathleen said, leaning forward with a groan as far as her baby belly would allow. She reached for the last custard tart on the centre table, taking a bite as she settled back in her seat.

'I have some chickens about to hatch,' Riley piped up with a smile from his beanbag, where Roger was now lying asleep beside him, his head on Riley's thigh. The dog had definitely worked his magic, and the women all turned to him, approving his idea with warm grins and nods.

'That's wonderful, Riley. We'll definitely take you up on that.'

Riley nodded with zeal, and Kate's heart just about melted on the spot. *This kid,* she breathed, her hand over her chest.

The room fell quiet, but Kate's mind was ticking at supersonic speed. She glanced up with sudden inspiration.

'What if we ran a car wash?' Admittedly, the blank stares directed her way were a little unsettling. But there was merit in it. She continued before anyone could douse the idea. 'We could use the water from the fire truck to wash them. Or we could promote the fair on the beachfront.' She was desperate to keep them listening. 'If we publicised it widely, people would come and not only buy our produce but buy from the bakery and the General Store as well. It could get our little town some much-needed notability.' She shot Meg an encouraging gaze. 'I'm sure they'd stay and buy lunch from the café, and Hughey could do a sausage sizzle again. His sausages are legendary around here now. He could even run a mobile butcher with a portable cold fridge alongside it. People might taste how good they are and want to take some home. If we can make visitors feel like they want to come back again, they might bring others. And stay overnight at the caravan park.' It might be overgrown and dishevelled thanks to neglect, but it was nothing that a fast-acting working bee couldn't fix.

Kate's wide eyes glided from one woman to the next, willing them to respond. Just when she'd accepted her grand ideas were about to be canned, an eruption of voices all began at once.

'I love it, Kate,' Nola said.

'Will you run it?' Brenda said.

'Someone needs to start writing these ideas down.' Meg dug around for her pen and paper in her bag.

'We'll have to set a date soon,' Patsy said, glancing about the faces of the women with eagerness.

Kate sat back a little, a thankful smile rising on her lips as her gaze shifted from woman to woman. 'Fantastic,' she said in a voice loud enough to stem the excited chatter but not enough to dull it. Now, all they had to do was make it happen.

'Kate, this is just what we need,' Nola said, all smiles. 'Graham can take charge of the car wash. But my car is first in line!'

Unified laughter erupted, and chatter began again as the kettle boiled.

But the most crucial question in Kate's mind was about Gus. Would he be prepared to get on board with the town fundraiser this time? As much as she didn't want to admit it to herself, she liked spending time with him, and this was the perfect opportunity to do so.

'The guy point-blank refuses to open up, Meg.' Kate blew out an exasperated puff of air that lifted whisps of hair draped around her face as she rubbed her hands together to warm them. The café was quiet, not surprising given it was a brisk Tuesday morning.

Graciously taking the mug Meg handed her, Kate slipped her hands around its warmth, sipping her mocha as Meg made herself a latté before they moved to the table by the window. The crow cawed on the gutter above them.

'I mean, he comes over—' Meg's eyebrows lifted with interest. 'No, no. It's not like that. He comes to spend time with his best buddy, Riley.' She found it hard not to let her tone sound miffed.

'Sure.' Meg smirked before hiding it by taking another sip from her mug. 'Something's up with you two. I can feel it.'

Kate gave Meg a warning finger.

'Honestly, the guy won't talk about himself, ever. He's infuriating.' Didn't he get she was struggling, too? Would it hurt him to try and understand her? Her kisses didn't come for free. She was an all-in kinda girl, not one to waste her time or anyone else's with an airy fling that was going nowhere. Not that she was looking.

'You like him,' Meg teased as she let her eyebrows dance with double enthusiasm above her mug once more.

'How can you like someone who clams up the moment you choose to make yourself totally vulnerable? When I was telling him about Jenna, it was like he froze on the spot.'

'Well,' Meg's serious expression intensified, 'did he say anything about what happened to him?'

'No. Brenda said he lost everything.' Kate slowly blinked.

'Maybe it's because he does like you and is scared he won't be able to save you either . . . if something happened to you.'

'What are you talking about? I don't need saving.' She tried to ignore the warmth rising inside her at the idea he might care so much.

Meg nestled herself back into her seat, eyeing Kate for a moment before she continued.

'You remember how you told him the fire brigade was incredible when they were there for Jenna? Well, Gus made it to lieutenant, one rank below Hughey. But after the accident, he—'

'Gave up.' Kate finished her sentence, stealing a breath.

'And he blames himself.' Meg gave a sad nod.

'He'd been the model citizen when he'd saved Carl from the car. But when Gus couldn't open the driver's door—' Meg's voice trailed off, and Kate reached a hand towards her friend's, clamping it tight, leaning towards her.

'It was crushed, and there were fumes.' Meg's eyes grew wide, staring through Kate as they glazed over. 'The fire erupted, but Gus was desperate to get her out. He was burnt trying to save her.'

Kate's heart thudded as she drew back, her mind reanalysing the way Ash Evans had treated Gus that first day outside the café. She unknowingly rubbed her own forearms, unable to comprehend how he'd managed to get through the ordeal. Or had he? She was no psychologist, but she'd gone through counselling after Jenna had passed away. It had been one of the hardest things she'd ever done, but she was adamant that without it and the ongoing support around her, alongside the love of wonderful family and friends, she would've blamed herself over what had happened.

'But it wasn't his fault.' Kate's words faded as it dawned on her what Gus was going through, staring at Meg in disbelief. He had to believe that. There was nothing they could've done for Jenna. Fate was cruel sometimes. She'd suffered immensely from the guilt of being the one to rise before dawn, taking Riley on an early morning hike that fateful day while Jenna had slept a little longer. Kate's mouth dried, and the memories she worked to keep well away from the forefront of her mind were now taunting her like clinging tentacles. She'd never forget the fits of laughter they'd shared with Riley the night before around the campfire, eating sticky marshmallows and playing charades. She'd been Daffy Duck and Jenna had resorted to squatting like a duck, eventually quacking so she could guess who she was.

Kate clasped the locket around her neck that Jenna had worn, holding it tight. She missed her so much.

But there was nothing she could do to change what had happened, and the most important thing now was to love Riley with everything she had and keep him safe, even if it meant he'd hate her for it.

CHAPTER 30

The golden evening sky did little to temper Gus's mood as he stomped around to the back of his house. 'Where the hell have they gone this time?' He stood staring, disbelieving what his eyes were telling him, that his paddock was empty of the lambs and ewes he'd assured Kate were staying put for good.

This couldn't be happening. He lifted his hands to the top of his head. It was like some damned puzzle he couldn't solve, and he wanted to get to the bottom of it.

Speedy danced in front of him, eager to join in the anticipation of her owner's angst, laying a manky old tennis ball at his bare feet. They shouldn't be far, he tried to convince himself. They couldn't be. The occasional lamb calling to its mother echoed in the distance. But with the fresh ocean winds buffeting him, it made it near impossible to determine the direction the noise was coming from.

Gus squinted past the open paddock, concerned they may have found a way out on the far side of his property. If they had, it would mean they were roaming through council land, which was completely uninhabited, wild and, more concerningly, unfenced. Finding them would take a month of Sundays, not to mention how he was meant to get them back again, given his less-than-average stockmanship savvy.

But the call of another lamb in the air had him paying closer attention. He could've sworn it was in the direction of the boundary fence, and he took off at a sprint, heading towards the noise and believing they were hiding somewhere amongst the scrub.

But the more he hunted, the closer he found himself

approaching the gate between himself and Kate at the top of the cliff . . . still with no sign of them.

Speedy ran ahead, disappearing amongst the dense undergrowth where bracken fern had taken over. A rabbit darted out, side-swiping Gus with Speedy hot on its tail, making him jump to avoid her body knocking him off his feet.

'Speedy, no!' Gus forgot the sheep, taking off after her before pulling up in an abrupt skid, throwing his arms in the air as he puffed loudly. 'Great. Now I've got a missing dog to boot.' He blew out a puff of air, still wilfully hoping his missing sheep might simply be a figment of his imagination. They had to be under the next cluster of bushes, so he pressed on.

It was only when he arrived at the corner of the cliff that he accepted the inevitable, the evidence overwhelmingly clear. The gate was *open*.

Gus stood there, stumped. He scratched his ear as each scenario he thought through came up short. How? He'd checked it himself after Kate had put his sheep back the other night. Not even the wind could have jiggled the latch with enough intensity to unhinge it. He cursed under his breath, marching through the gate, setting a direct course for his neighbour's house. Maybe they were on their way to her verandah and he'd be able to intercept them, swing them around and have them heading for home before—

Gus broke through the scrub to the opening in front of her house, pulling up short at the sight before him. Not only were his sheep settling themselves in for yet another night at their favourite camping spot, but Kate was there, arms crossed, staring straight back at him.

Not the welcome he would have picked, if he had the choice.

And in that exact moment, he couldn't deny the way his heart thwacked inside his ribs as her eyebrow rose and her mouth threatened to reveal that damned assured smile, he was all too aware both antagonised and attracted him way too much.

'I see Monica missed me.' She held his gaze with her dry tone, and he lowered it, hoping the rapidly dulling light hid his reddening glow. He drew in a quiet breath to compose himself.

What should he say? That the ewe had extremely good taste? No. Way too revealing.

'I tried to warn her that hunting down your roses could mean certain demise, but she wouldn't listen.' He angled for humour—it might just work.

Kate burst out with a chuckle, and it sounded so good, he found himself smiling back, more out of loving the sound than the relief he might not be in too much trouble. How long had it been since he'd been able to make a woman laugh at something witty he'd said?

Too long. Until Kate.

But just as he sensed his body relaxing, she called out.

'Riley.' Her tone was immediately terse.

Gus made to step towards her, pretty sure he knew what she was thinking. He opened his mouth to speak when Riley came through the door and onto the verandah. Monica nudged past Gus's leg and waltzed inside with authority, leaving him with Kate who was now on the verge of shooting daggers, most definitely his way.

But as quickly as her intense gaze latched on to him, it shifted towards her nephew. 'What did I tell you about leaving the gate open, Riley? Now you'll have to go and help Gus get these sheep home.' He was grateful she didn't use the word "again" for the hundredth time. It was overused and, well, overused. She shook her head in frustration, marching towards her produce, which she was clearly worried might have been hoed into. Monica bleated from inside.

The look of sadness and hurt was clear on Riley's face and it threatened to break Gus. He had to do something.

'Kate. Wait.' Gus raised the palm of his hand, but the expression on her face as she looked over her shoulder, told him if he got much closer than he already was, she'd be willing to have a good go at ripping his ear off.

'It wasn't Riley.' His voice pleaded, and her steps slowed. She turned to him, her head tipped to the side, her eyes narrowing.

'So . . . it was . . . you, was it?' She angled for him to answer with her self-assured glare and I-knew-it eyebrow. He was certain Riley hadn't done it, especially after their chat the other day, but what other explanation was there? Regardless, he wasn't about to let her lay blame on the kid and give her more assumed ammunition to hold against him. Riley had enough to deal with.

'Look, I don't know how, but—'

'You don't know how?' Her mouth slackened, and he shifted his shoulders, urging the tightness in them to dissipate. He hated the way she crossed her arms over her chest, drawing his attention despite his efforts not to look.

'Okay,' he said with a low breath. 'I did it. I left it open last night after a walk. I'm sorry.' He held his hands in front of his chest, palms outwards as she studied him. What else could he say? Riley didn't deserve her anger. Neither of them did.

'Don't you know the rule about gates? If it's open, leave it open. If it's shut, re-*shut it.*' Her stare declared indignance along with disbelief. Would she ever cut them some slack? He couldn't see it happening anytime soon, thanks to his ratbag flock.

'Listen, Riley said he didn't do it. What's so hard to accept about that? Are you ever going to take him at his word?'

Had he gone too far? By the look in her eyes, yes. But the kid deserved to be given some kind of assurance that someone had faith in him rather than being blamed all the time.

'Oh, and you're qualified to decide for me? This coming from a guy who hides from the community and his friends, all because he's too scared to trust himself.'

Whoa. Gus took a step back as though her words had slapped him in the face. And they had. He frowned, unable to hide the shock and confusion rushing through his mind. What had possessed her to say something like that? But was she wrong?

No. He knew it.

Regardless, he had some kind of life to live, and it wasn't about to include her; of that he was damn sure. He'd lock that gate with a ten-tonne padlock for good measure to know she'd never blame Riley, or him, ever again.

'Now you've done it, Kate Harris.' She pushed the front door shut with her backside, leaning her weight against it as she hid her face in her hands, shaking her head. When she looked up, Monica eyeballed her from the top of the table with such accuracy that she knew the ewe had the complete upper hand. She was the queen of the dining table and Kate was her inadequate minion, there to serve her with one scant glance from those large brown eyes that locked onto her in a firm glare. If only a sheep could give her advice on how to retract the heartless words she'd so easily dished out to Riley and especially Gus, without meaning to. It was in the heat of the moment. And it resulted in her disgrace at her poor actions. She'd been defensive, certain it was the right thing to do. And yet now? Well there was no coming back. Mortification settled on her like a heavy woollen blanket.

Riley and Gus had urged the sheep to move, and she glanced at the mob through the front window as they disappeared into the scrub, heading towards the cliff gate, all except Monica. It seemed she'd decided to stay despite the consensus of the mob.

Kate tugged herself away from the door and pulled out the frying pan, throwing four lamb chops on to sizzle on high heat. She didn't care that Monica was joining them for dinner. In fact, the company would be kind of nice, given Riley was undoubtably going to give her the silent treatment tonight, and rightfully so.

She couldn't be bothered doing veggies, so she marched out to the veggie patch and picked the remaining scraps of some cos lettuce leaves Monica had so graciously left for her, a lonely tomato still hanging on by a twig before winter fully set in, and a poor excuse for a cucumber. With a bit of cheese and some dressing, this sad salad would have to do.

It was fully dark when Riley stepped through the front door, his movements stilted as he shied from her gaze. It took everything in her to bite her tongue and not growl about him taking so long, spending even more time with Gus. She couldn't lose Riley, too.

She took a step forward but held herself back from moving too close. All she wanted to do was reach out, put her hand on his head and hold him tight to her, never letting go. But that wasn't going to happen unless she said sorry. And she wanted to. But she worried if she did, he'd take it as an admission it was okay to lie. She couldn't apologise for wanting to teach him right from wrong.

'Riley, I—' Her words were lost, along with the confidence that she could be the person Jenna had trusted her to be. How had her sister ever believed she could be the kind of parent figure Riley needed? She'd failed. Riley's face told her so.

Kate envisioned the phone call to her parents, the one where she would eat humble pie and admit defeat, returning with no home because she'd have no choice but to sell up, with her tail between her legs. And then Riley might finally be happy.

The offensive smell in the air arrested her introspection and she spun around, racing towards the kitchen and her lamb chops.

'No, no, no!' She dived for the pan, removing it from the heat and dumping it in the sink. The sizzling chops were charcoal black as smoke filled the atmosphere.

She flapped her hands in the air to clear a way for her to see, spying Monica twisting her head around, baaing her disapproval, probably at the smell of charred lamb. She hoped the ewe understood from the stern finger pointing her way that she'd be next on their menu if she didn't keep her thoughts to herself.

But it was when Riley's sad eyes shifted from the sheep to hers for those few long seconds before he trailed down the hallway that her heart broke the most.

CHAPTER 31

The new day had started off far better than Kate had expected. Riley had actually looked at her when she'd said goodbye at the school drop-off. He might've given her his don't-think-this-is-over-by-a-long-shot look alongside it, but she was counting it as a win.

With her spirits lifted, Kate walked into the café all smiles. 'Morning,' she said.

But Meg's widening eyes as she approached arrested her.

'Is there a spider on my head?' Satisfactorily scaring herself, she swiped at her hair, jumping back, straight into a body that, with the six-pack she felt, was definitely not Graham or Neil.

Spinning around to apologise, looking more like Cousin Itt from the *Addam's Family* with the imaginary spider still inching its way down her shoulder, she took in a surprised breath, her hands gripping his lower arms. Her eyes locked with his. He was warm to the touch, and when she moved her fingers subtly over his skin, he flinched.

'Gus.'

Interest flickered across his face as though she'd intrigued him, not disappointed him, and Kate gulped a breath to gather her composure. No, her racing heart. No, more like her outrageous delight at seeing his face.

'Um.' She wet her lips, her cheeks igniting with heat, grateful her hair hid most of it.

What should she say after the way she'd treated him last night? *I'm sorry.* No, not enough.

How about *I was an idiot?* Hmmm, getting closer, she acknowledged to herself. She pressed her eyes shut. Could she just disappear instead? She opened one eye, reluctantly searching his face. Not a chance was the uncomplicated answer.

'Morning, Gus,' Meg said. 'Your usual?'

'Ah, yeah. Thanks,' he said, his eyes remaining on Kate, reading her like she was some novel he was completely engrossed in. They were still touching. A rush of adrenalin coursed through her veins, leaving her stomach in knots.

With her feet frozen to the floor, all she could do was blink. Even when Meg curled around the counter to pass a mug of mocha to her, she had to force her hand to let go of his. Why was it that every time she came to hang out with Meg, he managed to hang around like some sexy sea urchin looking for someone to love?

Love? She didn't just say that, and she stepped back, risking a sip of her drink, knowing full well she'd score a burnt tongue for it. In all her dizziness, she'd still picked Meg had taken longer than required to heat the milk.

'Gus is fond of mocha's too, Kate. Were you aware of that?'

His mouth twisted in a shy smile as he released her remaining hand that was still clenching his. He took a step back, accepting the coffee from Meg.

Annoyance flared in Kate at the way Meg kept her voice all innocent and cute. When she did manage to get herself out of this pickle, she and her soon-to-be unfriended friend would be having words. She'd blurted out her heart and soul along with several tears and a red nose only days ago, only to have Meg try and couple them up? Kate's mouth moved up and down helplessly.

Mocha? Her brain fought to catch up. 'He is?' She shoved the hair from her face.

'Got rather fond of them after you bought him one. Remember?'

Kate's eyes were now at bulging status. 'What are you

trying to do?' she mouthed to her friend as she turned her back to Gus, but like it was water off a duck's back. Meg continued making her own drink.

Traitor. Kate's face twisted with annoyance, frustration and a fair share of exasperation as she glared at Meg. He'd want to disown her after the way she'd treated him, not get together with her.

'I've padlocked the gate,' he offered gently, stepping up beside her at the counter, his expression telling her he wanted to say more but refrained.

'Oh.'

Gus nodded his thanks to Meg for the mocha, paid for it, and then left the shop without another word.

And against all the meddling images swimming around in her mind, only one kept floating to the forefront. And it involved the way Gus had smiled at her with understanding.

And how much she was going to miss it.

'Seriously?' Kate whispered, leaning closer to Meg by her kitchen sink so the other CWA women couldn't hear. 'I can't ask him, not after everything I said.' Kate stole a glance behind her with caution, wishing Meg would keep her voice down. These women were a mixed bag, but every one of them was as sharp as a tack. If they so much as sniffed a romance within the ranks, she'd be toast. And it wasn't true. Fortunately for her, Patsy, Erin, and Brenda were sufficiently distracted by Kathleen's new baby girl cradled in Nola's arms. Lexi was licking her fingers from the vanilla slice Kate had made earlier.

Meg took a seat on the dining chair she'd dragged over to the coffee table in Kate's lounge, and Kate followed. Patsy had the flu, so they'd all converged on her place as tonight's venue. The fire brigade fair was getting closer and they needed to sort out the finer details.

'Yes, you can. What's the worst he can do?' Meg raised her cup of tea for another sip, her voice still too loud for Kate's liking.

'Don't look at me like that,' Kate whispered in a harsh tone and she turned away, wishing someone needed another cup of tea even though she'd just finished the rounds.

'Besides, he'll only say no.' To her own surprise, she recognised the note of sadness in her voice. Since when had she been worried about someone turning her down, especially over a fundraiser? There was always someone else to fill the gap. But she wanted Gus to be involved, believing maybe it would help him deal with his demons.

'Just ask him,' Meg urged, raising her eyebrows in a way that drove Kate mad. For a good friend, she sure was pushy, especially when her hunky next-door neighbour was involved.

'Alright,' Kate said in a hissy voice that was louder than she'd intended, her eyes widening as the rest of the group went quiet, directing their attention towards her. She straightened, her wary eyes landing on each woman, offering them an awkward chuckle, heat rushing over her cheeks as she tried to hide them behind her cuppa.

'So,' Kate piped up, desperate for a change of topic, 'we've set the date. The fundraising fair will be on the sixteenth of May, next month.' The art of distraction worked like a charm and the ladies pivoted. But that didn't stop Brenda, Nola, Erin, and Kathleen from exchanging intrigued looks between themselves in the meantime.

Focus, Kate. The man's no good for you.

'How much do we need to raise to make sure Fire Rescue Victoria helps us?' Brenda said, not missing a stitch.

'Graham was told we'd need at least eight thousand dollars,' Nola said.

There was stunned silence amongst the group. Kate hadn't expected the figure to be quite so high, but then again, trucks weren't cheap.

'Well, we'll just have to make extra sure it's a fair not to be missed,' Kate said, ploughing on with the meeting in Patsy's place. 'I'll make up some flyers and distribute them to places like Torquay and Apollo Bay. I'm going to Geelong so I'll take some there too. The wider the word is spread, the better the turnout might be.'

Kate breathed in a shaky sigh, taking a seat once more, desperate to push Gus's rosy windblown cheeks to the back of her mind and throw away the key. So, she sat down and stuffed a piece of vanilla slice into her mouth.

The ladies began to chatter amongst themselves again, and movement from the corner of her eye drew her attention. Riley had strayed from his room, heading for the bathroom. Was he a little pale, or was it their poor lighting? She reminded herself to get new light bulbs with stronger wattage for all the rooms in the house.

Kate gave a baffled frown. He'd appeared okay earlier. Didn't kids do that sometimes, seeming flat for no good reason? But she struggled to push aside her concern.

To make up for tonight, she'd promised him a Friday night fishing session at the beach tomorrow. She'd thought it would be fun to give him some practice for the fishing competition at the fair, but he'd shown little interest. She'd have to ask Graham if he'd come along.

Kate didn't finish the last of the dishes off until well after eleven that night, leaving them to drip dry in the drainer on the sink. She hadn't been able to unwind after all the excitement and planning they'd completed. If they could show Fire Rescue

Victoria they would do everything they could to raise funds, they might come to the party and help them get that second truck they needed, even if what they raised was below the suggested amount.

The wind picked up outside, rattling the branches as she tugged out her laptop, opening a fresh Word document, her mind coming up blank for a few minutes. How exactly could she make the fundraiser wildly appealing to entice crowds from near and far?

With fingers to the keys, she began scanning images. It had to be eye-catching and it had to have everything they were planning on offering or selling. She settled on a beautiful photo of the beach she'd snapped when she'd first arrived in Forest Gully. It was the perfect background to advertise the fair.

Kate's eyes were hanging out of her head by the time she'd finished, but the mock-up poster was done. *Not a bad job, Kate Harris,* she chimed, admiring the poster one last time before closing her computer. Now, all she had to do was drop by Patsy's and get her to print off some colour copies. Then she'd head off and deliver them on her round trip to buy more pots and soil ready for her new seedlings to grow in.

CHAPTER 32

Kate stretched in the driver's seat as Riley hopped from the car, his back to her as he walked away. Her heart sank. He was pale, and he had a sniffle but nothing bad enough to stay home for. He was prone to hay fever, and she was sure that's all it was, reminding herself to get some **antihistamine** tablets for him from the General Store.

'Have a good day,' she called from the wound-down window, but her words fell on deaf ears as Riley walked across the oval at a pace enviable to a snail. He still wasn't the least bit excited about their fishing adventure, even when she'd pumped it up with the promise of Twisties and chocolate. Kate pressed a hand to her forehead and closed her eyes, willing her pulsating headache to subside.

The sun was shimmying over the white-tipped waves, the wind buffeting her car as she made her way to Patsy's along the Great Ocean Road, the reflection making her head throb all the more. She parked, then walked to the store, skipping over a fallen branch lying on the curb.

'Morning, Patsy,' Kate smiled. 'I sent you a link for the poster last night, well, this morning, actually. Did you get it?'

'Hi, Kate. I most certainly did. They're printing as we speak. Thought I could pop them in letterboxes on my postie run.'

'Great idea. I might grab myself a coffee while I wait. Think I'm going to need a few to get through today.' She gave a tired chuckle. 'Would you like one?'

'No thanks, dear. I've had my one for the day, and that's enough for me. But take these copies already printed if you like. Might want to put them up in the café and the bakery on your way.'

Patsy passed Kate a few copies of the poster. 'I love the beach background.'

'Thanks, Patsy. Let's just hope it works.'

The wind shook the posters in her hand as she briskly walked to the café, shoving the door open with her hip. It was humming with the chatter of a few customers, and Meg looked up with a smile as Kate made a show of looking longingly at the coffee machine.

'I'm desperate,' Kate said, letting her arms lay over one another on the counter and placing her head on top of them.

'I can see that,' Meg said with an understanding giggle, firing up the machine.

With her mocha in hand, she diligently dropped off flyers to Lexi and then Nige at the hardware store.

It was early afternoon, and she was in the outskirts of Geelong delivering the last of the flyers when her mobile rang.

'Yes, okay. I'm a bit far away, so I'll send someone soon.' She hung up, the call deflating her improving mood. The school had rung. Riley needed to be picked up. He'd made a turn for the worse, and she was nowhere near Forest Gully. She'd promised Hughey she'd book a portable cold fridge, wanting to see them for herself, but decided to look online instead and ring to book. Her mouth tightened in a knot. How was she meant to do everything, let alone do it well?

Kate pressed her fingers to her nose, urging some great plan to come to her, her heart filling with concern. Who could she ask to pick him up so he wouldn't have to sit in the school nurse's office for the next hour or two alone until she could get to him? An overwhelming urge to hug him came over her, and she sniffed back the emotion rising hot and fast.

But who could she contact? Nola . . . no. When she'd dropped by the General Store this morning, she and Graham were unloading stock for the store. It was an all-day job, apparently.

Brenda . . . no. She'd likely try and make Riley wind up copious balls of wool.

Patsy . . . now that was a worthwhile consideration. She would have finished her mail run by now. Riley loved Roger Dodger. But that was no good either. Patsy was leaving for Adelaide to visit her brother.

Gus . . . Absolutely not.

Meg . . . she was the last one on her list who didn't have other children who Riley could infect if this was, in fact, some kind of flu bug he had. But Meg was too busy with the café. She couldn't expect her to have a sick kid in a shop where customers were coming and going.

Kate scrunched up her face, desperately trying to block out the image of the one person who would be able to help and the *only* name she didn't want to ring.

'Thanks, Gus.' She hung up the phone, a mixture of humiliation and annoyance clinging tight. Of course he was happy to pick up Riley. Why wouldn't he be? They were besties. The thought niggled, but he was getting her out of her pickle, which she was grateful for.

Kate's urgency to get home grew the closer she got to Forest Gully, relief swathing her as she pulled into Gus's driveway. The new gate was open—wonders never ceased—and her tyres bounced over the abundant potholes and sand lining Gus's driveway.

All was quiet, almost too quiet, as Kate knocked on his door, her fist hovering in the air as she turned to check out the paddock with his sheep and lambs in it. The only member of the flock missing was Monica, and besides the fact that Gus had padlocked the gate, Kate wasn't in any rush to return her. She was the size of a house, thanks to her belly swelling with a lamb, or two, but the ewe was keeping her company and didn't show any urgency to rush back to the flock.

The door swung open, making Kate jump.

'Oh, hey.' She couldn't help but give a nervous smile, relieved she was here for Riley and not just her good-looking neighbour. Her senses awakened immediately at the sight of a bare chest toned to perfection—and those abs . . . she glanced away quickly—from surfing. If she thought he'd been breathtaking when walking back from a surf, his hair bedraggled and his wetsuit resting on his swaying hips, then now, dressed in jeans that fitted insanely well, she was captivated.

He tugged on the T-shirt in his hands, then rested his shoulder against the door frame, studying her with those deep eyes she'd melt under if she allowed herself half a chance. And the way he smelt of sandalwood and lemongrass . . . she wasn't sure she should step inside for fear it wouldn't be safe. A distinct heat inched its way over her cheeks, and she shied from his gaze.

'Uh, how is he?' She desperately wanted to get inside, see Riley and give him the hug she'd been holding in her heart, and break the moment she was utterly sure Gus was also feeling happening between them. Thankfully, he stepped aside, urging her in with a wave of his arm. The air was charged between them as she brushed past. She closed her eyes, secretly soaking it in.

Allowing her eyes to adjust to the darkness inside, she recognised the comforting smell of chicken soup. Riley lay on the couch, fast asleep, a box of tissues next to him. Speedy rested beside him, her head on his legs. The dog watched Kate approach, her tail softly slapping the blanket.

'I gave him a cool drink of lemonade, and he was out like a light. Wouldn't eat a thing.'

Kate's insides squirmed, feeling Gus's eyes on her, unable to pluck up the courage to meet his gaze for fear fresh heat would rush back to her face. So she nodded instead, staring lovingly at her nephew. He looked so peaceful. Should she leave him here where he was settled or wake him and take him home? She was certain he'd be happier here with Gus, the thought sobering.

Kate looked about her, curiously taking in Gus's home. Everything in his shack was simple and necessary, nothing more. It was a bachelor's pad, and she couldn't help but feel it lacked something, like the small things that made a house a home.

'Would you like a drink? I'm making coffee.' He headed towards the kettle, setting it to boil, looking as equally uncomfortable as her. When he faced her again, his smile was kind, genuine.

Kate opened her mouth to speak before the deep sparkle in his eyes managed to steal her voice. She'd admired them from the moment she'd met him, but right now, they were gazing at her with an intensity she couldn't decipher, much like when he'd kissed her at his sheep yards. She'd thought they'd spoken of tenderness, even yearning, but now she wasn't sure.

'Um, coffee would be great.'

She took a seat, staring at Riley's chest as it rose and fell peacefully. A soft smile crept over her face, and she was grateful for the distraction. Why had she agreed to stay for a cuppa? Thank goodness she wasn't alone with him. Her crazed emotions would never cope.

Twisting her lips together, she offered Gus a brief smile as she struggled with what to say once she'd thanked him for her drink and he sat down opposite her.

'I reckon you could do with a plant in here. It would spruce the place up a bit. Succulents are easy enough to keep.' She cautiously side-eyed him, not trusting herself to face him front on as she caught another waft of his scent.

'Plants take one look at me and shrivel up on the spot.' He

chuckled, causing her own smile to rise. He couldn't be that bad, could he?

The room fell silent again, its awkwardness making Kate shift in her seat. They might have butted heads in the past, but it was always with a sense of underlying teasing towards one another, warm and well-intended, something she loved about him. Where had that gone?

'Thanks for picking Riley up for me. I was dropping off flyers for the fair.'

His relaxed brow morphed into a wary scowl that hovered, stealing the smile from her lips.

'I'm sorry.' Guilt consumed her, and she looked away. 'I forgot to tell you. We're doing another fundraiser.'

'Oh. How fun. What for this time?' The cynicism in his voice was all too clear, and she lifted an eyebrow his way.

'Our firies in Forest Gully. We're aiming to raise enough money to get Fire Rescue Victoria to pitch in and buy us a new truck.' There was a moment where Kate was sure she'd seen a flash of horror whip across his face before he checked himself, disguising it.

'Right.' He took another sip of his coffee, cringing as if it had burnt his tongue. Her eyes narrowed. Especially after everything he'd gone through, this had to be a good thing.

'You'll help, won't you?' She waited to catch his eye, but he refused to look her way.

'Bit busy that day.'

'You don't even know the date.' Her nice-try smile crept softly onto her lips, hoping it would encourage him to change his tune.

'Doesn't matter.' He continued to avoid eye contact.

'Yes, it does, Gus. This town is for all of us. And you know we need another fire truck.'

His face turned grey, and Kate sat forward in her seat. She reached out, touching the top of his hand. Her heart ached for the painful reminder his burns had to bring him every day.

He lightly shook his head, his eyes still hazed and distant, but her gentle words drew him back.

'You know the team would come if there was a fire threatening this place. They'd be here in a heartbeat.'

'Don't talk to me about heartbeats, alright?' He looked up at her so directly that a deep shiver raced over her body. He let her hand fall away. 'I said no, and that's the end of it.' He stood, walking to the kitchen and tipping most of his coffee down the sink. 'Too hot to drink anyway,' he muttered.

Kate took the hint and stood, wishing she didn't have to wake Riley, wishing Gus could see reason. Her eyes flicked across the rug on the floor as she dug deep for her confidence.

'Would you like to talk about it?' From her experience, speaking about the things that threatened to break you was the best medicine.

'Listen, I don't need a lecture from you about why I make the decisions I make, and I don't need your help. So just let it go, alright?' Gus pressed his hands heavily on the edge of the sink, his back to her.

She wasn't about to leave like this.

'But you—'

'But nothing.' He spun around to face her. 'This conversation is done.' He walked to Riley, rousing him. 'C'mon, buddy. Time to go home.'

'Okaaay.' The breathy word escaped Kate's mouth, and she stood, shocked. Was he kicking them out? All because he didn't want to front up to his demons?

'Isn't it about time you put your selfish fears aside and got on board for the better good of the community?'

'And what's that, Kate? I'm the legendary hero turned zero, the one who couldn't save his fiancée. What more do you want? There are people in this town who don't want me. The only reason I'm here is because I can't afford to go anywhere else.'

CHAPTER 33

Gus gave her the cold shoulder, pressing his fingers to his eyes, and Kate inwardly gasped. She hadn't meant to break him. She only wanted to wake him up to how he was acting and to make him see some sense. She gave a slow nod, regretting how the night had ended but relieved Riley had fallen back to sleep without hearing a word.

The bloody nerve.

Gus forced himself not to slam the door as Kate's rear lights disappeared down his driveway. Like the previous night, the wind was picking up pace, blowing rogue leaves inside his doorway.

Slumping on the couch and far from ready to face the real cause of his eternal fear—why he could never forgive himself—he snatched the remote, turning on the TV before promptly turning it off again with a jab of the remote. Nothing she could say was going to change his decision because, as of this moment, he was stepping right back, further than he already had, out of sight of the community that, deep down, he knew he loved. He was the guy who'd let everything he'd been taught in an emergency fly out the door in one agonisingly crucial moment.

The memory of that pivotal day rocketed back to him like it was yesterday, hitting him with the same intensity of emotion and panic. They'd been ordered to evacuate, the bushland surrounding them alight and moving towards them with fearful speed. Gus's heart rate sped up. He'd been travelling behind Kelly and Carl as they took the inland exit rather than the Great Ocean Road. They'd been ahead of the main fire front at that stage, and taking this route meant they'd have more escape options if one road became impenetrable by fire. But then a bloody wombat had to scuttle onto the road, wild-eyed and skittish.

Gus shielded his face with his hands as he recalled Kelly's shining eyes. It was her love for others and her knack for knowing just what to do for them that had been so attractive to him. She'd helped him become the man he'd wanted to be. She'd been loyal to a fault, but who was he? Nothing but the one who'd betrayed that loyalty.

Sucking in a gulp of air as his stinging tears flowed with ease, he dragged both hands down his face, a deep sob surging from his throat. How could he have forgotten the critical training he'd been taught to attend to the most seriously injured first? But in his panic, and his blind love for her, he'd foolishly listened to her begging him to help Carl first. Would things have turned out any different had he done what he'd been taught and dismissed her pleas?

Would she still be here?

Or would Carl be dead too?

The same sickness that hit the pit of his stomach every time he slipped up, remembering, came over him with agonising familiarity. After that fire, residents left in droves. It was the final straw for so many who'd endured past catastrophes like it. And he knew why.

While havoc and devastation had afflicted their township—a risk you chose to accept if you wanted to live here—with homes lost and stock destroyed, townsfolk accepted they could rebuild, choosing to because of the Otway's stunning tranquillity and beauty. It had been many years since a person had died, so losing someone they'd all loved dearly was beyond heartbreaking.

Ash Evans had every right to hold his bitterness with an iron grip. It's exactly what Gus deserved. He'd be content as the hermit of the town where no one knew his business. Now, he just had to stick to it. Then, just maybe, he could manage to live with himself.

Gus squinted against the early morning brightness shining into his room. Pushing the doona aside, he let his feet hit the floorboards, his toes curling at their coolness.

Dressed only in his boxers, he scruffed his bedraggled locks as he yawned and walked through to the kitchen, reaching inside the fridge for the orange juice. He set it down, resting his hands on the sink, peering out of the window with tired blinks. More branches to clean up, he murmured to himself as Speedy came to stand beside him, pressing her head against his leg.

That suited him just fine, because today, he was going back to living as the old Gus.

With his OJ in his hand, he stepped outside and stood under his verandah. Thank goodness his sheep were still in the paddock, the lambs bounding around a large fallen branch big enough to act as a tunnel obstacle. The ewes had their noses down, nibbling the dewy grass with such content it made him envious. Speedy broke his trance, nuzzling his free hand.

'Yeah, girl, I'll feed you. Then we might go for a swim, hey?' No need to start a job that wasn't going anywhere. He had all the time in the world now.

Speedy wagged her tail as her tongue lolled from her mouth, smiling up at him.

'Well, at least you like me.' He rubbed her on the head, relieved her enthusiasm for hanging around him never seemed to diminish.

While Speedy gobbled up her breakfast, Gus went to make a coffee so he could face the day. 'Ah, damn it,' he growled, looking at the empty jar he'd forgotten he'd finished off yesterday when Kate had arrived, exacerbating his annoyance at both her and his fate in life. Would he ever catch a break, or was this how it was always going to be?

Speedy stopped eating, licking her lips clean and looking up at him with a quizzical tilt of her head. He slowly blinked at her, letting out a long sigh. Contrary to his grand pledges last night, now he had no choice but to go down the street.

Gus chose to park down the side road in between the block of shops, hoping his discreet hiding spot would keep him from certain prying local eyes. He strolled towards the café as casually as he could, his eyes not veering anywhere other than his destination. It was only when he went to push the door open that a poster loomed in front of him on the glass door, stopping him in his tracks.

He gritted his teeth. It didn't matter how much he tried to avoid the goings-on in Forest Gully, he couldn't escape them, or more directly, *her*.

Kate Harris. At the thought of her caring disposition, her dancing eyes and her cheeky smile, his heart somersaulted. But hang on one minute. He was not about to be thwarted by her motives and good intentions for this town or for him. He was free to do as he chose and live the life that suited him. Couldn't she just stay out of it and leave him alone?

Frustrated, he shoved the door open harder than necessary, marching up to the counter.

'Just a mocha, Meg.' His words were terse before he lifted his head, realising Meg was gazing at him with more than astonishment. Her eyes narrowed on him.

'Well, someone got out the wrong side of bed this morning.' She leaned forward, and he didn't miss the guilt she was nudging his way.

'Please,' he corrected himself with a curt tweak of his head. Since when was he rude to Meg? Like never. He offered a regretful shake of his head. 'Sorry, Meg. Didn't sleep well last night.'

'That's easy to pick.' He looked her way once more, and she offered a kind smile.

'So, are you going to help?' Meg's questioning eyebrows lifted as she warmed the milk, watching him closely. He didn't like where the question was leading.

'With what?' He could play dumb.

'I saw you checking the poster out. So, are you?' Her keen eyes dared him to say yes, even begged. Turning down Meg was like never eating dessert again.

'Bit busy that day.' His weight shifted from one foot to the other. Why was she taking so long to make his coffee?

'You could donate some more sheep poo. It was a hit at the cinema night, a lot like Margot was actually.' Her cheeky grin almost undid him. He wouldn't have minded seeing *Barbie* if they'd screened it somewhere else, and he could watch it alone.

'Kate was floored by the enthusiasm and demand for it. I bet you'd sell a lot more if—'

'Sorry, Meg. Like I said, unavailable.' Forever. He looked away.

'Oh, okay.' Meg dragged out the word with a slow nod, as though she was playing along. She passed him his coffee, and in his haste to pick it up and get out of there, he swivelled on the spot, just about spilling the hot beverage down the front of—

'Kate.' His eyes grew wide.

Where the hell had she come from? He hadn't heard the doorbell. He hadn't noticed much at all other than the guilt poking him fair in the chest with a gnarly finger. And forget that damned gorgeous smile he didn't need or want, especially when it sent his body into a jitter and his mouth dry.

'You're in a hurry,' she grinned, tucking her chin into her neck, checking the front of her top. He followed her gaze, and when their eyes met again, her cheeks flushed, a low smile lifting his own.

'Um, yeah, I am.' He peeled his eyes away, feeling like an idiot for gawking at the most beautiful woman he'd ever seen. How did she undo him with such ease? He rolled his lips tight against his oncoming flush of embarrassment.

He stepped sideways to pass, but when he reached the door, he hesitated, talking over his shoulder. It was safer that way.

'Has Monica outstayed her welcome? I'll come over and get her if you'd like.'

He gave a disbelieving chuckle to himself at the fact the other sheep hadn't escaped since he'd padlocked the gate, glancing at Kate's profile from the corner of his eye. Her arms were crossed, watching him closely. He let his glance drop away.

'You might need to leave that thought a little longer now.'

Gus summoned the courage to look back at her. 'Why?'

'Well, I've kinda grown fond of her, but this morning she went into labour. She's had twins.'

So, just when he'd believed it was possible to cut all ties with his hottie next-door neighbour, his damned sheep kept the pendulum swinging, tethering them together longer than he thought he'd be able to cope with. Was he happy about this? Hell no. The risk of letting himself believe otherwise was fraught with too much danger.

Gus drove home, his coffee bitter, matching his mood. Thanks to his blasted neighbour rattling him yet again, he'd left town without a new jar of coffee.

CHAPTER 34

The crisp ocean breeze floated gently over Kate's face, and with the warmth of the sun, she soaked it in with a smile as she walked towards the bakery. She sipped her mocha, still grinning as she lowered the cup from her lips to push open the door. She spied Lexi out the back, pulling out the next batch of bread from the oven. The aroma was divine, making her hunger pains pinch. Hughey nodded goodbye to a customer as she strode up to the counter.

'Great effort with the poster, Kate. Customers are already talking about the event.' He threw a large cut of rump meat onto the cutting board and began to expertly slice it.

Kate thought back to Gus, regretful he'd left in such a hurry from the café. She'd wanted him to stay longer, talk about coming over to visit Monica, show him her babies— Have him over for tea again. She'd thought having the ewe at her place was the perfect opportunity for him to do that. But the way he'd left just now, perhaps there wasn't a chance for them after all. She pushed away the flurry of regret rummaging inside her chest.

'Hughey, do you reckon Gus might run the car wash if I ask him? We could use the water from the fire truck. That way, everyone would remember what we are raising money for.'

Hughey's eyes flicked to her from the steaks he was carving, and he shook his head slowly, doubt all over his face.

'I don't reckon so. Sorry, Kate. The truck is kinda like his nemesis. The day that happens . . . well, actually, it probably won't.'

'Oh.' Genuine disappointment welled inside her.

'Gus believes he let our team down because he didn't follow protocol. But nothing could be further from the truth.'

'Then he was a hero.'

'Not in his eyes.' Hughey stopped cutting the meat. 'Months before the fire and Kelly's crash, he'd saved Brenda's grandson from drowning in a rip this side of The Point. At the time the whole town kinda put him up on a pedestal. But to his credit, he never let it go to his head.'

Hughey's words went straight to Kate's heart, and she was powerless to look away. From the day she'd met Gus, she'd been drawn to his smiling eyes, teasing grin, and impenetrable exterior, which she was gradually chipping away at. Now more than ever, she wanted him at the fair to help. But above that, to be near her. Regardless of him pushing her away, she felt safe around him, like he'd look out for her and Riley at all costs.

'When Kelly passed away, she'd lost a lot of blood. The crash had ruptured the fuel line, which made things so much worse than the bushfire already pounding down on us. Gus tried desperately to get her out, but the door was jammed.' He stopped to take a deep breath, and Kate could see the pain on his face from the memory.

'It wouldn't have mattered what he did, Kate. We'd almost exhausted our water reserve fighting the fire. Even if he'd been able to open the door—' He shook his head slowly. 'She could never have been retrieved, not before the explosion. There was nothing any of us could have done. There was no time. But Ash still blames him for it.'

'Ash couldn't see it wasn't Gus's fault?'

'Gus was there. To Ash's way of thinking as a parent, Gus should have saved them both.'

Kate's chest tightened as she listened. It wasn't right, but it made sense why Ash acted the way he did around Gus. That's why

Gus held his fears so damned tight, refusing to get on board whenever she'd asked. A wave of guilt filled her for being too hasty in her judgment. She wanted to take her words back, but he'd made it clear he preferred she stayed away.

'He refuses to be a part of the team now.' Hughey gave an empty stare. 'But I guess I can't blame him.'

It was so different to her experience. The whole community had gathered around in grief and in celebration of Jenna's beautiful life cut short by a tragedy that could happen to anyone.

CHAPTER 35

Another week had flown by when Kate arrived home after dropping Riley off at school. She swung by Patsy's to collect the parcel her mother had sent. Now, sitting down at the dining table with the package, a sense of nostalgia and sadness rose in her. She laid her hands on the box as though she might sense the love it came with, acutely missing her parents and their doting ways, especially when it came to Riley.

She opened it, putting aside the pairs of socks and chocolate for Riley, smiling as she took hold of her mother's original recipe book. Copies were okay, but the real thing? Her heart skipped a beat.

There was a letter attached to it. She opened the envelope, retrieving the note.

Dearest Kate,

Here is my cherished recipe book for you to keep. I don't seem to be cooking as often with you and Riley gone, and Dad only complains he's getting rounder by the day and is unwilling to waste anything I make. Such a sweet tooth, which is probably where you get it from!

On the page I marked with Riley's name, there's a recipe he always loved. It's my special lasagne, and he swore it was the best he'd ever tasted. I'm sure it's the only one he's ever had, mind you. So, I thought you might like to make it for him.

Miss you, love.

Hugs and kisses,

Mum xoxo

Oh, Mum. Kate hugged the book to her chest, not realising

a tear had trickled down her cheek until she felt it drip from her chin. This book was entwined with memories of her childhood with Jenna, of spreading too much flour over the kitchen bench and using cookie cutters to make gingerbread. Then there were the cupcakes she'd always managed to convince her mother needed just that bit more chocolate than the recipe suggested to make them taste perfect.

Opening the pages randomly, a reminiscent smile graced her cheeks. She ran her fingers over the dried cake mix and grease marks, which were now permanent features of so many of the pages. These were treasured memories, a tender reminder of how much she missed her parents, her home. Jenna.

She held the book in front of her, staring at the tatty cover as more tears spilled. She sniffed, glancing at the note once more. Without a doubt, she could read between her mother's words, the heartache and longing, that she wanted them to come home to Tenterfield. Riley should have been growing up with grandparents who would teach him right from wrong, the same way they'd done for Jenna and her. The temptation to go home and let her mother make the lasagne tugged at her and she could almost smell it. If she did, there'd be relief in knowing Riley was being looked after with a wealth of experience, something she couldn't offer him. But Jenna had believed in her unreservedly.

Placing the recipe book on the table in front of her, she picked up the envelope, returning the note. She tapped the letter on the palm of her opposite hand as her mind whirred with an idea. What if she put gift boxes together to sell at the farmgate? Excitement at being able to share her produce in a new way gave her a light-headed giddiness. She'd given one to Erin when she'd come home from Melbourne after spending a week caring for her sick sister. Erin was single, and she'd included her white chocolate macadamia biscuits and a quick re-heat spaghetti Bolognese meal along with some homemade scones and a dozen eggs. She'd even managed to scramble together a tiny posy of her flowers that hadn't been ravished by Monica and Co. Erin had been delighted. She'd also given Kathleen a baby-themed one, stealing the celebration at the baby shower. The idea had to have merit.

Kate picked up her phone. She needed to sound it out, and there was only one person to call.

'I love it, Kate. If you want, you can sell some in the café. Maybe the ones that have more perishable goods in them? That way, they'd sell faster and not be exposed to the elements at your front gate.'

Elation, sincere and deep, filled Kate that Meg loved the concept. But achieving it would mean sourcing boxes and ordering stickers with The Seaside Bouquet printed on them. She'd already spent hours designing her logo, with tufts of beach grass on the left and a hand-drawn box with a bottle of homemade lemonade cordial, biscuits, and fruit. If she could buy boxes of various shapes and sizes, she could put the sticker on the front for advertising and wrap the contents in cellophane with a ribbon. Kathleen had a huge lemon tree, and Riley's friend's mum, Jenny, made handmade cards. She could commission her to design some. The more professional they came across, the better the appeal.

It was in the darkness of the new day when Kate closed her laptop, her mind exhausted but exhilarated by the vast array of boxes available online and her ideas spilling from her mind like a fountain. She wanted her gift boxes to be unique, customisable, and made especially for every occasion. She could even get some ready for the fundraiser if she got a wriggle on. She just needed to talk to the ladies at their next meeting. If they could contribute with their knitted garments, it would be another avenue for them to share their talents and get paid at the same time.

Gus pulled up outside his front gate, having seen Meg for an extra early mocha and two of Lexi's custard tarts, his eyes narrowing like an eagle about to nab its first unexpecting mouse of the day. What on earth was that confounded woman up to now? Obviously, Riley was the gofer, delivering whatever hair-brained scheme she'd concocted. The poor kid's wheelbarrow was so overloaded that he struggled to keep it upright.

'Heya, buddy. Whatcha up to?' Gus leaned towards his passenger door and attempted to wind down the sticky window, but with Speedy in the passenger seat, standing as she spied Riley, it was now nearly impossible. It managed to jam on itself a couple of times, and Gus cursed under his breath, wishing he'd bitten the bullet six months ago and given his ute the overhaul it didn't deserve but desperately needed, since he wasn't going to be buying a new one any time soon.

Riley dropped the handles of the wheelbarrow, and it landed with a thud before he ran over to Gus's ute, his face revitalised with a smile.

'Auntie Kate's selling encouragement boxes.' His mouth pinched at the side, telling Gus he was indifferent about her latest scheme.

Boxes? Who needed boxes for something like that? Gus's brow pinched, fighting where his mind wanted to go, thoughts of his intriguing neighbour hanging in front of him like an irresistible chocolate bar.

'Wanna go to the beach for a walk?' He hesitated. 'That is, if your Auntie Kate is okay with it? Speedy's itching for a run.' Gus appreciated the way Riley had never assumed or judged him, even after he'd told him about his burns. The fact that the kid still wanted to hang out with him was a testament to his loyalty. But what about Kate? Was he being disloyal to her by spending so much time with Riley? He was beginning to love the kid like his own nephew. Riley was as good as one he could've ever wished for. He didn't want to replace what Kate was to Riley, but if he could help, he would. Besides Hughey and Meg, the kid was filling a vacant space in his heart that had been missing for far too long.

'She won't mind.' Riley raced back, stacking the last of Kate's encouragement boxes before forgetting about the wheelbarrow, instead leaping into the ute with Gus.

'Now, are you sure, buddy? I don't need to be in any more trouble than I already am with your auntie.' His mouth tightened at the side; his expression cautious despite his light smile.

'I told her I was going to say hello to Speedy after I did the farmgate.' His nod was good enough for Gus.

When they arrived at Gus's house, he put the tarts inside as Speedy leapt from the ute and took off, her nose to the ground with the scent of an exciting chase on the wind. Riley ran after her, laughing as he looked over his shoulder.

'C'mon, Gus. Let's see what she's found,' Riley beckoned with his hand before disappearing into the scrub.

'Wait for me.' Gus gave a breathy laugh before breaking into a jog and following. This kid was either going to wear him out, make him fit, or both.

They reached the gate and Speedy panted, turning to watch them approach as she waited for the gate to be opened. Gus unlocked the padlock with the key on his keyring, put the keys in his pocket, and patted it. He'd wait until Monica had returned home before he'd lock it again.

The trio made their way down the steps Gus had painstakingly carved as a light shower of rain shimmied overhead. The clouds were building, but that was nothing new, especially for this time of year, despite the fact no further storm had graced them so far.

The ocean wind struck them in the face, blowing Gus's hair and almost knocking Riley off balance as they stepped onto the sand. Gus stepped forward, catching him by the shoulders.

'You right, little mate?' he said, smiling.

Riley gave a nod, not dissuaded.

The waves whooshed to the shore in angry breaks and folds as they stepped towards them. The surf was great on a day like this, and Gus wouldn't have minded bringing his board down to catch a few. Maybe he could come back when Riley went home.

'Have you gone shopping for a wetsuit yet?' Gus kept his tone upbeat, thinking about how he might start Riley's surfing lessons off on a calmer day than this.

Riley's bright face changed quickly to disappointment, and he shook his head as he looked over at a seagull taunting Speedy. Had he asked Kate about it? By the expression on Riley's face, he guessed not.

'Not to worry. We'll work something out so we can give you a go on the waves when it's not so rough.' Gus grinned, expecting Riley to show some enthusiasm, but he remained quiet, even retrospective, as he picked up a stick and threw it for the ever-eager Speedy.

CHAPTER 36

Kate bounced her finger in the air as she counted the boxes lined up on the dining table, all filled with a mixture of her shortbreads and choc chip cookies, cheesy dry biscuits, homemade lavash, and some pecans coated with a delicious spicy dry mix. Even Lexi's niece was entering the entrepreneurial world, making chocolates and styling them in small trays and individual bags that would fit inside Kate's boxes. Those would only be available in Meg's café, where they wouldn't melt.

The boxes had been all-consuming for Kate, and it was only when she glanced up to see it was dark enough to turn the lights on that she realised the time. She had no dinner plans for them, and it was too late to go to the shops.

'Riley?' She stole a breath, glancing about the house as she stood up from the dining table. He would've finished putting out the boxes on the farmgate shelves by now. So where was he? No doubt he'd got distracted by some ant nest or a rabbit burrow and stopped to investigate, which she loved to see. That's what being a kid was all about.

Kate switched on the lights and moved to the door. Opening it, Monica rose to her feet in a slow, easy stretch, her lambs springing up beside her, baaing with a sudden urgency to have a drink. Monica blinked patiently at Kate as her lambs dived beneath her belly, searching for her udder. Their tails wiggled as they suckled.

'Don't go getting any fancy living ideas, Miss Monica,' Kate said, waving a knowing finger at her despite her lambs' cuteness. 'Stay right where you are. I don't need your children trashing my house.'

Monica gave a bleat of objection, or so it seemed, and Kate's mouth widened in a smile. If the ewe kept this up, there was a high chance Gus may never get her back.

The dusk horizon was illuminated by brilliant purples and oranges amongst the approaching darkening clouds, and Kate shivered, shying away from the threatening sky. The last thing they needed was another ravenous storm. She wrapped the long cardigan she was wearing around her chest, crossing her arms tightly to keep out the evening chill working hard to settle in.

Scanning the failing light of the yard for the wheelbarrow, she frowned over its whereabouts as the crashing waves sounded in the distance, wild and angry. Ahead of her, approaching from the ocean side of her property, two figures emerged with casual ease from amongst the scrub. Her heart gave a skip as Gus's outline came into view, his hair blowing in the breeze and his athletic body drawing her eyes despite warning bells sounding wildly in her head. There was a heartwarming chuckle amongst their animated voices and warmth swelled inside her at the sight of her nephew's face, relaxed and happy as he looked up at Gus adoringly, thriving on his company.

And that's when it struck her. Riley loved Gus like a big brother or an uncle, dare she think it. It was a precious sight to see, and Kate found herself pressing a hand to her lower neck, a gentle smile caressing her lips. She'd wanted Riley to find a true friend in Forest Gully, one who'd be there for him through thick and thin. But Gus—all dishevelled and unpretentious through his easy-going way of living, simply enjoying her nephew for who he was. Did that friend have to be Riley's own age?

And what was more, it was abundantly clear to her by his doting eyes that Riley loved him more than he loved her. Or at least that's how it felt, and the realisation plunged hard and fast into her ribcage with a painful blow. How had she been so quickly replaced, the favourite member of the family of all time? How was she meant to convince Riley she was the one he needed most when Gus had stripped her of her only title, the one she'd rightfully deserved as a family member?

She studied the two of them as they walked, unaware she was watching. Would there be a time when she'd connect with Riley as a parent figure and not feel utterly inadequate, completely unprepared, and totally useless? She shook her head in a slow, steady arc.

As they moved closer, a new feeling surfaced, pure and raw. Annoyance. What gave Gus the right to step in, taking charge and acting like the guardian she was supposed to be?

'Where have you been?' She stepped in front of the lounge room window to allow the backlight to reveal her, eyeing Riley and ignoring Gus. If this vexing man were smart, he'd get the message and leave. Immediately.

Riley's mouth opened, then closed again, his happy disposition sharply replaced with apprehension as he searched the ground about him like he was looking for a two-dollar coin. Her heart thudded. She didn't want to upset his little apple cart, but he was driving her to distraction with his knack of disappearing. She'd tried loosening the reigns to let him have a bit of freedom and look what she'd got for it; a gutful of worry and discontent. She pictured Jenna leaping from the grave to throttle her.

Gus lifted his palm into the air as he approached, the action meant to pacify the scene. All it did was raise Kate's hackles higher, her eyebrows folding inwards as she sucked in an impatient breath. At least he had the good decency to offer an apologetic smile, stirring delightful shimmers over her skin at his handsome face greeting her.

Gus offered a hollow half-chuckle, wisely taking the stance

of a man about to be chastised for his misbehaviour. 'I was showing Riley the spot I call Shark Tooth Corner.'

Was that meant to sound like a *safe* place to her? She was glad he read the concern on her face.

'It's pretty cool with caves and rocks and—'

And that damn smile. Why did he have a knack of pulling it out when she wasn't ready to accept it or enjoy it?

'You mean you've taken my nephew to a place that sounds to me like it's creepy, jagged, and shark-infested, *without* my permission?' She pushed back on one foot, her arms now crossed over one another in a tight grip, hoping he was going to say she'd heard it all wrong. And perhaps *sorry.* That word would be mighty helpful right now. Her finger tapped on her forearm in a fast beat. Was this what it was like for a grizzly mamma bear when she thought her child might be in danger? She certainly felt like shredding him right now. Or was this how Jenna had felt the moment she'd heard the branch breaking, realising she'd never see her son again?

'You had no right. And you didn't text.' Her words came out in a rush, harsh and full of fear. It was so unfair of him to rob her of her job description, even if she did suck at it. She turned to Riley, narrowing her eyes on him. This time, she'd put her foot down, and like it or not, her nephew was going to listen. That or she'd set a date herself for them to return home before her parents beat her to it.

'I don't want you going near any point, or rock, and *especially* not near any cave, ever. Do I make myself clear?' Her voice rose, and she hated herself for it, but giving them this new opportunity in this town was her way of showing herself she could be everything to her nephew. But if Riley kept jeopardising her chances, she'd have to admit she'd failed Jenna. She couldn't do that a second time.

Kate's heart lurched as Riley resisted addressing her with his gaze, his bottom lip quivering, and it crushed her more than she'd thought possible. A stray tear fell down his cheek before he looked up at her, his jaw tightening and his expression morphing into the full resentment and outrage of an eight-year-old ready to dive into a full-on tantrum.

'You're not my mother. I hate you.' Before the words could sink in, Riley rushed past her, slamming the door.

Monica gave a lone bleat as she watched him, then looked back at Kate.

And just as fast, the door swung open again. Kate turned towards it, a split second of hope rising in her that he'd somehow come to his senses. Was he going to tell her he loved her as much as she loved him? To the moon and back?

'And I never wanted to come here.'

The door slammed shut again, making Kate jump, leaving her fragile and vulnerable. What just happened? Was her whole relationship with her nephew so close to broken that if he had the choice, he'd leave her?

Gus's eyes averted from hers deliberately as she gazed in his direction, waiting for him to say something, anything, in the dim light of the verandah.

She spoke through the agonising silence.

'You've done this,' and she pointed towards the house where Riley was no doubt hiding in his room, her voice quiet, defeated. 'You've somehow managed to turn him against me when everything I've done has been purely for him.'

'Me?' Gus raised a hand to his chest, not sure if he was hearing correctly. 'And how did you arrive at that conclusion?' How dare she smart-mouth him when she had no clue what her nephew was feeling or living through. When would she wake up to the fact that she needed to actually ask him?

'Don't you get it? If I fail at making a life here for us. 'Kate broke off, her chest shuddering as she grappled to gain her composure, 'I'll have to leave.'

'But why?' This made no sense. Never mind the hollowness the thought left him with.

'Mum and Dad couldn't understand why Jenna had left guardianship to me, and quite frankly, neither could I.' Her chest heaved, and she began quietly sobbing, her head down and her hands covering her face. 'And I'm failing dismally,' she cried, through distraught breaths.

Gus held the base of his neck with his hand, tipping his head back. The middle of the year . . . it was almost here.

'The kid has no one, Kate.' He took a tentative step towards her, his previously rising frustration now being cushioned by her pain and the thought of losing her.

'That's not true.' She glared at him, the night bearing down on them. 'He has his friends. And he has me.' She pointed to herself, her finger shaking and her voice hollow, sad.

He hurt for her, deeply. But he had to make her understand what she couldn't see. If he didn't, she and Riley might up and leave, and his heart reeled at the thought.

'What friends, Kate? Where are they? Can you tell me their names?' He was careful to keep his voice soft and controlled. Riley had confided in him that he'd never asked to have a friend over because Auntie Kate was always too busy.

'I've given him lots of chances to have friends over, but he always says no.' She sniffed loudly, her sobs calming a little.

'That's because you're always running off to some CWA meeting, dragging him with you. He hates those meetings, Kate.

Why don't you try asking him what *he* wants? I promise you, it won't be much. He's too good a kid.'

'Oh, so now you know my own nephew better than I do?' She ran the back of her hand under her nose, sniffing, then folded her arms rigidly across her chest once more, her reddened eyes wide and accusing. 'I'm doing all that stuff to help this town be safer. Hughey deserves it, and so do the firies. You, of all people should see that.'

Oh no, she wasn't swinging this on him. She had no right.

'If you'd back off a bit from all your do-gooding, maybe you'd see he does want to be with you. But you won't give him a chance to show you.' He waved his arm in the air, dismissing her excuses as he glared at the faint outlines of the shrubs, almost entirely cloaked in darkness now. If she couldn't see what Riley wanted—*her time*—then she'd never fully secure his devotion and love.

The incessant scratching of a rabbit digging out a burrow interrupted the acute silence of the still night and the awkwardness resting between them. He lifted his eyes with concern. Where was her smart rebuff now? A tangle of guilt filled him as he spied her expression in the dim light, and dare he say it, she looked broken. Had he gone too far? Everything in him wanted to step forward and take her in his arms, comfort her with a reassuring hug, soak in her softly scented perfume. He wanted to let her know she could still have the relationship she wanted with her nephew. She just needed to make some minor changes. And if she did, there was no doubt Riley would come around.

'I didn't ask for this, Gus. I don't have some parent guide on the shelf telling me what I'm supposed to be doing and how to achieve it. I'm oblivious when it comes to being a mother.' Kate put her face in her hands again, sucking in more ragged sobs.

'Are you sure you have to be a mother?' Gus hesitated as

he spoke the words, worried she might take them the wrong way. She looked up at him with questioning eyes, but he continued.

'You know what he'd like? The two of you should go to Torquay. Maybe you could take him out for lunch.' Would she pick up on his hint to take Riley wetsuit shopping? He'd wanted to take Riley himself, only he'd been certain he'd end up with his head on the chopping block. And he hadn't been wrong.

'Since when did you become the expert on parenting?' She blinked through her tears, her eyes glistening in the faint light that filtered through the lounge room window.

'I'm not.' He shook his head as he kicked away a stick at his feet. 'But he talks to me, Kate because I hang out with him. He's a great kid. He loves maths now. And were you aware the boys at school pick on him? They don't let him play footy because he's an out-of-towner.'

'But when am I supposed to find the time to do that? The fundraiser is only two weeks away.' Her brow tightened; the pressure of her promises deeply static.

The stupid fundraiser again. Gus fought not to tip his head to the rich full moon rising steadily overhead, the clouds now gone. Did the woman never let up? If she'd just let go of the do-gooder caper, he'd be a happy man.

'And speaking of which.' She regarded him with renewed anticipation in her glassy eyes.

Here we go again, and this time, he didn't hide the sigh that left his lungs.

'You are going to help, aren't you?' It was a statement more than a question and she blinked long and hard, staring him down. Was that meant to convince him?

'We need someone to run the car wash. We're going to use the fire truck for water to hose down the cars.' Her voice brightened, her damned gorgeous smile toying with his insides despite the tear streaks on her cheeks.

But his body tightened at the words "fire truck", and by the way her forehead scrunched into light folds, she wasn't about to accept that as an excuse. Bad luck.

'No, Kate. You don't need me.'

'Yes, I do. We do.'

Did she mean that? Did she need him? Could, and more so, should he believe a woman would feel anything but a simple friendship for him again? He resisted looking down at his arms.

'Maybe it would be good for you.' She spoke through her snuffly nose, almost pleading with him and for a split second, he wanted to say yes.

But he couldn't. Not now, not ever.

'What do you mean, good for me?' His protective walls were rebuilding faster than he could say 'Forget it.'

'You've got to get over your fears, Gus. And don't give me that look.' She pointed a finger towards him, and he hated the way it effectively silenced him, warming his insides and making his midriff pinch from the genuine care she was showing him.

His hand raked over his whiskers, and he blinked to refocus his thoughts and push aside the ones he found hard to discard.

'I've been there, but unlike you, I refused to let it warp me into someone who thinks the whole world is against me,' Kate said. 'You think I don't feel guilt over Jenna's death? Do you think I don't blame myself for leaving her to sleep inside that tent instead of waking her? Do you think there's a day that goes by where I don't think it should've been me instead of her?'

'Whoa, hang on a minute. That's what you believe I'm doing?' He hadn't seen that one coming, especially from her. Well, she could take her cute little backside and march back inside her house right now because no one was allowed to accuse him of not dealing with his stuff. He was dealing with it just fine, if people like Ash Evans and his motley crew would damn well let him live his life. Alone.

From the look on her face, she evidently wasn't convinced and his forehead lifted, his eyes avoiding hers.

'So, the reason you were late and didn't stay for Hughey's fundraiser and now won't help at the brigade fair, for a cause I could remind you was something I'm thoroughly aware you loved, is because—' He opened his mouth to object, to cut her off. But she put her index finger in the air, silencing him. *That damned finger.* His lips pursed tight. 'You're *too* scared.'

Too scared? 'Hang on one minute. That's not—'

That damned finger again. His lips clamped shut as he turned away, shaking his head. Could she be any more vexing?

'And don't think I haven't noticed the way Ash and some of the guys dismiss you, turning a cold shoulder when you're nearby.' She went quiet then, her smug little eyebrow sending the crystal-clear message that she was more on his page of woe-is-me self-accusations than he'd realised. But how did someone come back from a tragedy that wasn't only a devastating loss for himself and the immediate family but for the whole community?

Gus's heart raced. He eyeballed Kate, dumbfounded.

'You've got to stop believing that lie, Gus, or you'll never be able to fully live out your best life.' Her eyes pleaded with him as if pain hid behind them, or was it affection lurking deep in her gaze? Was she telling him something he'd refused to admit to himself? Was she saying she'd take a chance on him if only he'd do that for himself first?

CHAPTER 37

Kate slouched at the dining table, her head in her hand, relieved to be mesmerised by the steam rising from her mug of tea. An out-of-towner? Hadn't Riley been making friends? He occasionally went over to Jenny's house to play with her son, Jack, after school. But Gus's words rang loud in her mind, causing her to check herself. When was the last time she'd insisted Riley have a friend over or organise a playdate as a surprise? The truth weighed heavily.

She hadn't.

And there it was, another thing that revealed to her how totally out of touch she was with her nephew. It ground on her confidence to think maybe Gus was right. Perhaps she did need to ease back on her commitments. But people were relying on her for the upcoming fair, which was only two weeks away. If she could just get past that, then she'd be able to give Riley the time he needed.

Kate soaked in the dawn light appearing on the horizon behind clambering patches of cloud through the kitchen window. She finished her drink, tipping the dregs into the sink. Riley was still asleep. She'd let him have a bit longer before she woke him for school.

Dressed in shorts and a T-shirt, Kate opened the front door to find Monica strewn across the entrance of the doorway, baaing loudly. She couldn't decide if it was from being woken far too early or because she hadn't been offered her usual slice of bread. That was another bad habit she'd regretted starting.

Taking a high-step over the unmoving ewe, she headed

towards her front gate on foot, mindful not to trip over the protruding roots jutting out at ridiculous angles. She rubbed her hands together to fight away the chilly nip in the air. After a restless night of toing and froing, she was desperate to gain some perspective before the meeting with the ladies later that morning. But even more than that, she wanted to sort through what Gus had said the night before.

She let out an irritated huff, and a kookaburra tipped his head to the side as he looked down at her before ruffling his feathers as though he wasn't the least bit interested in what she had to say anyway.

She stared down the front gate like it was her enemy. How dare Gus come over all sexy and beach-like, then proceed to tell her what she was doing wrong as a parent. From what she understood, he had little or no experience with kids. She ignored the suspicion he might have been doing something right all this time with Riley, something she obviously couldn't work out for herself. She squinted against the glimpse of sunlight peeking through a gap in the trees.

Her fingers pressed against her lips as she continued to pound the driveway. She'd never neglected Riley, always including him in everything. She'd even gone to the extra effort to cook his favourite sweet treats, and the ladies had loved her for it too. They enjoyed him coming along to the meetings and chatting with him, but that was when he wasn't absorbed in his Lego or truck book or his school computer. Maybe at the end of the day, she'd take him to Meg's for his favourite, a banana thick shake. Meg always spoiled him with his choice of cake or slice from her cake counter too.

Standing a little taller, she nodded with satisfaction. Gus had it all wrong. And as for Riley yelling at her, saying she wasn't his mother—darn right she wasn't. She was the fun auntie, and that was how it was going to stay. Only, that would mean discovering where that woman was actually hiding out. Her shoulders sagged beneath her breath as she reached her front gate, the wheelbarrow empty and tipped on its side. Not ready to head home, she took a detour, fighting her way through the gnarly scrub and gangly trees, shuddering through the spider webs that consumed her block.

By the time she'd arrived back at the front gate, she was covered in scratches, her mood thicker than the custard in her vanilla slice. But two cars had pulled over, one in Gus's driveway and another on the opposite side of the road. Kate pulled out a warm smile, her spirits lifting and she waved her thanks as two of her encouragement boxes headed for new homes. When she stepped through the gate and approached her shelves, to her surprise, only two of the six boxes Riley had put on the shelves the night before remained.

Kate gave a satisfactory nod. At fifteen dollars a box, they were already becoming popular, and she collected the money, a tidy thirty dollars profit for her hard work after taking out the costs. She tucked it in her pocket. That would go towards the chicken wire she'd need to Monica-proof her veggie patch. And the boxes would become even more appealing once she added homegrown eggs, hand-knitted goodies from Brenda, Erin, Kathleen, Nola, and Patsy, and the other bits and bobs listed in her ever-growing ideas notebook.

The week whizzed by in a blur for Kate, the final preparations for the fair fundraiser in full swing the following Saturday at her house. She couldn't believe how fast it had come around, and they'd had good feedback about the project. Alongside the flyers they'd distributed, the Forest Gully Fire Brigade's Facebook page was generating a lot of interest. If the number of likes were any indication, they'd be catering to a large crowd, and she'd need enough hampers to sell.

'Okay, ladies, let's get this production line happening.'

Kate had laid out everything on the dining table, the excess spilling around the loungeroom floor, ready to either be bagged as smaller gifts or placed into the array of boxes donned with shredded crêpe paper Riley had cut up for them. With all manner of donations like chilli jams and tomato relish from Lexi alongside her apple cakes and hedgehog, to the abundance of knitted and crocheted baby clothes and blankets, Patsy's plethora of eggs, and the beautiful eucalyptus gum and fern bracken branches Kate had assembled as native arrangements, the boxes were themed and ready for them to make a roaring trade.

Teacups clunked on saucers as her house became a hive of activity, and by the end of the night, each box, one hundred and twenty in total, were wrapped in cellophane with an array of assorted bows to tie them up. Jenny's cards hung from each ribbon.

Kate stood back, hands on her hips, a satisfied grin on her face. Most of the boxes were going to be donated for sale at the fair. She hoped they'd be as popular as her farmgate ones had been.

'Well done everyone. No one will be able to resist these.' No chance they were going to be ignored by Fire Rescue Victoria now.

The room gave a cheer, but Kate found herself stepping back into the sanctuary of her kitchen, watching Riley quietly disappear down the hallway to his bedroom. Tightness welled down her neck, and she rubbed it, giving a weary blink. Only one more week, she reminded herself, then she'd make sure she made it up to him.

And as for the handsome local who happened to live right next door? She drew in a contemplative breath, her finger tapping her parted lips. She'd done what she could. Now, it was up to him.

CHAPTER 38

Gus squinted against the illuminating glare of the morning sun, the day bright and breezy as he bounced his way down the corrugations of his driveway. If he timed it right, he might be back with enough time to get a surf in.

'What is that woman up to now?' Gus groaned as he pulled up at the entrance of his driveway, putting the ute into neutral. His ute door gave an ear-curdling objection as he opened it and hopped out. Running an impatient hand through his hair, he marched to his closed gate, stopping to glare at the scene unfolding in front of him. Thanks to a line-up of cars outside his entry, not to mention the cascade of cars parked across the road, there was no chance he'd be getting to town and back within the twenty minutes he'd banked on.

The Fair. Was that today? A seasoning of guilt sprinkled over him. He'd stayed away from the main street so he could forget about it, but by the looks of things, Kate had other ways of reminding him. That woman was bothersome, infuriating, and glued to his perception so tight that even an abrupt shake of his head wouldn't release her from it. Why couldn't she choose to inhabit someone else's mind with her constant side glances and heart-warmingly beautiful smiles?

'If there's a collision,' he growled, his fists curling as he shoved the gate open and stomped back to his ute, 'it's not going to be on me.' He slapped his hand on his thigh hard enough for it to sting.

'Morning, young Gus,' Graham said with a wide grin, firm hands clutching two of Kate's encouragement boxes to his chest like it was a matter of life or death as he walked over to Gus's ute, stopping him from departing. Gus stared at him, baffled.

'What's the frown for?' Graham paused in front of Gus's open window, leaning in. 'I'm grabbing these for Nola.' He looked down at the boxes under his arms. 'She wants them for her sisters. Figured there may not be any left by this afternoon.' He gave a chuckle, way too cheery for Gus's liking. 'Kate's hit onto something big here. My Nola wasn't wrong when she said she's a go-getter.' The way Graham let his eyebrows dance with approval made Gus fume, not missing Graham's hint he wasn't about to admit to. Since when had he indicated to anyone that this maddening woman might be worth his trouble?

Gus waved his hand in the air dismissively, ignoring Graham's pretend look of indignation.

'All us locals are grabbing the extra gift boxes Kate made up. 'Cause they're her own produce, the money's going to her. Everyone's so proud of how much she's poured into this. It's the least we could do. The ones for sale at the fair are all going towards the new truck.' Graham's face beamed. 'And not a moment too soon, if you ask me. Things are too dry already, thanks to hardly any autumn rain. The summer is shaping up to be a doozie, according to the predictions.'

For the briefest of moments, Gus gave thought to getting one for Patsy, just to thank her for the veggies she never failed to supply him with. But as fast as the idea came to him, a crush of goosebumps rose on his skin, and he uncomfortably stretched out his arm. Did they honestly think the fundraiser could raise enough to be taken seriously?

Gus tilted his head away from Graham with a hesitant nod as he headed back to his vintage truck. That left Gus staring straight at Kate's shelves, now stripped bare, thanks to the entourage, the cars all gone, leaving him with a hollowness he didn't understand. He had to give it to her. The momentum she'd built up left a buzz in the air he might even consider being a part of.

If he were good enough.

But he wasn't.

Banking on all the locals heading home after their Seaside Bouquet frenzy, he decided to take his chances, making his way down to the main street. He couldn't have been more wrong. The array of utes and cars parked haphazardly in, around, and behind blocked-off areas took him by complete surprise. Tents were being erected all over the foreshore, and people were moving about like organised ants.

Gus let a growl hover deep inside his throat, checking his clock in the ute—one of the few things still working—before scanning the proceedings once more. It was only eight a.m., for crying out loud, and things were either close to done or ready to go. What was it with these people, and what was happening to his quiet town?

Parking was nearly impossible, but he found a spot three streets away from the main drag. With any luck, he could get to the General Store, grab another jar of coffee—his life source since being in perpetual hibernation—and get out of there.

Gus risked a glance towards the fire station as he walked past. He received all the unmistakable glares he was expecting in return, like a direct hit to the gut. He'd definitely made the right call. The less he was around them or the people in this town, the better. He reached the shop, shoving the door open.

'Oh, Gus, I'm so glad you're here,' Nola said as she finished serving someone he'd never seen in town before. He gave them a polite nod of acknowledgement before stepping around them, his jar in hand alongside a two-litre bottle of milk.

'Good to see you too,' he said, reaching for his wallet in his back pocket. The quicker he got this done, the better.

'Now you're going to be helping today, aren't you? Kate did say you would.' She beamed a heartening smile his way as she presented the card reader for him to pay.

Had he masked his oh-she-did, did-she face adequately enough? Well, he had news for her and everyone else in this tiny, way too nosey town. He looked anywhere other than Nola. As far as he was concerned, he'd be making himself totally transparent. Invisible. Unavailable. He'd be out of here faster than Graham could say, 'She's a little ripper'.

The doorbell rang behind him, and loud chatter buzzed with the mood of the day.

'Hey, Gus.' Carl Evans led the way, followed by several of the other young locals, all with the exuberance of the world and the naivety to go with it. Carl was wearing the bright CFA turnout gear like a badge of honour, bright orange and impossible for Gus to miss. A shiver ran over his body, and his gut clenched.

'Carl.' He acknowledged him with a firm nod, hoping it sent the message to leave the conversation at that. If he had to keep his eyes on that outfit a moment longer, he couldn't guarantee his breakfast would stay down.

Beaming, Carl continued to engage in conversation, his excitement sickeningly clear. 'Can't wait for my first fire turnout.'

'What the hell for, Carl? Wasn't it enough to lose Kelly?' Gus's fists clenched so tight his knuckles turned painfully white, his unforgiving glare a direct hit at Carl. He was sorry the words had flown from his mouth before he could stop them. But how could Carl almost die alongside her and still be busting to attend a fire? What was wrong with him?

Gus's jaw clenched, a hot mixture of fear and grief overriding his emotions. If he didn't get out of here soon, he'd say something else he'd no doubt regret, especially when Ash heard about it. And with the others all listening on, that was a surefire guarantee.

'I've gotta go.'

Gus threaded through Carl's followers to escape them, the shop, and this whole charade being undertaken today. But as he pushed the door open and stepped onto the footpath, he came face to face with the girl next door, the one he cursed at night when he couldn't sleep, visions of her soft-flowing hair wrapping itself around her long neck and golden eyes sucking all sleep from him.

He stopped breathing. Of all the people he didn't want to run into today, she was at the top of the list. Only Ash could trump her.

'Hey, Gus. Glad you're here.' She angled her head to the side, her narrowed eyes tugging at the deepest, most private parts of his soul as her warm lips curved in a luscious smile he wanted to keep imprinted in his memory. And yeah, she had him worked out. She could pick a runner when she saw one.

'Just here for the coffee,' he interjected, holding up his jar, determined not to allow her to interfere with his moves or decisions for the day. In a valiant try, he took a step around her, but she held her ground and blocked him.

'No latté today? You're hanging around, though, right?'

He could see it in her eyes. That question was loaded with more ammunition than he could handle. He squared his shoulders, urging the tightness to abate. Well, that was a waste of time.

'Look, I'm on my way home. Sorry, Kate. I've gotta go.' He nodded politely, hoping his apology would be good enough. But even if it wasn't, he couldn't chance another glance her way to see her disappointed face. Standing so close to her, the perfume she was wearing dancing around his senses—he was as good as standing in front of a firing squad the way her scent threaded inside him, pinning his feet to the concrete footpath. As it was, he'd been way too close to pushing his doubt aside and taking her lips to his there and then, desperate to feel their softness, to soak in the tenderness of her kiss like they'd shared last time. A kiss that might restore some faith he kidded himself he might deserve.

No, there wouldn't be another kiss. He couldn't let it happen. Her charm be gone. Everyone's safety depended on him staying as far away as possible.

And when were things going to get any easier? He quickened his pace, heading for his ute, but when he arrived, his head angled to the ground in defeat.

'You've got to be kidding me.' He ran a deflated hand down his face. He'd been boxed in, and one look at the culprit car confirmed it. Of course, it was. Ash Evans. The bastard's move was a good one. He'd more than likely done it on purpose, giving Ash and all his buddies something to laugh about at his expense.

He pressed a hand to his mouth. 'Unbloody believable,' he muttered, looking about him while trying to decide what to do next. But what choice did he have? Everyone was at the foreshore, and the fair was about to start. He didn't know who was parked in front of him, and he wasn't about to sidle up to Ash, politely asking him to move. He'd have to ride this one out as gracefully as he could, as long as grace didn't carry too high a price.

Foreboding clouds crept towards the town with alarming stealth, and Gus looked up as he opened the passenger door of his ute, frowning. They were dark, but his guess was the threat of rain wouldn't hit anytime soon. That at least gave the fair a fighting chance to raise whatever money they could. After the effort Kate and everyone else had put into it, he didn't want to see it not do as well as it could.

He shoved the coffee and milk into the footwell. The milk would more than likely be curdled by the time he could get his ute out, so he made a mental note to buy another bottle before heading home.

He slammed the clunky door, again regretting why he hadn't bothered getting the problem looked at. He glanced about, hoping no one had noticed.

His gaze went to the beachfront in the distance, the hive of activity keeping his attention. His eyes flicked in every direction, his heart notching up a beat at the sight of the fire truck, big, cumbersome, and red, making its way down the street. It pulled up at the curb where a line of cars was waiting beside the team of volunteers—the men and women he'd once loved calling his mates—holding buckets and cloths to wash the cars.

So, he'd do what he needed to do. Hide amongst the building crowd, avoid Ash, and wait out Kate at all costs.

CHAPTER 39

Kate wiped the sweat from her brow with the back of her hand, replaced her cap and re-scanned the grounds for Gus again with the same amount of luck as she'd had most of the day. Absolutely none.

Dogs and their owners pottered along the beachfront happily after the high jump competition. Kate had left her stall to Brenda, especially to watch the chook run contained in a long rectangular pen on the grassy hilltop. Feathers had flown in the air and laughs burst out all around. It had taken grown men fifteen hilarious minutes to actually catch the chooks Patsy had donated.

Riley had won a prize for the ten-centimetre fish he'd caught, and he hadn't been able to wipe the smile off his face, according to Hughey. All his chickens had sold with orders for more, and Lexi's pizzas had satisfied everyone's eager appetites, alongside Hughey's sausages, to which he had run out of over two hours ago.

'Did you see the gumboot toss?' Meg was dancing up and down as she came up to Kate.

'No.' It was a relief to feel the smile on her cheeks.

'I won. Now I'm the boot chick,' she laughed, showing off her trophy which was a piece of wood with a spray-painted kid-sized boot nailed onto it. 'It's going on the shelf behind the coffee machine.'

The fair had been a bigger success than any of them had predicted, and Kate had run out of gift boxes, the last one being sold five minutes ago. It was a great feeling, but now it was time to pack up.

With her hands on her hips, she fought against the persistent urge to check on the clouds, which were growing darker and heavier by the second. A foreboding quiver ran over her body as she forced herself to watch people moving back and forth to their cars, utes, and trailers, packing away their dismantled tents and tables. She peered through the crowd, looking for Kathleen and Jenny. Between those two capable women, they'd juggled a newborn and a two-year-old, appearing and disappearing children wanting more money to spend, and been the drop-off point for all the funds raised, exchanging coins for cash where needed and being the central go-to for anyone who wanted to pay by card, much like Hughey's fundraiser. Each stall had two people manning it so that one could escort the customer and allow them to pay. It had worked a treat.

Kate ducked and weaved amongst the business, offering nods and smiles as she headed towards the ladies. If they'd managed to raise enough, then the FRV would look favourably on them. Showing they were a committed community determined to get a second truck mattered more than anything.

Kate hadn't seen Riley since he'd asked for money to buy lunch from Hughey and a touch of worry wove into her core.

'Kate.' Ash Evans drew her attention away. 'You've done a good job here.' His tone appeared genuine.

'Thanks, Ash, but it was a team effort. And a new truck is what we need. I think it'll help Forest Gully reconnect again.'

Ash's face greyed a little at her words, apprehension filtering down her spine.

'Well, you were the driving force and we can't thank you enough.'

'Well, a bit of hope never hurts anyone.' Her smile turned into a curious frown as Ash left, her thoughts cascading as she watched his back disappear behind a tree. Had he ever thanked

Gus for saving Carl's life? She was certain she knew the answer. The guy's words carried weight around Forest Gully. There weren't many who dared to challenge him, and she doubted few ever would.

Meg was wiping down the portable coffee machine while shooing away her favourite crow, who'd managed to find her amongst all the stalls, when Kate approached.

'You haven't come across Riley, have you?' Kate rubbed her arms with her hands as a fresh chill from the wind whipped about them, a splat of rain landing on her forehead. She wiped it away, yawning from her five-a.m. start and squinting at the moody sky. Was that thunder she'd just heard, or was it the roar of the fire truck's engine?

'He's over with Hughey, officially employed. Hughey has been paying him in sausages to put them into bread with onion for the customers all afternoon.'

Meg and Kate shared a laugh as her heart swelled for the friendships she'd made. They not only had her back, but they had Riley's, too. Maybe someday he'd recognise how amazing the community of Forest Gully truly was.

'I'd better go find him,' Kate said, waving goodbye and heading for Kathleen. She was dying to know if they'd made at least six thousand dollars, the figure they'd set as a benchmark. But as she looked over at Hughey's site, it was all packed up, the only evidence they'd been there his soft tire marks as rain droplets splatted the sandy ground.

Kate gave a light smile. Riley loved hanging out with him, so perhaps he was helping Hughey with his gear, taking it back to the bakery. No matter. He'd be safe. She'd text him soon to organise picking Riley up.

Kathleen and Jenny were frantically packing up when Kate halted abruptly, ducking instinctively as a crack of thunder disturbed the air. Thankfully, there was too much daylight for the lightning to be noticeable, but as she straightened again, a lone figure with a slouch hat drawn over his head in the distance, caught her attention.

Kate set her shoulders, studying Gus as he leaned against the tree, one foot resting against the trunk and his head down as he checked his phone. Had he been here all day and not offered to help? He hadn't shown his face to her. Any wonder. Most likely guessing she'd dob him in for something, which she would've, but not before she gave him the what-for over hibernating in the anti-volunteer camp he was so fond of. He'd keep.

Her eyes narrowed at him before turning away. She didn't have time to go over and listen to his soppy excuses right now, the black clouds rolling in the sky taking precedence over her brooding thoughts.

Overhead, a deep crackle rumbled, low and steady in the distance but close enough for her discomfort to hitch up another notch. She dug her hand into her pocket, pulling out her phone, hoping there would be a message from Hughey. She pressed a hand to her chest.

Hey Kate. Riley is with me. Is it okay if I take him home to your place? If you're not there, we'll drop in and see Gus. Just let me know when you get home, and I'll drop him back. He's an awesome kid. Helped me all day. I'll pay him some money on Monday when I'm back at work.

Hughey.

Kate breathed a sigh of relief, holding the phone close as an almighty clap surrounded her. She shrieked, hurriedly pulling her phone down in front of her to text Hughey back, asking him to stay with Riley until the storm passed. Her free hand rushed to her brow, her phone shaking as she stared at the towering trees above, swaying in the building breeze. Another clap slapped the air moments later and she bobbed down, rushing her hands over her head before bolting to her car and leaping inside. She slammed the door after her as though it might keep the storm and its bad mood from reaching her. Her tent could stay right where it was until this angry squall was over. She wasn't hanging around a moment longer.

Intermittent droplets bounced off her windscreen with building momentum, and she eyed them with misgiving. Her fingers fumbled with her keys as she tried to find the ignition. She glanced over her shoulder at the tree where Gus had been standing.

He was gone.

Her heart skittered then plummeted; at the loss of his reassuring presence or at the relief of it, she couldn't tell. The guy was a pure nuisance, invading her mind in all manner of uncomfortable and exasperating ways, making it impossible to evict him day and night. And she'd tried, many times over.

Her key finally found the ignition when there was a tap on her window.

Kate jumped, her eyes wide and her mouth agape as she hung on to the steering wheel with both hands, peering through the drizzle at the face low-smiling back.

'What the hell, Gus?' she yelled through the closed window. 'You damn near scared the daylights out of me, and there's not a lot of that left.' She snuck a look at the angry sky tumbling behind him, wishing his body could block it from her vision completely. Droplets began to drench his windcheater.

'C'mon, hop in,' she urged, indicating with her hand for him to get into the passenger side. He might be the last person she wanted to see, but she'd never subject someone to the impulses of a raging storm when they were so close to tree branches beating savagely to the rhythm of the wind, no matter how much they drove her mad.

He jogged around the car, and she chastised herself for watching him. He opened the door and hopped in, pulling it shut before removing his hat and letting it fall to the floor in a soggy mess. His damp locks dripped, his low man bun bedraggled yet managing to take her attention from the storm. The force of the rain intensified, drumming against her car.

Kate's gaze found its way to his inviting lips, the droplets resting quietly on them until his grin, so wide and radiant, made her heart run unchecked. She was staring, unable to pull her eyes away. Her own lips parted as she questioned what might happen next if she slowly inched forward. Was she prepared to follow everything her body was calling her to do, to lean in to kiss him softly, tenderly? Did every part of his body turn to complete mush when he was around her, too? If it did, he'd done way too good a job of concealing it.

A flash of lightning illuminated the beachfront, snapping her out of her trance as her face reddened, and she gnawed her bottom lip, turning the ignition on. How could one man make her wild with frustration and weak at the knees so effortlessly?

'Want a ride?' She could feel his gaze trained on her because her skin was prickling. Did her voice sound casual, calm, everything she was most definitely not feeling right now? Closing her eyes, she drew in a calming breath, letting it out slowly, steadily, as her psychologist had taught her. It was just the thunder making her nervous, nothing more, and she'd worked to overcome that fear. Only, right now, she questioned how successful her sessions had really been.

'Yeah, that'd be great. Ash Evans has conveniently blocked me in.'

Kate's eyebrows rose, relieved at the change of subject even though she couldn't trust herself to look at him, her eyes utterly untrustworthy.

'He did?' Her questioning brow lifted, and she sucked in her cheeks to pull down the smile desperate to appear. The act was far from acceptable if Ash did, in fact, do it on purpose. But what she couldn't believe was that he'd been stuck at the fair all day. It served him right, considering he hadn't offered up one finger to help.

Gus nodded, his focus now on the trees. 'I'll come back tomorrow and get it. No biggie.'

No biggie? Ha. He couldn't fool her, and Kate nodded slowly, pretending to agree before pulling away from the curb. Her wipers struggled at double speed against the pounding rain now hammering down, making it nearly impossible to see. She had little choice but to pull over again.

'There's no way we can drive in this.' She let out a despairing huff. Was Riley okay at home in this storm, even with Hughey? Was the tree leaning dangerously close to her verandah being shaken of all its leaves? Would a branch fall on the roof? He'd just started sleeping through the night, the realisation escalating her guilt about moving to Forest Gully. She rubbed her sweaty hands down her jeans, fighting to keep hot tears from her eyes. He'd be so frightened, and she wasn't there to help him through the thing he feared the most. He *needed* her. And more than that, she needed him.

A quick memory flashed in front of her, of him during the last thundery night they'd had. He'd run into her room at one a.m., and as she'd woken, reaching her arms out to him, he'd slunk away again. She'd followed him back to his room, but he'd already jumped back into bed, curled up beneath his doona, pretending to be asleep.

Her stare grew distant as her heart clenched. Was she ever going to be able to reach him?

Would he ever let her?

Her brow crinkled. Was she doing such a terrible job at parenting her nephew? She'd undeniably felt that way after Gus had spoken to her about what he thought Riley needed. Perhaps he'd been right. With everything she'd done for the community, she'd put Riley second every time. She was living her own life even though she tried to convince herself otherwise. And Riley was tethered to her by circumstance against what he really wanted.

Kate blinked away her sadness as the rain continued to spill down all around them. She'd deal with this and make changes from here on when she got home, as long as Riley was okay until she could get there.

CHAPTER 40

'Why didn't you help today?'

Kate's words broke through the pelting rain hammering the roof of the car and Gus blinked several times to refocus. He'd been worlds away, in a place and time where he'd been planning a wedding the whole town would celebrate.

He gulped against his dry throat. How did he answer her? He didn't want to. She'd assume he was being weak. She'd said he wasn't prepared to face his fears and maybe she was right.

Stuff them all. He didn't need anyone. All he needed to get by was a mate like Hughey, who'd been there when Kelly's car had burned to smithereens. Hughey had been the one to drag him away from the flames. And Gus had fought against him, ignoring the stench of his burning, charred skin, desperate to get to her. But his pain was nothing compared to what she'd suffered.

Gus pulled his arms in tight to his chest, layering his hands over each forearm, feeling the deformity. It was his daily reminder . . . of how profoundly he'd failed. He coughed down his emotion.

'Had a few other things to do.' He didn't miss the less-than-convinced eyebrow Kate shot his way. He wouldn't risk looking at her, not after his insides had turned to a pulp as she'd stared at his lips like she longed to kiss them. He'd wanted nothing more than to experience again how they fitted so perfectly with his. But in reality, it was better they hadn't. He could never give her what she wanted or deserved.

He was too damaged.

'Didn't look like it to me.' She continued to stare his way, but he kept his gaze neutral, focused on the windscreen wipers vigorously swiping back and forth. He didn't owe her an explanation. Why did everyone think they had him all worked out?

'Yeah, well, you were too busy being Little Miss Do-gooder to even know.' Had she seen him? He thought he'd stayed hidden.

Ouch. Where had that come from? He didn't mean it. He was just sick of the attention and blame always being pinned on him.

Blustering wind gusts rocked the car. Kate laced her arms, her glare set firmly on him. 'So it's better to keep your head in the sand, for the umpteenth time, is that it?' She rolled her eyes in an I-give-up gesture, and he swung his head towards her. If he hadn't been so angry, he might have been amused.

'And this coming from the one who won't give her nephew the only thing he wants. Your time, Kate. That's it. That's all he wants.'

He could see it in her face with the subsequent illumination of light, her eyes welling and her mouth quivering, but it was too late to take back what he'd said.

'I've learned you can never get back time, so you have to grab every moment you can.' He quietly stared out the windscreen.

'But you can't let circumstances define you either, Gus. I'm doing exactly what you're saying. I wanted to give to this community because it's my home.'

'At what expense? Riley?' His head jerked back towards her, hurting as it jarred, but he wasn't about to let it show. 'You think I *like* avoiding everyone? You try living in this damned place long enough when at every corner you turn, someone's rubbing your failure in your face with salt.' He crossed his arms, glaring out of the side window. She was just the same as everyone else. Why had he thought any different? Delusional, that's what he was. And an idiot for not seeing through it. That was the last time he'd be led astray by his runaway feelings.

Thunder surrounded the car like it wanted to consume them, and Gus looked across at Kate's phone in her hand. Was she shaking? His lips tightened. He wanted to reach for her hand, reassure her by taking her fingers in his, but he couldn't do it, not after what he'd said.

'Damn it.' He spoke to himself, rushing impatient fingers through his tangled hair as Kate let her phone drop to her lap, her head tipping back against the headrest. He stared at her.

'There's no signal. Riley is home and—' Her voice vapourised as she took the phone again, shaking it, desperate to see the blank screen light up with a message. 'I just need to find out if Riley is okay.'

How long were they going to be stuck here? The rain continued to pound the car, making it hard to hold a conversation. Gus shouted over the wave of rain hitting them with ferocity.

'We can drive slowly. I'm sure we can make it home if we're careful.' He felt the anxiety for Riley, too. A storm was enough to scare the daylights out of any kid, but especially him.

Kate shook her head vehemently, shouting back. 'No. I'm not driving in this.'

'Then let me,' Gus said, determination in his eyes. 'I know this is scary for you, but if we can get home, you'll feel better.' And he would, too. Riley was as good as a little brother to him these days.

Kate hesitated for a long moment; her eyes tormented with fear as she watched him. He nodded, urging her to consider it.

'Okay, but you *have* to be careful.' Her eyes pleaded with him.

'I will.'

But the next problem was swapping places in the car. Hopping out wasn't an option. He'd end up as wet as when he went for a surf. He cast a casual gaze over her flowery top showing off her feminine shape, then her skirt accentuating the outlines of her thighs. He sucked in a breath, blinking as his stomach did that strange tightening thing it had a habit of whenever he was around her. Strands of her hair dangled at the side of her face, and he reached out, tenderly brushing them aside to see her profile more clearly. He'd waited a long time to do that, and her gaze penetrated his.

Stunning. He stole a steadying breath.

'Just reach your legs over and sit on my lap. Then I can slide from beneath you and we'll swap sides.' His body writhed. Had he actually said sit on his lap?

Hell, Gus, what are you doing, man?

'Um, sorry.' Kate cringed as she kicked Gus's leg with her heel while attempting to manoeuvre herself towards him. Her heart bounded and she sucked in half a calming breath, reeling in the comfort of his reassuring body now pressed against her back. In that moment, all she wanted was to let herself seep into him, drawing on the strength he exuded, the strength she couldn't seem to find for herself.

Another crack of thunder fizzed the air outside, waking Kate back to reality. She wiggled as fast as she could, edging towards the passenger door so Gus could slide from beneath her to reach the driver's side.

Thank goodness he'd offered to drive, saving her from the angst of facing it. Kate reached for her belt, clicking it in, then let her gaze settle on Gus's face, a complete picture of calm and confidence as he moved back onto the road. She wasn't sure she'd ever overcome her newfound fear of storms, but for the first time since Jenna's death, she thanked it. Even the way he'd gently placed his hands on her hips, purely to help steady her as they'd switched places, had been ridiculously comforting. He looked across at her, a sympathetic yet completely understanding smile filling his face.

She smiled back.

Kate found herself straining forward against the pull of the seatbelt as they drove blindly, the white lines off to the side of the bitumen the only indicator they were staying even remotely on the road. Gus remained vigilant, both hands holding the steering wheel tightly. He carefully wound his way around fallen branches of varying sizes as they came upon them, sending a cold shiver down her spine. If they'd been in a car any bigger, they wouldn't have made it through.

Torrents of water greeted them at her driveway, streaming down the grooved ruts they'd gouged into the gravel.

'We're never going to get through.'

'Yes, we will. You open the gate. I'll get us there.'

He made those words so believable that she found herself leaping from the car door and bolting for the gate without a second thought. Saturated, she swung her body back into the car, wiping away the droplets on her face with her equally wet hands. Gus edged the car forward, his forearms straining as he peered through the windscreen, dodging the ruts of running water with slow momentum. Kate found herself studying his disfigurement. The damage to his left arm ran up past his elbow. Both arms spoke of pain and heartache, but it didn't bother Kate. She saw them for what they were, the arms of a man who'd dared to fight with unconditional love and total commitment for someone he'd loved. Her heart leapt.

The sky filled with fresh blazes of light, thunder following with fervour. A medium-sized tree branch fell across the driveway ahead of them. Kate shivered, both at the coldness of her wet clothes clinging to her and the idea of exposing herself to the storm again.

Jenna, she thought, a sad longing hitting her hard. And Riley, who she needed to hold close to her so desperately her body ached.

Gus pulled up in front of the branch and without hesitation, Kate jumped out, gingerly running to it. It was heavy, but her adrenaline kicked in, her mouth set as she heaved it aside. Gus rolled up to her, and she hopped back inside the cabin, leaning forward, her eyes cast towards her home.

Everything about her house was lonely and dark as they approached, not what she'd been expecting. Had they lost power? Concern flooded her. Where was Riley? She squinted against the rain, desperate to focus, to think. He'd be inside, hiding beneath his doona with Monica beside him. He'd be okay once she reached him.

Both Gus and Kate ran from the car towards the house, Monica's baa barely audible underneath the verandah as they approached. She was already standing, and her lambs sprang up. Kate pursed her lips, dampness sliding from her chin.

Pushing past Monica, Kate reached for the handle of the door, a frown filling her forehead. It was locked. That couldn't be right. If Riley was home and he'd locked it after letting himself inside, then he had to be deathly frightened. She stared at Gus, confused.

She fumbled with the keys Gus passed over, her shaking fingers obstructing her ability to slide the correct key inside the lock. Gus reached out, covering his large hand over hers and squeezing it gently. A rush of warmth hit her and she looked up with surprise, his eyes impressing reassurance as they locked with hers.

If only she could believe that.

She reluctantly eased her hand from beneath his, and he fitted the key, opened the door, and stepped back. Kate burst inside. Auntie, mother, what did it matter? All she needed was to find her nephew and tell him she loved him.

'Riley?'

Gus entered the house, closely followed by Monica. Her lambs bounced after her, nosing the air with apprehension before darting towards their mother's side.

'Riley!'

Kate's eyes widened with worry as she checked the kitchen, then the bedrooms. She ran back down the hallway towards Gus, stopping short of sliding into his arms. She wanted to press herself into them, but if she did, she couldn't say when she'd be able to pry herself away.

'He's not here.' She couldn't hide the trepidation lacing her voice, and she checked the couch a second time, hoping she'd simply missed seeing him asleep at first glance.

She pressed her shaking hands to her mouth, desperate to channel her line of thinking into some rough kind of order before she tugged out her phone from her skirt pocket. One bar of reception and a message from Hughey. Kate put her hand to her heart, relief flooding her. 'He must still be with Hughey,' she breathed, and for a moment, her raging heart steadied. But as she read the message, her body began to shake.

Hey Kate. Have you made it home yet? I was at your place with Riley, but the doors were locked. He said he'd go and get the spare key. I waited more than ten minutes and when he didn't return, I got worried. I've spent twenty minutes calling and searching for him but he won't answer. I've called the CFA boys to alert them for help, but there are trees strewn everywhere. They're working their way here, cutting them off the road as they go. I've gone to Gus's to see if Riley's there. Let me know when you get this.

Hughey.

Kate checked the clock on her phone. Hughey had left that message an hour ago. Her heart plummeted as she turned to Gus, her face stricken.

'What's wrong?'

'Riley has disappeared, and Hughey can't find him.'

CHAPTER 41

Renewed black thunderclouds tumbled across the sky from the west like a ferocious monster keen to devour anything in its path. Gus eyed them from the doorway of Kate's house, his eyes narrowing. This storm was lasting longer than he'd thought it might.

Remaining calm, Gus swivelled his body back inside, scanning every nook and cranny he could spy in the lounge room, not ready to believe Riley wasn't inside.

He pushed his hands over his wet hair, cringing against the tug as his fingers stuck to it while he redid his man bun to keep it out of his face. His mind whirred. Where would he go if he were young again and scared of a storm?

Gus's face paled. He shied from Kate's desperate eyes, instead studying the carpet.

No. He wouldn't have . . .

Kate stepped forward, reaching for his arm and squeezing it tight. 'What? What is it, Gus?'

It didn't matter if her fingers were shaky and cold or holding his vulnerable skin. Her soft touch was a comfort he'd long forgotten he needed. He looked down at her eyes burning into him. How could he tell her? Riley had promised he'd never go anywhere near Shark Tooth Corner. But that cave was his own favourite haunt, and it had become Riley's, too. He pressed a hand to the top of his head, straining to convince himself Riley might be somewhere else. With the weather like it was, the ocean would be pounding the cave with brutality. He checked his watch.

The tide was in.

Memories slapped at his face and he broke her hold, turning for the bathroom, afraid he might lose what little he'd eaten. But with long slow breaths, he urged the nausea aside. What was he meant to do? At least he could get down to the beach with relative ease, thanks to the steps he'd built. But then what?

He strode back to Kate, her face drawn tight and his hand pressed to his forehead as he pushed another wave of sickness down.

'What, Gus? Tell me, please.' She moved a step closer, reaching for both of his forearms this time but he took a step back, keeping her at a distance. It was guilt, pure and simple, keeping him from touching her. How could he ever forgive himself?

Her face revealed her shock. But it was nothing compared to the impending fear rising inside him over Riley's safety. If he was, in fact, at Shark Tooth Corner, then this was all his fault.

'Where is he?' she begged. 'You know, don't you?' This time, it was she who stepped back, her eyes staring him down as they morphed from distress to accusatory.

'No, Kate, I don't. But I can have a good guess.' He stopped, unable to make himself speak the words.

'Tell me, Gus.' She stepped towards him once more, this time the fear in her face meshing with the fragrance of her perfume he'd appreciated in the car only moments ago. This was why he didn't want to get involved with anyone ever again. If he couldn't find Riley—

Gus shook his head in disbelief at the situation unfolding. Was he living this nightmare all over again, with another life in danger? What could he tell Kate, and what the hell was he meant to do? Could he make himself that vulnerable again? There were enough people in town ready to fire arrows his way. All they needed was another tragedy, and they'd shoot for real. Then he'd have to leave for good, with nothing but his few meagre possessions and Speedy to remain his closest friend.

'Gus.' Kate broke his trance, stepping into his face and watching him as if she wanted to slice his throat open if he gave her the wrong answer. And that's exactly what he had to give her, the answer she didn't want to hear.

Light-headedness washed over him and he stumbled backwards, only to have her step into the fresh space he'd created.

'I'm taking a guess he's gone to the cave.' There, he'd done it, said the words that were his inevitable death sentence, both for his chance at anything more with Kate and for his history. He'd sealed his fate.

'Well, we've got to go and get him,' she said, making for the door as the rain continued to pound down on the roof like it might break through at any moment.

Gus chased after her, and they ran out into the rain, but he stalled, certain he could make out the sound of barking coming from what sounded in the direction of their boundary gate. He listened desperately, hoping beyond belief that he was right.

Kate swung around, water dripping from her hair down her face, her body streaming wet as she shivered. 'What are you waiting for?' she yelled above the next tumble of thunder, her anger and frustration fully directed at him.

'Listen,' he pleaded, his breathing heavy. He locked eyes with her, certain he was right. 'Did you hear that?'

'Hear what?' She was squinting, and he ran over to her, turning her body towards the ocean. His hands held her shoulders tight. She had to hear it too.

'That.' Gus squeezed her shoulders before pointing, realisation registering on Kate's face. 'It's Speedy, I'm sure of it. I think she might be with Riley.' Relief flooded him. If he was right, the direction her barking was coming from told him they weren't anywhere near Shark Tooth Corner.

Kate took off, running towards the barking, but Gus hesitated, edging back towards the house, away from the thought of what might have happened. He couldn't do this. He shook his head, wishing his neighbour had never arrived and woken his destitute heart. He wasn't ready for any of this again, not a relationship and certainly not a rescue. It cost too much.

But Riley . . .

Gus flicked away the dripping water from his face as Kate skidded to a stop, turning and staring at him in disbelief. He wanted to go, but his feet were stuck to the ground.

Kate ran back, her expression livid. 'What are you waiting for? We have to find him.' She pointed angrily towards the gate.

'No, Kate. I can't.' He could feel the tears stinging his eyes as he begged her to understand.

'What?' Kate recoiled from him, covering her mouth with her hand before turning back.

Guilt writhed inside him, and he welcomed the self-loathing descending upon him in a firm grip.

'You've got to be kidding me,' Kate yelled, the rain on the tin roof so deafening he barely made out what she'd said.

'I'm not who you want me to be, Kate,' he said, shaking his head, water dripping from his nose and chin.

'And here I was believing you were the hero people had told me about.' She planted her hands on her waist, her don't-you-dare-mess-with-me stance hitting him hard and fast.

Hero? Now he knew she had him all wrong.

'Well, you're not one at all.' She poked at his shoulder with her finger, making him wobble. 'Not even prepared to get out there for Riley. Is that what you do for all your besties?'

Kate emphasised the word, and it ground deep into his soul. He more than cared for Riley. In fact, had he considered anything could come of whatever it was he and Kate had, he would have been more than proud to be a father figure to him. But that could never happen.

'You have no clue what you're talking about. I've been to more funerals than I care to recall.' He yelled through the rain. 'I turned up as a mark of respect for the grieving families.' It was his turn to spit out his words. Car crashes from dangerous driving, rock climbing, and mountain bike accidents all added up. His chest hitched as he fought against the pain.

'We've wasted valuable time when Riley needs us, all because you won't step up,' Kate yelled back, water streaming from both their faces. 'Well, don't worry about it. I'll find him myself.'

Her words were a slap in his face, Speedy's abrupt bark filling the air again, the rain unrelenting.

Something inside him snapped.

'So, all of a sudden, you want to be the parent? Don't you get it, Kate? You're still avoiding him.'

'No, I'm not.' Kate's eyes widened despite the renewed downpour. 'You don't know how hard it's been. And now I'm about to break my word to Jenna when she trusted me. Fine job I did of doing that. *When* we find him, I'll pack up and leave for home. That's what you wanted, wasn't it?'

Her words stung to the core. She couldn't leave, not when he was sure they were onto something between them that truly mattered, however that looked.

'Why do you think he's nicked off in this storm, Kate? He's already lost one mother, and the other one doesn't want to own the fact that she's become one. You just don't get it. All he wants is *you*.' He stared, his eyes pleading with her. 'And besides, I'm no good to him.' Now his voice softened, wishing he could reach down and take her beautiful face in his hands, kiss away the desperation in her eyes, and show her how much he wanted her to understand him. 'I can't do rescues anymore.'

'Yes, you can. You're trained for this. Why won't you help me?' Her reddened eyes begged him, and his heart broke. He wanted to. He just couldn't.

'Your sister wouldn't have died if the CFA had got to her in time.'

Kate's face screwed up, not comprehending what he was saying.

'No, Gus. There was nothing any of us could do.'

'But if I go out there—' Gus's mind travelled to where the steep cliff dropped away to the sand far below, 'he might . . . *die* . . . on my watch.' He angrily swiped the rain from his face.

He'd been privy to too much heartache. Enough was enough.

CHAPTER 42

Was Gus wrong?

Kate closed her eyes against the sting from the rain, disbelief dripping from her. Was that what she was doing, avoiding being Riley's mother? Her foot tapped nervously on the soggy ground.

Of course, she was. She was never meant to turn into the mother of her nephew. Kate's face crumpled at the loss of Jenna and at the way she'd let Riley down. She wanted to hand him back to his mother to deal with all the problems and discipline.

But now it was she who pulled Riley into line. The only problem was he hated her for it. She didn't want this job anymore.

'I couldn't do anything to help Jenna. I'd been holding the branch off her body as best I could, but it was too heavy to make any difference. The firies urged me away when they arrived and took over.' Her lashes dripped but her eyes held him firmly. 'It was no different for me, Gus. We all knew each other, but that's what communities are around you for, to have your back when you need them.' Her voice hushed, and a hot flush of tears stung her eyes. 'They're there for you when you suffer loss.'

She stood taller, her resolve building as she bristled. 'So don't tell me you can't get out there and help. I don't have your training. Riley needs you. And I need you.'

She does? Gus blinked rapidly at Kate like she couldn't have meant what she was saying. But her face told him something different. Dare he think it, there was love in her eyes and a desperate urgency rose up inside him. He was helping no one if he continued to hide, all for the sake of a few angry locals. Sure, they were allowed to feel grief, but they had no right to treat him like an outcast when, in fact, he'd done everything he could at the time and borne the cost.

'Gus, you didn't do anything wrong for Kelly,' Kate broke in, interrupting his trance. 'She was no different from Jenna. No one could do anything to make that kind of difference.'

She stepped towards him, placing her shaking hand gently on his chest. His heart leapt. In the distance, he heard Speedy barking again, then as the wind abated for a brief moment, there was a voice.

Riley!

'Did you hear that?' He reached for her, begging her to have heard what he hoped he had.

'Ring Hughey right now. We might need all the help we can get.' He focused on her hard and fast, his face no more than a hand span from hers. 'I'll get him, Kate. He's going to be okay.' He pressed his wet lips to hers in a firm but swift kiss before he grabbed the torch in her hand and took off towards the gate.

CHAPTER 43

Kate was a nervous muddle of apprehension as Gus ran into the fresh onslaught of oncoming rain. She put her shaking hand to her mouth, his heartfelt kiss meshing with her worry, making her brain scramble. She fought between the desperation to have Riley back in her arms and her immediate urge to wring his neck for doing something like this. He knew what storms were capable of.

She bolted back to the house, ignoring Monica, now lying on her new lounge rug, her babies snug against her side. Monica's look suggested Kate shouldn't come inside when drenched like a sewer rat.

Sinking to her knees at the coffee table, the ewe blinked what Kate could have interpreted as concern, even understanding. Kate leaned forward, her elbows on her knees, hiding her face in her hands as her body rocked and water pooled beneath her.

What if I lose him, too?

Hughey! She snatched up her phone sitting on the table and flicked it on, her hand trembling as she fumbled to scroll for his number.

'Hughey, it's Riley. He's out in the storm. Gus has gone to look for him, but . . .'

She swallowed as hot tears sprang, strangely warming her cold cheeks.

'Okay. I'll stop looking at Gus's. Graham's messaged me. He and Neil are nearly at your place with the fire truck. We'll be there soon, I promise. Do you have any clue where they might be?'

'Somewhere near the cliff. That's where Speedy's barking.'

Kate hung up, pacing to the kitchen and back, Monica

eyeing her every turn with interest.

The siren of the truck startled her. She raced for the door, but Hughey beat her to it, pushing it open and stepping inside, fully kitted out in his rescue gear, which he kept in his ute. He opened his arms, and she lunged into them.

'Follow Speedy's bark, Hughey,' she whispered into his ear.

Nola, Patsy, Meg, Lexi, and Erin strolled in next, all business-like, clearing her dining table and placing loaves of bread and ingredients down as though they'd known all along that this was going to happen. Lexi wrangled a large box of cold pies and sausage rolls from the bakery, and Brenda shuffled through the door, lugging the big urn beside her, the cord dragging behind and her knitting in the other hand.

Hughey stepped aside as Meg raced to Kate, gripping her in the tightest of hugs.

'He's going to be fine, just you watch,' she whispered in Kate's ear before she pulled away, holding her by the shoulders. 'I promise.'

'Don't promise something you can't guarantee, Meg.' Kate's tears sprouted again as she reached for her hug once more. 'I can't lose him too,' and she shivered, burying her face deep in Meg's shoulder. A sensation of fury at her nephew's recklessness rose inside her, but it was what she deserved. She'd pushed him to it, just like Gus had said. And what if she never got the chance to turn things around? What if he didn't come home? Deep sobs heaved from her body.

'And you won't. The boys won't let anything happen to him.'

Kate stood back from Meg, wiping her face with her palms, wishing she could genuinely believe her words.

'Now go, get out of that gear, or I'll be wringing my clothes out, too, if you keep hugging me like this.'

'No, I have to go and help.' She made a move for the front door, but Meg pulled her back by her hand.

'Hughey's already gone.'

'Gus is there,' Kate said, unable to deny the hope she was pinning on him.

Meg held Kate at arm's length, her serious gaze penetrating her to the core. 'Well, there you go. Now, go get dry clothes so you don't get a chill. We don't need to be worrying about you too.'

Kate sniffed, offering a feeble nod. She was running for her bedroom when a loud gasp from the lounge room stopped her in her tracks. What's wrong now?

'There's a sheep at the coffee table.'

Kate's gape drew in at the sides as she turned to see Brenda with a hand over her heart. Monica blinked at Brenda, unperturbed.

'You can make her a cuppa if you'd like,' Kate said, relieved that's all it was.

'Well, I never,' slipped from Brenda's lips.

Kate changed quickly, leaving her wet clothes in a soggy pile on the bathroom floor before she raced back to the living room, her breaths stalling at the sight.

Her dining table was laden with sandwiches in the making, and the smell from the oven suggested Lexi's goodies were being warmed up. Nola spied Kate staring at the slices in utter surprise.

'We had some leftovers from the fair. Rather timely, don't you agree?' Nola moved to Kate, giving her a side squeeze. Kate's appreciative nod became a disbelieving shake of the head. These women, her friends, they were the best.

She raced outside, tugging on her waterproof jacket as she awkwardly took off towards Speedy's louder, excited barks.

CHAPTER 44

Gus ran towards the boundary fence, sliding on the sludgy mud, making it to the gate in record time.

'Riley?' Droplets dripped from his hair into his eyes as he scanned back and forth with the torch. Nothing. Could Riley even hear him amidst the howling winds? The severe cliff drop was crawling with rock ledges jutting out at peculiar angles, and Gus shone his torch towards them. If Riley had fallen onto one of those, he might have a chance. He might also have a broken bone . . . or more, and he gulped down his worry.

The image of Carl's broken wrist appeared without warning, and Gus drew back, rubbing at his own arm in response. All he had to hang onto was the faith that Riley hadn't got himself into serious trouble.

The gate was still unpadlocked, and he silently thanked Kate for not returning Monica. He flung it open in readiness for the truck, then ran towards Speedy's anxious barks.

Gus ran along the cliff top, searching left and right, but there was no sign of his dog or Riley. Could he have fallen to the base of the cliff amongst the scattered rocks and waves belting against them? Gus's heart leapt to his mouth as horror gripped him. This couldn't be happening. Gus pressed his hand to his forehead. Maybe they were at Shark Tooth Corner after all.

He'd earlier kicked himself for being so wound up with his own problems that he'd forgotten to lock Speedy inside. But now he was grateful.

Gus ran towards the stairs, the rain thrashing him in intermittent bursts as the wind whipped him, sending fresh shivers scurrying over his body. It stung, making him cold to the core. As he reached the razor-sharp rock face, he stopped. He wrapped his arms around his chest, shivering as he looked about, flicking the rain from his face.

Speedy scooted up from the cliff to his far left, barking urgently at him before turning and running back down.

'That'a girl.'

Gus ran to where Speedy had disappeared, the cliff edge looming dangerously close. For all the good intentions he'd had for Riley with his warnings, boys were always going to be boys.

'Riley,' he called, cupping his hand around his mouth.

Gus skirted as close to the edge as he dared, his torch swinging to and fro. The pounding from the ocean at high tide was battering the rocks, frustrating him as he tried to listen in case Riley called. He stood, drawing a breath, his hand falling to his side despondently.

Would he have to prepare himself to find a small body?

What was he going to tell Kate?

'Riley.' He belted out the name and waited. Listened. If Riley wasn't answering, then—

'I'm down here, Gus.'

His heart leapt, and he whispered a silent prayer of thanks. Riley was alive. That's all that mattered right now. But with the cliff face too steep and the rain hammering against it, there was no way he could chance trying to get down there without a rope or some help.

'Are you hurt?' Gus called again as he leaned forward, the juts in the rocks making it impossible to see Riley. He waited for an answer, but either Riley couldn't hear him for the howling wind and the wild swell belting below or . . . worse.

Gus's imagination taunted him. Had Riley lapsed into unconsciousness? Or . . .

Gus gasped in a breath, desperately looking about him for something, anything that he could use to lower himself down.

There was nothing.

As if on repeat, his sense of uselessness overwhelmed him, clawing him back to the day when his life changed so dramatically, faced with his inability to help and his desperation to try.

There was a tree that had a long, low-lying branch. He ran to it, tugging it hard, testing it for strength. He leaned back, allowing his full weight to be held by it. It could work if . . .

His hands, sweaty and wet, suddenly lost their grip on the branch.

'Oh hell!' Gus stumbled, and he fell to his backside, sitting dangerously close to the edge. He stole a jagged breath, calling on all the calm he could muster before shuffling to safety and standing again. His heart raced, and he flicked the sandy mud from his hands with a swift shake before cautiously peering over the looming drop once more. Was the branch long enough to reach? It'd be close. It was all he had.

He knelt. 'Riley, you still with me, buddy?' He tipped his ear to the side, straining to listen for an answer as water streamed over his face.

His eyes narrowed on the branch once more. Even if it held long enough for him to get down halfway, he might be able to slide the rest of the distance to the ridge.

But what if he overshot his mark?

'Damn it.' This was impossible. Gus stood, pacing back and forth. He felt useless all over again, the impulse to ignore protocol—intentionally this time—so strong he could hardly bear it.

He had to do *something*.

The fire truck siren sounded in the air as the rain eased off a smidgeon and Gus spied the flashing lights as it wound its way along the fence line towards them. He laid bets Hughey would've rung the State Emergency Service (SES) to help, but the closest assistance was in Lorne, and given this weather, they'd be run off their feet with incidents within their jurisdiction.

'Riley, I'm coming down. Just hold on.' He had to trust that, by some miracle, Riley had heard him.

'Gus. Is he all right?' Kate's face held panic as she emerged from the scrub, her voice breathless and her eyes frantic as she stood at the fence line.

What did he tell her? That her nephew might be hanging out on a precipice ten metres below with a forty-metre drop below that? His brow tightened. No, that was his concern right now, not hers.

'I hope so.' Would she leave it at that? He shook his head in the softest of shakes. She'd never.

'Gus, tell me he's okay. Please. I . . . I need to know.'

His heart twisted as her face crumpled in on itself, her voice hitching.

'I'm unsure if he's hurt, but he called out to me.'

Her hand flew to her mouth, and she bent forward, clearly frightened to take a step any closer. All over again, his heart leapt into his mouth, his entire body tense. What he wanted to do was go to her, wrap her shivering body with his and reassure her. But right now, Riley needed him more.

'Gus, what's it look like?' Hughey's deep voice cut through the rain as he stepped up beside Kate, calm and focused like he always was in an emergency. He hopped the boundary fence in one stride and walked to the edge, peering down before turning to face Gus, his face drawn. Gus knew his best mate was assessing himself as much as the situation to be sure he could cope.

He had to prove not only to Hughey that he could do this but to himself.

'Not real good. I don't know how stable this ledge is, and I can't easily communicate with Riley, so it's unclear how badly injured he is.' Gus stole a glance towards Kate, his heart aching at the sight of her distressed face from behind the fence where Graham now kept an arm around her shoulders, probably to hold her back from joining them.

Graham had seen many a rescue and knew precisely what to do. If his nerves hadn't been so tightly strung, Gus would've offered his fellow lieutenant a smile of thanks for keeping her safe.

But he needn't have worried. Graham gave him a short nod that spoke louder than any words could, filling Gus with something more potent than his inadequacies. Hope, raw and authentic. Now, all he had to do was come through by helping Riley.

Ash Evans, their fire captain, wasn't on the scene, so Hughey took charge as first lieutenant.

'Carl, grab the ropes with Nige and Graham.'

Carl? The name halted Gus, and his eyes narrowed against the brightness of the truck lights, shining directly at him through the opaque lighting. Was he here? But instead of anger, relief washed over him. And pride. Regardless of his own opinions, Carl was standing up for what he believed in, just like he had once done, and right now, Gus was grateful for the extra set of eyes on the job.

'I need to get to him, assess him, then secure the accident site,' Gus said to Hughey.

Hughey walked towards him, rope in hand and an expression of wariness on his face.

'Listen, mate, are you up for this? I can go if—'

'No.' The word came out sharper than he'd intended, but he meant every bit of it. 'I have to do this.' He agonised over the sheer will and grit he would need to call on, staring at Kate's desperate face once more. 'Besides, I'm a whole lot lighter than you.' He managed an amused expression, enough for Hughey to get the good-natured jibe he was sending.

Hughey stood silently, nodding while deep in thought. 'Yeah, mate, you're right.' He stepped in, giving Gus's shoulder a reassuring grab with his hand. 'I get it. So, let's get this rope wrangled into some kind of harness and get you down there.' Hughey stepped back, wrangling the rope like a pro.

The wind whipped around them, lightning flashing across the angry surf churning up the ocean as Gus stepped into the makeshift harness. He looked up at Hughey, a mutual silence between them speaking so loudly that Gus suddenly wished he could swap roles with his best mate. It would save him from facing every damn fear surging through him right now. But Riley deserved so much more than that. So did Kate.

At the thought of her name, a wave of warmth swelled inside him. He would do this for them, and he needed to do this for himself if he wanted to believe there was a chance of a future with them in his life.

'When's the SES getting here?'

'Dunno, mate. Let's just do what we can 'til they do, hey?' The smile Hughey gave him was meant to be reassuring, but it was wasted on Gus.

'Here, put these on. You look like a drowned rat.' Hughey passed him his fire jacket and helmet.

Gus hesitated, his eyes full of caution and fear. He hadn't worn those since . . .

He dug deep into his resolve, taking the reflective coat and shuffling it over his sodden jumper. His helmet fit like a glove.

Hughey tossed the remainder of the rope to Nige, the one who'd taken his desperate call during their fire evacuation that fateful day, and Gus clenched his teeth. Nige had been one of the guys inclined to shun him down the street, and here he was now, putting his trust in the guy to tie him off securely and not let him crash to the angry waves below. His fierce grip on the rope tightened another notch.

'All tight and secure,' Nige called, tugging the rope to show Hughey and Gus it was ready.

Gus willed calmness into himself by releasing his pent-up breath, his capable hands shaking with trepidation as he clutched the wet rope. He gave Hughey a firm nod before allowing his eyes to settle on Kate one last time.

'I'll get him.' He mouthed the words because he couldn't bring himself to say them out loud, her pleading eyes almost too much for him to bear. She gave him a trusting nod as her hand pressed against her mouth.

More sirens rang in the air. He had to hope it was the SES arriving with a stretcher to winch down to Riley. But Gus had to get to him first.

Drawing on every ounce of focus he could, he turned on his helmet light, then lowered himself over the cliff edge, tugging the rope to continually test its strength before he took a new step. He eased himself down, the mud-caked rocks causing his foot to slide more than once.

The wind battered him, whipping against the rocks as it came and went in bursts, the rain pelting his helmet and falling from it like a waterfall. Gus was halfway down when he glanced over his shoulder, first seeing the wild salty water beating against the bottom of the cliff and then Riley in his torchlight. His heart jolted at the sight. Riley was lying on his back, his head to the side, eyes closed.

Gus urged himself to move faster, losing his footing, smacking his elbow against the rocks as he rushed his footholds.

'Riley?'

He looked down, desperate to catch some form of recognition from Riley at the sound of his voice. A movement, anything.

Nothing.

The rain rose in tempo, whipping him on the back as he neared the ridge. He squinted, concentrating on Riley and his next foothold.

With one last bounce off the rock, he planted his feet behind Riley, his body dangerously close to the jutted edge. A scattering of small rocks shifted beneath his feet, falling to the hungry upsurge below.

Gus glanced at the dark sky above him, the same one he'd normally admire, now barely able to make out Hughey's form. He waved anyway, tugging the rope to indicate he'd reached Riley and was okay.

'How is he?' Hughey called out.

'Not sure.'

Hughey's voice was pure relief to his ears, and he pressed his helmet to the rope as he clung to it, desperate to draw enough courage to see out this rescue.

Gathering all his resolve, Gus bent down to Riley, directing the headlight attached to his helmet on him, taking his small hand in his. It was white and cold. Gus blew out a shaking breath. He leaned over Riley, putting his cheek near his mouth to feel for any sign of breathing as he gave him a gentle nudge, hoping Riley would rouse at his touch.

C'mon Riley! he pleaded, his heart just about jumping out of his chest. The smallest of soft breaths fingered his cheek. It was weak, but it was there.

He gently felt down the boy, looking for any sign of lacerations. Nothing appeared broken, but the full extent of his injuries wouldn't be determined until they got him proper help.

That kind of thing was beyond his skill set.

'Riley, can you hear me?'

'Hmmm.' A faint murmur.

Gus's eyes widened as he stared at Riley, willing him to respond more. He put his hand to Riley's cheek, troubled at how cold he was. Riley's shivering was slowing. He was getting colder.

'Riley?' Gus's desperation grew, and he shrugged off his heavy fire jacket, placing it over his little mate's weak body. He edged himself next to Riley, mindful of the severe drop he was so close to. Gingerly, he stretched out so he could lay snug beside him to both warm and protect him from the rain, ignoring the deathly chill on his own back. Acting as a windbreak would increase Riley's chances of survival. Loose rocks tumbled from the edge as he moved.

'Gus?'

Riley's faint whisper reached him. At first, Gus dismissed it, sure what he'd heard was the wind beating in his ear. He'd been so focused on checking up top for any sign the SES rescue team had arrived with a stretcher he'd almost missed it.

Instant relief flooded him. 'Yeah, mate. I've got you.' Riley's eyes fluttered open, then closed again.

'Gus, they're here,' Hughey called from the top. He heard Speedy give a quick yap.

Gus gave a thumbs-up just as the portable stretcher appeared over the cliff edge, its reflector strips shining in the light of Gus's headlight, making him squint.

'Can you get him in it yourself? I don't reckon there's enough room on that ledge for anyone else but you.' A large torch flashed down at him.

'Yeah, I can.' He gave Riley a gentle shake again and his eyes fluttered open.

'We're gonna get you out of here, okay.' He raised his

eyebrows at Riley, who gave a small nod.

CHAPTER 45

Kate pulled at the stray hairs gripping her wet face, straining through each flash of lightning to watch the rope dangling from Hughey's hands. They'd sent the stretcher over the edge, and Hughey had given her the thumbs up with a nod. Why weren't they coming up already?

Rain continued to pelt the night sky, and Kate's heart double-skipped at the sight of the SES crew walking past her. They were the image of concentration, only talking to Nige and Graham—who'd left her side only to confirm with them the situation—before he appeared again, apparently dubious she might break free from his hawk-eye supervision. And he was justified in doing so, she had to admit. It was the third time she'd considered bolting from his side, but the continual lightning and thunder had put an abrupt halt to that idea.

Another rumble and flash filled the atmosphere, and she shifted from one foot to the other, her wary eyes looking on helplessly as everyone worked calmly, confidently, and professionally. A huge night light provided by the emergency service truck lit up the scene as Kate's eyes darted from the cliff edge to Hughey, then to the cliff again. How long was it going to take before she could see her nephew?

Oh no, and her heart sank with sudden sadness at her thought. Her parents. What would they say when they heard about this? She clenched her eyes tight as she stood still, chewing at her nails. She was the one with Riley's life in her hands, even though they'd told her they would be happy to raise him. He was their only grandson, and she'd not only taken him far away from them, but now she'd lost him too.

You can't look after yourself, let alone someone else, Kate Harris.

She wasn't worthy of being Riley's carer; she knew that now. She couldn't make him happy. The thought twisted its jaws into her with a stabbing jab. She might as well call it quits and take him home to her parents if she got him out of this predicament. They'd raised two kids, proving they could do a much better job than her.

And Gus . . . Riley was drawn to him like some supersonic magnet. What did he have that she didn't? Gus didn't like hanging around anyone, especially her. So why Riley?

A spasm of guilt hit her with such force she sucked in a paralysing breath. What had Gus said? Riley wasn't happy at school.

And Jenna. Riley hardly talked about his mother to her. Did he feel the guilt of not wanting to make her feel bad about being his mother's replacement? Or was he always quiet because she said no to everything he asked, even when it wasn't much? When had she become so parent-like and sensible? She'd made a gigantic mess of his life and hers, and she couldn't see a way to recover from any of it. Had she simply been selfish this whole time, dragging him across the countryside and expecting him to accept all her choices while she didn't ask him about the things he wanted in this new life?

Speedy stood beside Hughey, looking over the cliff, her tail still. That couldn't be a good sign.

Her eyes widened as Graham stepped away to talk with Hughey. What were they saying? Was it good? She strained to hear through the wind, her leg jiggling nervously as the men exchanged nods and quiet murmurings, no doubt so she wouldn't hear. Her eyes narrowed, droplets dripping from her lashes as she held her hair back with a hand against the cold wind blasts.

Graham appeared by her side again, reaching out and putting his comforting arm around her shoulders, giving her a squeeze. She examined his expression for any clue, any indication of what was going on.

He offered a crooked smile. 'Hughey just told me Gus has him safe 'n' sound. But you need to be ready.' He looked down on her with a warning gaze. 'We can't say if he's hurt or not. You need to prepare yourself in case it's not good.'

The prickle of tears hit fast, and she choked, turning from Graham, fighting away the sting of bile. With one hand swiping her wet face and the other pressed to her stomach, she watched every intricate move Hughey made.

He looked back and caught her desperate gaze, giving her a nod, his smile a grimace.

Kate's shoulders folded inwards.

'Right, let's pull 'em up,' Hughey said, and Graham hopped the fence, standing behind Nige, Carl, Hughey, and the rescue crew before they began to draw the rope towards them as a team. Ash Evans breezed past her, leaping over the fence to assist.

It was an agonising ten minutes before she glimpsed Gus's head, his helmet light pointing directly at her as he emerged from the cliff face. Speedy's tail flew back and forth.

Jumping the fence with fresh disregard for the thunder and lightning, she skirted around everyone, ignoring their objections as she ran towards Riley. She dropped to her knees, the puddles soaking her jeans as she pressed her hands to his tiny, icy face, her mouth turning down when he didn't respond.

Tears welled, and she sniffed back the emotion, swiping at her running nose with the back of her jacket sleeve before pressing her warm fingers to his face. She'd held it together for months after Jenna's death because of her parents and for him.

'Riley? Riley? I'm here,' she whispered, lowering her forehead to his, begging him to wake up. Her fingers shook as she sat back, staring at his lifeless form, so small, so helpless.

The SES crew gently moved her aside, picking up the stretcher before walking to the waiting ambulance, and Kate sat back on her haunches, staring with helplessness. Her mind was a mish-mash of what-ifs and what could have been. But the painful memory of Jenna's lifeless body being taken away by the ambulance once they'd determined there was no chance to revive her . . .

Kate's hand flew to her mouth at the memory as she sucked in a desperate gasp. They hadn't let her travel with Jenna. If Riley was going to die—

Gus came to her and squatted down. She grabbed his drenched clothes with her fists, holding tight as she pressed her face into his chest. His arms wrapped securely around her, the deep sobs that she should've released all those months ago for Jenna, now raking her body.

Kate could hardly focus when she sat back, taking in Gus, his gaze full of concern and patience alongside the deep empathy that reached into the depths of her heart. She rubbed at her eyes and struggled to her feet, her legs wobbling like jelly. She leaned against Gus's reassuring body.

'I need to go with him.'

All Gus did was nod, holding her elbow for support as she gained her balance.

'Auntie Kate?' Kate's eyes widened at the whisper-soft voice as she stepped up to the ambulance. If he was calling for her, did that mean he was going to be okay?

Kate reached forward, grabbing his hand beneath the warm blanket now covering him, squeezing it tenderly as she softly smiled. Riley's eyes closed again, but his fingers wiggled ever so slightly beneath her hand.

CHAPTER 46

Gus paled as the ambulance drove away. Even with so many people about him right now, he'd never felt more alone with Kate and Riley gone.

He squinted against the steady rain falling, the wind making his cold body double up in a shiver. He rubbed at his arms as the last glimpse from the ambulance lights disappeared. Inside that vehicle were the two most important people in his life. But would Kate move back home after this? His throat clenched tight. He couldn't lose them, not now.

Gus looked about him as equipment was returned to the trucks and people were debriefed post-rescue. He remembered when they used the pack-up time to check how everyone was coping after an event or a recovery. He'd always gone through this process, talked it through and moved on.

But not anymore. If he truly wanted to go after the things in his heart, a future with people he wanted to do life with, then he had to make changes. And that not only included the way he acted around Graham, Nige, and Hughey, the guys he'd had full confidence in what felt like a lifetime ago. Guilt weeded its way into his veins. They'd not only saved Riley.

They'd saved him tonight.

And Ash Evans . . . The guy halted, rope in hand, as he locked eyes on Gus. His gut pitched. Unable to read Ash's face thanks to the darkness of night, he wondered if that might be a good thing, visualising the social shunning from Ash's main mates in the days to come. He'd have to lay low for several months, if not years, from now on.

Gus spun around at the footsteps approaching him.

'Hey, mate. Reckon you'll need this again.' Hughey offered a cheeky grin like the true mate he was, handing Gus his fire jacket with a glint of solidarity in his eyes. 'Give it half an hour, and you'll be an ice block.'

Gus reached for it, hearing loud and clear the *other* agenda Hughey was suggesting, but that could wait until another day to chat about.

'Feel like one too.' He gratefully took the jacket, surprised at how it didn't make him quite so squeamish as he put it back on. He stared at his muddy boots, unable to look Hughey in the eye as he wrestled with the words he wanted to say.

'Hey, listen, thanks . . . for today.' He paused, attempting to compile the matted thoughts rattling through his mind, unsure what he wanted to say next. He'd been a blockhead and then some. 'I couldn't have done it without you.' He scratched at his whiskers sheepishly, unable to look at his best mate who hadn't given up on him, not once. Sometimes, you only got one shot at a friend like him, and he wasn't prepared to lose him now.

'That's what mates are for, you goose. And don't go forgetting it.' Hughey pointed a teasing finger his way. 'I'll need you one day, and there's no one I'd rather have there for me.'

Gus's eyes widened and he urged himself to look Hughey in the eye. Hughey stepped forward, slapping him on the back, but Gus opened his arms, unable to stop himself from embracing his best mate in a full-on man hug, his eyes watering.

The CFA and SES crews made their way back to Kate's house for a well-deserved feed and warm cuppas after their long day and night.

'You comin'?' Hughey tossed his head towards Kate's house.

'Yeah,' but Gus's voice trailed off. 'Just might use the night air to take a breather. I'll be there soon.'

Hughey gave him an I-get-it wave before he left.

Gus waited until Hughey was out of sight. The storm was moving slowly out to sea, but a misty drizzle continued to fall, the wind blustering him in haphazard waves as the sky continued to light up. He closed his eyes, breathing in the smell of fresh rain as he walked. He slowed beside the fire truck, reaching a hand out to it. What Kate had done, raising money for another truck, was a good thing. They could have done with a second one today.

Gus froze, his eyes widening. Someone was near the back of the truck, hovering in the shadows.

Watching him.

Ash Evans approached Gus slowly, and Gus's body tensed. Was he about to cop a mouthful of abuse, or was he going to hit the deck hard and fast from the right-hander Ash had long wanted to give him?

Or both.

Ash stopped not three feet from Gus, his face set, eyes boring into him.

'I might not agree with how you went about things today,' and Ash lifted his chin a little higher. 'Bloody reckless if you ask me, but—' Ash stopped. He gave a slow swallow before he continued. 'Good job today. From what I hear, you were the hero.'

Gus's whole body turned rigid at the word, and when he attempted to speak, it came out horse.

'I'm nobody's hero, Ash. I never have been.' He cast his eyes down in shame. 'I nearly couldn't do it.'

'But you did do it. That cliff drop is brutal. There wouldn't be too many prepared to risk their own lives in a freak storm as wild as this one to do what you did. There's carnage all over the roads. That's why I was late. Lucky I got here at all.'

Gus snatched a glance towards Ash. Now the guy had him

on the back foot. Was he being lured into some kind of trick conversation where he'd be tripped up at any moment? 'When you're ready, you're welcome back on the team.' Ash broke the intensity of their discussion with a glance over his shoulder as he continued to speak.

'And for what it's worth, I should've told you that a long time ago.' To his credit, there was a shimmer of remorse and even a dusting of shame in his words.

The frown on Gus's face was telling. He hadn't missed how hard it was for Ash to say the word *welcome*. And after believing he was the outcast of Forest Gully by the man he should've been related to by now, had all things panned out, Ash Evans was sorry? Gus couldn't decide whether to feel relief or caution, let alone how he'd manage to front up to the next brigade meeting for the formal emergency briefing and training day. But deep inside him, he knew he would.

Ash gave him a cursory nod, then moved towards his car.

CHAPTER 47

If Gus could measure the weight of his worry, he was currently ten kilograms lighter. He let out a light chuckle as he neared Kate's verandah to see Hughey waiting for him. Monica was standing a few metres away from the door, her look of indignance loud and clear.

'It appears the Queen Bee has been exiled from her hive.' Gus grinned as he kicked off his boots, waiting for Hughey to do the same.

The ewe swaggered away, baaing as her lambs bounced about her.

'More like Queen Lamb Chop,' Hughey said, and both men burst out laughing as the ewe stopped and turned back, bleating another loud objection like she understood exactly what they were suggesting.

Kate's house was warm and smelled of all things comforting. He moved towards the fireplace, which was crackling with heartening eagerness. These late autumn nights were hit and miss, and tonight was one that definitely required an injection of cosiness.

Gus sat quietly on the couch, a towel beneath him to soak up his sogginess because Brenda couldn't cope otherwise, contemplating the night's events as everyone engaged in chatter and warmed themselves with cuppas, and a surprising realisation dawned on him. It felt good to be around these folk again.

In fact, it was reassuring. He'd denied himself permission to want it, let alone enjoy it, until now. This was his community, the one he'd immersed himself in and called home. He'd forgotten how much he'd both missed it and needed it.

Two hours later, everyone packed up, said their goodbyes, and left, leaving Gus alone with Kate's house and his rattling mind. He was too wound up to sleep thanks to the warming coffees Brenda had been determined to drip-feed into him, not to mention Nola force-feeding him hot sausage rolls and party pies because he was still skin and bone. But all this did little to quell his rioting emotions. Speedy lay at his feet, her thick fur floofed thanks to the rain, and he tossed another log onto the fire before sitting back, allowing himself to be mesmerised by the flames as they flickered about.

What did his future look like now? He scratched the back of his head.

And would he allow it to change?

Did Kate have her phone with her? Gus sat up in a panic, taking a moment to realise where he was. He'd fallen asleep on Kate's couch, the birds now chirping in the early daylight and a hoof pawing at the front door. Gus rubbed his eyes, wrestling with renewed thoughts of rushing to Geelong Hospital where Riley had been taken. Had she stayed there with him all night? Was Riley going to be okay? How long would he be there? Did Kate need fresh clothes?

Then he stopped, surprise filling his features. Since when had his mindset shifted to thinking of them as . . . family? But that's what you did for family, or at least that's what he'd pictured himself doing. His heart stirred gooey-warm at the thought.

Speedy lifted her head from her paws, panting with a smile.

'Hey, girl.' He reached down and patted her head gently, her tongue licking his hand before he stood, moving towards the kitchen.

Gus tapped his finger on the sink with increasing pace as he waited for the kettle to boil. He was in desperate need of a coffee before he could think about any plans. Did Kate even want to lay eyes on him after everything that had happened? Hell, she'd had to convince him to go and find Riley in the first place, something that mortified him now. He'd understand if she banished him from her property and her life forever.

Gus scrubbed his face up and down with both hands, letting out a frustrated growl and Speedy stood, tipping her head to the side as she watched him.

'I'm a certified idiot, Speedy,' he said, shaking his head and closing his eyes. When was he going to get his act together and give himself a chance at life? He was starting to believe he might deserve it.

Taking his coffee with him, he dropped down onto the couch. Speedy hopped up, laying her head on his lap, her big seal eyes staring adoringly at him. What could he do to help Kate? He looked about him. The CWA women had removed every last crumb of evidence to suggest they'd been there, but maybe he should check on Monica and throw her a bit of hay. She did have a growing family to feed.

The dampness and havoc of the storm hung heavy in the air as he stepped outside, the ground soaked, broken branches hanging from trees or spread over the landscape as far as Gus could see. With Monica fed, he decided to head into town for one of Meg's mochas, which was way more appealing than Kate's dull flat white. His eyes wilted at the thought. Riley and Kate had occupied so much of his night and even though he could tell he was going to be paying a fair price for it all day, he didn't care. Even his still-damp clothes didn't bother him.

Tugging on his heavy jacket, he strode to Kate's car, the

sun now shining in the mid-morning sky. The breeze was gentle but chilly, and leaves from the gum trees that lined her drive dripped and glistened with a damp sparkle.

His phone dinged, and he dug it out of his pocket, reassured to see Kate's name in the incoming text message. His heart flipped with excitement.

Riley's going to be fine, but he'll need to stay another night for observation. Thanks for everything you did. I'll see you tomorrow. Love Kate. xo

Gus closed his eyes with sheer relief, nodding. How he might have lived with himself had Riley not pulled through, he couldn't say.

Gus's steps steadied as he approached the café, the tables full of unfamiliar customers chattering as they wrapped their hands around mugs of hot beverages with carefree smiles.

But it was when he pushed the café door open and headed inside that his eyes widened. People eyeing Meg's emporium selection of jams, cookies and, of course, Kate's encouragement boxes. Others were sipping lattés as they chatted, and quiet laughter filled the space. Meg had managed to fit two more table settings inside, all three occupied.

'Gus. Could you go out the front and pluck the feathers off that wretched crow? It's becoming a town hazard.'

Gus couldn't resist a smile, her happy-exhausted expression revealing unconditional friendship towards him.

'He's become *your* arch enemy, but yeah, sure.' He grinned her way despite her frustrated snarl.

With the crow sent on its merry way, Gus joined the queue. It was only when he'd reached the counter that Meg stole a long breath, her flushed cheeks puffing and her eyes widening with steadily rising panic.

'I can't keep up, Gus.' She shook her head while still managing a tired smile, filling the jug with milk for his order. 'I'm going to need more stock by tomorrow if it keeps up. And more help. Kate's not available and—'

'Is there a wedding we don't know about?' Gus leaned in, his eyebrows teasing her as he pretended to act all-knowing and suspicious.

Meg put down the jug of milk with a thud and aimed the tea towel at him, missing his ear by millimetres. 'If there is one, it had better be yours.' She shot him a don't-keep-us-hanging glare.

'Did you see the turnout of caravans on the other side of the road as you arrived?' Meg started warming his milk again. 'People have been pouring into the General Store, booking camping sites at the showgrounds. Nola left Graham to deal with them while she came to get coffee, desperate for a break. It's as if it's school holidays. Gus, these people are choosing to stop here. That hasn't happened in, like, forever.'

'Maybe it's the grey nomad holidays.' Gus chuckled. Whatever it was, the town was feeling more alive than ever.

Meg handed Gus his mocha, her voice turning serious. 'Have you heard from Kate? I've been so strapped for time, I haven't been able to ring her.'

'Yeah, just before. He's all good, but they want him in for another night, just to be sure.' His chest danced with warmth. Saying this aloud, Gus realised what he wanted. To have them back in his world as fast as possible.

Meg held a hand to her chest, moving around the counter and reaching out to Gus, a big smile on her face. He closed his eyes as she rested her cheek on his chest, hugging her in return. Knowing someone accepted him just for him mattered, deeply. He didn't have to live in the stench of his past. He could choose better than that, having wasted enough time and opportunities. He needed to make some changes, and he wasn't going to wait any longer.

'That's such a relief,' Meg said as she stepped from his arms, her voice tight. 'I hardly slept last night but didn't want to text or ring in case I was disturbing the bit of rest they might be getting.'

'Give Kate a ring. I reckon she'll want to talk to you.' He smiled, picked up his coffee, gave her his go-do-it-now raised brow and left.

CHAPTER 48

Two days later, Gus and Hughey were busy checking over his sheep in the yards, a stitch of apprehension skittering through Gus.

'They're growing out real well.' Hughey walked around them before he rested his gaze on Gus. 'Reckon we'll be able to do something pretty tasty with them in another few months.' He waggled his eyebrows as his smile grew.

'Listen, I've had a change of heart.' Kelly's sweet smile flittered in his mind.

'Oh?'

'Yeah, I'm not going to sell them. They can eat down my grass.'

'I get it,' Hughey said, turning down his lips with an understanding nod.

'Thanks, mate. Hey, has the insurance company got back to you yet?'

'Nah, not yet. But they have agreed it was an electrical fault and there shouldn't be any trouble with the claim. I'd like them to hurry up though. I'm itching to start on the new building.'

'Do you reckon Meg will come on board?' Gus could see the anticipation almost carved into Hughey's expression about Meg launching into a joint venture with him. And now with his old building burnt to the ground, it was as good a time as any to do it.

Hughey hopped out of the sheep yards, scratching his ear. 'I dunno. For a while there, I didn't think so. But with the café making a roaring trade, if that holds up, she'll need to expand.'

Hughey went quiet and Gus offered a small grin. How

would his best mate handle it if Meg still said no?

'C'mon, mate, give it to me,' Hughey said. 'I know you want to.' His expression held trepidation at what his best mate might say.

'Hey, man.' Gus held up his palms in the air, 'I'm the last one to be giving out relationship advice, but I reckon you should ask her again. There's hardly any room to stand, let alone sit in that café these days. I say you should strike while the iron's hot.'

Hughey's eyes widened. 'Yeah? So, does that go for you too? When are you going to pull your finger out and do something serious about Kate?'

Gus's face warmed with heat. What exactly was he going to do?

CHAPTER 49

They'd kept Riley in a third night, and Kate was keen to get home now they'd been discharged. Erin and Kathleen had been good enough to drive her car to the hospital. But first, she needed to drop off an encouragement box of sorts that she'd quickly put together at the shops on her way home.

Hughey's ute was parked in front of Gus's place when she arrived. Voices were coming from the direction of the sheep yards, but she decided not to go and say hello, wanting to get Riley into his own bed. She hoped what she was leaving on Gus's doorstep was enough to convey her heartfelt gratitude for everything he'd done.

After all that had happened, it felt like a lifetime since she'd been home, and as Kate stepped out of her car, she smiled. It was good to be back. But could she stay? She softly shook her head. Right now, she just didn't know.

Slowly entering her home, she rested her hands on Riley's shoulders and looked about her. On the dining table was a large vase of freshly picked cottage and wildflowers, and beside that was a chocolate cake laced with oozy fudgy icing, the smell filling the space with a delicious aroma. But it was the smell from the oven that had her begging to sit down at the dining table.

'How about you go and have a snooze, hey?' Kate dipped her head to the side as Riley gave a tired nod, agreeing with her for once. She appreciated the feeling, squashing down a small smile at his sweet face.

Her gaze followed him as he trailed off to his bedroom. She went to the verandah and glanced about for Monica. She figured by her absence, the ewe was off grazing, so she collected a few bits of wood Graham had cut for them. The fire lit easily before she moved to the kitchen, eying the lasagne that smelled uncannily like her mother's. Had Meg dropped off a meal for them? Kate bent down, peering through the glass on the oven. That was weird. It even looked like her mother's baking dish.

Kate stood back up, frowning as she searched about her. Maybe it was Patsy or Nola. They were of the same vintage as her mother, after all. But that smell—she closed her eyes, breathing it in again, only distracted by the sound of a car pulling up. Monica had resumed her post, offering her customary welcome from the verandah, one of her babies also bleating. Could Monica number two be in the making? She chuckled.

When Kate opened the door, she stood still, floored.

'Mum!' She lunged at her mother, her hug long and emotional. When she finally managed to let go, she hugged her father before ushering them inside. She gave Monica the warning finger, and the ewe stopped short, feigning innocence as she blinked, avoiding Kate's glare.

'What are you guys doing here?' Had they heard what had happened and come to take them home? A sudden wave of nausea bombarded her.

'Well, we missed you both.' Her mother glanced at her father before grinning her way again. 'And we have something for you. It's from everyone at home.'

'What do you mean?' Kate frowned.

Her mother's face morphed into a crumpled mess, and she was momentarily lost for words, so her father stepped in.

'What your mother is trying to say is that everyone misses you. But they understand why you needed to leave, so they sent down a gift for you both.' He moved to the door, stepping out to the side of the house, grabbing two large objects under both his arms before wrestling them inside.

Kate stepped forward, curiosity filling her face.

'You mean you're not coming to take us home?'

'Heavens no. Why would we do that?' Her mother's lips tightened, her now-wary brow pinching above her nose.

Kate's dad stepped forward.

'You did so much for everyone back home, they just wanted to say thank you. They would've done it before you left,' —he gave a fatherly chuckle— 'but you beat them to it. You're always in such a bloody hurry, Zippy.'

Kate blinked, staring at her father like he'd come from a foreign country. 'But I—'

'Just take one, will you.' Her father shook his head. 'You haven't changed one bit, my girl.'

Kate and her mother giggled, and Kate believed it was mostly true, all except one thing. She had changed when it came to who she wanted to be for Riley. She'd always be his auntie, but she had to work this strange new role in a different light. She loved him like her own, and she wanted to give him the world. And after the cliff incident, she believed she just might be able to do it in her own way.

Kate held the taller surfboard with both arms, studying it, a shimmer of excitement running through her.

'Why? How?'

'Everyone back home figured these were pretty appropriate considering you're a beach babe now.' Her mother beamed.

Would Gus teach them to surf? She hoped so.

'Kate.' Dad smiled. 'You were always the go-getter, making things happen. And from the talk downtown the last two days, you've done exactly the same here.'

Kate's eyes all but popped out of her head. 'You've been here two days?' Did they know about Riley? A feeling of dread filled her belly, and she unconsciously placed a hand over it. 'How did you get in?'

'Oh, that lovely boy next door gave us your spare key.'

Of course he did, and she grinned to herself, recalling telling him where it was when Riley had been unwell. Had he been the one to tell them about what she'd been doing here?

'We've driven down with the caravan, and we're stopping at the showgrounds. We wanted to surprise you.'

'I . . . I'm speechless.' Kate stared at them, thrilled they were here with her and Riley but scared of where it might lead. She'd definitely be facing some home truths now.

She put the kettle on to buy herself some time as her mother took out some mugs. They made the cuppas together, and just as they sat around the coffee table, Riley appeared from the hallway, sleepy-eyed and scruffy-haired.

'Gran, Pop!' Instantly, he was wide awake, running towards them. He lunged into the arms of his grandfather first, then into his grandmother's for the longest time. Goosebumps ran over Kate's skin, tears threatening as he refused to let them go.

But in that same moment, inadequacy surged through her. Here was Mum doing and saying exactly the right things. She could even hug way better. Riley was a testament to that. When Kate tried hugging him, he flopped in her arms like a limp fish.

'Hey, look what they brought you, kiddo.' She dug deep, fighting her emotions by turning to her father, who'd picked up Riley's new surfboard from against the wall.

'No way!' Riley ran over to it, taking it in his hands and admiring it like it was a trophy. 'Gus can teach us to surf,' Riley said, spinning to her, his face beaming.

Did he say *us*? She pressed a palm to her cheek to steady the joy wanting to burst out, managing to nod instead, unable to hide the happiness showing in her welling eyes.

'Yes, he can. That'd be great.' The words lodged in her chest as she blinked against her fresh tears fervently. Hadn't she shed enough of those already?

Kate slowed her breathing, determined to face the difficult topic of Riley's misadventure head-on. If she didn't, someone else in the community was sure to tell them all the juicy details.

When she'd finished, her mother offered a sympathetic smile, squeezing her shoulder on her way past to get the lasagne out of the oven. Kate sat back, a tentative smile filling her face as she looked lovingly at her father, who snuggled with Riley beside him. Even though he was listening to Riley's rundown about the new Lego spaceship he'd finished while he was in hospital, thanks to a special delivery from Meg—and Hughey, although Meg didn't want to admit to that fact—she didn't doubt her father had heard every word she'd said.

Kate hopped up, her stomach in knots, fully ready for her mother to say they would take Riley back home with them. She wasn't cut out for this crazy, nerve-racking role.

But her heart ached heavily. While it was the obvious choice and the best option for Riley, why couldn't she say it to her parents?

CHAPTER 50

Gus halted, cautiously eyeing the box sitting at his front door before he glanced about him. Was Kate here? His heart did a flip, and his belly filled with jiggling butterflies as his hopes grew. Were they home? But when he took a closer look at the box, a nervous nuance filled him.

What was this for? It presented like another one of her encouragement boxes, and *not* something he needed.

Inside was a card, a coffee jar, which he couldn't help but softly chuckle at, and a small succulent in a terracotta pot.

A plant? But then he remembered the day when Riley had been sick, and he'd brought him home to his place. He gave a soft chuckle as he held the box. Did she remember their kiss as keenly as he did, reliving it over and over like an old record he couldn't stop playing? It didn't matter. They hadn't kissed since. It wouldn't change the way he felt. He was smitten with her giggle, her sassy eyebrow, and her deep capacity to share everything she had.

But then he remembered she'd mentioned the fair. It was the passion killer he'd needed to ensure he didn't make a fool of himself. She didn't really want him, not then, and especially not now, after everything that had gone down. And no doubt her parents were ready to whisk her and Riley back home with them. Why else would they be here? This was a thank you for everything and a goodbye gift.

He shook his head. He wasn't the one who needed encouragement. He just needed to get on with life. On his own.

But as he took the box inside, placing it on the kitchen

bench, he couldn't help but lift out the succulent with a grin. Speedy gave a quick bark.

'Yeah, yeah, I know. She was right. Don't remind me.'

Gus put the plant on the corner of the bench and stood back. It didn't look half bad after all.

He made himself a coffee and took it to the couch where he sat back, opening the card.

Dear Gus,

This is just a small thank you for all you've done for us and I couldn't imagine life without you. After all, you are Riley's best mate!

Love Kate, Riley and Monica xx

P.S. I think I'll let Monica stay.

Gus's chest welled with elation and relief as he re-read that last line. She's keeping … Monica? Not only had she made a claim on his sheep, but it also sounded like she was planning on hanging around. His stock handling had definitely improved since the ewe had stayed next door. He gave a hearty chuckle.

Kelly came to mind. She'd been the kind of girl everyone loved. Kate was no different. Would she be proud of him?

The answer was a resounding yes.

And somehow now, his well-guarded motto of Keep the Solitude Secure no longer mattered.

CHAPTER 51

Riley sat cross-legged on his upside-down surfboard in the loungeroom, fiddling with his fingers, unable to give Kate his complete attention.

'C'mon, Riley, you can tell me,' she urged softly. Her heart was aching for him. He clearly didn't want to tell her the truth about what happened the night of the storm, and she was scared he'd tell her that he'd been trying to run away.

He blinked, opened his mouth, then closed it, his head moving with the mildest of shakes. She hopped off the couch and grabbed her surfboard leaning against the wall and laid it down next to his. Perching herself on it, she waited patiently. If only he could understand how much she loved him. If only she could find a better way to show him.

He took a cautious glance her way from beneath his fringe before lowering it again.

'Speedy was here when Hughey brought me home. I told Hughey I was going to get the key, and she followed me until she took off as a huge clap of thunder roared above us. It was a rabbit she'd seen 'cause I saw it in a flash of the lightning. I called and called her . . . but she wouldn't come back.' His shoulders collapsed and his face rumpled in shame, slow sniffs catching his breath. 'I had to go after her, Auntie Kate,' he pleaded. 'I didn't want her to die in the storm.' A violent shiver ran over his body.

It was all too close to home, Riley's actions and why he'd done what he had. He loved that dog so much that he was prepared to look past his own fears of the storm to go after her. Proud auntie vibes filled her innermost being. She reached over, rubbing his back, remaining silent.

'She was barking near the edge of the cliff when I found her. I went to take her by the collar, but she leapt forward, disappearing beneath some scrub down the cliff. That's when I slipped.' His soft sobs steadied, but his fingers were interlacing one another over and over.

Kate didn't think she had any more tears left to shed, but he proved her wrong.

'Oh, Riley.'

He hadn't run away from her after all, even though she'd failed him over and over. He was the bravest kid she knew.

Storms represented so much horror to her, but she couldn't let them dictate how she should react. There'd always be a level of fear with them, there was no denying that, but she was never going to allow them to paralyse her again. 'All that matters is you're okay.' She bent forward, her hair falling around her face as she coaxed him for his attention.

'Will we go to the surf shop sometime soon and choose a wetsuit each for our birthdays? I'm going to need one if I want to dip my big toe in that freezing water anytime soon,' she grinned, a fluttery shiver surfacing down her back. Was she seriously committing to this ludicrous idea? She wanted to believe Gus would be impressed.

He beamed up at her, nodding eagerly, and it was the best thing she'd seen since, well, ever. Parenting was a tough gig, but it was worth every ounce of agony just to have him look at her like that. And before she realised what was happening, Riley stood up, pulling Kate to her feet and wrapping his arms around her waist so tight she thought she might burst.

'To the moon and back,' he said, reaching on his tiptoes to kiss her on the cheek.

Kate slowed, glancing up as she yanked another tuft of pesky weed from the garden bed and tossing it to Monica standing nearby. She grinned. Her handsome neighbour was striding towards her, his free-flowing hair blowing with the breeze. He wore a smile that messed with her mind and her heart, sending it skipping out of rhythm the closer he came.

'I see you have a captive audience,' he chuckled.

She giggled. The only captive audience she wanted right now was him.

'Well, that's not hard when the offerings are green and juicy.' Her eyebrows danced.

'Hmm, I'm not sure she's going to love me then.' Gus frowned.

'Oh? Why's that?' Could he get any cuter? This guy had it all: the eye-catching looks and the wit that left her wanting for more. He moved towards her, his enticing lips drawing her like a damned drawstring, and she stepped into him, their toes touching.

'Because I've come to take her home. She's lived here rent-free for long enough.'

Kate's heart gave a sudden thud. Was he feeling this, too? His eyes, full of longing and intensity, told her he was.

'Hi, Gus.' Riley bounced down the pathway to greet them both before she could respond to him, and she took a swift step back, casting her suddenly shy gaze downwards. She released a pent-up breath, the closeness of Gus and the fact she'd almost been caught in one highly embarrassing auntie moment she wasn't ready for her nephew to witness, shadowing her face. She'd been so close to kissing him, the air between them electric.

'Hey, Riley. Wanna help us get Monica and the kids back

to my place?'

Kate's heart surged as Gus smiled at Riley, the gooey fuzziness inside her chest at bursting point. Ever since Gus had saved Riley, something had shifted between them, visible and unmistakable. They just needed a moment of time on their own, but with the winter school holidays underway, she wasn't sure how that was going to happen.

The three of them made their way towards the gate, following Monica and her mischievous twins as they bounced and darted unpredictably from one side to the other.

'Looks like she's ready to admit she's missing her buddies,' Kate said as the ewe ran ahead of them like she knew exactly where they wanted her to go.

'Yeah. She could've done that sooner, saving me a whole lot of grief.' He gave her a teasing glance from the corner of his eye. 'With my neighbour.'

'Maybe your neighbour wanted them to stay, so *her* neighbour might come visit.' She waited for Gus's reaction, the twinkle in his eye telling her everything, and she moved closer to him, the backs of their hands brushing one another's before Gus clasped her hand in his, and her chest whooshed with warmth. His touch sent a fierce charge through her body and she risked a glance his way, her cheeks flushing with heat.

Riley took off ahead after Monica and in that opportunistic moment, Gus slowed, tugging her close. He lowered his mouth to hers, kissing her long and slow, making her toes curl and her lips smile beneath it.

Forgetting about Riley, and Monica for that matter, she reached her arms up around his neck, kissing him back deeply, their lips refusing to part. Every nerve ending came alive as her eyes closed, their lips lingering, so much so she didn't hear the footsteps slowing next to her.

'It's about time, Gus. I thought you were never going to do that.'

Gus and Kate broke out in laughter as they stepped back from one another, smiling down at Riley.

'I think it's about time, too,' Kate said, ruffling Riley's hair good-naturedly before smiling back at Gus, his unmistakable adoration for her radiating from his whole face. Riley beamed at her.

'I want to show you something.' Riley beckoned them to come with him.

Kate gave Gus a surprised frown as they held hands, following Riley.

It wasn't until they were in sight of the gateway near the cliff that they stopped, staring at the gate, and Monica.

'It was her the whole time,' Riley said, bouncing up and down as he pointed to the ewe. 'See, I told you I didn't do it.'

'Well, I never,' Kate said as Monica impatiently tugged at the chain with her mouth, tossing her head up and down until the chain finally fell to the side of the post. She nudged the gate with her nose, waltzing through it with her lambs in tow.

CHAPTER 52

The road was busy with cars and caravans poking along, searching for an elusive park along the main street of Forest Gully. There was a buzz in the air, and it wasn't just because the holidays were underway. The town was beginning to get some serious traction from travellers, and between the General Store, the bakery, and Meg's café, they were increasing their stock orders weekly to keep up with demand. And that included orders for Kate's cooking.

Gus stood with his back to the café, the sunshine streaming down on him as he surveyed the proposed building site on the beachfront where they'd held the fair. Hughey came and stood beside him, giving him an enthusiastic slap on the back.

'So, mate, are you ready to do this?'

'I am.' Gus looked at Hughey, stoked they were going to go into the butcher business together, giving himself a sure future after the letter they'd received approving their building plans. Only, they'd be sourcing their meat elsewhere.

'So, who's gonna turn over the first sod of dirt?' Hughey's eyebrows jiggled as he grinned at his best mate. Meg and Kate came and stood between them, and Gus hooked his arm around Kate's shoulder, dipping to give her a sweet kiss on the lips before taking in the sight, a wide smile on his face.

'It's gotta be you, Hughey,' Meg said as she scrutinised the big guy.

Kate and Gus watched on, their eyes narrowing with interest. Had Meg's eyes sparkled when she'd held Hughey's? Gus gave Kate an I-reckon-so wink.

'Aww, Megsy, thank you,' Hughey said, his eyes locked on

hers adoringly. He received a swift thump from her to his upper arm in return.

'Here's some good news,' Hughey said, shifting their attention. 'Graham spoke with Fire Rescue Victoria yesterday. Our nine thousand, six hundred and forty-eight dollars has been accepted. We're going to get a new truck.'

Gus tugged Kate a little tighter to him, his relief palpable as he stared out at the glistening ocean, the water gently lapping along the shore. After everything that had happened, there was no better news. Forest Gully was thriving, and the risk of fires and accidents was always present, so having two trucks would make a world of difference in saving lives.

'I've got something to tell everyone,' Kate said, breaking his earnest musings.

'You're engaged!' Meg spun to her, grabbing her left hand with excited expectation before glancing up, disappointment written all over her face.

'No.'

Gus shied from Kate's astonished gaze as her cheeks flushed pink in a flash. He couldn't deny it was at the forefront of his mind, but he had plans about how he wanted to do it, and it wasn't with Hughey and Meg around, regardless of how great their friendship was.

Kate did an about-turn, making them all follow her move as she made a point of considering the shops on the main side of the road. 'Not only did I get the job at the school to run the veggie garden, but I'm also thinking of turning my farmgate into a shop front. I'll call it The Seaside Bouquet.' She grinned at each of them, her eyes lingering on Gus, then back to the shops, unable to hide her ecstasy.

'I like it, Zippy.' Gus angled a teasing glance her way as her mouth dropped open, her eyes narrowing. He'd been waiting for the perfect moment to call her by the name, and her reaction didn't disappoint.

'That's perfect, Kate,' Meg beamed. 'Which one?'

She gave Gus one last suspicious look before she turned back to survey the empty shops. 'I haven't worked that out yet, but there are a few to choose from.' She chuckled, as did the rest of them. Gus pulled her to him, his chest filled with pride and relief. Kate wanted to stay as long as he did. Forest Gully was where he lived, but together with her and Riley, they'd make it *their* home.

ACKNOWLEDGEMENTS

What a journey this book has had. It has crossed the careful eyes of many writers far better than me, and I am deeply grateful for their feedback, which has shaped my writing and, hopefully, improved it.

Lisa Ireland, Ida Brady, Leanne Lovegrove, and Kerryn Mayne, you have all been with me during this story, keeping my plot lines behaving and my sanity from turning to mush.

Pamela Cook, thank you for your wonderful insight into writing. *Your Turn Up the Tension* course opened my eyes to new ways to see this story and where it needed to improve. And to all the ladies who did the course with me, thank you for your input also. Growing and improving came from so many wonderful places.

Tania Ryan and Amy Doak, thank you for our endless long cuppas and pep talks to keep me on track when I was wondering if this story would ever make it. You were there through some tough times these last two years, and I am so grateful for all the hugs and love you gave.

Dee Burton, Kristy Sargeant, and Skye Egan, thank you for reading early drafts and lovingly giving me the feedback I needed to hear.

Annie Seaton, a huge thank you for not only your wonderful eye for editing but also for your support to see me get this book over the line. I couldn't have done it without you, literally! And to Roby for your proofreading prowess, and just when I thought there were no more misbehaving commas and semicolons!

Tess Woods, thanks for the chats and pep texts in amongst your busy writing life. You are one in a million.

Leonie Kelsall. Wow, what a gun you are, and an incredible writer of this wonderful genre. Thank you for all the organising you did to bring our SA book tour adventure together. May there be many more, with even more laughs along the way!

Samantha Wood. You are a true inspiration, and I'm so grateful we met on this crazy, inspiring writing journey. You are so generous with your time and advice. Hugs. xo

Kelli. You are the lifeboat I've needed so often, holding me up when I thought I might drown. You told me "I can" when I believed I couldn't. THANK YOU. You deserve the biggest squishy hugs I can give!

Dave Jenkins and Mike Kinsman, thank you for sharing your experiences of the CFA and for willingly reading parts of a rural romance. That's a first, I'm sure! And to Alex Lewis, Steven Hull, and Rod Henders. Every detailed experience counts as great fodder for a story.

Lois . . .words can't say. But I'll give it a try. You have been on this crazy ride with me from the beginning, encouraging me even when my stories needed work—and lots of it! Not only are you a treasured friend, but you have an incredible eye for 'the little things' in the manuscript. Thank you for proofing the review copy of *Sheep Gully Road*. Sorry, but you've got the job for life! And to Sonn, for also proofing the review copy, helping it to make it the best it could be.

To all my wonderful RWA friends and the many incredible people I've met through social media. Franceen, my expert peanut gallery and cheerleader extraordinaire, and Jeanette, for having the phone handy for our life debriefs, the wins and the losses.

To our two amazingly talented daughters, Corinne and Anna, whom I am so proud of, and to my incredible extended family. You have not only supported this crazy ride I've been on, but you believe in me. I couldn't have a better cheer squad.

My heartfelt gratitude to my wonderful readers, Neroli, you're in there (!), who have waited patiently for my next book to see the light of day. Thank you for your continued enthusiasm and support. I hope you love Gus, Kate, and Riley's story as much as I do.

 Laurelle xo

ABOUT THE AUTHOR

Laurelle Cousins is a wool classer who lives in the country, with all its unique vibes, sounds, and smells—some of which are more tolerable than others. She loves writing characters with strength and sass, her heroes and heroines always getting their happy ever afters, but she'll put them through the wringer to get there.

Laurelle has been runner-up for favourite debut author in 2022 with ARRA for *The Lonely Paddock* and has edited a feature piece, Childhood Memories, for *Rural Women's Day* magazine.

She has a ratbag kelpie named Jazz who loves sticks ten times her size. She also loves to stay in touch with her wonderful readers and would be thrilled to hear from you. You can find her at:

Website: Laurelle@laurellecousins.com
Instagram: laurellecousins.writes
Facebook: Laurelle Cousins
        Laurelle Cousins Writes
Newsletter: https://shorturl.at/P8erW
Pinterest: pinterest.com/laurellecousins

Sheep Gully Road

Other books By Laurelle Cousins

The Lonely Paddock

KATE'S STICKY CARAMEL CAKE

If you've read *Sheep Gully Road*, you may have worked out that my character's favourite recipes are, in fact, mine. And if you've gone to the recipe first before reading the story, you've made a great move. It's exactly what I would have done. Cook it and sit yourself down with a big oozy slice beside you, then enjoy the journey of Gus and Kate as you munch to your heart's content. And if you feel extra inspired, Ross's favourite chocolate brownie recipe is in my first book, The Lonely Paddock, available through Harlequin Escape and in libraries near you. And if it isn't, I'd love for you to request it. They will get it in, and the love story between Ross and Flick can reach more readers. As always, please let me know what your tastebuds think.

In essence, this is a sticky date cake or slice. I use a large square tin so I can cut big pieces that turn out about 5cm tall. The recipe is also extremely versatile. I've cooked mini cakes in an individual rose mould tin (or muffin tins), and the recipe freezes perfectly. I thaw individual pieces completely before warming them up. The sauce keeps in the fridge and is thick and sticky. Put a generous-sized scoop on top of the slice and warm them gently in the microwave. And like Meg says, a good dollop of double cream adds to the enticement.

INGREDIENTS:

170g dates, stoned and chopped
1 teaspoon bicarbonate of soda
300ml boiling water
60g unsalted butter or dairy-free butter

¾ cup caster or brown sugar (i use brown as it adds to the colour)

2 eggs

170g self-raising flour or gluten-free self-raising flour (same quantity)

½ teaspoon pure vanilla extract

100g of pecan or walnuts, chopped, or dark chocolate optional (for a little change-up)

sauce:

400g brown sugar

1 cup thickened cream –I use Zymil lactose-free, same quantity

250g unsalted butter

1 vanilla bean, split.

METHOD:

1. Preheat oven to 180 degrees C and line an 18cm square cake tin with baking paper (my hint is to scrunch it first, then unfold and fit it to the tin. this works a treat for keeping the paper staying in place).
2. mix dates and bicarbonate of soda in a small bowl. pour boiling water over this and leave to stand.
3. cream the butter and sugar, then add the eggs, one at a time, beating well after each so they don't curdle.
4. fold in the flour gently.
5. stir in the date mixture and vanilla *and pecans or walnuts or chocolate if you're using one of them. (only bake for 20 mins if using small moulds, as they'll cook faster, but check with a skewer first).
6. pour into the prepared tin.
7. bake for 30 – 40 minutes. i test with a skewer to see if it

comes out clean.

Sauce:
1. Put the sugar, cream, butter and vanilla in a saucepan and gently bring to the boil.
2. Reduce the heat and simmer for 5 minutes.
3. Remove the vanilla bean.
4. Pour a little sauce over the warm cake and return it to the oven for 2 or 3 minutes, making sure the sauce has had a chance to soak in.
5. Remove the cake from the tin and on a cutting board, cut the cake into generous squares.
6. Place on a plate with extra caramel sauce (the more the better!) and add Meg's dollop of cream (or she may just have words with me).
7. Let the remaining slices cool before placing them individually in the freezer for that special treat you're hankering for or haven't got time to make.
8. Enjoy! Xo